IN YOUR EYES

IN YOUR EYES

SANTINI & JAMISON Vol. 1

Pywacket Press
Murrells Inlet SC 29576
www.pywacketpresssmall.wix.com/pywacketpress

First Edition © 2013 by L. Thomas Cook. All rights reserved
Cover Photo © Adrienn Orbánhegyi | Dreamstime.com
ISBN-13: 978-0615835815

To my husband who is also my best friend. Thank you for all the love and support.

This story is dedicated to anyone who has ever been in love and knows what an amazing gift it is.

Special thanks to Trilby Plants, author, editor, publisher, and all around terrific lady. She may not like exclamation points but she makes her point and drives a writer to dig deeper. Hugs, Tibby. You're not only a wonderful friend but the best mentor I ever had. This book would not have come to life without you.

1

May 1983

Detective Jay Jamison lowered the binoculars from his strained eyes.

From the passenger seat of the cherry red Mustang he watched the street, but his patience thinned each time his partner, Sonny Santini, in the driver's seat, drummed his fingers along the steering wheel.

Jay turned toward Sonny, and, as the drumming grew rapid, he couldn't take much more. "Will you knock it off." He rolled his eyes.

"What?" Sonny said.

"That." Jay imitated the sound by rapping on the dash. "Just sit still for a minute. Can you do that? Please? Before I reach over and strangle you?"

"Little too much coffee there, partner?" Sonny smiled. He drummed once more before he put up his hands to surrender.

"Very funny," Jay said and rubbed his hand down his tired face.

Focused on their target like hawks in a tree surveying their surroundings waiting for the right moment to swoop, they had been there for hours. The early morning sun finally crept over the rooftops. The light revealed the ugliness of what they faced.

Downtown Oakland City, Florida. Graffiti-covered walls lined the blocks. Ravaged stucco buildings with broken windows were abandoned except for the rats. This was their urban wilderness filled with dark corners to hide in and desperation so thick it actually had its own odor. Sonny and Jay were the hunters faced with the task of protecting the innocent. Except the identity of the innocent blurred so much with the guilty that sometimes it was hard to tell the difference. Both men did the best they could to stop the violence. Sometimes they were too late.

"Cobra Three," the police car radio squawked

"About damn time," Sonny said and sat up in his seat.

"Cobra Three," Jay answered. "Go ahead."

"Suspect spotted at 321 Talon Street. Hotel Cypress. See the lobby clerk."

Jay looked at his partner.

"Trotter," they both said at the same time.

"Proceed with caution," the radio warned.

"Always do," Sonny replied to no one in particular. He floored the gas pedal. The car responded like a stallion let out of the gate. Jay's head jerked back. Sonny tightened his grip on the steering wheel. Squealing tires created a cloud of smoke.

Jay stuck the police dome on the roof. The swirling red light parted the sea of buses and trucks. Cars hugged the curbs. Cobra Three blew past them all without question.

The corners of Sonny's mouth curled into a grin.

Jay laughed at his partner. "You love this part," he said.

"Friggin' love it," Sonny said.

Two blocks from the hotel, Sonny slowed and shut off the dome light.

The hotel at 321 Talon Street was a rundown, ten story concrete building. It sat on a block with other bedraggled buildings. All of it should have been torn down years ago. Instead of the clean-cut neighborhood of the 1970s, it was now overrun with the worst the city had to offer. This block and others like it were a far cry from what Florida, the Sunshine State, was known for – sandy beaches and Disney World.

"We're home, dear," Sonny said and eased the Mustang to a stop.

Jay nodded. His partner was right. These streets had been their home for almost four years.

"Think this place would be sick of seeing us by now," Sonny said.

"Just as long as they don't know we're coming." Jay pointed to a side alley.

"Right you are, Blondie." Sonny pulled into the alley and turned off the ignition. He patted the car's door as he got out like a cowboy patting his horse.

"Waiting for backup?" Jay said. Sonny headed straight for the hotel, and Jay shook his head. "Hey. Hey," he called his irritation to his partner, but it was too late, Sonny had gone inside.

Jay hurried to join him, and with steady strides they walked across the lobby. Dressed nothing like police officers, both men were undercover detectives who wore jeans, plain shirts, sneakers, and light jackets to cover the bulges of their gun holsters.

The radio at the front desk played the latest hit song by Joan Jett & The Blackhearts, "I Love Rock N' Roll." The clerk known as Trotter barely looked up when Sonny leaned on the counter. There was no need to flash badges. Trotter knew them: Oakland City Metro PD. Trotter gave a quick nod and, after Sonny pointed to the radio, he turned it down.

"You rang, dear?" Sonny said.

Even though Sonny acted casually, Jay sensed Sonny's body was tense and ready. Jay scanned the lobby. Anything was possible. This could easily be a set-up and, if so, he and his partner could be served for breakfast to the vultures that drooled.

A bum with a dingy Miami Dolphins' cap over his eyes was passed out in the corner. Head slumped over, he clenched a brown paper bag in his filthy hands. Other than that, the lobby was quiet. Not necessarily a good sign. Rats loved to hide in the shadows.

"I got who you want," Trotter said. He lifted his gray face and stuck out the open palm of a tobacco stained hand.

"I'm just supposed to take your word for it?" Sonny said and peered over the top of his sunglasses.

"He's here," Trotter said. "I wouldn't waste your time. Or mine."

Sonny glanced down at the racing form spread out on the counter. "Any good tips?"

"Yeah. Don't get shot. I hate cleaning up blood." Trotter's thin lips curled upwards.

"It won't be my blood." Sonny turned the racing form around so he could see it. "I like this one. In the second race. Winner Takes All. Good name."

"He's a mud runner. Ain't gonna rain today." Trotter slid the form back in place.

"Ya never know," Sonny said. "It could pour. Storm clouds can come up real quick."

"Not today," Trotter said. "I hear someone paid them to stay away." He put out his hand and wiggled his fingers. "Ninth floor. Room 9C."

Sonny handed the man a fifty dollar bill, but when Trotter kept his palm open, Sonny said, "What? Rate going up?"

"There's two others with him. Don't know 'em. Don't wanna. I figure twenty-five more apiece."

"How do I know they're worth anything to me?" Sonny said.

Trotter smiled yellow teeth. "You want Diller? The other two might try and stop ya. If they're with him, they're worth a hell of a lot more."

"Oh. So this is your snitch sale." Sonny laughed toward Jay and slapped another fifty in Trotter's hand.

Trotter nodded and returned to his racing form.

Sonny made a loud rap with his knuckle on the counter and, when the clerk eyed him, Sonny pulled off his sunglasses. "You know the drill, Trotter. You make one sound to warn 'em, and I'll be all over you like a horse on a carrot."

The clerk waved him away.

A few steps from the front desk, Jay turned to Sonny. "Horse on a carrot?"

"Just came to me." Sonny shrugged his left shoulder and put his sunglasses in his pocket.

Jay took the stairs two at a time, Sonny one step behind. At the first landing, Jay peered around the corner and checked the hall. He lowered his hand to signal it was clear. They continued up the stairs.

With Sonny right behind Jay, they reached the ninth floor and took cautious steps down the dim hallway. A single bulb suspended from the ceiling in the middle of the hall flickered on and off. The stench of urine and vomit was strong. A radio played a soulful tune. They approached the door of room 9C and listened.

Jay, his back pressed to the wall, drew his gun.

Sonny, his gun firm in his hands, nodded at Jay and kicked in the door.

The door frame splintered and the door slammed open. They burst into the room.

"Police," Jay shouted. "Freeze."

Two men reached for weapons, but Jay's semi-automatic pistol was on them tight, and they put up their hands.

The third man wasn't giving up so easily. He flipped the table where he'd been sitting and ran for the open window. He made it through and climbed down the fire escape.

Sonny took off after him.

Jay handcuffed the other two men to the cold radiator and scrambled to the window. Below him was the curly hair of his partner, and the real reason they were there – Dice Diller, wanted for three murders.

Dice turned and fired his weapon. Jay heard an instantaneous metallic ting. Dice leaped four feet to the ground and stumbled.

Sonny jumped from the metal ladder and landed on Dice like a tiger pouncing on a grizzly bear.

Dice, who outweighed Sonny by a good fifty pounds, fell to the ground. His gun flew out of his hand. He flipped Sonny off his back and landed a punch straight to the jaw. Sonny went down. Dice couldn't locate his gun. He looked back at Sonny and took off running again.

Sonny got to his feet and sprinted after Dice. Jay spotted Dice's abandoned gun by the dumpster, grabbed it, and joined the chase. He headed into the alley, rounded the corner and lost them.

A garbage can crashed. Sonny shouted, "Freeze," and then the scuffle of feet on dry pavement.

Jay worked to make his legs run faster and then…there was silence. The worst kind of silence. The kind that made Jay freeze.

He stopped at the corner. His chest heaved. His heart pounded. Jay gripped his gun and inched slowly around the wall.

Sonny was on the ground. Dice Diller stood over him. He had Sonny's gun aimed right at Sonny's head. His left eye squeezed shut, Diller let out a raspy chuckle.

"Guess it just ain't your day."

"Hold it," Jay ordered and took a step.

Dice darted his eyes toward Jay. Sonny swiped his legs and kicked Dice's legs from under him. Dice tumbled backwards. The gun fired into the air. Jay charged Dice just as Sonny got to his feet. They both grabbed

Dice, whirled his bulky body around and slammed him face first into the concrete wall.

Sonny handcuffed him and hissed close to the side of Dice's face, "Try to use my own gun against me?" His lip bleeding, he whipped Dice back around and smashed his left fist into the man's nose with a crack. "You're a real prick, you know that?" Sonny growled. Blood oozed from Dice's nose.

"Cool off, partner," Jay said. He pressed Dice hard against the wall and began to read him his rights.

Sonny trailed his shirt sleeve across his mouth, retrieved his gun, and spoke to it. "It's okay, baby. I don't blame you."

Two police cars screeched to a stop in the alley. Four plainclothes detectives stepped onto the pavement, but only one smiled.

"Figures the A-team got here first." Detective Weiss in a wrinkled brown suit grinned behind his gold rimmed glasses.

"Just saving the taxpayers' money," Sonny said. He pushed Dice Diller toward the huddle of cops. "Mind dropping him off for us? We've had a long day."

"Gee, thanks, Sergeant," Weiss said. "So nice of you to let us play."

"Our pleasure." Jay handed over Dice's gun. "Give him a nice room. Maybe one with a view of a fire escape."

Sonny grinned a crooked smile that exposed the dimple in his left cheek. "Oh, hey. Let's not forget the other two upstairs."

"Oh, right, right," Jay said. "Take care of it, would you?" He tossed his handcuff keys to the other detectives.

Weiss smirked. "Bagged two more? You don't get a commission, you know."

"Don't buy into their bullshit," Detective McCann, unsmiling, stared Sonny and Jay down. "They're both just a couple of damn showoffs."

Sonny laughed. "I heard that."

"I don't give a shit, Santini," McCann said. "You are. A damn cocky showoff."

"I only show off in front of you, McCann." Sonny snickered. "That's 'cause your approval means *so* much to me." He strutted toward the older, stern-faced man and grinned. "It means *everything* to me. You just" – he shrugged a shoulder– "turn me on."

"Get away from me," McCann growled.

"Thanks, guys," Weiss said. "We'll take it from here."

"No need for thanks," Sonny said as he strolled away. "Just bow when we walk into the room."

"One of these days, smart ass," said McCann, his voice rising to a warning tone, "you're gonna have your head handed to you."

"Put it in a memo, Detective," Sonny said, walking backwards. "I'll read it on a snowy day. Oh, wait. That's right. It doesn't snow in Florida. Oh well." He tossed up his hands and shrugged.

"Why do you love to egg him on?" Jay said after they returned to the Mustang.

"He makes it too easy." Sonny smiled while he took off his navy blue nylon jacket and tossed it into the back seat. "Long day." He rolled up his sleeves to the elbows, adjusted the strap of his gun holster, and then climbed in behind the wheel. With the windows up, he turned on the air conditioner full force. A cool breeze blew out from the vents. Sonny put his face as close to it as he could.

"Worked up a sweat, did you?" Jay watched the air blow over Sonny's damp hair. "You thinking what I'm thinking?"

"Yeah. Sloppy Joes and a pitcher of beer," Sonny said and sat back.

"That's *not* what I was thinking."

Sonny widened his eyes with mock innocence. "It wasn't?"

Jay recognized that glint. "*Now* you're thinking what I'm thinking."

"Home?" Sonny wiggled his dark brown eyebrows.

"Home." Jay nodded with an immodest grin. "And then? You and me time."

"I'm with ya, partner," Sonny said and winked.

2

With warm sunlight streaming through the window, Jay woke wrapped in Sonny's arms.

"Good morning," Jay said.

"Is it? Morning already?" Sonny replied. He blinked soft dark lashes over sleepy blue eyes and squinted at the light.

"Morning already," Jay said. "And by the looks of it, a nice one. Hey, you awake?"

Sonny's eyes were closed. Jay grinned and placed his lips to Sonny's mouth.

The kiss didn't disappoint. A spark like a match set to a fuse sizzled through Jay's body, and by the way Sonny groped his hair, Jay knew Sonny felt it too.

"I am now," Sonny said, breathless.

Jay wrapped his arm tighter around his partner and smiled sheepishly up to the ceiling. He loved what they shared from the intense heat of the city streets to the extreme heat under the sheets. Years of closeness, trust and friendship had brought them here. This new part of his relationship with Sonny felt more than right. It felt inevitable.

Jay didn't want to move from his spot on the bed. A warm breeze through the open window caressed his naked body.

Combing his hand through Sonny's thick, dark hair, he twirled a curl around his finger. "You took a big chance yesterday," Jay said.

"Don't say that." Sonny rested his head on Jay's bare shoulder. We agreed when we started this that nothing else would change. We'd do what we always did."

"And I am. I always worry about the chances you take."

Sonny chuckled deep in his throat. "Yeah? Well I didn't hear you worry too much about the chance I took last night. That was one hell of a position, partner."

"Dirty boy." Jay smacked Sonny's arm. "Get your mind out of the gutter for a minute. I'm serious. You rushed in with no backup."

"Slows me down."

"Dice Diller shot at you."

"True. But I knew you'd be right behind me."

"What if I hadn't been?" Jay continued twirling Sonny's hair, trying not to think of the consequences.

"Ah, but you were," Sonny said. "A little slow though."

"Slow?" Jay said. "You took off like a damn jackrabbit on fire."

"You gotta get a little quicker, Jamison."

"I do, huh? Well, you're missing the point. The point is, you were on the ground, and Dice had *your* gun aimed at *you*."

"Uh, no, Blondie, *you're* missing the point," Sonny said. "The point is, that wasn't the first time a piece of scum tried that. Ain't the last either."

"I'll say it again. He got your gun. He had it aimed right at you."

"And I'll say it again. Those are the risks."

Jay stopped playing with Sonny's curls. "That's it? Those are the risks?"

"Listen, we're cops," Sonny said. "Damn good ones too. It's all part of it. That's what we do. That's what we are."

"Really? That's what we are?"

Sonny sat up and faced Jay. "Do you think I'm good at what I do?"

"You're the best…."

"But?"

Jay sighed. "But you're cocky. You don't take precautions."

"Precautions? Are you serious? Precautions could get me killed, or worse…you killed. Nope, ain't gonna as long as I know what I'm doing and how."

"So we throw away the book? Forget about playing it safe?"

"We play it safe like always by backing each other up like always," Sonny said. "But playing it too safe can get in the way sometimes."

"And what about this?" Jay said. "Is playing this safe getting in the way too?"

"In the way? No. This is us after we leave the sewer. After we take off the guns. This is just for us. No one else."

"No one else?" Jay smiled at his lover with the warmth of his body pressed close to Sonny's flesh. "And here I was hoping for a threesome."

"Now whose mind is in the gutter? You're a bad influence on me, Kenneth Jamison."

"Me? On you? No one would believe that. You strutting that bubble butt of yours around. Batting those blue eyes. Pouting those full lips. You should be some Calvin Klein model, for Christ's sake. How was I supposed to resist all that?"

"Somehow you managed for years." Sonny began to move out of the bed.

Jay pulled him back and smiled into the most beautiful face he knew. "I barely managed. It was the hardest thing I ever did." He pulled Sonny toward him and kissed him with a hungry longing. Sonny groaned. That throaty moan fueled Jay's desire for this tantalizing man even more, and he grew stiff between his legs

Jay loved this man. Michael Sonny Santini at the age of twenty-five with his Brooklyn accent, his thick, dark brown curly hair, and a body that made Michelangelo's *David* look wimpy, was the best thing that ever happened to him. Not a day in the past few months had gone by that Jay wasn't thankful for the courage to have, what they called *The Talk*.

Sonny lingered with the kiss and then abruptly reversed positions so he was on top. He smiled down at Jay with a playfulness Jay never grew tired of.

He gazed up at Sonny. The man's body burnt hot against his. This was all he'd ever wanted from the first moment he allowed himself to be honest. Once he stopped trying so hard to push aside his true feelings and admitted there was more between them than simple friendship, Jay's real struggle was whether to tell Sonny or keep it a secret. He was glad he decided to tell even though it hadn't been easy.

The bed squeaked. The headboard banged against the wall. Jay rocked in unison with Sonny, both their bodies covered in lover's sweat, and he knew it was all worth it.

Afterwards Jay rested exhausted and sated against Sonny. Sonny placed a fresh kiss on Jay's mouth and slipped off the bed. Naked, he padded to the bathroom and called back over his shoulder, "Hey, ya know what today is, don't ya? Six months."

Jay remembered. The shower turned on, and he stretched out his long, lean body. The feel of Sonny still with him, he grinned with eyes shut.

Six months ago today they had confronted one another after a long, sometimes scary, history. All those years Jay hid his feelings, never really knowing if what he hoped he saw in his partner's eyes was more, or whether it was just wishful thinking.

Jay grinned again at the memory but not the fear. He had been scared. Scared the first minute he laid eyes on Sonny when they met at the Florida Police Academy. Afraid every time his heart beat faster when Sonny walked into the room. Scared of feelings he'd never experienced before, but somehow, deep down, didn't completely surprise him.

Everything he felt was so much more than just how gorgeous Sonny was. Everything about him took Jay's breath away. His voice, silky and smooth. His confident strut. The way he teased. The way he smiled. His street smarts. His determination. An inner strength that glowed. And those eyes. Those deep sapphire eyes that seemed to mystify, nearly hypnotize, could not be forgotten.

That was nearly five years ago. Since then, they had graduated and worked together as uniformed police officers and friends. Soon, they were promoted to detectives and took on the dark and dirty side of crime everyday side by side. They had come to know each other well…but not the secret that Jay kept guarded. It was so well guarded that Jay even managed to convince himself it wasn't what he thought. Until Emma Mills.

Jay turned over in bed. The sheets still warm where he and Sonny had made love. He crunched his pillow under his head, and his mind drifted back to that time of uncertainty.

* * *

Emma Mills was a pretty blond with a slim body and long legs. She was a loan manager at the bank where Sonny had gone to get an educational loan for his younger sister, Rachel, so she could complete college. That's the way Sonny was and one of the things Jay also loved – Sonny was about family.

Next thing Jay knew, Sonny was dating Emma. But it was different from the other girls he had dated. It was the way Sonny acted. He was preoccupied and talked about the relationship in a way that made his face flush, and Sonny never blushed. Jay tried to push aside his jealousy. All he wanted was for his partner to be happy. But still, it hurt. It hurt like hell.

How could he tell Sonny that he had fallen in love with him? How could he admit it and risk losing him? Either way, the heartache would be unbearable. Even now, as Jay lay on the pillow, his eyes stung from the memory of that fear of risk and the uncertainty of the outcome.

Then one day Jay was alone with Emma. They were at Sonny's apartment and, on Emma's request that Sonny get a specific bottle of wine for her, he had left. She faced Jay.

Emma, who always wore low tops to show her best features, had grinned patronizingly at Jay.

"So," she said. "How are things?" Her voice sounded condescending.

"Fine. How about you?" Jay said and put down the car magazine.

"Same. Good. Michael and I are doing better than good." She smiled. "He's really…something," Emma said and smiled more. "Really…something."

Jay nodded. "Yeah. He's something, all right."

"I've practically moved in," she announced.

Jay noticed she waited for a reaction. "Really? Good for you." He swallowed the knot in his throat and awkwardly went to the window. It felt safer to have his back to her.

"Yes," Emma said. "Of course, after we're married, we'll have to get a bigger place. This is just too…small, don't you think?"

"Married?" Jay said. His face burned. Running a sweaty hand through his fine blond hair, he tried to steady his voice. "I-I didn't know. I mean that-that it was…that you and Sonny were…."

"Serious?" Emma giggled. "Oh, I'd say it's very serious." She ran her hand along the arm of the chair. "Look at this old thing. It's a mess. This will be the first to go. I have my eyes on some beautiful things at Ethan Allen."

"Furniture?" Jay said and coughed to clear the squeak. "You-you're buying – ?"

"New furniture? Of course. And a new big bed. Cherry, I think or mahogany. Lots of leather too."

"Sounds...expensive," Jay said.

"Expensive? Of course it's expensive. It's time for Michael to come up in the world."

"Michael. Right. Well, he has a cop's salary. That isn't much. Guess you make more at the bank."

"Oh, I don't plan to work after the marriage," she said and crossed her legs.

Jay ran his hand through his hair again. "A new place? Furniture? Takes money." He turned to face her.

"Once Michael gets that new job, we'll have plenty."

"New...new job? What new job?"

"Working for my father. At the security company. Michael will be the Director of Supervision. My father is making up the position just for him."

"Michael...I mean, Sonny, will? Wh-what kind of job is it?"

Emma waved her hand. "I don't know. My father will figure it out."

Jay eyed her. "So it's just a bogus job." He lowered and shook his head. "You know he loves being a cop."

"A cop?" Emma laughed and waved her hand at the thought. "Not with me. Long hours. Lousy pay. I can't very well take my husband to the country club and tell people he works as a cop in downtown Oakland City." She looked as if she had tasted something repulsive. "That would never work."

Jay's stomach twisted. Was she for real? "Does...does Sonny know about this? I mean, he never said anything."

Emma uncrossed her legs and looked back at the front door before she eyed Jay. Quietly, she said, "He doesn't know. Exactly. I've hinted at it. That's why I need your help."

"Me?"

"You're like his best friend, right? I need you to convince him that my idea is best for him. I mean, he'll still be able to do some of that police stuff. He'll be in charge of security for some very influential clientèle. No more creepy, disgusting perverts. It will be good, honest work with plenty of perks."

"Police stuff? Look, Emma, I don't know if you know the same guy I do. Sonny loves that…ah, police stuff. Okay? It's…it's in his blood. You can't change him."

"Oh, can't I?" Emma glared at him with a snotty look. "I'm pretty sure I have a good idea on how to change him. He'll listen to me."

"Then why would you need my help?" Jay said, an edge to his voice.

"I just thought it would make it easier. But if you're not willing, I can get him to do this."

"You're sure of yourself, huh? Sonny's pretty stubborn."

She waved a manicured hand at him. "Please. Putty. Pure putty. He knows I know what's best for him."

"You know what's best for him? You?"

"Of course. I've already gotten him to go to the country club. At first he laughed, but then he went."

"He did? You introduced him as a cop?"

"Good God, no. I told him to pretend he was undercover. He played along as a business associate of mine from corporate."

"Sonny? My Sonny did that?"

Emma frowned. "*Your* Sonny?" She laughed and relaxed her face. "He had a good time playing along."

"Playing along. But it wasn't real."

"Believe me, he'll be just fine."

"My parents tried to change me too, you know," Jay said. "They didn't like the idea of me being a cop either."

"Michael mentioned it. They disowned you."

"I didn't like the country club crowd anymore than Sonny will."

"Oh, he will. You just watch. He never liked to drink wine either. But when he comes back, you watch. He won't have a beer. He'll pour us both a glass of wine. And it won't be from a box, either. Eighty dollars a bottle."

"Eighty dollars a....You don't know him. You don't know – "

"Know what?" Sonny said, as he came in the front door. He bent to kiss Emma and took the expensive wine out of the bag. She had been right. He poured a glass for them both, offered a glass to Jay, and then sat on the arm of the chair next to Emma sipping wine that Jay just knew he hated.

* * *

A towel snapped in front of Jay's face.

"Hey. Jamison. You here?" Sonny said.

He towel dried his hair.

"What's the sappy grin for, Jamison?" he said.

"I'm here." Jay pulled himself back to the present. "No place else I'd rather be."

"Good for you," Sonny said. His naked body glistened with beads of water. He took a tee shirt from the drawer and began to put it over his head.

"Hey. Come back to bed," Jay said with a sweet smile.

"Hey," Sonny said. "Get your ass outta bed. It's nine o'clock. It's Sunday. No work today. Weather is perfect. Come on. Move it."

"That's exactly why we should spend the day in bed."

Sonny tossed the tee shirt aside, came over to him and kissed his shoulder. "You're a maniac. You know that?"

"Can't help it if I can't get enough of you," Jay said. He couldn't resist. He caressed Sonny's arms and then pulled him down to the bed. With his partner completely his, he placed kisses along Sonny's silky left shoulder until he felt Sonny's arms around him.

Jay ran his hand over Sonny's moist chest until he reached the area just below the naval. This was his favorite spot. It was where the fine black hair on Sonny's stomach narrowed, and led a path to ecstasy.

Sonny moaned and arched his back. His taut muscles relaxed while Jay massaged him with his hands and mouth.

The taste of Sonny was sweet. Jay's heart pounded with joy as the real-ization, still so fresh, captured his mind. Here he was with the one person that completed him. The one person he had feared he could never have. Now they belonged to each other. Sonny held his heart.

Once more, Jay's eyes burned as he recalled their journey. Here he was in the arms of the man he loved, but, even so, the desperation that all would-be lovers felt – that persistent fear that the one person who meant more than the next breath might not feel the same – was still present.

It was not because the person Jay loved was his best friend. And not because Jay was worried that a relationship might damage their friend-ship if it didn't work. No, it was more complicated than that. Jay was in love with another man who was also on the police force. The police department had its own culture and rules. The people they worked with were a close family who knew Jay and Sonny lived as bachelors, dated women, joked about marriage and having a family, but who didn't know in all this time that Jay had fallen in love with his partner.

Tears streamed down Jay's cheeks. He never meant for all of this to happen, but it did. And he wasn't about to take it for granted.

"I love you," Sonny whispered.

Those words. Jay never thought he'd hear them from Sonny. It made his heart want to burst. Sonny moaned and Jay felt the man's body react the way he hoped. When he glanced up at Sonny's smile and that gleam in his eyes, it said all that Jay needed to know. He moved into Sonny's arms and they held each other.

Quiet, they rested until Jay reluctantly eased out from the crumpled sheets. "You're right. We should do something to celebrate today."

Sonny smiled. "I thought we just did." His curly hair was still damp from the shower, and his body was covered in fresh sweat. "Guess I need another shower."

Sonny eased out of bed and followed Jay into the bathroom.

"So." Sonny teasingly nudged Jay. "Whatta we gonna do today?" He combed his hair.

"You decide," Jay said, going back into the bedroom and picking up mangled sheets from the floor.

"Me? You're the romance guru of this operation. If it was up to me, I'd say let's get some beers and watch the football game."

"You would too," Jay said and laughed. He turned, and the sight of Sonny made his flesh tingle. He admired the way the light shone on Sonny's dark hair. It was a complement to Jay's wispy straight blond hair.

"Stop looking at me like that," Sonny said as he came closer. "We'll never get out of here if you don't." He picked up the white tee shirt from the floor and pulled it over his head.

Sonny's hair sprang from the neck of the shirt. That hair along with Sonny's rich olive complexion was a contrast to Jay's fair skin.

Sonny pulled on a pair of cut-off jeans and then stood next to Jay at the mirror. Jay admired their reflection. He and Sonny complemented each other in both shape and size. Jay, six feet, almost three inches taller than Sonny and, at 180 pounds, five pounds heavier. Both men were lean and muscular with strong chests and arms. Sonny more solid. Jay longer in the legs. Jay's eyes a light sky blue. Sonny's a blue that changed in the light and with his moods, from deep violet to sapphire.

"You're doing it again, Jamison," Sonny said. He patted Jay on the back. "I'm leaving this room now before I get trapped here all day. Join me. Time to eat. And yes, I mean food." He left the bedroom laughing.

Jay smiled. Their personalities and temperament, while different from one another, also balanced each other. Sonny was a kidder. A natural born practical joker. He used his humor to protect his vulnerability with others. He was kind and good-hearted, but didn't trust easily or often. He could be moody. Upbeat one moment and wanting to be alone the next. Jay had gotten good at reading him over the years. He knew when to push an issue and when to leave it alone until Sonny was ready to deal with it.

Jay went into the kitchen. "What do you want to eat?"

"I don't know." Sonny was tying a trash bag to take it out. "Surprise me. And I don't mean by being buck naked when I come back."

Jay shook his head. Life with Sonny. A dreamer who believed in fairy tales, who loved happy endings, scary movies, dancing, Christmas, and just plain acting like a kid.

Jay was two years older and not quite as social as his partner. More shy where Sonny was outgoing. More clumsy where Sonny was at ease. Jay was into history, philosophy, and nature. Sonny's idea of an evening home was pizza out of a box, beer and loud music. Jay's was reading a good book and listening to country ballads.

Jay was the thinker. The romantic. The logical one who, for some strange reason he could never understand, trusted too easily. That was the flaw that allowed him to be hurt more than he cared to remember.

The rattle of the garbage can outside brought Jay back to the moment. He glanced out the window. Sonny stuffed the trash bag in the can, tried to squeeze the lid down to fit, and cursed when it didn't. Sonny went back to the garage to get another can, but not before he stopped to check his car. The cherry red Mach 1 Mustang he loved.

Again, Jay shook his head. Sonny was a fanatic about cars and junk food. Jay enjoyed quiet walks, wine and gardening. He didn't know a damn thing about cars, but he grew beautiful roses.

That's what Jay loved. They were different, but the same. They both enjoyed jogging together, the beach, basketball and old movies with Bogart or Cagney. Jay loved to read the comics to Sonny. Sonny loved to take pictures of Jay with his camera.

Jay got coffee ready to perk for Sonny. There was the sound of a metal scrape from the other garbage can Sonny slid out of the garage. When Sonny began to toss a bag of trash inside it and the bag ripped, Sonny cursed again. From the window, Jay laughed. This was his partner. The one he fought crime with, and the one who moved in perfect sync with him on the streets or under the covers.

Jay fixed his health drink. Sliced bananas, vanilla yogurt, granola, and wheat germ with skim milk all placed in the blender. He let the machine whirl, blending the mix, and shut it off as Sonny came through the back door of the kitchen.

"So, partner?" Jay said, trying not to laugh, "how'd you make out with the trash? Did you arrest it for resisting a police officer?" He poured the lumpy concoction into a glass and snickered.

"I beat that scum to the ground," Sonny said. "Taught it who's boss, and tossed its stinky ass in the can." He washed his hands at the sink, turned and stuck out his tongue at what Jay drank. "How in the hell, Blondie, can you stomach that crap? It's disgusting."

"Right. And three-week-old pizza is what? A taste fest?"

"Better than that stuff." Sonny took the glass, sniffed the contents, and handed it back. "That is so gross. It looks like – "

"Don't," Jay said and put up his index finger.

"Vomit," Sonny finished.

Jay set the glass on the counter, grabbed Sonny around the neck and wrestled him to the floor.

Sonny laughed as he maneuvered Jay so he was on top. Victorious, he raised his arms up over his head while he straddled Jay.

"Don't mess with the Santini," he said in his best Italian Brooklyn accent.

Jay cupped Sonny's groin. "Or what?"

"Don't do it, Blondie."

Jay began to squeeze the package.

"I mean it. I bite."

"So? Bite."

Sonny tickled Jay under the arms. Jay roared with laughter and begged him to stop.

"Okay. Okay," Jay finally said, winded. He put up his palms. "I give. No messing with the Santini."

"Better believe it," Sonny said and got up. "They make us tough in Brooklyn. You're from Indiana, of all places. You don't know these things. Like my Uncle Tony always said," – Sonny shadow boxed around the kitchen – "Jab and dance, kid. Jab and dance.'"

Jay rose, leaned his back against the counter and took a drink from his glass while he watched the show. "Are you done? Or is there an encore?"

Sonny punched his fists into the air while he bobbed back and forth. "Gotta stay strong. Gotta stay hard, kid."

"I really think you need counseling."

Sonny stopped sparring and poured himself some coffee. "Oh, you had it easy growing up. My family? Now that was tough."

"You think so, huh?"

Sonny was close to his mother and younger sister, while Jay wasn't close to his family at all. Sonny's father died when Sonny was fourteen.

Jay's parents preferred to travel the globe and make money to spend on expensive homes and cars, than spend any real time with their only son.

"You met my mom," Jay said. "Once. Remember? You took me out so we could get drunk when she left."

Sonny fixed his coffee. "Hey, look. I know your parents are…."

"Weird? Strange? Egomaniacs?"

"Yeah. All that. But come on, you met my Uncle Tony. He's not the type you wanna mess with."

"True. I wouldn't."

"I mean, he's a hell of a New York City cop, and…."

"You love him."

"Yeah, sure. That too. But man, when he got pissed." Sonny whistled. "Duck."

Sonny's Brooklyn accent was still intact, especially when he spoke like this. He had grown up on the streets. His mother worked two jobs to support him and his sister after her husband died. Uncle Tony tried to help, especially after Sonny got into trouble. Jay, on the other hand, grew up in a mansion with a nanny, a gardener, and went to private school.

Jay patted Sonny on the back. "You survived. Somehow we both did." He finished his breakfast drink and asked, "Have you seen my watering can?"

At the kitchen window, Sonny gestured toward the front door. "Out on the steps."

"Hey? You okay? You started talking about your uncle and now you have that Santini frown."

"Yeah. I'm good," Sonny said, but his expression said something else.

"What is it?" Jay said and stepped closer.

Sonny turned back to the sink. "I just got to thinking about my mom and our families. I wish sometimes….I don't know. That we didn't have to lie about us. Sometimes."

"You never mentioned that before. Are you sure that's what it is?"

"Yeah," Sonny said without looking at Jay.

Jay turned Sonny so they could face one another. "Well, hey. You said yourself, it's not a lie if no one asks." He smiled a bit to lighten the mood. "It's our business. Right? Our life. Why worry about what anyone thinks or how they'll react. Besides, who knows what could happen in a couple of years. Maybe the world will change."

Sonny snickered. "Yeah. Right. I know what'll happen in a couple of years. I'll still be stuck with you, and my mom'll wanna know why I haven't settled down and given her grandkids. Then my uncle'll say he'll knock me in the head if I don't marry a nice Italian girl. You think I should tell him I'm already married? To you?"

Jay's eyes opened wide, and he blushed. "You are? I-I mean…you-you think we're married?"

"Get the stars outta your eyes, Blondie. What do you think this commitment is?"

"Married? I-I didn't think…." Jay faced the sink and turned on the water.

Sonny shut off the faucet. "You aren't getting all watery-eyed on me, are you? I mean, I just figured this is for the long haul, ya know? For keeps, right? Unless you want something else?"

"Me? No. I-I want…you know, this. Us."

"Yeah? Then look at me, Jamison. Oh, shit. You *are* turning on the water works. I swear, you are way too sensitive." Sonny hugged him. "That's just one of the things I love about you. So, we're committed right? You. Me. This place and all our bills?"

Jay nodded and wiped his damp eyes. "You, me, and our bills."

"Any chance you got a little bit of Italian in you? No? Well," Sonny sighed. "Mom'll be disappointed. Guess she'll have to deal."

"Are you sure you're okay with all of this?"

"Oh, Christ, Jamison. How many ways do I have to say it? Or show it? Yes. I love you. I love our happy little home. You and me. Partners. Always. Okay? Now let's go celebrate. How about you make sandwiches, and we head out along the coast? A nice long ride somewhere secluded and maybe…just maybe, I'll make out with you in the backseat of my car."

They kissed long and firm with deep moans and lusty desire.

Sonny pulled away first and shook his head. "Oh, no, Jamison. I know your wild ways. You're not getting me back in bed."

"You going to skip your run this morning?"

"Yeah. But that doesn't mean a run in bed."

"I want a ring," Jay interrupted, his lips feeling puffy from the kiss.

"A what?"

"A ring," he repeated and pointed to his left ring finger.

"What?" Sonny shrieked. "Are you nuts?" When Jay laughed, Sonny shook his head. "You're crazy, you know that? Insane. I'm going to get the newspaper." He whistled as he left the kitchen.

* * *

Sonny opened the blinds in the living room. He heard Jay humming, and it made him smile.

All he wanted in his life, besides taking down the bad guys and staying alive, was to keep Jay safe and make him happy.

Sonny glanced out the window at the quiet suburban neighborhood where they lived miles from the sewers they worked every day. They had decided to rent the one story ranch house on Tremont Street four months ago. Sonny had never been happier. All the pieces in his life finally fell together, and for that, he was grateful.

He went out to the front steps searching for the morning paper. The neighborhood was quiet. A family friendly residential suburb, it also leased to single professionals. Two secretaries rented the house across the street. Fran and Michelle were both in their twenties. They met in college and decided they should room together while looking for Mr. Right.

An elderly couple lived next door. They often waved when Sonny and Jay took walks or drove past.

Two doors down was a family with three children. Doug Connor and his wife, Molly, had lived in the one story brick ranch for three years. Doug worked construction, and Molly stayed at home to care for their two-year-old son and five-year-old twin girls.

At the end of the street lived Mrs. Lowe. She was a widow known for the collection of rocks, assorted sizes and shapes, she used for her rock gardens.

The neighborhood suited Sonny and Jay. The house was perfect. The owner was decent, and best of all, no one questioned why he and Jay lived together. Everyone seemed to like the idea of having two cops so close. The other detectives they worked with and their own captain said it made sense to combine salaries and live in a decent place. The pact that he and Jay had made was working.

"Where the hell is that paper?" Sonny mumbled.

The grass in the yard was a deep green despite the fact that it hadn't rained in over a week. He had to mow it, but it would have to wait.

"Okay, kid, where'd you toss it today?" Sometimes Sonny found it in the bushes. Sometimes on the driveway peeking out from under Jay's rusted Chevy.

He spied the rolled-up newspaper under the mailbox. "Ah. I win. You lose. They don't call me detective for nothing."

The weather was mild. Highs in the mid seventies. Not a cloud in the sky. A perfect day for a drive along the coast.

From where he stood just at the edge of his lawn, Sonny spotted Doug and Molly's son, Danny, riding his wooden scooter up and down his parent's driveway. For a two-year-old, Danny was a big kid with strong legs. He loved to push that scooter with his feet, and Sonny often kidded Molly that Danny could probably outrun the Mustang.

Molly was in her front yard. She waved to Sonny as she watered and pruned her flower garden. "Beautiful day isn't it, Michael?"

"Sure is," Sonny called back. "Your yard looks good."

"Thanks," Molly said. "I was wondering if you could help me get the ladder. Doug's not home, and I wanted to cut some branches off that tree."

"No problem." Sonny crossed the street, went into the garage with Molly, and a second later, carried out a wooden ladder that he placed against a tree on her front lawn.

She pointed to a small green bush. "I just planted this yesterday. It's jasmine. I saw the ones you have. I love the scent."

"I'm not the one that planted them. Jay knows that stuff, not me." Sonny smiled and turned with a wave toward his house at Jay who stood on the front steps.

Molly glanced over her shoulder. "How do you do that? How did you know he was there even before you looked?"

Sonny grinned and shrugged.

"That's kind of spooky," Molly said with a giggle.

"When you do our kind of work, you get a sense for that sort of thing," Sonny said and began to walk back down Molly's driveway.

Danny, on his scooter, zoomed past him.

"Whoa there, cowboy," Sonny said. "Slow down."

An engine raced. A car down the street picked up speed. The driver wove back and forth from one curb to the other. Danny's momentum and the slight decline in the driveway pushed the child toward the road. The car sped faster. Sonny reached for Danny, but the toddler moved too quickly.

A scream. The glare of the car's bumper headed toward them. Danny was within an inch of the street. Sonny grabbed the child, lifted him up, and tossed him back on the grass. The car slammed into Sonny.

Sonny flew over the car. His back smashed down on the pavement. His head struck the row of gray rock at the edge of Mrs. Lowe's lawn, and the world went black.

* * *

Jay watched in stunned disbelief. Someone screamed.

The car plowed into a mailbox two houses down. The hood of the car bent inward, around the post. The rear tires spun in place. Steam poured out from under the hood. The engine sputtered and died. The driver climbed out. Dozens of empty beer cans fell around his feet.

Molly scooped up a crying Danny. Sonny lay motionless.

Jay ran so fast his feet barely touched the ground. He knelt down.

"Sonny," he said. Blood oozed from the side of Sonny's head and from his nose. Sonny moaned. "Easy buddy. Take it easy." Jay took Sonny's hand in his. More blood dripped from ripped skin. "I'm right here. Hold on. Hold on."

For a brief second Sonny opened his eyes. The whites were bloodshot. The irises gray and cloudy. He gazed at Jay and then shut his eyes.

Jay felt him begin to slip away. "No. Sonny. Stay with me. Stay with me," he begged.

"I called an ambulance," someone said.

Jay glanced around at the crowd that had gathered. All their faces blurred together. He rubbed the back of his hand across his watery eyes.

He knew he shouldn't touch Sonny. Instinct kicked in, and he tried to assess his partner's condition.

"Just stay with me, please. Don't leave me." He sucked back a sob.

Sonny's lids barely opened, his lashes damp. Blood dripped from his forehead. More trickled from the corner of his mouth.

"No. Oh, God. No," Jay cried out. "Hang on. You gotta hang on. Where the hell is that ambulance?" He brushed away a bloody strand of hair from Sonny's forehead. The right side of Sonny's head was in a puddle of blood. The pool slowly widened until Jay's knee was soaked.

Sonny's breathing was shallow. He turned colder under Jay's touch.

Jay squeezed Sonny's hand. It was limp and clammy. He held it firm as if it would give his partner strength. "Please," he pleaded, "don't leave me. Stay with me. Hold on to me."

Sonny's lips parted, trying to form words. Jay leaned closer.

"J...." Sonny said, and then there was nothing but air.

The police and ambulance pulled up with sirens blaring. Jay felt a hand on his shoulder and half heard someone ask him to move back. Another hand helped him up, and two men with a stretcher came forward.

A paramedic checked Sonny's pulse. He shined a light into his eyes.

"Easy," Jay said as they worked on Sonny.

Two uniformed officers – Jay knew them – Harry and Stan, took the driver into custody. Jay rushed the man and shook him hard.

"What did you do? What did you do?"

The officers pushed Jay back.

"Easy, Jay," Harry said. "Just take it easy,"

"Get this piece of shit out of my sight," Jay shouted. "Get him out of here."

He turned his attention back to the paramedics, Tom and Rick. He knew them slightly from other police emergencies that usually involved a dead victim. Jay cringed, afraid to look at them because he knew that if he saw them pull a white sheet over Sonny's face he would drop and never get up again.

"Jay, come on," Stan said and led him to the patrol car. "Come over here with me. Let them do their work. Just take it easy."

Jay barely acknowledged him. He looked back toward Sonny sprawled on the street and then back at Stan. It still didn't register.

"I'm gonna call it in," Stan said and spoke into the radio. "Dispatch, this is Unit 31. We have a 10-50." Stan eyed Jay. "Victim is Detective Michael Santini."

Jay heard it. The code 10-50 meant accident, fatal, personal injury. Sonny's name. He heard the words, but none of it made sense.

"T-tell them you want Captain Colby," Jay stammered. He was dreaming. His own voice sounded odd.

"I will," Stan said. Again, he spoke into the radio mic. "Transporting to Memorial Hospital. Request Captain Colby. 10-95. Subject in custody. 10-77. Hold." He turned to his partner. "Harry? How long till the medics are ready?"

"Fifteen," said Harry, his face grim.

Stan keyed the mic again. "Dispatch? ETA 15 minutes. Unit 31 out." Stan hung up the radio. "Captain Colby will meet you at the hospital," he told Jay. "You okay? Maybe we should get the medics to check you?"

Numb, Jay shook his head. The medics had placed Sonny on a stretcher, but the imprint of where he landed, all the blood, still painted the pavement red.

"I'll ride with him," Jay said as they loaded Sonny into the ambulance.

"Can't, Detective," Rick said. "He needs all our attention."

Jay wasn't about to take no for an answer. Through gritted teeth, he said, "He's my partner, dammit."

"I know who he is," Rick said. "But you know the rules."

Jay was nearly nose to nose with the man. "I don't give a shit about rules."

"Jay?" a woman said from behind him.

It was his neighbor, Fran. "I'll drive you." She placed a sympathetic hand on his shoulder.

Jay's face was damp with tears and sweat, his body trembling. He slowly nodded. The ambulance pulled away with its siren screaming.

"Let's go," Jay said and hurried into Fran's car. During the entire trip, he never spoke. He kept his eyes on the ambulance while he rubbed his hands up and down his thighs.

At the ER entrance, Jay leaped from the car. The paramedics opened the back doors of the white and red ambulance and rolled out Sonny's stretcher. They quickly wheeled him inside the entrance. Jay, close behind, followed. Sonny wasn't moving. He wore an oxygen mask, was sandwiched into a neck brace, and hooked to an IV in his arm.

The stretcher barged through the emergency room doors where two doctors waited. The minute they saw the stretcher, they circled it.

A nurse stepped forward. "Trauma Room One," she said.

"Is he all right?" Jay said. "Is he going to be all right?"

He got no answer and followed behind, but as the stretcher was guided through another door, a nurse in a bright printed uniform held back. The door swooshed shut.

"No, you don't understand," Jay said. "He's my….I'm his….I'm a police officer."

The nurse tried to calm him. For some reason, the yellow happy faces on her shirt began to bounce in front of Jay's eyes while she directed him to a waiting area.

"Someone will be out as soon as they know anything," she said.

Swoosh. She and her happy faces were gone.

3

J ay was left alone still in shock and drowning in a stream of fear. In that moment, he realized he had dried blood caked on his hands, his pant leg and on his shirt.

The swoosh of the hospital door, a nurse walked past him. Another swoosh, and more people walked by. He tried to look in through the small window of a door marked Emergency, but all he saw were more hospital staff, drawn curtains, and machines being wheeled in and out.

Tears strained. He closed his eyes. It didn't help. He could see it all so clearly in his mind. He had gone out to the front steps to water his plants. Sonny waved to him from Molly's driveway somehow knowing he was there. Sonny smiled. Little Danny on the scooter rolled by just as Sonny reached out to grab the child. The car. Jay's stomach gave way as the car struck Sonny. The impact flung Sonny up and over the car like a rag doll. He didn't land until a few feet later. The sound. A god-awful crack when Sonny landed with such force, Jay was surprised the ground didn't split open and swallow him.

Jay's heart beat almost out of his chest. He got to Sonny's side and saw the blood. Internal injuries. There was no doubt. Try as he might as the emergency room door swooshed open and shut, he couldn't fool himself into believing that Sonny only had minor cuts and scrapes. Under his breath he prayed, "Oh God. Not fatal."

"Jay? Jay?"

Was that Sonny's voice? Jay's trance broken, he jumped with a start when he heard his name again, and a hand touched his shoulder. When he turned, Captain Hank Colby stood by him.

"How is he, son?" Colby said, his usual gruff voice softened to almost a whisper. He was dressed in a dark brown suit and brown striped tie as if it was any normal day, but it wasn't, not to Jay. Nothing about today was normal.

Hank Colby was the Captain of Detectives for the Oakland PD. He had worked his way up through the ranks and been assigned as captain seven years ago. He was a dedicated police officer who also knew how to be hard edged when necessary. As one of the few black police officers in Florida – let alone a high ranking one – he had to be tough.

Jay owed Colby a lot. He was a good mentor and commanding officer. He was the one who had the foresight to assign Sonny and Jay as partners.

"I-I don't know," Jay said and stared at the hospital door. "I don't know."

Colby placed a strong hand on Jay's shoulder, but it didn't calm his shaking. "Let's sit down."

Colby was an inch shorter than Jay and about eighty pounds heavier. A usually serious man with a stern manner that reflected in his wide, somewhat heavy face, he hardly smiled. With a small mustache that he grew only to shave and grow again, he often barked orders out of the side of his mouth, a mouth that seemed forever in a downward slope.

Captain Colby was respected by his men, and he respected them. A by-the-book-no-nonsense kind of cop, Jay suspected the man had a soft spot for him and Sonny. Their antics with each other always seemed to amuse him, even when he tried not to let it show.

Jay let out a deep breath that he held since this whole horror began. "They took him in there. I haven't seen anyone yet."

Colby gestured toward some chairs. He guided Jay to them and somehow managed to get him to sit. "What happened?"

Jay's eyes were glued to the door. "A car. He…Sonny grabbed Danny, our neighbor's little boy, before the car hit him."

"Is the child all right?"

Jay nodded.

"God bless Sonny," Colby said. "I'm sure he saved that child's life."

Jay nodded again and rubbed his hands together. "What's taking so long? Why haven't they come out?"

"It takes time. It always seems worse from this side."

"It's bad, Cap. I'm sure there's internal injuries." Jay's eyes pooled. "He landed so…hard. And…." Jay's mind drifted to that sight again and that horrific sound.

"He's been in tough spots before," Colby said.

Jay cleared his throat and shook his head. "Not like this." He looked again at the blood on his hands until he felt Colby tap his shoulder and point at a nurse.

"Excuse me," the nurse said. "Did you come in with the young man from the ambulance?"

Jay leaped to his feet. "Yes. How is he?"

"He's still with the doctors. I need some information for our records." With a clipboard in hand, she signaled for Jay to sit back down and began her questions.

Jay gave her the information she needed and explained that Sonny had been in this hospital nearly a year ago for a gunshot wound.

The nurse, whose name was Helen, according to her uniform badge, asked if Sonny was allergic to any medication or if he had any distin-guishing marks on his body. Jay blushed, but tried to hide it. Knowing that Sonny did have a birthmark just below his right buttock was not information that simple police partners, or even best friends, should nec-essarily know.

The nurse thanked Jay and shook his hand. "As soon as the doctor's ready, he'll be out."

"Miss?" Colby said. "Is it possible to get Detective Jamison a change of clothes?"

"Of course," she said.

Colby offered to get Jay coffee. Jay refused. When the nurse came back with a pair of green scrubs, the captain said, "Why don't you go in the bathroom. Clean up. I'll be out here waiting for the doctor."

Jay nodded. "I won't take long."

Safely locked behind the bathroom door, Jay was glad for the excuse. He needed this moment because the tears he fought so hard to hold back fought him harder. Finally alone, they won and flowed down his face.

"Come on, Jamison, snap out of it," he said. This wasn't like him. He'd dealt with worse than this in the past, and the possibility of tragedy was part of everyday life for him and Sonny. But…this had come from no-where, for no logical reason. This was supposed to be a day to celebrate and not have the bottom drop out.

He started to wipe his eyes but caught sight of his hands in the mirror. They were sticky red. What had been Sonny's warm blood had grown cold and hard. His shirt and pants were crusted heavy with blood as well. His stomach churned with a sick feeling. The health shake he drank that morning decided to come back up. Jay rushed into the stall. Everything in his stomach exploded from his mouth until he had nothing left.

Jay sank to the cold floor. The front of his shirt was a mixture of vomit and blood. The smell alone made him sick again. He gagged and swallowed. Another wretched gag, he knew he couldn't hold it. He fumbled to reach the toilet just in time and puked until his throat was raw.

Shaky, he stumbled out of the stall, pulled off his stained shirt, and looked at himself in the mirror. What stared back wasn't Jay's face. It was the face of Sonny. Sonny with his crooked smile, with his dancing eyes, and that damn playful laugh. Jay shut his eyes. None of this could be real. What felt real was yesterday when they had busted Dice Diller and this morning, before the nightmare began.

"Paging Dr. Wells," the hospital intercom called.

Jay's eyes snapped open. Tears ran down his cheeks almost as fast as his feet had run when the car slammed into Sonny.

Once more his mind replayed the events. He had come out to the front steps, picked up his watering can, smiled when Sonny spoke to Molly, and then stepped to the driveway to get the hose. The roar of a car engine. A scream. The car's front bumper hit Sonny at just the right angle.

Jay could still feel their last kiss and touched his lips. His mouth pulsated just with the thought of Sonny.

"Commitment. You and me. Always." The last thing Sonny said. He could feel Sonny's arms around him. The man's warm breath. His heated touch. Jay throbbed. He felt Sonny's caress. Felt Sonny everywhere inside and out of his body.

"I love you," he heard Sonny say.

Jay trembled. He washed his face with shaky hands and tried to steady himself. He gripped the white porcelain sink and cried. Quiet, inaudible sobs that shook his body from the inside out. There was no place for his pain to go. Nowhere for the fear to be released. He gripped the sink and squeezed with white knuckles.

"You're too damn sensitive, Jamison," he heard Sonny say. It made him chuckle through his tears.

"And that's why you love me," Jay replied and took a deep breath to compose himself.

Combing his damp hands through his hair, his mind flashed to the time a little over a month ago when Jay was so sick he had to be hospitalized. Sonny never left. He sat day and night by his side.

"Come on, Jay." Sonny called to him, and even in a fevered delirium, Jay had heard him. "You're tough. You know you are. You can make it. Hang in there. Hang in for me okay, partner?"

Jay leaned forward with his forehead pressed to the mirror and held on to those words. "I could hear you then, partner, so I need you to hear me now. Hang in there, okay?"

With a deep breath, he opened the bathroom door just in time to see the doctor walk up to Colby.

"I'm Dr. Dixon, the neurologist here at Memorial." He shook Jay and Colby's hands as they introduced themselves.

"How is he?" Jay said, not realizing he still held the doctor's hand tightly in his own.

"We need to talk," the doctor said.

4

D r. Thomas Dixon looked to be in his mid-fifties, with greased-down, thin black hair that was receding. He wore a white collared shirt and dark blue striped tie under his starched white medical jacket. His skin was pallid compared to most Floridians – an indication to Jay that the doctor worked long hours indoors and rarely got out.

Dixon stood eye to eye with Jay. "Michael is in critical condition."

Jay's stomach flipped.

"Does he have family here?"

Jay shook his head. "His mom lives in New York. I'm the closest family he has."

Dixon nodded. "His injuries are significant. There is damage to one kidney and his spleen. We believe we have it under control. My main concern, however, is his head injury. Michael sustained a traumatic head injury that damaged the brain. He has edema…swelling. The brain is pushing against the skull. We have him on medication to reduce this and minimize the damage. Right now, he's in a coma. He's breathing on his own, which is a good sign, but he's not responding to painful stimuli. Our primary goal is to reduce the swelling without surgery. If he doesn't respond to the medication, and the swelling gets worse, we may need to relieve the pressure."

Jay tried to absorb what the doctor had said. It wasn't easy. He could hear the doctor loud and clear, but couldn't seem to focus.

"Will he be all right?" Jay said. It felt like time froze waiting for the answer.

The doctor glanced at Jay, then Colby, and back again. "We won't know for at least forty-eight hours. His vitals are stable, but we have to monitor his blood pressure."

Colby cleared his throat. "What's the prognosis?"

The doctor took a reluctant breath. "We can't rule out death. I'm sorry, but I won't hide any facts. There is also the possibility of permanent coma and vegetative state. If he does make it and regains consciousness, there is no doubt he will be permanently brain damaged."

Jay's breath caught in his throat. "Wh-what do you mean? Permanently brain damaged?"

"The spectrum is wide," the doctor said, his expression hardened. "We won't know until, and if...he wakes up. I'll be here checking him. If you have any questions, please have the nurse page me."

"Can-can I see him?" Jay said with pleading eyes.

"Yes. He's in ICU." Dixon pointed. "Through those doors and up the elevator to the third floor. Room 309." The doctor shook both men's hands again. "I wish I had better news, but for now, at least he's alive."

Jay felt the hammer in his stomach again. The same hammer that pounded his gut since this nightmare began.

In silence, Jay and Colby walked along the corridor. The *ting bing* of the elevator, and they were in the Intensive Care Unit. It was a daunting sight. Room after room with observation windows and patients hooked to monitors, IVs, beeping machines and respirators.

A nurses' station occupied the center of this mass of rooms. A perfect square, office chairs behind the counter, and TV monitors that displayed each room on the floor.

On the wall behind the counter was an erasable message board. Patients' last names and room numbers were listed with their primary doctor's name and duty nurse. Times were also written next to the names to indicate either when vitals needed to be checked or medication given.

The name Santini topped the list. Jay wasn't sure if that had anything to do with the seriousness of the situation or whether it was just a coincidence.

Disoriented for a moment, Jay stopped, and then his legs wouldn't move. Despite his desire to get to Sonny as quickly as possible, he simply couldn't move.

"Jay?" Colby said, an unexpected gentleness in his voice.

Jay nodded. He took a deep breath, but that didn't stop the pounding hammer in his stomach, or the urge to just turn and run.

"I think it's this way," Colby said.

In a fog, Jay noticed nurses and doctors as they came in and out of rooms and chatted to family members. He overheard one woman let out a heart-breaking gasp of denial and cry. Jay turned to see her embraced by a younger girl.

The entire wing in this area of the hospital was a quiet bustle of activity. Men and women wore starched white medical jackets that matched their equally starched white expressions. Nurses wheeled various machines from one room to another. The wheels of the machines squeaked as they moved along the glossy, white tiled floor. Patients, some old, some young, some large, some thin and frail, were wheeled on stretchers down the hall as young nurses or orderlies struggled to balance beeping machines and IV poles.

As they passed by another room, the door slightly ajar, Jay glimpsed a priest who gave Last Rites. The priest bent to place the sign of the cross on the person in the bed. Jay's stomach twisted.

"May I help you?" a nurse said.

Jay could not speak.

Colby cleared his throat. "Mr. Santini's room," he said and stood close by Jay.

The nurse pointed to the last room at the end of the hall right next to a smaller nurses' station meant only for that area. The hospital room door was propped open by a kick bar. A long observation window was on the left side of the door. The bed was positioned so that the foot of it faced the doorway. Jay could see Sonny's prone body, face-up, with a white sheet and blanket that covered him to his armpits. His arms extended to the sides.

Just the fact that Sonny was in this specific room so close to any assistance that might be required, told Jay the seriousness of the situation.

The fact that there were numerous machines in the room told Jay even more. He shuddered.

"Jay?" Colby said. "You okay? You need to sit down?"

"No," Jay said in a dry rasp.

Just outside the room, Colby stopped and looked in. Jay paused for a second and then went inside and stood at the foot of the bed.

Sonny lay with a white gauze bandage wrapped around his head like a turban. Both his hands were wrapped in bandages as well.

There were wires everywhere. Some came from Sonny's chest, some from his arms. He was hooked to a monitor that showed his heart rate and blood pressure. Black wires protruded from the gauze bandage around Sonny's skull. The wires led to another machine meant to measure brain waves.

Machines beeped and flashed numbers, arrows moved back and forth on graph paper. A clear plastic IV bag, suspended from a pole, dripped into a thin plastic tube, through an IV machine, and into Sonny's right arm.

Sonny breathed on his own. The doctor said that was a good sign. An oxygen mask covered his nose and mouth but, thank God, no machines to do the breathing.

Jay moved to the left side of the bed and gazed at the man he loved. Sonny lay there with his face pointed to the ceiling. Not a muscle flexed. Not an eyelid twitched. His motionless fingers poked out of bandages. Jay traced the form of Sonny's body with his gaze. Covered in the thin knit blanket that clung to him, Sonny was laid out like a wrapped mummy. Jay made out the form of Sonny's torso, his legs, his feet. Nothing moved except the slow up and down of Sonny's chest as he breathed.

Sonny's face was puffy. But other than that and the bandages, there were no outward signs of injury. Jay almost wished there were. If this were only a broken bone and a simple concussion, then one or two nights in the hospital and Sonny would be home. Jay would take care for him, and then life would return to normal.

There was nothing normal about this. The doctor had said to be grateful that Sonny was alive...for now. The internal injuries could still cause problems. The head injury was serious. Jay's eyes burned. Permanent brain damage. Oh, dear God, what did that mean?

Jay pulled over a chair. It squeaked on the floor. He looked at Sonny, worried the sound had wakened him, and then wished it had. He reached out and took hold of Sonny's bandaged left hand, unsure whether Sonny could feel his touch through the gauze.

"It's me, partner," Jay whispered. "I'm right here. You're gonna be fine. Just fine."

* * *

Hank Colby stepped out of the room and watched both men through the window. He couldn't hear what Jay said, but he could see him whisper to Sonny.

Colby hated seeing two of his best men like this even though he was no stranger to heartache. A cop's life wasn't an easy one. He had been in hospitals like this for his men injured in the line of duty. No one liked to think about it, but every cop knew deep down the risks and possibilities. A simple traffic stop could turn fatal. But this? Something so unexpected. He wasn't sure which was worse.

One thing he knew, Sonny and Jay were tough. They were two men he respected and admired. They were the youngest cops in all his years as an officer who'd made Detective Sergeants in such short time – no small feat.

But Colby hadn't been surprised. He knew the minute he met both men, fresh out of the academy where they graduated at the top of their class, that there was something special about them. Perhaps it was Sonny's street smarts and his doggedness. Or Jay's attention to detail and his allegiance to Sonny. Whatever it was, they complemented one another's style to get the job done.

Colby had assigned them to downtown Oakland City. The area was rife with robberies, murders, drugs, prostitution and gambling. Sonny and Jay took on the streets like Sundance and Butch Cassidy. They became known and respected. Two men above reproach. Loyal to the force and each other. It amazed Colby just how well they worked together. They seemed to communicate with facial expressions and body language as though they had some kind of psychic connection. It was almost eerie the way they sensed each other's needs.

Still watching them, Colby thought of his own partner when he'd been a detective. People who hadn't experienced that kind of relationship couldn't comprehend the closeness that came when a life depended on another's judgment and actions.

"Excuse me," Colby said to a passing nurse, "is there a phone I could use?"

5

Jay slid the chair closer to Sonny's side. The machines continued – *beep, beep* – every four seconds. The black strokes on the graph paper moved up and down with a consistent pattern. There was no movement other than Sonny's slow inhales and exhales. His hands were cool. His eyes pressed closed. No flinch. No twitch. Nothing to indicate dreams or distress or alertness of any kind.

"Hey," Jay said, his voice soft. "Come on, partner. Wake up. Give me something here, huh?"

Still nothing.

"Look, you're the great Santini, right? Tough guy. You aren't going to let a thing like a car take you out, are you?" Jay looked around the room. They were alone. "Listen, partner, you know I love you. You're my life, okay? Yeah, yeah, the sappy stuff. So what? We were going to take a drive today. Remember? You and me. Make out. Back seat. You can't stand me up, not today. Not on our six month anniversary. So, come on, wake up. Please. Open your eyes and look at me."

Nothing.

Jay rubbed Sonny's arm, stroked his cheek, anything to reassure him with words and touch. "Dammit, Son. I love you so much." Jay placed his chin on Sonny's unresponsive hand. "You have to come out of this. I know you will. Can you hear me? I need you. Commitment, right? You. Me. Our bills. We were going to celebrate. Six months ago. Our big talk." Jay shut his eyes, and a warm tear slipped down his cheek. "Our big talk," he whispered to himself, and the memories flooded back.

* * *

After Jay and Emma Mills had spoken in Sonny's apartment seven months ago, Jay saw less and less of Sonny other than at work. Even then, Sonny seemed quiet, different.

A few times Sonny invited Jay to come along with him and Emma. Emma tried to fix Jay up with some of her friends. But those nights were awkward at best. Jay found himself staring when Sonny held Emma's hand. He'd feel his face flame every time Emma leaned over to kiss Sonny. It didn't take long before he began to make excuses why he couldn't join them.

Nights were the hardest. He called Sonny late sometimes just like he always had with some lame excuse about work. The truth was, he just wanted to hear Sonny's voice. But now when he called, Emma answered. Jay hung up.

The ache Jay tried so hard and so long to ignore grew. He found himself driving past Sonny's house just to see if he was there. He was almost sick. He even got to the point where he tried to distance himself from Sonny.

"Focus, Jamison," he'd say to himself. "Concentrate on work. Just work."

It didn't help. All he could imagine was Sonny, and all the cold showers in the world didn't stop the ache. That's when he knew. He couldn't push the thoughts aside anymore. He had to face it and come to terms with it. He was in love with his partner.

One afternoon driving back to the police station, Jay summoned the nerve to broach the subject with Sonny.

"So, how are things?" Jay said. "You know, with, Emma?"

"What do you care?" Sonny said, looking out the window.

"What do you mean, what do I care? I care."

"Yeah? You haven't wanted to hang out with us."

"I–I didn't want to crowd you. Th-that's all," Jay said, hoping he sounded sincere.

"That's not the reason, and you know it," Sonny said.

Jay frowned. "Geez, you're in a mood today."

"I'm in a mood? You're the one who comes up with excuses not to hang out. You hardly talk. Shit, Blondie, we used to have fun, and now….what gives?"

Jay tried to focus on the road while his mind reeled. "Gives?" His voice cracked, and he coughed. "N-nothing gives. I just asked a simple question."

"Right," Sonny said and sighed. "A simple question. Like I said, since when do you give a shit?"

"I give a shit," Jay said and looked sideways at his partner. "I do. I just…."

"Don't want to hang out. I get it."

"No. That's not…that isn't it. I-I told you. I just don't want to, you know, butt in the middle of something. I mean, if there is something. Serious. Is-is there?" Jay looked back at the traffic but his attention was glued to Sonny's reply.

"I know that's not the reason. You can tell me," Sonny said.

Jay frowned again. "T-tell you what?" His voice ended an octave higher. He coughed to lower it. "What?"

"The real reason. It's because you're madly in love with me and you don't want to share me with anyone else. That's it, right, Jamison?"

Jay knew the color drained from his face.

"Hey, watch it," Sonny shouted.

Jay swerved to miss a car. He looked at Sonny who was busy watching him.

"Christ, Jamison," Sonny said, "I was just kidding. You almost got us killed back there."

Jay squeezed the steering wheel. Now? Should I tell him now? "Are you…happy?"

"Happy? With Emma?" Sonny turned his head, gazed out the window and shrugged. "Sure. Why wouldn't I be? Emma's…you know, terrific. I'm lucky to have her."

Jay swallowed. "Did she…did she mention anything about a bigger place? Furniture? A job at her father's company?"

Sonny laughed. "Oh, now I get it. That's what this is all about. She told you that stuff, huh? Yeah. She always talks about a bigger apartment or a house."

"What about the job?"

"That too."

"And?"

"And…I thought about it. I'm still thinking."

Jay pulled into the parking lot and turned off the car. Sonny got out. Jay watched him while he thought, too.

A week later things felt more strained between them. Sonny finally called one Friday afternoon and broke the ice asking if he could come over and talk.

Jay sweated from the moment he hung up the phone.

"Okay, Jamison," he said aloud, "this is it." He wanted his partner to be happy. Was he? Happy with a woman who wanted to change him? Okay, never mind that. If Sonny loved her. If he wanted to be with her then…. what could Jay do? Say, "Hey there, partner, how's it going? By the way, dump the chick and get with me?"

He laughed pitifully at himself. Combing a nervous hand through his hair, he shook his head. No, that wouldn't be the way to do it.

He paced the room and sat on the couch. He could say, "Sonny, for a long time now I've had…feelings for you. More than just friends. More like…I want to take you to bed and screw you." Jesus, Jamison, get a grip. He'd laugh in my face and run for the door.

Jay went into the kitchen where he gulped a glass of water and tried not to throw up lunch.

He couldn't do this. What good would it do? Sonny would either punch Jay in the mouth – and he'd seen Sonny punch. Painful. Or, he'd tear out of there so fast, there'd be rubber burns. Might as well face it. Wish him well. Put in for a transfer and get the hell out of Dodge.

The doorbell rang. Jay nearly leaped out of his skin. His heart raced. His cheeks burned. That was the worst part of being blond. People could always see him blush.

With sweaty palms he turned the doorknob, and there stood Sonny, tight jeans, shirt tails hanging out, sneakers, and that damn dimple when he smiled.

Jay stepped back and gestured for him to come in.

"How ya doing, partner?" Sonny said.

"Fine. You?"

"Bad day? You sick or something?"

"No. Why?"

"You look flushed. You got a fever?" Sonny reached to touch Jay's forehead. Jay pulled away.

"I'm fine. So what brings you here?"

"What? No beer? No chips?" Sonny moved like he always did – like someone at home in his own skin and very at home in Jay's apartment.

"You know where everything is," Jay said and gestured toward the kitchen.

"Right you are, Blondie," Sonny said. "You want anything?"

"No. I'm fine. Just…fuckin' fine."

"What?" Sonny called from the kitchen.

"I said I'm fine," Jay said, louder.

"Don't have to shout." Sonny came back with an open bottle of beer and a bag of pretzels.

Jay sat on the couch. Sonny eased himself into the chair across from him. Jay watched the man suck his beer and munch a pretzel.

"New plant?" Sonny pointed to a potted plant on the coffee table.

Jay nodded. "Trying a new seed mix."

"Working?"

"So far."

"What's the mix?"

"It's…hold on. Since when do you give a shit? Are we making small talk here?"

Sonny snickered. "Guess so." He put down his beer and rubbed his hands together to get off the pretzel salt. "Listen, I kind of wanted to talk to you. About Emma. I-I've been thinking, see? And what I've been thinking…well, I mean, her and I have been thinking, see? And…."

"This isn't like you," Jay said. "To stammer. That's more a me thing. So what exactly are you saying?"

Sonny grinned. "You're right. I don't know why I should be nervous. Not with you. Its just…well, this is kind of big and it feels…weird."

"Weird? As in not right? As in you aren't so sure?" Jay said, with a slight edge to his voice.

"You sound pissed, and you haven't even heard what I have to say." Sonny took another long swig of beer, wiped his mouth with the back of his hand and smiled again. "Emma thinks it's time…to, you know, move on."

"Move on?" Jay felt a twinge of hope. "Move on like move on to other people?"

"Other people? No. Other things," Sonny said. "The next step. You know."

Jay deflated. "Next step?"

"The big one. The M word."

Murder came to Jay's mind. "M word?"

"Marriage. You know. She thinks we should."

"And what do you think?"

"That…maybe…we should."

Jay's stomach twisted. He stared at Sonny and then slowly nodded. "Maybe you should," he said softly.

"You think?" Sonny blinked his blue eyes. "It's a big step."

"Do you…." Jay coughed. "Do you love her?" His stomach tightened more.

Sonny rose and went to the window and looked out. "Hey, who's got the Corvette?"

"I asked you a question," Jay said.

"I could do all right with her," Sonny said.

"All right with her? That's no answer."

"I…I love her. We…we could make it work."

"None of that sounds like you're committed, Sonny."

"I'm just nervous, like Emma says. It's a big step."

"This is something you should be sure about. Not just her."

"I am. I am," Sonny said and then sat on the coffee table in front of Jay. "What do you think? I mean, it makes sense to settle down, right?"

"Settle down? Or…just settle?"

Sonny frowned. "What's that mean?"

"What about all the things she wants? The bigger place? The expensive furniture? She's got you drinking wine, going to the country club. What about being a cop?"

"We could work it out," Sonny said. He looked down so all Jay could see was the man's long, dark lashes casting shadows onto his cheeks.

"Work it out? Sonny, you know better than anyone all the crap I went through with my parents. They didn't accept me or my decisions. That country club life. Is that what you want? Is that what would make you happy?"

Sonny went back to the window. "Nice 'vette."

"Answer me."

"I'm going to take that job. With her father," Sonny said without turning.

"What? I swear I heard…."

"I'm going to work for her father," Sonny repeated and slowly turned toward Jay. "It's better that way."

Jay practically flew off the couch. "Better that way? For who? You? Emma? She's changing you, Sonny. She's got you wrapped around her finger. That's no way to live or have a relationship. You're good enough for…for anyone just the way you are."

"I just…think it's better this way."

"You're not happy. I can see it. I know you better than anyone, and so help me, you're not happy."

"I better go," Sonny said.

"Hold on," Jay blurted. "Just hold on." He paused. His heart pounded. His legs shook slightly, but this was it. "Anyone who loved you…really loved you, wouldn't want you to change for them. They'd never get you to drink expensive wine or pretend to be undercover at some damn party just to make them look good. I lived with my parents who only cared about appearances for a long time. You remember when we first met. My confidence was almost gone. You. You helped me find myself again. I want you to be happy, partner. Really, honest to God happy. Not just pretending or thinking you could make it work. Anyone who was lucky enough to love you or who was damn lucky to have you love them, would want you to be happy."

"I...I think Emma does."

"She does? How? By getting you to work with her father and give up being a cop, which you love?" Jay stopped and looked longingly at Sonny. "I have to tell you something," he began slowly. "Something that I know won't make this any better. And it's selfish. It is. But I have to. I have to say it."

"What?"

"Don't. Don't look at me with those damn blue eyes. Just...just listen, okay? And after I tell you and before you run for the door, remember that you should be a cop because you're one of the best there is. I can transfer. I can leave. But not you. You have to stay."

"What are you talking about? Transfer? Why?"

"This is the big talk. Actually Sonny, this is the mother of all talks. I've put it off. I tried everything I could to handle it. I even decided not to say anything. But after everything you just said, I have to tell you. I just... don't settle. Not for someone who doesn't...who can't love you for who you are. I'm not sure how to do this or where to begin but I got to tell you before I explode inside."

Sonny creased his brows. "What? Jay, tell me. What is it?"

Jay took a deep breath, but it didn't stop the slight quiver in his voice. "It's about you and me partner. It-it's about how I feel." He sat on the couch again, afraid his legs would give out.

Sonny sat on the coffee table. He placed his hand on Jay's bent knee. "It's okay. You can tell me anything, you know that."

Jay accepted Sonny's touch, fearing it might be the last he ever got. He paused and wished this moment didn't mean the end.

Sonny squeezed Jay's knee. His eyes, now indigo, looked deep into Jay's face. "Go ahead. Tell me."

Jay opened his mouth. Nothing came out.

"Come on, partner," Sonny said, "you're scaring me now."

"Sonny…I…you know I love you." He looked down at Sonny's hand still on his knee.

"I know. I love you too," Sonny said. "And I know you want the best for me."

"No. You don't understand. I mean, yes, I want the best for you, but… dammit, Sonny. I love you." Jay stood.

Sonny didn't move from the coffee table. His eyes followed Jay.

Jay moved to the far wall and leaned on the bookcase to steady himself. "Okay, partner, this is it. Sonny. Sonny." He turned to face the man. "I'm *in* love with you. I love you more than anything or anyone in my life. I'm in love with you, and I can't hide it or fight it anymore. If this ruins our relationship, if you never want to see me again, it will be like someone took a knife and cut out my heart, but I can't lie and I can't deny it. Not anymore." He turned back to the bookcase and lowered his head. "I'm just so much in love with you that it hurts."

There was deafening silence.

Slowly, an inch at a time, Jay turned his head. Sonny still sat at the edge of the coffee table, his eyes even deeper blue than a moment ago, and his mouth slightly open. When their eyes at last met, Sonny looked away and to the floor.

Panic now struck Jay's whole being. "There's the door, partner. You've got plenty of room to run to it."

Was it stunned silence? Thoughtful reflection? Jay couldn't decipher it. All he knew was that Sonny didn't move. He didn't speak.

"Did you hear what I said?" Jay said.

Sonny's head bobbed slowly, his mouth still open until the word "shit," came out as a breath. Finally, the man found his voice.

"Oh…shit." He looked at Jay and then at the door. "I…I gotta…I have to…let's just…." He looked back at Jay. "Shit." He hurried for the door and rushed outside.

The Mustang started, the engine revved, and Sonny was gone.

6

D ee Santiago, with Crocket LaSalle beside her, waited in the hospital room doorway.

"Jay?" Dee said. "Captain Colby called." Her eyes were locked on Sonny's prone body. "Dear God, Jay."

Delores Santiago, who preferred the name Dee, had come to the States from Cuba when she was ten years old. She was a handsome woman with thick auburn hair. Street wise, bold and confident, she took no bull from anyone. She could drink a Merchant Marine under the table, and actually had a few times. A pool shark, a businesswoman who knew her way around, she trusted few people: only Crocket, her business associate, and Sonny and Jay.

A God-fearing, church-going woman, she wouldn't hesitate to fight like a tiger if she or the people she cared about were crossed. As tough as she could be, she had a soft spot, especially for Sonny. With him, she seemed to melt. She knew Jay suspected she had a small crush on Sonny.

At the age of thirty-six, she was three years older than Crocket. She had known him for nearly eight years, and together, they owned Smiley's Tavern.

A tall lanky man, Crocket, whose true name was Hector LaSalle, had smooth, chocolate skin. He was a comical and haphazardly attractive man who liked flashy clothes and funky music.

Born and raised in New Orleans, Crocket was truly the prince of cons. There wasn't much he hadn't done or been involved in just short of a felony. He knew the streets better than anyone and often said, "If you wanna know about the dirt, ya gotta roll in the mud." Dee didn't usually get involved in his dealings. As long as he kept the bar they co-owned out of the mud, she left him alone.

Smiley's Tavern was a bar and restaurant in a run-down building located in the heart of the worse part of Oakland City. The tavern served an assortment of customers from the downright weird to the casual tourist who happened to get lost in the wrong part of town. Its location, along with Crocket and Dee's reputations, made them the perfect informants and Sonny and Jay's best friends.

Sitting beside Jay, she kept a quiet vigil with him by Sonny's bed. After nine hours nothing had changed with Sonny's condition.

Occasionally, Dee sniffed and dabbed at her moist eyes. Silently, she cursed herself for those signs of weakness. Seeing Sonny, this gutsy, charismatic man she'd known for four years, lying in a hospital bed, just tore at her insides.

"How is he?" Crocket said, returning with three fresh cups of coffee.

"No change," Dee said, her eyes transfixed on Sonny and that damn monitor that kept a constant noise. She almost wished they could shut it off, but then the worse case scenario for that made her shudder.

"He's a hero," Crocket said. "First morning edition." He took a newspaper from under his arm and handed it to Dee.

It hadn't made front page, but on the second the headlines read: Local Off Duty Detective Saves Child.

The article did not include a picture of Sonny, and they misspelled his last name.

"Jay?" Dee said. "Jay?" She called the man's name three more times before he even glanced her way. "Have some coffee."

Jay shook his head.

"It's midnight," Dee said. "Why don't you go home and get some rest. I'll stay with our boy."

Again, Jay shook his head.

Dee looked over at Crocket for help. "We'll be here for him, Jay. I promise. Crocket could drive you home."

"Sure," Crocket said. "You look like hell."

"That's how you help, you ol' hound dog?" Dee criticized.

Crocket smacked his lips, and in his Cajun accent said, "Dang, woman, I ain't exactly certified in these matters. He does look like hell, and I bet he knows it, too."

"Oh, just hush up," Dee said.

Jay leaned forward in his chair and readjusted the blanket that covered Sonny. It had become his fifteen minute ritual.

Dee sat back in her chair. She closed her eyes for a moment. Flashes of Sonny played in her mind. There he was with his shiny, curly hair coming into the tavern, laughing at some stupid joke Crocket told, and flashing his amazing eyes at her. He could be a flirt. The waitresses melted whenever he was near. Women in the bar bought him drinks and asked him to dance. Their boyfriends wanted to fight him in the alley. Sonny took it all in stride – as if he wasn't aware of the impression he made or why there was such a fuss. He usually charmed the anger right out of the jealous boyfriend and before long, they'd all be tossing back beers.

She remembered when she first met Sonny and Jay. They had come into Smiley's in uniform, and Dee told them to get out unless they had a warrant. She didn't want any trouble in her establishment. Not from dealers who knew better than to deal so much as an aspirin fifty feet in either direction of the tavern, or pimps making arrangements with clients for one of the ladies on the corner. She especially didn't want trouble from cops, and a cop in her place was like a bear poking his nose in a bee's nest. Smiley's was a fight-free, drug-free, don't-mess-with-Dee, place.

"We're here to see a guy by the name of Crocket," Sonny had said, looking around the place. He faced her, and the moment she looked into those eyes, her legs turned to jelly.

Holding onto the bar, she straightened her back and swallowed the drool in her mouth. "What about?" She tried to sound tough.

"He called us," Sonny said.

She looked at him without knowing how long she looked. Then she heard a cough and realized Jay stood by this man that pulled her into his eyes and wouldn't let her go.

"Is he here?" Jay said.

She noticed him, his long blond hair, sheepish good looks, angelic. She found it hard to believe Jay was a cop. He seemed too soft compared to his partner's ruggedness.

"You're both new around here," Dee said. "Never seen you before."

"Yeah, well, get used to us, darlin'," Sonny said and leaned in toward her with a crooked smile. "That wouldn't be so bad. Would it?"

His voice was soft, sexy, and a chill ran down Dee's spine. She glanced over at Jay. He grinned at his partner's antics.

Dee composed herself. "If you plan to come that close to my face," she said to Sonny, "you better be ready for what comes next."

"Oh, yeah? What's that, sugar?" Sonny said with his dimple extreme.

"A slap in your damn face if you don't back up. Sugar," Dee said, and Jay laughed.

Sonny looked at her and then slowly smiled again as he backed away. Hands up, he said, "You got me. You're the sheriff in this place."

"Don't be foolin' with me, boy," Dee said. "Or I'll take off your balls and use them on the pool table."

"Understood," Sonny said. "How about two beers?"

"In uniform?" Dee said.

"We're off duty," Sonny said.

"Oh yeah? Well come back out of uniform and we'll talk," Dee said.

They did, and they had been friends ever since.

* * *

It was six in the morning when Captain Colby got off the elevator at Memorial Hospital and made the journey toward Sonny's room. He spotted Crocket in the hallway and stopped. "Any change?"

"Dang, Cap, you're up mighty early, ain't ya?" Crocket said with his characteristic snicker.

"I'm on my way to the station. I wanted to check in," Colby said with no smile.

"Nothing's changed. Jay's been by that bed all night. Dee right next to him. And me? I got a sore neck trying to curl up on that lumpy sofa in the waiting room. You know...." Colby walked away. "Hey? Dang. Nobody ever listens to me," he mumbled under his breath.

Colby stood in the doorway. He cleared his throat until Dee looked his way. She tapped Jay on the knee.

Jay turned, nodded toward the captain, and then patted Sonny's hand. "I'll be right back," he whispered to the comatose man.

Colby looked into Jay's red, swollen eyes, his pale, worn face and said, "Is there anything I can do? Anything you need?"

"No, Cap. Thanks," Jay said.

"There is something you can do," Dee said. "Order Jay to go home and get some rest."

"I'm fine," Jay said.

"Dee's right," Colby said. "If you collapse, too, that won't help anyone. I can give you a ride home."

"Then call Crocket," Dee suggested. "He'll come get you. And I swear, if Sonny so much as moves a finger, I'll call you."

Jay brushed a hand through his hair. "I could bring back my car."

"Only if you get some sleep," Dee said. "Go home. Shower. Change your clothes and take a nap. Eat something. I swear I'll call."

Jay sighed, looked back at Sonny and nodded. "I won't be long."

When Jay walked out, Dee took Colby by the elbow. "Try to get him to sleep."

Fifteen minutes later Colby pulled into Jay's driveway. He watched as Jay labored to get out of the car and said, "I'll come in with you."

"No, that's okay, Cap. Thanks. But I'll be fine."

"Just let me help, okay?"

Colby shuffled his bulk to get out from behind the wheel when his police radio sounded.

"10-35 in progress," it announced.

"You better respond to that," Jay said. "Gotta keep the streets safe." He flashed a weak smile.

Colby regretfully nodded. "You better get some rest. I don't want a call that you fell asleep behind the wheel."

"Copy that," Jay said and worked for another smile.

"I'll come by the hospital later today."

* * *

Jay turned toward the house. His and Sonny's house. The place that was supposed to be their safe haven.

Outside and in, it appeared as if nothing had happened except Jay's watering can was tossed on the lawn where he dropped it, and the front door wasn't locked. That was a good thing since Jay had neither his keys nor a wallet. Inside, all was quiet. Sonny's coffee cup, half full, still sat on the counter. The blender needed to be washed. A loaf of bread sat waiting for Jay to make sandwiches.

In the bedroom, the bed was a tangled mess of sheets and blankets. A pair of Sonny's jeans was tossed in the corner. The towel he used the morning before sat rumpled in the middle of the bathroom floor.

Jay moved as if he were sleepwalking. First, he turned on the shower, and then he turned it off. He began to fix the bed, and then dropped the sheets where he found them. He drifted down the hallway and passed the spare room. The room that was set up as if it was Sonny's with a hairbrush, a broken watch on the dresser, a pair of boots against the wall, and some clothes Sonny hardly wore in the closet. It was all made to look as if Sonny stayed in that room, but it was all show for those times when they had friends over to visit.

The real truth was in the master bedroom. Jay wandered back to that room and flopped on the bed. He inhaled Sonny's scent. Vanilla, cinnamon, and leather. Reality hit. The screech of tires. The horrific *crack* as Sonny landed. Jay closed his eyes, squeezed Sonny's pillow tight in his hands, and let the pillowcase soak up his tears.

No one knew the real depth of his pain. There was no one he could tell. That was the condition of this relationship all based on promises made six months earlier.

* * *

That day, after Jay had confessed and Sonny had run, Jay heard the screech of the Mustang and lowered his head. It was over. Sonny was gone, and he was left, barely standing, to sweep up his tattered dreams. And then, Sonny burst through the door.

Jay turned from the bookcase. Sonny's eyes were pools of blue.

"Now what?" Jay said. "You going to punch me in the face?"

Sonny walked to him and stood directly in front of him.

Jay felt awkward in his partner's gaze. He tried to think of something to save them both, but his mind wouldn't function. He had willed a miracle to occur. He knew it. There was nothing left either of them could possibly say.

Jay stuck out his chin and tried to be brave, even when his voice shook with heartache. "So, go ahead. Hit me. Hell, maybe I deserve it."

But then…Sonny placed his left hand on Jay's cheek. The touch was warm and gentle. Tears that Jay had tried to hold back welled up and spilled. Sonny swept them up with his fingers, and his own eyes turned watery blue.

Sonny looked deep into Jay's eyes, deeper than he ever had before. With the softest voice Jay ever heard, Sonny said, "I love you too." He smiled, tender and sweet. "I'm in love with you too, Jay."

Jay's eyes opened wide, and then he frowned. "I don't…how? I don't understand."

"I was scared. Too scared to admit it. But it's true. I love you."

"You-you feel the same?" Jay said.

Sonny nodded and smiled, his dimple deep in his cheek. They hugged, burying their faces in the warmth of each other's necks.

Jay tipped his head back, and what he saw wasn't much different from what he had seen thousands of times – except now he recognized it. All along what he had seen was the look of love, and not just between friends. That look that they shared with no one else. Jay now knew the depth of what it had always meant.

Standing close, Jay placed his hands on each side of Sonny's face. More than anything, Jay wanted to kiss him. He wanted to feel those soft, full lips. "You ran out of here. I thought…I thought I'd never see you again."

"I ran," Sonny said. "But not from you." He chuckled shyly. "I mean… at first from you. What you said. But…when I was driving away. All I could see was you. Shit. I almost hit a car."

"All you could see was…me?" Jay said, his voice still trembling.

"Yeah. You. Your face. Your blue eyes. Your damn goofy smile. That stupid laugh. I kept going. But then I heard you. What you said. You want what's best for me. I heard you say – "

"I love you," Jay said. "I'm *in* love with you."

"Yeah. That. And I kept hearing it," Sonny said. "And for a second everything was kind of mixed up all together. You and me. Side by side. Busting in some shitty room chasing a killer. Hair falling in your eyes." He moved a strand away. "Like now." He smiled. "You. Watering your damn plants and talking to them. Remember when I laughed at you and you – ?"

"Poured the water over you."

Sonny nodded. "You. When you pulled me back from going around a corner in that alley 'cause somehow you knew there was a creep waiting with a gun."

"Sonny, those are all reasons we're…friends. Why you love me in that way. But, *in* love, partner? That's a whole different thing."

"Hey," Sonny said and lifted Jay's chin. "Loving you as my friend and loving you as the person I couldn't take my eyes off the first time I met you is the same thing. *You're* the one that makes me want to be the best police officer there is. And you're the one that just makes me want to *be*." Sonny raised his shoulder and tipped his head smiling with his dimple pronounced. "So, I heard you, and I kept hearing you. And then I slammed on my brakes, did a U turn, and got back here before you skipped town." His eyes drifted to Jay's mouth. He leaned in, and their lips touched. At that moment, Jay felt as if he had grown ten feet. This is what he'd waited for all his life.

They looked at each other, self-conscious at first, until their lips met again. This kiss was more definitive. Their mouths pressed fully to one another, the tips of their tongues touched, hungry for each other. All the mangled pieces of the puzzle suddenly fit. When they finally separated, Jay was dizzy but whole.

"I love you, Jay," Sonny said, breathless.

"I prayed for this," Jay whispered. "I prayed so hard."

* * *

Jay opened his eyes, but instead of seeing Sonny's smile, instead of feeling his arms around him, there was the image of Sonny in a hospital bed, not moving an inch while the monitors kept a steady pulse.

They were supposed to be celebrating the life they created. Jay wished he had convinced Sonny to come back to bed. To hell with the damn newspaper. To hell with a drive. They were safe inside this world they made. That's what they decided, and that's what had worked.

Jay labored out to the living room. He sat heavy on the couch. The same couch where he and Sonny quietly sat side by side after the revelation that they were in love with each other.

Jay had been the first to break the silence. As the reality of their admission hit and so did the thought that the real world would be uninvited, he asked Sonny, "Now what?"

"Nothing. We go on same as always," Sonny said.

Jay frowned. "What? What does that mean?"

"What do you think it means?"

"I-I don't know. I never thought this far. I figured you'd be in Mexico by the time I finished telling you."

Sonny laughed. "Well, I'm right here, partner, and we have to figure this out."

"So what? You want to go back the way it was?"

"Yeah. No. I mean...."

"What exactly do you mean? *Partner?*"

"Don't get all pissed," Sonny said. "This is new for me too."

"So what then? Exactly? You think you'll marry Emma and sneak here to see me?"

"Emma. Oh, shit."

Jay huffed. "Yeah. Emma. Oh shit."

"I have to tell Emma," Sonny said.

"What? Are you kidding?"

"No. I mean. I have to say something."

"Yeah, well, I don't think telling her you're in love with me is the smart plan." Jay glanced at Sonny. "You are. In love with me, right? Or am I dreaming?"

"You're not dreaming." Sonny flashed his smile. "I am. You know… that."

"*That?*" Jay stood and looked down at the man. "Why am I not feeling so good all of a sudden?"

Sonny sighed. "I'm saying this all wrong."

"You think?"

"Sit down. Come on. We need to talk."

"We need to talk? I hate those words. It's usually not a good sign." Jay walked over to the bookcase where all of this began. "Don't bust my bubble, partner. Let me enjoy it for at least a few more minutes."

"I'm not busting anything, and would you please sit down? You're always so dramatic."

"I'm dramatic? Don't you think now is a good time to be dramatic?"

"I think now is the time to turn on the thinking cap, Blondie. You're the realist. The practical one. We have to figure this out."

"Okay. So figure. Where do we stand? And please, let me sit before you tell me." Jay sat in the chair.

Sonny sat on the coffee table in front of him. "Listen to me, okay?"

"Why is all of this so familiar? Oh, that's right. We began our little talk just like this. Me in this chair. You on the coffee table. Except I think your hand was on my knee."

"Will you stop being all doom and gloom? I love you, okay?"

"Say it again. My head is still fighting it."

Sonny laughed. "Okay. Real slow this time. I. Me. Love. You. Jay. Better?"

"Better. But I'm not about to be…somebody's mistress." He frowned. "Is that even the right word? What word is there for something like this?"

"I'm not gonna marry Emma. I'm not."

"Really?" Jay said.

"Really. Geez. Give me some credit."

"Well, if you knew you loved me, why did you plan to marry her?" Jay said.

"I thought it would be better. Hey, I never said I had it all figured out. I mean, I didn't know. You know. That you felt like this. I thought I'd better just cut my losses."

"That easy, huh?"

"No. Not easy. How about you?"

"Me? I'm the one who took the chance."

"And I'm glad you did," Sonny said and grinned. "When did you know? You know. That you loved me?"

Jay's cheeks burned. "From day one."

"Come on, tell me. When did you know?"

Jay took a breath. "I felt something the first time we met. A connection. I pushed it away. I tried not to think about it. But more and more over time it got harder. Being with you was hard. Not being with you was harder. Hell, the times we got called in on weekends, I didn't even mind so long as I was with you. The time you got shot. I couldn't leave you, and I found myself needing that. To take care of you. But I was never going to say anything. And then there was this thing with Emma. I figured one way or the other I'd lose you…what we had…so I might as well bite the bullet and go for it."

Jay took Sonny's hand in his. It still felt strange to show such outward affection, but exciting at the same time. "I really meant it, partner, what I said. I just want you to be happy. If I thought Emma could have done that for you, then I would have stuck my tail between my legs and let you go. I just didn't believe you were happy with her." When Sonny lowered his head, Jay said, "What's wrong?"

"Nothing." Sonny's voice was quiet. "It's just….I wish we could celebrate and not have to hide it. Jay, I've never felt this way before. I never thought I could about anyone. You were right when you said I was going to settle. I would have. It was like a piece of me was missing, and I just got used to it not being there. I know it shouldn't matter to me that you happen to be a man. It shouldn't matter if you had three heads and polka dots."

Jay laughed. "Gee thanks. I think."

"But…."

"There's that damn but."

"But let's face it. It does matter. We're cops. This is the south. There's that virus that's killing gays. This is a scary time for lots of people."

"Gay," Jay said thoughtfully. "I realize now that I never said that word out loud before. I-I'm gay." He chuckled and then smiled as if relieved. "I'm gay. And, I'm not ashamed." He looked at Sonny. "Are you?"

"I'm not ashamed either. I mean it. Having you is the best thing that could ever happen to me. I'm not settling. I'm not running."

"But we do have to hide," Jay said with sadness.

"It doesn't have to be so bad."

"You're right. I mean imagine announcing this. What good would it do?"

"None. Can you see the looks on the faces of all the guys? McCann?" Sonny whistled. "He'd make a plan with the others to shoot us in the back and claim it was a drive-by."

"True. We'd be open targets. And then there's department policy."

"Department policy? I didn't know there was one," Sonny said.

"Yeah. The one that says couples can't be partners." Jay smiled.

"Asshole," Sonny said and smacked Jay's arm.

"So what do we do?"

"That's the part I meant. Nothing. I mean nothing at work. Work is work. Business as usual. We do what we're good at same as always. Go in low – "

"And make the bust," Jay finished, and they slapped five.

"Just like always. If we could fool them before….hell, we fooled each other, then what's the difference? But…."

"Another but." Jay sighed.

"You'll like this one. But, after work, after we take off the guns and put down the badges, then it's us. You and me. Doing, you know, what people do."

"What people do?"

"Lovers," Sonny said, and he blushed.

"Right." Jay grinned. "Lovers. I like it."

"Thought you might."

"There's just one thing."

"Now what," Sonny said.

"Well, I-I've never…I mean, I don't know, you know. I've never been with a-a man." Jay's cheeks flushed.

"Me either. So, we do like always. We learn together."

"Like always."

"You got it, partner. Always."

"So," Jay said. "You. Me. Like always only with…perks."

They both laughed. "Perks," Sonny said. "Lots of perks."

Jay leaned forward and relished the feel of Sonny's mouth on his. They both stood with each other in their arms. The bulge between Sonny's legs tapped Jay's thigh. Jay was erect in his own pants so large he thought the zipper would burst.

The kiss ended, and they placed their foreheads together. "Are you sure? About this?" Jay said.

"I'm sure," Sonny said.

"Happy? Honest?"

"Honest. Happy."

They faced each other. "So we promise," Jay said, "to love each other. To keep it between us and no one else ever. Work smart. Play hard. You and me."

"We can't help who we fell in love with."

"I'm glad it was you," Jay said.

"Me too. So, agree?"

"Agree. We play it safe," Jay said. "Just one more thing. What about Emma?"

"Oh, shit."

"You already said that," Jay teased.

"I'll just tell her I don't wanna get married. I don't wanna work for her dad. I like being a cop. Believe me, she'll break up with me. She'll be so pissed, she'll throw that eighty dollar bottle of wine at me."

"Well, like your Uncle Tony always said…don't turn your back, but watch your ass."

"In other words – "

"Duck," they both finished and slapped five again.

They kissed once more. Wet. Warm. Seductive. Groans vibrated in their throats, and they clung to one another.

"Thanks, Jay," Sonny whispered in Jay's ear.

"For what?" Jay said. He inhaled Sonny's scent.

"For the talk." Sonny smiled. "I'm glad you were brave enough. I'm not so sure I would have."

"You would have gone through with the marriage?"

"I think I wanted you to stop me. For a long time I pushed it away."

"Did you ever feel like this before?"

"A few times. In high school. In the army. Around a few guys before, but nothing I'd ever admit."

"Oh. So, I'm not the first," Jay said and laughed.

"You're the first one I'm telling. The only want I want to tell. Hell, there's no way I'd ever admit it to my family. Even to myself."

"I know. It's the same with me," Jay said.

"I just thought it was part of growing up."

"Yeah. I convinced myself that it was just a normal thing all guys go through."

"Right. Then I'd find the right girl, settle down and be happy. I'd *make* myself happy. But then there was you."

"You and me," Jay said. "And I couldn't convince myself of anything else. I would never want anything else."

This was their world, their life, where no one else was permitted. Jay sadly smiled. He was back in the present, alone in their bed, gripping Sonny's pillow, damp with his tears.

"I love you, partner," Jay whispered. "You have to live."

7

Dee's eyes grew heavy, and before she knew it, her head dropped and she dozed in the chair by Sonny's bed. Feeling herself drift to sleep, she fought the urge and lifted her chin. When she saw the shadow of the tall blonde at the foot of the bed, she startled and gasped, "Oh my God."

"What?" Crocket fell with a thud out of the chair.

"You scared the spirit out of me, Jamison," Dee said and put her hand to her heart. She checked her watch. "I was hoping you'd take longer than three hours. Did you get any sleep?"

"Colby called me," Jay said in an angry tone that caused Dee to scowl.

Crocket picked himself up from the floor. "Sonny's fine. He hasn't moved."

"Oh how could you know, you old mule?" Dee said. "You've been sleeping."

"Dozing," Crocket said. "With one eye open, woman,"

"Jay? What's wrong?" Dee said.

"They arrested the guy that hit Sonny," Jay said. "This was his third DWI in two months."

"A drunk driver?" Dee looked toward Sonny and the equipment that monitored his life. "That son of a bitch. Excuse me, Lord," she said.

"He is a son of a bitch," Jay said and stood by the side of the bed. "And so help me, if I ever get my hands on him…."

"Hey," Crocket said, "how about we all get something to eat?"

"No. I just want to sit here," Jay said and slid a chair closer to the bed.

Dee glanced at Jay and saw the worry on his face. She tried to distract him by sounding upbeat.

"We've been getting cards and flowers," Dee said. "Everyone at the station is praying for him. The nurse told me that the hospital switchboard is getting lots of calls. Friends. Neighbors. Even some of your snitches." She chuckled, but it fell on deaf ears.

Jay focused on Sonny with his whole body pressed as close to the bed as he could physically get.

Crocket stood by Jay and said, "Yeah, man. He's got lots pulling for him. He's gonna come out of this. You watch."

"How about some water?" Dee said.

Jay nodded, still not taking his eyes off Sonny's motionless form.

"That damned crack...." he mumbled.

"What?" Dee said.

"Crack," Jay muttered. "Bone hitting pavement. It screams in my head. It's a sound I'll never forget."

* * *

Hours later Jay's tired body ached as he got to his feet. He placed his hands on the small of his back and stretched out the kinks.

He checked the monitor. He was getting good at reading the numbers. Everything was stable. He went to the window and looked out at another new day.

From a special place that was not a long ago memory, Jay had laid close to Sonny, the man's warm breath like a fever on his neck. Jay ran his fingers along the curve of Sonny's back. To be this close to him, to touch him in ways he'd only dreamt about, caused Jay to press in closer if only to reassure himself this was not a dream.

For years, in private fantasy, during quiet moments, when no one was around to see Jay's face flush or his mouth curl into a sultry grin, he would allow himself to picture what it might be like to make love to Sonny. To finally be lovers was better than any fantasy he ever had because it was real. Real but not in the perfect way only dreams can be. Real was better.

Jay trailed his hand along Sonny's stubbled cheek. He drifted casually to other places along Sonny's naked flesh. As his exploration of the man's body continued, and, Sonny made his arousal known, Jay asked him to open his eyes. Sonny did and looked directly into Jay's eyes, and Jay swam in the sapphire blue that always amazed him.

Their lovemaking was slow and still new to them. Sonny was patient, generous, and gentle. Jay urged him on, and their bodies pasted together by sweat and desire fueled his lusty need.

Jay's fingernails dug into Sonny's shoulders. Sonny groaned in a lover's tone. They were one, and the discovery complete.

Breathless, Sonny began to move off Jay but Jay held him there.

"Not yet," Jay said with a sated grin.

Sonny remained, his head resting on Jay's shoulder.

"You okay?" Sonny whispered.

Jay nodded and hummed. "I've never felt so…loved." He couldn't contain the silly laugh and covered his face in embarrassment. "I mean –"

"I know what you mean," Sonny said and rolled off to Jay's side. "I feel the same. I never knew it could be this…good." He laughed. "So, you hungry?"

"Don't change the subject."

"You're gonna make me do this, huh? Talk about it?"

"Sonny, I've wished for this moment for a long time. I think it deserves a little more than, you hungry?" he mocked. "I know you hate the sappy stuff, but go with me on this, okay?" Jay strolled two fingers along Sonny's chest and smiled. "You are so damn…beautiful."

Sonny chuckled deep in his throat. "I'm more than a pretty face there, partner."

Jay grinned. "I know that. I meant all of you."

"Hey, it's not like we never saw each other naked," Sonny said.

"This is way different than seeing you changing clothes in the locker room. Way different."

"You're beautiful too," Sonny said. "Your hair's like silk. You're body is…." His shoulders shook with laughter.

"Knock it off," Jay said. "Now you're being stupid."

Sonny tried to hide the chuckle. "Sorry." He cleared his throat. "But I mean it. It's just….I'm not good at this stuff."

"Just say how you feel."

Sonny shrugged. "Okay. It's like I never tasted chocolate cake before. I mean *really* tasted it."

Jay snorted. "So, I'm what? Chocolate cake?"

"No. Yes. I mean better. Better than anything I ever had. Or knew I could have."

"We're damn good together, partner," Jay said, and his mouth widened into a wry grin.

It was true. Everything seemed right. No one was the wiser at the station or anywhere else. They continued as always. Horse play, playful insults. They still argued and even annoyed one another and that was part of what made the *real* perfect. And just like always, they continued to depend on each other. For over four years they had risked their own lives to save the other so many times, even they couldn't tell where one began and the other left off.

And there was the added reality – they were lovers. Jay's dream was complete. They communicated in ways no words could.

"When did you know you were in love with me?" Jay turned to face Sonny and relaxed on the pillow they shared.

Sonny scrunched his face. "Not this again. Please."

Jay laughed. "I like the story. Tell me."

"When? The first time? Or the second time?"

Jay smacked Sonny's chest. "No jokes, Bozo. Tell me."

Sonny bit his bottom lip. "Okay. Let's see." He looked up at the ceiling and grinned. "It was when you were in the shower."

"What?" Jay squealed and sat up. "That's not how the story goes."

Sonny chuckled. "Who's telling this? You or me?"

"The shower? What shower?"

"At the academy. We just got done running eight miles. Man, it was freakin' hot that day. I remember I couldn't wait to take a shower. My tee shirt stuck to me, and I tore it off."

Jay laughed. "Yeah. I remember that. You ripped it in two."

Sonny stared up at the fan whirling above them and grinned even more. "I turned that water on to freezing."

"I was right next to you," Jay said.

"You and twenty other guys. Man, it was rough taking showers like that. All those bodies covered in soap."

"Hey. Knock it off," Jay said. "This is supposed to be about me,"

Sonny laughed deep in his throat. "It is. You wanna know why I turned that damn shower all the way to cold? 'Cause you were there, and I tried hard to keep my eyes off of you. I thought for sure the Marshall would give me away."

Jay frowned. "The Marshall?"

Sonny lifted the sheet and pointed down. "The Marshall."

"Oh," Jay said with a head bob. "*That* Marshall."

"Yep. I knew then."

"Hold on. While that's a nice memory, it isn't the story I wanted to hear. I mean, I know how hard, and I do mean hard, it was for me when we took showers, but that isn't exactly the love part."

"You really like the mushy stuff, don't you?" Sonny grinned up at the ceiling fan again. "Okay. It was…gradual, ya know? I felt something when I met you and then, when we studied together and talked, it all just… came. But I wasn't about to say it. I couldn't admit it to myself. That's why I tried to make myself get serious about Emma. I just thought if I did that and took that other job, I'd forget about…us. That's the real reason I came over here and talked to you. I guess deep down, I was hoping you'd try and stop me from marrying her."

"And I did," Jay said and laced his fingers together with Sonny's.

"And you did," Sonny said and kissed Jay's hand.

"I fell in love with you the minute I saw you," Jay said.

Sonny snickered. "Bullshit."

"I mean it. I was in the hall of the academy looking for the registrar's office."

"I remember. Lost as shit."

"I was confused. And there were a bunch of people bumping into me, and then I see you. It was real quick. And then that damn crowd passed by, and I could only see parts of you. You pointed the way to the registrar's office. Next thing I knew, you were gone. I thought, shit, I'll never see him again." Jay smiled. "But then I was sent to bunk in Steinmart's room…."

Sonny laughed. "Oh, shit. Remember him? Marty Steinmart. What a nut."

"He idolized you," Jay said.

"That guy couldn't find his way to a fifteen story building burning right in front of his face."

"When you came into his room and smiled? I swear I couldn't breathe."

"So how did we fool each other all this time?" Sonny played with Jay's fingers.

"Guess that's why we're so good as undercover detectives. We keep a poker face." Jay turned over on his back, and as the fan above his head rattled just a bit, he said, "When did you lose your virginity?"

Sonny laughed so hard he nearly choked. "What?"

"You heard me. When?"

Sonny lifted up the sheets and looked under it.

"What the hell are you doing?" Jay said.

"Just checking what's between your legs. I swear sometimes you sound like a girl."

"Ha, ha. There's nothing feminine about me."

"Right. Except for your soft hair and your fuzzy face," Sonny said. "Come on, Blondie, admit it. You look like a damn cherub."

"Knock it off."

"Okay," Sonny said. "Don't get pissed. I'm just kidding."

"I'm tough enough. Managed to take down Felix Mortez yesterday with no trouble."

"That you did, Blondie. And I must say, you did it without breaking a nail."

Jay slapped Sonny's arm. "Is this how it's going to be now? Girl jokes? Get out of my bed. Go, and don't let the door smack you in that pretty bubble butt of yours."

Sonny laughed. "Okay. I give. You handled Felix the Fink like a damn Marine. He never knew what hit him. Of course, you got a new dent in the hood of your car, but what's one more?"

"Damn straight," Jay said and stared up at the ceiling. "And don't ever call me a girl again. I'm just…."

"Sensitive," Sonny said.

"No. Dammit. I'm…romantic. So, when did you lose your virginity?"

"Oh, for Christ's sake. I don't know."

Jay huffed and sat up in bed. "You don't know? How can you not know?"

"Okay. Okay. I was…thirteen."

"Bullshit."

"I was. She was seventeen."

"Shut up. You're lying."

"I swear. Mary Jane Geonette. Half Irish. Half Italian. I think it was the Italian half that was the horniest."

"I bet I know which half. Are you serious?"

"What can I say? Girls just…liked me."

"And of course you could never say no."

"Are you nuts? Girls left bras in my locker. I couldn't walk across the football field without one of them jumping me. Once, I came home from baseball practice and found one of Rachel's girlfriends naked in my bed. She was like fourteen. I was seventeen. I told her to get out. She started to cry."

"So you did the only thing you could."

"I kissed her and said that's all she got till she turned a lot older. She's still calling me every week."

"You poor helpless stud," Jay said. "How did you survive?"

"Wasn't easy. My Uncle Tony found me once in the backseat of Angie Comastille's car. He told me if I got a girl pregnant he'd stuff my *coglione* down my throat. He meant my balls."

"I guessed," Jay said.

"How about you?"

"Me?" Jay coughed. "Well…I-I, you know, I was kind of – "

"Under-developed?" Sonny laughed.

"You really want to go there, Santini? No. I was…shy."

"So when? Fifteen? Sixteen?"

"Nineteen."

Sonny tried not to laugh. "Nineteen? Really?"

"What's wrong with that?"

"Nothing. Did you live with Wally and the Beaver too?"

"That's it, Curly. You are so going down."

They wrestled under the sheets. Jay won but suspected Sonny had let him.

Jay smiled at the memory, and then the sharp, high pitched scream from one of the monitors shook him back to reality.

Nurses rushed into the room.

More alarms went off in unison. The shrill was piercing.

More nurses. One ran to the phone and paged Dr. Dixon, STAT.

"What's wrong?" Jay said. "What's happening?"

Hands pushed Jay back until finally someone moved him into the hall.

Dr. Dixon rushed past him. Jay stood, stunned. A nurse swept the curtain around Sonny's bed shut and then closed the door.

"Code Blue," the speaker over Jay's head announced.

"No, no," Jay whispered. He wanted to run into the room, hold Sonny's hand, and tell him this was not how it ended – it couldn't be how it ended.

A cart pushed by a team of people rushed past him. From under the curtain, Jay saw feet move quickly, remain still, and then move around more.

The curtain was ajar now, enough for him to see that they ventilated Sonny. The nurse pumped the bag hard and steady, forcing air into Sonny's lungs. The black bag expanded. The nurse squeezed. The bag deflated. The nurse pumped. The bag expanded. Over and over again, and each time Jay took a breath right along with his partner.

Another doctor ran into the room. He checked the monitor. The steady beep was a flat line. The doctor took two paddles from the cart. He placed one on each side of Sonny's chest.

"Clear," the doctor ordered.

Sonny's chest lifted and dropped.

"Clear," the doctor ordered again. Sonny's body arched, lifted and dropped enough that the bed moved.

The doctor held up the paddles and waited. Watching the monitor intently, he wasn't the only one.

"Come on, Son," Jay pleaded. "Come on, buddy."

The monitor alarm still shrilled. The line was still flat.

The nurse continued to pump the bag.

Another nurse checked her watch.

In Jay's mind, he heard Sonny. "I love you, Jay. Always will."

Tears ran down Jay's cheeks. "Don't leave me," he whispered. "Stay with me."

"Clear," the doctor demanded louder than before.

Dixon glanced over at Jay.

The doctor pushed the paddles down hard. Sonny's whole body jolted. He went up and then back so abruptly the bed moved from the wall.

Jay remembered Sonny's arms around him and saw his sweet, dimpled smile.

"Don't do this, partner," Jay whispered under his breath. His hands laced behind his head, he waited with the others for what seemed way too long.

Beep beep...beep...beep. The constant, steady sound grew stronger. The medical team relaxed.

The curtain was finally pulled back all the way. The paddles placed back on the cart. Dr. Dixon spoke quietly to the other doctor. The nurses repositioned Sonny's limp body and tucked the blanket up to his chin.

Dr. Dixon looked concerned as he walked from Sonny's bed and spoke to another nurse.

Frantic in the doorway, when Jay's eyes met Dixon's, he begged for answers.

"Detective Jamison," Dixon began and took Jay by the arm.

"Ken."

"Ken," Dixon said and led Jay down the hall. "Michael just made it through a serious crisis. His blood pressure dropped dangerously low, and his heart stopped."

"What caused it?"

"A form of shock. The body is reacting."

"Th-that's good, right?"

"Not exactly. We had to restart the heart. Technically, he was dead for nearly a minute and a half."

Jay pressed against the wall to keep himself from falling. "D-dead?"

"He's back now, but our concern is the oxygen level. Especially to the brain. He doesn't need more complications. We have him on a stronger medication and we'll try to minimize the damage."

Minimize the damage.

"What does that mean?" Jay said.

"It means…keeping him alive. The probability for something permanent is significant. What we're hoping for is to minimize the worse case scenarios. We don't want another recurrence of what we just had." Dr. Dixon looked directly into Jay's eyes. "Right now, we're working to keep him alive. I'm sorry, but the longer he remains in a coma, the more permanent that may be." Dixon went to the nurses' station and requested Sonny's chart. "Did Michael ever mention a DNR?"

"DNR?" Jay said.

"Do not resuscitate."

"Do not res….Whoa. Hold on. What are you talking about?"

"It's a formality. Some patients feel strongly about a DNR. Sometimes it's their wish."

"Well, it sure as hell isn't Sonny's wish," Jay said.

"It just means – "

"I know what it means," Jay said. "And, no, he's never mentioned it."

"I just thought as police officers, he might have discussed it with you," Dixon said.

"We've never discussed it. Sonny and I are fighters. He would fight."

"I understand that. It's just that given this last incident, it may be something to consider. Another occurrence like this one and – "

"And what?"

"It wouldn't be good," Dixon said. "His body. His major organs and his brain can only take so much. Another incident could very well leave him in an even worse state."

"Th-that isn't something I even want to think about. Not right now," Jay said.

"That's understandable. But it is something you may need to decide with his mother," Dixon said.

Struggling to find words, Jay had none. With still shaky legs, he left Dixon and went back into Sonny's room. He was almost afraid to approach the bed, which felt odd. He had never been afraid of anything to do with Sonny before – except for the fear of losing him.

"Please, partner. P-please, wake up. No matter what, we can handle this together, but you have to wake up. Open your eyes."

Jay took Sonny's hand in his and sat with his face within inches of the sleeping man.

"I need you. Can you hear me? Please try. Don't give up. I love you too much. I can't….I can't be alone. Without you, I…." Jay covered his face while his shoulders shook. "I won't be anything good."

Sonny's pale, cool hand felt like a dead weight. Jay clung to it. Sonny's whole body was like a shell. It almost seemed hollow.

There was only one other time Jay had felt something remotely like this. It was nearly a year ago, when Sonny had been shot in the line of duty. Jay heard the blast. He ran so quickly, his legs almost didn't stay under him. When he got to Sonny, the man was lying on the ground bleeding. Jay skidded to his partner's side and grabbed him.

Sonny asked Jay how bad it was. Jay told him that the bullet was in his shoulder. Sonny chuckled and flinched with pain. "Shoulder? That's all?"

The ambulance came, and Jay rode with his partner, staying close by. Sonny gave a weak grin. "You look more scared then me," he said.

"No," Jay responded. "I'm just jealous of all the attention you're gonna get from those pretty nurses."

"You lie better undercover. It's okay to be scared. I was scared too. But ya know? I think I'm gonna be all right…once it stops hurting."

Jay grinned. "Hurts, huh?"

"Like a bad toothache. Except all the teeth are hurting at the same time. Hey. Did you say pretty nurses?"

Jay laughed. "Yeah. All wanting to take care of you."

"Yeah?" Sonny sucked in his breath and squeezed his eyes shut with the pain. When he finally could breathe again, he asked, "So, how do I look?"

"Like crap," Jay said.

"Go back to lying."

Jay hurt seeing the intense pain on his partner's face. "Just hang on, okay?"

Breathing heavily as the ambulance raced down the street, Sonny had said, "Ain't going nowhere, partner."

8

After two hours of sleep at home and a quick cup of coffee, Jay tossed on a shirt and headed back to the hospital. The shirt was one he had worn two days ago, and it was stained at the edge of one sleeve. He stepped off the elevator, rolled up his sleeves, and heard the page he feared the most – Code Blue.

The speakers along the corridor shouted Code Blue once more. He heard the shrill of alarms and took off running.

A cart pushed by nurses flew out of a side room. Jay was two steps behind them. The team of doctors joined the race.

"Code Blue," the intercom announced again.

The team rushed down the hall. When Jay stopped at Sonny's room, the cart and nurses kept going. Two rooms down, they ran inside.

"It's not Sonny," Dee said from the doorway.

Jay bent over and put his hands on his trembling knees. He glanced up, and for a second, he was grateful.

Dee put her hand on Jay's back as if reading his mind. "I know. Thank God it isn't Sonny." She looked down the hall and added, "I just pray whoever it is will be fine."

Jay's pounding heart slowed, and he took a deep breath. "Yeah. Me too."

"It's okay. To be glad it wasn't Sonny."

Jay peeked into the room. "How is he?"

"Same. I've been telling him about my plans to renovate the tavern. He didn't have much to say about it." Dee plucked a piece of lint off the blanket. "In some ways, it reminds me of talking to Crocket. Except he usually grunts and walks away."

"I'm just glad he's resting." Jay chuckled, but it sounded weak even to him. "Sick, huh? That I'd rather he sleep than" – he glanced out the door, and from the expressions of the medical team who passed by, things hadn't gone well – "than have them in here."

He looked at Sonny. "No more scares, okay, partner? No more scares."

* * *

Another day came and went. No more close calls. No change other than the swelling of Sonny's brain stabilized. The doctors hoped Sonny would begin to wake or, at least respond to stimuli, but he didn't.

The machines, except for the one that measured brain waves, remained in place. The oxygen mask was removed. Jay had an unobstructed view of Sonny's face. It was ashen except for the purple-red blood vessels along his cheeks. They were like thin, spidery veins running in short tracks. His skin appeared leathery, his lips dry and cracked.

The bandages on Sonny's hands were gone. Cuts caused by reflex when he fell, were scabbed. The bandage around Sonny's head was still in place as was the IV and heart monitor. The machines continued their rhythmic beep. Sonny remained motionless, covered in a white knitted blanket, still without so much as a twitch. He slept as if frozen in some dimension unreachable by anyone – including Jay.

Jay watched the monitor that beeped with its green jagged edges that spiked upwards and dropped down, curved, and spiked again. The green neon numbers flashed a steady pulse. If it weren't for that, Jay would have sworn Sonny was dead. He couldn't even feel the man in the room with him. Jay felt dead as well, and the only reason he knew he wasn't was because he willed his heart to beat in time with the machine.

Jay sniffed. In a quiet voice, he spoke to the monitor. "I remember the first time you called me Jay." He grinned bittersweet but didn't turn toward Sonny. It was the monitor that let Jay know Sonny was alive. Looking at the body in the bed didn't prove a damn thing.

Jay sniffed again. "I laughed and said, 'That's the best you got? Jay? Not too original is it?' And you said, 'Whatta ya want me to call ya? The

Rock? Face it, pal, you ain't built like no rock.'" Jay chuckled. "I said I wanted something tougher sounding, and you grinned with that damn stupid dimple and said, 'Hey, they call me Sonny. Ain't exactly a tough nickname either.'"

Jay reached up to touch the monitor, realized he shouldn't, and dropped his hand. "You know why the guys called you Sonny? At the academy? Almost all of them had some kind of nickname. Bill Dutcher was Dutch for obvious reasons. Mike Blake was Z-Man 'cause he always fell asleep in class snoring till we kicked him under the desk. Remember? His head shot straight up and he was all confused. He'd say, 'What? What? I'm awake.' You called him Z-man, and it stuck."

Jay turned to his partner. "But you they called Sonny. You said it was because of your sunny disposition. That wasn't it. Mark Johnson gave you that name. Johnson, the Swiss, 'cause he was always eating Swiss cheese. He called you that because of Sonny in the Godfather movie. Remember? The brother who was always ready to fight? And you were. You never backed down. The Sergeant would give you the biggest, toughest sparring partners to take down and you never gave up. Never. He had to pull you off of those guys a few times."

Jay ran a trembling hand over Sonny's buzzed hair. "You'd hate your hair like this. It reminds me of the picture your mom has. The one when you were in the army. You were tough then too, huh? Sonny?" His voice cracked. "Please, don't back down now. Don't give up. I need you." A tear slipped down Jay's cheek, and as he glanced at Sonny's mouth, the urge to feel the man's lips on his grew too strong to resist. Jay began to bend his head and was suddenly aware of someone in the doorway.

Jay brushed a tear away before he turned. In the doorway stood Emma Mills.

"Emma?" Jay said, suddenly awkward and uneasy. As he pretended to fix the blanket over Sonny, he knew full well that one second more and the young woman would have seen the truth.

"Hi. Ken," Emma said poised on the threshold as if something kept her from entering the room. She looked at Sonny like she expected him to wave and smile at her. "I heard. About the accident. Is he asleep?"

"No. Emma. Sonny is…he's in a coma," Jay said.

Emma gasped and placed her hand to her mouth. "I heard it was serious, but I didn't know how bad. A coma? He's really in a coma?" She stepped into the room, her high heels clicking on the tile floor. Her skirt was short and tight. The blouse a low cut V-neck. Her blond hair was swept up in a bun with loose strands around her made-up face. Jay smelled the scent of lilacs even from six feet away.

Jay glanced down at Sonny. No way was he about to reconfirm what he said.

Emma came to the bed and studied the motionless man. "He's so... pale," she said in a soft voice. "Is he going to die?"

"No," Jay said, angered by the thought. "He's going to be fine. He will."

Emma's eyes filled with tears. "He won't stay like this, will he? He'd hate that. If he was...like this."

"Why did you come, Emma?" Jay said.

"Why? We were in love with each other, Ken. We were almost married. Remember?"

"I remember. And then you broke up. You said you never wanted to see him again."

"Thanks to you," Emma said with a sneer. "Oh, don't look so surprised, Ken. I knew it was because of you. I've always known."

"Known? Known what?"

"Mr. Innocent. You never fooled me. You like to think you did, but I know if it wasn't for you, Michael and I would be married."

"Emma, this isn't the time or the place – "

"Time? Why not? I know it's your fault. You're the one that convinced him."

Jay frowned and looked out to the hall. "Keep your voice down. I never convinced him of anything."

"Oh, please." Emma let out a bitter laugh. "You convinced him to stay a cop. You're the one that told him I didn't know what was best for him."

"D-did Sonny tell you that?"

"No. He would never say anything about the oh so wonderful Jay. Well, you know what? I know you're not oh so wonderful. You couldn't stand the fact that he was happy. That *I* made him happy. We could have been married right now. We *should* have been. He'd have a house, a real home, and a good, decent job. He wouldn't be lying here now. Like…like this."

"What's happened has nothing to do with him being a cop."

"Oh and that's supposed to what? Make it okay? Well, it doesn't. I've never forgotten him. I still love him, and I plan to let him know that. As soon as he wakes up. He doesn't need you keeping guard over him, Ken. You're…you're like obsessed with him or something. I could see it every time you hung around. Well, the truth is, I do know what's best for him just like I know *you're* not."

Jay's jaw muscles flexed. "Get out," he said.

"Me? I have as much right…even more right than you to be here."

"Get out," Jay said again and strained to keep his voice low. "You don't have any rights. Not now. Not ever."

Emma smirked. "You were always jealous. Jealous because he had me, and you were all alone."

"I was never…." Jay ran a hand through his hair and tried not to scream. "I was never jealous of anyone for that reason. Sonny finally woke up and recognized you for the selfish, greedy bitch you are. You wanted him to give you things and show you off. No, the real truth is, you wanted to show *him* off like he was some damn puppy you trained. Well, he's not. He has his own mind, and he knew what he wanted, and lady, trust me, what he wanted wasn't you."

"How dare you."

"How dare I? You come in here all dolled up to what? To seduce him again? Well, here's a shocker for you. He's in a coma. Yes. He *really* is in a coma. And if he wakes up, he'll more than likely be brain damaged. So how does that sound?" Jay moved closer to her. She backed away. "How do you think he'll show at the country club? Think he'll get a ribbon? Think Daddy will still want him as Director of Supervision when he's the one that just might need to be supervised? Come on, Emma, come a little closer and take a real good look at our boy now."

He reached to take her arm, but Emma pulled away.

"If I thought for one second," Jay said, "Sonny would have been happy with a cunt like you, or that this wouldn't have happened at all if he was with you, believe me, sweetheart, I would have driven him to you with a bow on his head. Now get out, or so help me, I will pick up your skinny ass and throw you out."

In the doorway Emma glanced past him to Sonny's unmoving form, the monitors that beeped, the IV bottle that still dripped liquid into a tube, and then she looked at Jay again. "Brain damaged? I...I didn't know that either."

"Next time, check first," Jay said.

"I better go. Tell Michael...." She looked back at Sonny, her face pale. "No. You don't even need to tell him I was here." She whirled, bumped into the medication cart a nurse pushed and rushed down the hall.

Jay rubbed his hands down his face. Back at the side of Sonny's bed, he huffed. "Sorry about that, partner. All the stuff I said. You aren't going to need to be supervised or any of that crap. I just wanted her to get the hell out of here. Jealous?" He snorted. "I sure as hell was jealous but not for the reason she thinks. And I never convinced you of anything. You were the one that was convinced. You love me. I know that. You and me." He checked the monitor again. "Is he *really* in a coma? Tell me I have no right to be here." He looked at the door again. "Just stay away from him. Stay away from *us*."

* * *

At ten o'clock in the morning, just outside of Sonny's room, Jay gave an occasional grin at the nurses and orderlies he had gotten to know the past few days. They greeted him with pleasant nods and polite hellos.

Right on time, Captain Colby and Dee paraded down the corridor. It had become the morning ritual. Colby brought coffee. Dee brought an egg sandwich usually on burnt toast. Jay had become accustomed to this and to pretending that everything tasted good when in fact, it all tasted like rusted tin. It wasn't the coffee or Dee's cooking to blame. They could have brought Lobster Newburg, and that would have tasted like crap too.

"Jay, can we talk for a minute?" Colby requested.

"I'll sit with him," Dee said and went into the room.

A few steps down the hall, Colby turned and faced Jay, a bit nervous, which was unlike him. "I don't want this to sound the way it's going to," the captain began, "but, Jay, I need you back at work."

"Are you joking? I can't...."

"Jay, it might do you some good."

"How? Huh? And you plan to what? Stick me with some temporary partner?" Jay recognized the look of doubt on Colby's face. "That's what it would be, you know. Temporary. Sonny *will* pull through this."

Colby lowered his dark brown eyes. Perspiration beaded along his forehead, not that unusual for the robust man. His dark skin glistened under the fluorescent lights. "Look, son, I know what it's like to lose a partner."

"I haven't *lost* Sonny."

"I understand all too well just how close partners can be," Colby said.

"You do, huh?" Jay said, bitterness in his voice.

"Yes. I do. I lost my partner and best friend in the line of duty. I have a damn good idea how hard it is."

"Sonny is going to pull through. He is," Jay insisted.

"Well until then, you have a job."

"Morris was able to take family leave, why can't I?"

"Jay, his wife was in intensive care."

"And so is Sonny."

"I know you and Sonny are as close as brothers, but even so, you aren't family, and I can't twist policy to fix that. I can't."

"Then put me in for all my vacation. I'm serious. In what? Four years, I've only used one week. I've got it coming and sick time too."

"You want to use all that?"

"Yes. And if I run out, then I'll put in for a leave of absence."

"Jay, this won't help. Sitting here day and night."

"Maybe. Maybe not. But I wouldn't do any good on the streets. I couldn't concentrate."

"You could do desk work. I've got reports up the wazoo."

"Not going to happen, Cap. I belong here and here is where I plan to be."

"I understand. I do."

"No. I don't think you do," Jay said.

"Jay? I care about Sonny too. Not just because he's one of my best, but I like to think of him and you as friends. Even so, I have a department to run. If I can't have both of my best detectives, I need at least one of them."

"I wouldn't be the best. Not like this."

"Work could get your mind off this."

"Nothing, Cap, and I mean nothing, could get my mind off this."

"All right. Don't be upset. It isn't easy to be boss and…well, a friend."

Jay softened. "I know," he said and touched the captain's arm. "I get it."

"I'll let Human Resources know," Colby said. "I have to get to the station. Call me if – "

"I know the drill and I will," Jay said. He turned back toward Sonny's room where Dee met him halfway.

"Jill, that sweet nurse?" Dee said. "She asked me to leave the room so she could check on Sonny. I'm going to the ladies room."

Jay nodded and walked into Sonny's room. Jill looked up and smiled. She had a plastic bin all set up with a washcloth, shaving cream and a razor. "I'll only be a few more minutes," she said and drew the curtain around Sonny's bed.

Excluded and helpless once more, Jay stepped back. He glanced into the room next door. A wife shaved her husband. Across the hall, a man combed his wife's hair and then squeezed out a washcloth from a basin before he drew the curtain shut.

You're not family. Jay heard Colby's voice.

No one knew. No one knew just how hard this all was.

With drooping shoulders, Jay roamed the corridor. It was strange how the days slipped into one another. It hadn't seemed like that much time passed and yet, it felt like an eternity. With all the hours Jay spent at the hospital, he had become familiar with some of the patients. Some had introduced themselves. Some he overheard the nurses talk about. Some he just caught glimpses of whenever he left Sonny's room to stretch his legs.

The patient in the room next to Sonny's was a man in his seventies that had suffered a stroke. His wife sat with him every day until six in the evening when the man's two sons came. They sat briefly, always seeming anxious to go, and then they took their mother home. Both of the man's sons were in their thirties, and all they did the entire time they visited was complain about how stressful their lives were.

In the room two doors down from Sonny's, was a young woman who was involved in a car accident. She was speeding when a tractor trailer changed lanes. Her car flipped and rolled three or four times before it landed upside down. The police had to use the Jaws of Life to remove her from the wreckage. Doctors discovered she was paralyzed from the neck down. Her back broken. The woman was brought to the hospital two days ago. Her mother and father came every day. Her boyfriend came once. Jay hadn't seen him since. The woman remained unconscious.

In between that room and the last one down the hall there were two patients in permanent comas, awaiting beds in a specialized facility. One, a young man, was neurologically damaged to the point that he couldn't speak or recognize that anyone was present.

Cases like that one frightened Jay the most. The spectrum for brain damage, Dr. Dixon had said, was wide. That could mean anything. Sonny could be completely helpless. Unable to walk, to speak, to move. He could be left with no ability whatsoever to communicate. Or, he could be a total invalid. He might be reduced to the mind of a young, helpless child or suffer from such damage that he should be institutionalized. Jay refused to allow himself to dwell on any of those possibilities.

He wandered to the very last room. Mrs. Murphy came out of the doorway wheeling her seventeen-year-old son, Peter, in a wheelchair. Peter groaned sounds with head permanently tipped to the right. He drooled. His hands spasmed, and his legs twitched uncontrollably.

Peter had a swimming accident while at school. He was on the varsity swim team. During practice Peter attempted a dive that caused him to hit his head on the diving board. The boy landed in the water and was submerged for two minutes before anyone could get to him. He suffered massive head trauma and oxygen deficiency to the brain. The outcome was permanent brain damage.

"Hi Ken," Mrs. Murphy said.

"Hi. How are you? How's Peter today?" Jay smiled down at the young man.

Mrs. Murphy grinned warmly. "We're off to physical therapy. I think Peter enjoys it. He got excited when I told him."

Jay had met Mrs. Murphy the first night Sonny was admitted to the floor. She was an optimistic woman in her late thirties with a younger daughter and another son at home. Peter had been in the hospital for two weeks. The first forty-eight hours were the worse, Mrs. Murphy had told Jay.

Peter's mother usually left the hospital late at night. Early every morning she returned with her medium length brown hair combed back and wearing a clean set of clothes. She carried a thick novel, but the bookmark never seemed to move. At different times, when Jay took his stroll, he overheard Mrs. Murphy on the phone. It sounded as though she was arguing with one of her children about them helping out at home while their brother was in the hospital.

Her husband, a tall heavyset man, found it difficult if not impossible to be anywhere near a hospital let alone come there to sit. Jay had only caught sight of Mr. Murphy twice and then for less than an hour each time.

Jay had overheard Mr. Murphy tell the doctors that if his son was now retarded he wanted a facility for him immediately. He could not face the boy the way he now was.

In addition, he was suing the school and expected them to pay for all his son's medical bills and treatment. There was no way he intended to foot the bill for any of this.

Jay felt such sadness for Peter and his mother. From what Jay could tell, Peter had been a handsome, athletic young man.

Jay smiled again at Peter. "I guess physical therapy can be fun, huh?"

Peter grunted.

"How's Michael?" Mrs. Murphy said. "I heard they removed his oxygen."

"I think better. His blood pressure is good."

Mrs. Murphy nodded she understood. "Don't give up hope, Ken. It's all we have in times like this."

"I know," Jay said. "Thanks. Well, don't let me hold you up."

"Come and talk any time, Ken. It's good to have someone to share this with. I wish Peter's father would come….It's just so hard."

Jay nodded sadly. "See ya later, Peter."

"I mean it, Ken," Mrs. Murphy said. "It's good to have someone to talk too."

He knew how right she was. And how impossible it would be at the same time.

9

On the sixth day, Sonny was moved to the Brain Trauma Unit of the Neurological Wing. Located on the seventh floor, the room faced the parking lot. Jay looked down from the window. It made him feel like a displaced God of some weird kind who hovered above tiny cars, and all those people unaware he watched.

By the end of the day, Jay was bored with counting the number of cars that came and went. By the seventh day, he had calculated the percentages of cars by color. Red was in the lead with white a close second.

He talked to an unresponsive Sonny, read to him, even kidded that Sonny was his captive audience and if he didn't want to hear any more about Shakespeare, he damn well better wake up soon.

Dee sat with Jay often. Friends stopped by in clusters. He was grateful that Dee dealt with all the well wishers – he just didn't have the energy. It was also uncomfortable for Jay to have so many people see Sonny this vulnerable. The pity on their faces, the shocked looks, none of it helped, even though they all meant well.

"Jay?" Dee quietly said as he stared off into space. "Doug and Molly Connor are here."

Jay cleared his dry throat and ran a hand through his hair with a nod. He turned to see Molly in the doorway, crying softly on her husband's shoulder.

Jay walked to her, and she hugged him. "I'm sorry," she said. "I'm so very sorry about all of this."

She glanced past Jay. "He's so frail." She cried more. "He saved my little boy. That car. And Michael. Oh, Ken, he risked his life to save my baby."

Doug took hold of Jay's hand and shook it up and down non-stop. "If it wasn't for Mike, Danny would be dead. How do we repay that?"

Jay was speechless.

"He'll make it. I just know he will," Doug said and finally released the hold.

Molly sobbed more and then handed Jay a crayon picture of a huge red and yellow sun and two stick people. "Danny made this. For Michael. He calls him his hero." The young woman broke again and buried her head in Doug's chest.

"I better get her home," Doug said. "If you need anything…anything, you let me know."

"Thank you," Dee said. "We'll put the picture right here. On the bulletin board."

"Yes," Jay said and roughly cleared his throat again. "Thank you and tell…tell Danny…we said thanks."

"Excuse me," a nurse said. "Detective Jamison? Mrs. Santini is on the phone."

"Okay," Jay said and, to the others, explained, "I have to take this call. It's Sonny's mom." He took a deep, shaky breath and went to the nurses' station. "Maria?" he said into the phone. "No. No change. He's settled in the new room."

"Ken," Maria Santini said, "you sound exhausted." The older woman, whose smile and humor often matched her son's, cried on the other end of the line. "I should come. I should be there."

"Mom," which Jay called her sometimes, "there isn't much anyone can do right now." He adored this woman who always made him feel like part of the family – Sonny's family. "It's a long trip. There's no point in just sitting here." He wanted to protect her, the way Sonny would have.

"If it wasn't that everyone here had the flu, I'd be there."

"I know you would," Jay said.

"Call me every day, please. If Mikey's not better by the end of the week, then I'm coming," Maria said. "God bless you, Kenny. You look after my boy."

Tears sprang to Jay's eyes. "I will. You…you know…." he choked, "I will."

* * *

The bandages on Sonny's head were removed. Jay could see black and blue just under Sonny's hairline above his forehead. His head had been shaved. Hair was starting to grow back. It all made Sonny look so young and helpless. Although he was still extremely pale, he looked more comfortable with all the wires and machines removed. All that remained was the IV and its endless drip through the tube.

He was still on medication to control the brain swelling. Medication to prevent seizures. Medication to prevent infection to his kidneys and spleen. And even more medication to control his blood pressure and pain.

"How the hell do they expect him to wake up if he's on all those drugs?" Jay constantly asked the nurses and doctors, and then he apologized for his own frustration.

They regarded him with a pity Jay came to resent. He refused to believe that Sonny wouldn't wake.

"He's a fighter. He won't give in. If only they took him off all these damn drugs," he'd say to Dee. But what he didn't say aloud was his true desire – If I could just hold him. If only he could feel me next to him.

Other than when the nurses moved Sonny in the bed, Sonny did not move on his own. Round the clock, nurses propped him to one side or the other with pillows stuffed behind his back for a few hours.

Sonny never flinched. There was no response. They pricked him with needles, shouted his name and even moved him about roughly. Sonny never gave any indication that he was aware of it. Not a reflex. Not a groan. Nothing. His dark lashes cast shadows on his face, but his eyes did not open. He was manipulated in whatever position the nurses decided. His body accepted the IV liquid. He lay like a flat board on the bed as the nurses lifted, pulled, pushed and tugged on him to change the bed sheets or clean him. All he did was sleep, a deep, empty sleep that Jay imagined was as close to death as a person could get.

Jay watched for any sign. Sometimes he stared so intently that he imagined he saw a movement. A flicker of something. With bated breath, he waited and coached his partner but then…nothing.

There were times, late at night, when Jay sat close to Sonny's face just to feel the man's warm breath. It was the only sensation there was. Sometimes Jay imagined himself shaking Sonny and shouting at him to wake up. In his wishful dream, Sonny woke, laughed, and sighed. "Okay. Okay. What's the problem?"

Sitting until his butt was numb, Jay watched. He rubbed Sonny's arms, his legs, his head.

For short periods of time, Jay slept. It was a restless sleep where he dreamt that Sonny called to him, trying to find him.

The clock ticked slowly on the wall. The Trauma Unit was quiet. A distant *beep-beep-beep* could be heard from down the hall. Jay sat with eyes closed and listened to the rhythm of the machine.

He stood and stretched. A woman dressed in a black skirt and jacket with a white blouse underneath, was about to knock on the open door. She was about forty and petite with black, curly hair pushed behind her ears and hanging just to her shoulders.

"Excuse me." She glanced at her chart. "Mr. Jamison? I'm Nell Pratts. A social worker with the hospital's trauma unit." She extended her hand and looked with mild interest down at Sonny. "I understand that you're a friend of the family." She took a chair and moved it next to Jay.

"What can I do for you?" Jay said as the woman sat uninvited.

"I'm very sorry about your friend's accident. I hear he saved a little boy's life," Nell said as she read from the chart.

Jay nodded. "That's right."

"Mr. Jamison, I know how difficult this is. Situations like this are never easy for family or friends. I am afraid, though, that we have to talk about what is in store for Mr. Santini. What the plan will be for his care."

Jay frowned. "What do you mean?"

"The prognosis seems to be that this coma is permanent. I understand that he has a mother?" Nell again read off the chart.

"His mother and sister live in Brooklyn."

"I'll need to contact her," Nell said. "To discuss arrangements."

"Arrangements? What sort of arrangements?"

"For his long term care," Nell said.

"Long term care? He-he's going to wake up. He's going to be okay."

Nell looked at Jay with eyes that said something different. "Mr. Jamison. I hope that Michael does wake up. But we do need to plan for his care in the event that he doesn't. And in the event that he does wake up, he's going to need intensive care for himself." She pulled out some pamphlets. "I have a list of long term care facilities and rehabilitation hospitals for his family to review. There are several in the area that are very good. If Mrs. Santini prefers, I can locate some in New York. May I have her phone number?"

"Look lady," Jay said. "There's no way in hell that my…my partner, is going to some long term facility. I'll take care of him. He'll come home with me."

"That's very generous of you, however – "

"Generosity has nothing to do with it."

"However," she began again, "I don't think you understand the amount of care he'll need. I've seen loved ones try this in the past. They end up exhausted and sick themselves. There is a great deal of stress, not to mention around the clock care. I think that Michael would be more comfortable – "

"Lady, you don't know a damn thing about him. He'll be more comfortable at home with me," Jay said and fixed Sonny's blankets.

"I am sorry. I never meant to upset you." Nell rose. "I'll leave the information." She went to the door. "I will need to speak to his mother, though. She'll have to reach a decision."

Alone again, Jay fussed with the blanket. "It's okay, partner," he said. He glanced back at the door. "Bitch."

He worked to calm himself and then grinned at Sonny. "She's just doing her job. Hell of a job, huh? What does she know? I'm not leaving you. Gonna stay right here. I know you'll wake up. I won't let them take you anywhere except to bring you home. I promise. You just rest and get strong. I'm right here."

He returned to rubbing Sonny's arm. "I know you can feel me. I know you can hear me. Feel that? That's my hand. It's on your forehead. I'm holding your hand with my other hand, too. Feel that? I squeezed your hand to let you know I'm here. Now I'm touching your cheek. I'm tugging on your earlobe now. Can you feel it?"

Jay was lost in the amazement that was Sonny. Every curve on his face. Every feature. He was mesmerized by the detail. The shape of Sonny's nose. The curve of his upper lip. The slope of his chin. The laugh lines that appeared around the corners of his mouth. Jay had touched and kissed all of it at some point.

He longed for his lover's touch. The feel of bare skin together. The passion they shared. The way they communicated without words. It was always gentle, soothing, filled with indescribable pleasure.

Jay could always read Sonny's body. The arch of his back. The movement of his hips. The way Sonny groped his hair or fisted the sheets. It all meant something, like lover's code, that only they shared.

The urge to kiss him grew strong again. He took Sonny's hand in his. "I love you. And when I get you home, Mister, I'll show you how much."

From the corner of his eye, Jay saw someone in the doorway. He turned. Whatever it was, was gone. Jay went to the door. The hall was empty. He returned to the side of Sonny's bed and took his partner's hand once more. "When we get home, we'll get a case of beer and watch the damn football game. Now you know I love you because I freaking hate football."

Jay's eyes burned. There could never be a love like this again. Never. He would never love this way again.

* * *

That evening Dee Santiago stood in the doorway of Sonny's room. The pain resonating from Jay penetrated her heart. She put on a brave face and knocked at the door. "Hey there. How did I know I'd find you here?"

Jay struggled for a grin and then simply nodded. He didn't even bother to disguise the tears.

"I think his color looks better today. Don't you?" Dee said and moved closer to Sonny.

"Yeah. I-I think so."

Dee eyed Jay. He looked beyond exhausted. Anyone who didn't even know him could see that. He looked as though with each second that passed, a part of him died.

Dee busied herself watering the plants that were set all around the room. "A new one. From…."

"Ellen and Captain Colby," Jay said and sniffed.

"Hey," Dee said, "when was the last time you ate anything?"

Jay shrugged. He folded and refolded the flap of the blanket.

"Well I'm here now, buster, and I'm not taking no for an answer. I want you to go home. Shower. Shave, for heaven's sake, and eat something. I'll stay here with sleeping beauty. When he wakes up, I'll tell him he took too long and you had a date with some hot nurse. Serves him right making us wait so long."

"No," Jay said. "I-I should just stay here."

"Ken Jamison, you look at me right now. This is Dee you're talking to. I already asked nice. I won't ask nice again. Now, you know me. Am I the type to take no for an answer? Huh? No, I am not. So, you go out that door right now. Do not even think of arguing."

Jay let out a tired sigh. "Okay. But I'll be back in an hour." He fussed with the blanket one more time. "Don't...don't leave him, okay?"

"An atomic blast couldn't get me to move. I swear."

Jay walked to the doorway and looked back as if he were about to say something. He didn't. With bent shoulders, he walked from the room.

Dee pinned her hair back and sat in the chair Jay had occupied. She dabbed at her wet eyes. Black mascara stained the tissue.

Taking Sonny's weightless hand in her own, she said a silent prayer.

"Sonny," she whispered. "Sonny, can you hear me? I think you can. I think you can hear all of us. Listen. I know you're tired. I know you're doing your best to heal and get better but...but, Sonny? Jay needs a sign. Something. Anything to give him hope. Oh, it's not that he's giving up. You know better than that. Jay would never...will never give up. It's just that he's so tired, you know? He needs you, Sonny. You're his...well, his best friend in the whole world. You know he doesn't have anyone except us. And if...if he ever lost you, he'd never be the same. He needs you to give him a sign that you can hear him. We all do. A sign that you're working your way back to all of us. Can you do that, Sugar? Can you give us a sign? I wouldn't ask except if I know Jay, he's probably telling you just to sleep and rest and get better. That's fine. But Jay would never ask for himself."

She straightened the blanket.

"So," Dee continued, "if you could just try to give him something. Anything. A twitch. Lift a finger. Anything is fine. We all miss you so much, but Jay? He's hurting, Sonny. I've never seen him hurt like this before. I don't mean to worry you. It's just that Jay is so tired. But if you could give him a sign then maybe…maybe he'll let himself rest a little. Please, Sonny."

Dee sat quiet for a moment, looking upon her friend. "Okay. Well you just think about it. Work on it, okay?"

10

―――――――――――――

Two hours? Really?" Dee said when Jay walked into the hospital room. "That's all the time you took?" She looked at her friend who wore wrinkled clothes and whose hair was still damp. "I bet you didn't even eat, did you?"

Still pale with red eyes, Jay thanked Dee and then took his usual spot next to the bed.

Dee tossed up her hands and sat quiet.

An hour later, Jay moved to the window. Dee stood to stretch. She glanced down at Sonny. His eyes were open.

"Sonny?" she called quietly. "Sonny? Jay? Come here."

Jay rushed to the bed. Sonny's deep blue eyes *were* open. Glassy, fixed, they stared straight upwards. No blinking. No movement. Just a blank, empty stare.

"Sonny?" Jay said. "Can you hear me? It's me. Jay. Can you hear me?"

"I'll get the nurse," Dee said.

Sonny remained motionless, his gaze rigid.

Dr. Dixon and a nurse hurried into the room. Dixon waved Jay back and then bent to examine Sonny.

Jay glanced at Dee with the first smile he had shown in days. Dee crossed her fingers.

Dixon shined a penlight into Sonny's eyes. He poked him. Pressed on him. Even pinched Sonny's arms. He checked Sonny's blood pressure and breathing and then stepped back and gestured for Jay to come out of the room. Dee followed both men.

"He's waking up, right?" Jay said, excitement in his voice. "He's coming around, right?"

With a solemn expression, Dixon said, "What we have is a higher level of consciousness, but he isn't conscious. It's a reflex. An involuntary reflex. It's a step though, and a good one."

"So he is waking up?" Dee said.

"Yes and no," Dixon said. "He's at a higher state, but not alert. Not focused. He's actually sleeping with his eyes open, still unaware of his surroundings or any stimuli. From this point on, we may see more random movements. All reflexes."

Jay's face mirrored Dee's own disappointment.

"I don't want you to lose hope," Dixon said. "Really I don't. He could continue to move forward or….This may be all the progress he makes."

"No," Jay said. "He's coming back. I know he is."

Dixon placed his hand on Jay's arm. "I hope so too. Just be aware that this may be the level he remains at…indefinitely. Ken, I know you spoke to Ms. Pratts, the social worker. We've been in touch with Michael's mother. We sent her information so she could think about long-term care. I know this is hard for everyone to hear. But you should know that there's a bed opening up at the end of this week in a very good facility. I plan to transfer Michael to it until Mrs. Santini makes other arrangements."

Dee's stomach sank.

Jay shook his head adamantly. "No. Absolutely not. I'll take care of him. I'll bring him home."

"Ken," Dixon said, "that's very generous of you. However, the care that Michael will require is beyond your scope. Please. Do what's best for your friend."

"What's best for….What do you think I'm doing? He is not going to some facility or institution. Not now. Not ever."

"This isn't your decision to make. I'm sorry, but it's up to Michael's family. You may try to convince them to let Michael stay with you, but I *will* recommend something different. The care he'll require is too much. How will you manage? You're a police officer, correct? You work long hours. And what if…what if something happens to you? Then what? No, in all good conscience, I cannot recommend home care for Michael. Not at this time anyway." Dixon removed his glasses. "I'm sorry, but I never hold back information from my patients, their family, or their friends."

Dixon nodded at Dee, then turned and left. Jay, head bent, walked back to Sonny's room. Dee followed. Sonny lay in the bed. Eyes closed again.

"Jay?" Dee touched his shoulder. "Maybe it is best. You're exhausted." Sadly, she added, "It's just a different kind of hospital."

"It isn't best," Jay said. "If Sonny goes there, he might never….Dixon can't do this. Dee? Stay with Sonny." He hurried out of the room.

* * *

Down the hall, Jay caught sight of Dr. Dixon.

"I need to talk to you," Jay said.

Dixon handed off a file to a nurse and nodded. "My office is this way."

Inside the paper-cluttered room Jay paused awkwardly. He ran a hand through his hair. "You can't move Sonny to that…that place."

Dixon stood behind his desk. He considered Jay for a moment and then gestured for him to sit. "I know how much you care about your friend, Ken. And I respect that. But hospital policy and – "

"I don't give a damn about hospital policy. Sonny is not going to be moved to some damn institution."

"Is there something you'd like to tell me?"

"I just did."

"Ken, there is such a thing as patient-doctor confidentiality. That can also apply to family, even extends to close family friends, so whatever you need to say to me is kept in trust."

Jay frowned and then sighed. He wanted to say it, but there was the promise. The one he and Sonny made. No one was ever to know about their private life even if something happened to either of them. They had to protect themselves. One of them would be left to face the repercussions, and that also meant endangering their careers.

"It's confidential," Dixon repeated.

"For us too," Jay said.

"Then let me ask. Are you and Michael…?"

"A couple?" Jay eyed the man, swallowed, and then said, "Yes."

Dixon sat back in his chair and laced his fingers. "I see."

"Do you? Does that mean something? Is he less of a concern for you now?"

"Of course not."

"Really? Something tells me you suspected it. Is that why the need to transfer him is so urgent?"

"No. You really don't understand the severity of his condition, do you?"

"I understand."

"But you're in denial. That won't help him."

"And neither will giving up on him. Sonny and I are...a couple." Jay rose and ran a hand through his hair. He huffed. "That's the first time I ever described us out loud to anyone."

"So, no one knows? Not even that woman who's always here?"

"No one. We're cops. You do the math on the rest."

"I see." Dixon rocked slightly in his office chair.

"You do? What exactly do you see?"

"Does his family know that you're...?"

"Homosexuals? No. But none of that changes anything. His mother told me I was in charge of calling the shots for his care. She's counting on me."

"I know. She told me."

"Then what's the problem?"

"Like it or not, the hospital has no policy for this sort of thing. Family. Spouses. Even engaged couples may have the authority to decide care, but not...."

"Gays. Well, doc, I don't know what to say to you except, screw your policies. Sonny's my partner, and unless I hear different from his mother, I'm all you've got."

"Mrs. Santini needs to understand all the facts."

"Did you ask her? About me and Sonny?"

"No. Of course not. This conversation is between us. I respect your right to privacy. You have to respect the hospital's policies. I can't make exceptions. I wish I could."

"Do you?"

"I'm not here to judge anyone. My first and only concern is for the patient. Ken, Michael is very...ill. It isn't going to just disappear. Even if...

and that's a big if. Even if he wakes up, he *will* be brain damaged. To what extent, I can't predict. But right now, as things look? He's in a vegetative state. That could go on for months. Years."

"There's hope." Jay swallowed his uncertainty. "There's always hope."

"I understand how hard you're fighting for Michael."

"No, you don't. We're more than just two gay men. He's my partner. You ever put your life in someone else's hands? You ever face a man with a gun about to shoot you and have your partner push you out of the way ready to take the bullet himself? Sonny is everything to me. Everything. You might as well get out the broom and sweep me off the floor if anything happens to him."

"I understand."

"Don't say that if you don't."

"I do," Dixon said. He turned a photograph on his desk. "This is…was my wife. I lost her two years ago in a car accident. They had to sweep me off the floor, too. Somehow, I had to put the pieces back together."

"Not sure I could, Doc. Not sure I'd want too."

"No need to make any decisions today. Let's see how it goes in a few more days."

"And his mother?" Jay said.

"I'll consult with her and you. You have my word."

* * *

Throughout that night and into the next day Jay kept track of Sonny's condition. Sonny continued to open his eyes and close them. No focused gaze, just opened eyes fixed upward. Glassy. Empty.

It was spooky to see. He just seemed to…stare without blinking and then, nothing. Sometimes his lids partly opened. Sometimes only one opened as if he were peeking out. A minute. Two minutes. Closed again.

Dee cried when he did this and left the room.

The arm movements began shortly after that. Once more it was misplaced hope. Involuntary movements that only meant he'd have to have restraints so he didn't accidentally pull out his IV.

Jay looked down at Sonny's failing body like he did when he was the god who hovered above the parking lot watching the tiny cars. What he forced himself to see was that Sonny was shrinking. He had lost weight. His muscles were flaccid. He was ghostly white. His cheeks sunken. His eyelids were like the white knit blanket that covered his motionless body. Sonny looked small in the bed encased inside a shell. Buried alive and unable to call out.

Jay shivered. Hours of watching had turned to days. Thirteen days since the screech of tires and the sound of bone hitting pavement.

Crack.

With a shaky breath, he moved toward the window. He had to think. Think about what he was going to do. But every time he tried, he felt like he was letting Sonny down and, just as painful, like someone was cutting off bits and pieces of his flesh.

"I'm not giving up, partner," he said from across the room. "I just… need…." His voice quivered. "To think." His mind wandered just as it did every time he tried to think beyond the realm of Sonny coming back to him. It was getting harder and harder to concentrate. And harder to fight the dizziness that had started a day ago.

It was dawn. The sun slowly floated up from the horizon. Two large, dark clouds appeared in the sky. Finally, drops of rain. The sun fought a gallant battle. Dim rays of light became stronger until the storm clouds had no choice but surrender.

"Dixon wants to speak to me today," Jay announced to the window and the new day. "We both know what that's about." He drove a trembling hand through his hair. "That isn't a conversation I want to have, but…."

He turned around and once more Sonny's eyes were open, staring upward. "I swear I'm not giving up. But maybe that other place can do…." He looked at Sonny and frowned. A step closer, he said, "Do…something." Another step, he frowned harder. Was that a blink? Jay was by the bed. "Maybe I'm the one who's asleep." There it was again. A blink.

Jay rubbed at his own exhausted eyes. Two rapid, undeniable blinks. "Sonny?" Jay said in a whisper at first and then louder. "Sonny? Are you looking at me?" He felt his heart skip. "Sonny? S-squeeze my hand if you can hear me. Try. Squeeze."

Jay held his breath. There it was. It was weak, but Sonny squeezed his finger.

"Holy….Oh my God," Jay said. "You did it. Are you awake? Are you looking at me?"

Slowly, like a hinge that hadn't been opened in decades, Sonny's jaw moved, and a deep, dry breath said, "Yes."

"Yes. You said yes." Jay was ready to do a somersault. "D-don't go away." He headed for the door and then came back to the bed. "Stay right there, partner. Don't leave."

He ran to the hall and shouted. "He's awake. He woke up. He spoke."

Nurses pushed past him, and Jay shouted it to them again. "He said yes. He looked right at me and said yes." Jay grabbed one nurse and planted a wet kiss on her mouth.

Dr. Dixon hurried into the room. Jay bounced up and down like someone on a caffeine rush.

Dixon shined a light in Sonny's eyes. They were glossy. When asked to squeeze the doctor's hand, there was a pause and then a response.

"You see? See?" Jay squeaked.

Sonny looked straight up at the ceiling. There was no reaction other than his eyelids that opened and closed slowly.

"Do you know where you are?" Dixon said.

Sonny's eyes darted. "H-hospital," his frail voice confirmed.

"Hospital? Did you hear that?" Jay beamed like the proud papa of a one hundred and sixty pound male.

Dixon stood up straight and for the first time smiled. "This is a very good sign, Ken. A very good sign."

"I knew it. I knew it," Jay said and smiled even wider.

"Let me examine him," Dixon said.

The nurse led a bouncing Jay out the door. "Just give us a minute," she said.

Jay laced his fingers behind his head, ready to dance. He smiled at everyone who came down the hall, and then he saw Dee. He ran to her, lifted her off the floor and twirled her around. "He woke up. He spoke. He spoke."

"What? Sonny?" Dee said.

"Of course Sonny. I told you he's a tough little shit. He knows he's in the hospital. He said it."

Dee threw her arms around Jay. They laughed and cried at the same time.

"I want to see him," Dee said.

The door was open. Jay held tight to Dee's hand and brought her inside.

Sonny was still awake. He looked at them, and Dee gasped.

"Do you recognize anyone in this room?" Dixon asked Sonny.

Sonny creased his brows.

"Sonny?" Jay said. "It's me."

Sonny frowned more. In a breathy voice, he said, "I-I thought you... you said my...my name...was Michael."

"Sonny is your nickname," Dixon explained. "Do you know anyone in this room?"

Jay stepped closer. "Hey there, buddy."

"Who?" Sonny said.

"It's me, partner," Jay said with a wide smile.

"Who...are...?" Sonny faded and drifted to sleep.

11

"He'll sleep on and off for a while," Dixon said and handed a chart to the nurse.

"He-he's just a little confused, right?" Jay said. He looked back and forth at the doctor and then Dee. "That's normal, right?"

"When he wakes again, see if you can get him to talk." Dixon patted Jay on the back.

"You-you heard him, right?" Jay said to Dee. "I'm not dreaming, am I?"

"No," Dee said. "I heard him."

"He's just confused," Jay said. "Who wouldn't be? But Dixon said this is a good sign." He repositioned the blankets around Sonny. "He's coming back to us. He is."

"Why don't we get something to eat?" Dee said.

"Are you kidding? He might wake up again." Jay fussed with the blanket once more.

"The doctor said he'd sleep on and off. This might be a good time to take a break."

"No," Jay said and smiled. "I'm not leaving. I'm going to be right here." He settled in the chair, eyes glued on Sonny. "When he wakes up again, I want him to know I'm here."

* * *

"Hey there," Jay said the moment Sonny woke. "You look even more awake then before. That's a good sign, partner. I knew you could do it. Come back. The doctors…well, they thought….But hey, never mind. I knew you could do it."

Jay waited for a response, but all he got in return was a strange stare. He grinned past it. "You know where you are?"

Sonny moved his lips slowly. "H-h-h…hospital."

"That's right. That's great."

Sonny began to lift his left arm, but the restraints still attached prevented his movement. "Wh…why am I…tied?"

"That? That's nothing. Really. It's just so you couldn't pull out the IV. They'll take them off soon."

Sonny tried to move. His head and shoulders dropped back on the pillow. He tried once more like a newborn foal trying to find the strength to stand. But, once more, too fragile, he dropped to the pillow. Jay steadied him.

"Easy, partner," Jay coached. "You're not ready to run the marathon yet."

Sonny's eyes darted around the room. Once more he tried to move. Once more he flopped back.

"Easy, buddy. Just relax," Jay said. Gently, he pinned Sonny's shoulders. With a sweet smile, he adjusted the IV tube. "You never were a very good patient. But in this case? You have to stay put for now."

"I don't…know.…Wh-why can't…?"

"It's okay. I know you've got lots of questions. I'll tell you everything. But for right now, you have to take it slow. Okay?" Sonny relaxed, and Jay sat in the chair next to him and went back to smiling. "That's good, partner. You're doing fine."

Sonny held up a hand the little that he could. He bent and unbent his fingers. "Ev…everything…h-h…hurts."

Jay's muscles tightened. "I know. I'm sorry."

"Wh…what happened?"

Jay leaned in closer. "You were in an…an accident. But you're okay now. Everything is going to be okay."

Sonny frowned. "Wh…who *are* you?"

"Me?" Jay's smile began to cave. The thought that Sonny was kidding occurred to him. But the look in Sonny's eyes wiped away what little smile Jay had left. "I-I'm Jay."

The frown didn't leave Sonny's face. "I don't...I can't...." The earlier agitation returned and so did Sonny's attempt to move a body that literally refused.

Again, Jay worked to soothe him. "It's okay. You've been out of it for awhile. You're just...confused."

Dr. Dixon rapped at the doorway and came in with two nurses. "Awake? That's good." He checked the chart one nurse offered and said, "You remember me? Where you are? How about this man?"

"Sssss...stop," Sonny slurred. "My...head hurts."

"Well, that's to be expected," Dixon said.

"Wh...why can't I...m-m-move my legs?" Sonny said.

Jay tossed a panicked look at Dixon who acted perfectly calm.

Dixon went to the foot of the bed and with a long pin, poked at Sonny's toes. "Can you feel that?"

"Sssss...some," Sonny said, his eyelids beginning to shut.

Dixon looked at Jay. "I don't see this as a problem. The swelling caused some muscle damage but we'll get him into physical therapy once there's more improvement."

Puzzled, Sonny creased his eyes. "What?"

"Never mind," Dixon said to him. "Just keep up the good work and rest."

Sonny's eyes were closed before the doctor finished the sentence.

"Ken, let's talk. Outside," Dixon said and led the way. In the hall he had a serious expression not unlike most of his expressions. "We need to run some tests."

"Of course. But this is good, right?"

"Did he recognize you?"

"No...but he just woke up after almost two weeks. He's confused."

"Ken, I told you to expect this. He may never recognize you."

Jay ran a hand through his hair, looked back at his sleeping partner, and huffed. "He will. Why do you always write him off so easily? A few hours ago, you called him a vegetable. Now, just because he's a little mixed up, you want to tell me he won't get better."

"I don't want to tell you that. It's my job. I've seen cases like this before."

"But he's talking. Answering questions. He's looking at us."

"I'm glad he made that much progress," Dixon said.

"And he'll keep making progress," Jay said. "You watch. I know my partner." He went back into the room and sat once more by the bed.

* * *

An hour later Jay said, "Hi," when Sonny opened his eyes again.

Slow and weak, Sonny replied, "Hi." There was no expression on his face. Blank, he simply looked at Jay and then looked away.

"You just missed Dee," Jay said. "She went to get something to eat." Still no reaction. "I've missed you so much."

Sonny strained with each word. "Wh…what? Why…why am I…?"

Jay leaned in and took Sonny's left hand. "Why are you here? You saved little Danny's life, buddy. You got him away from that car. But you couldn't get yourself away fast enough."

Sonny frowned at his hand in Jay's.

"You're going to be okay," Jay said. "You will."

Sonny squinted at Jay's hand still holding his. "Sssssstop."

"It's okay. It's just us," Jay said and smiled.

"Go…go away," Sonny said in a breathy voice.

Jay's eyes grew large. "Go? Away? Sonny? It's me, partner. Jay."

"I-I don't know." Sonny pulled his hand out of Jay's, and it dropped like a weight by his side.

"Shhh. It's all right. Just be still. You just came out of a coma. It'll take time, that's all."

"Who…are you?"

Jay's knees went weak. "Who am I? It-it's me."

Sonny was asleep again. Jay sank into the cold, hard chair. His mind fought with what he didn't want to know and what he hoped.

Dee walked in with a brown bag and sodas. "So, how's the sleeping prince?" she said. One glance at Jay, and her smile disappeared. "What's wrong? Did something happen?"

Jay sat forward and cleared his throat. "No. He woke again. The doctor was in. They need to do tests."

"Jay, I know you. When I left, you were as high as a kite, and now you look sick. What's going on?"

"He…Sonny, doesn't…he doesn't know who I am."

Dee looked at the sleeping Sonny and back at Jay. "Well, that's normal. Isn't it? I mean, after a coma?"

"I-I thought so too. At first. But…I don't know. Something isn't right."

"Don't worry so much. He woke up. Remember? A few hours ago you were afraid he'd have to go to an institution and now, he's awake. Let them do the tests and give Sonny a little time."

"I guess you're right. He just needs some…time."

12

T hroughout the day Sonny woke a few times, and each time was no better than the last.

"You? Again?" Sonny said. His expression was either a perplexed frown or an unconnected indifference.

He rolled over to his side. With his back to Jay, he stared with no purpose at the wall.

Jay coaxed him. Sonny ignored him.

Each time Sonny reacted that way, Jay's smile evaporated. His optimism was slowly being drained from him. He was recharged when Sonny woke, believing it might be different this time, and then drained again within a matter of seconds.

It wasn't just Sonny's reaction to Jay. It was his reaction to everything and everyone around him.

He didn't recognize Dee or Crocket. He looked away from them all and stared at the wall once more. In almost a dry growl that caused Jay's stomach to knot, he told them all to leave him alone. And whenever Jay reached to touch him, to calm him, he recoiled as if Jay were poison.

Jay walked out into the hallway. He read the faces of the hospital staff. They hesitated to go in Sonny's room. They hurried in, changed his IV, gave him his medication, tried to ignore his threats and cold stares, and then hurried back out again.

"Get. Out," Sonny shouted so loud that Jay heard him from down the hall.

Jay quickened his steps. In the room, there was the distressed nurse, her hands on her hips, and hostility in the air so thick it smoked.

"I am going to report this to Dr. Dixon," the outraged nurse said in a stern voice. "Do you hear me, young man?"

She stood over a brown, chunky mess on the floor and turned when she noticed Jay. "Do you see this? This isn't the first time he's thrown his food tray."

"Get. Out," Sonny screamed. With one swoop of his hand, the plastic glass of water on the bed tray was also flung to the floor.

"Sonny, take it easy," Jay said.

Sonny looked at Jay like a viper ready to strike. "Who the fuck are you? I'm sick of you. Her. And this whole goddamn place. Get out," he shouted as three other nurses came in behind Jay. "I mean it. All of you. Leave me alone." He tried to move too quickly, cried out in pain and wrapped his arms around his head.

"Sonny," Jay said and rushed to his side.

"My head," Sonny cried. "Hurts. Hurts." He had his eyes squeezed shut, and he cringed with each moan.

The nurses came to him, and he batted them away until Jay took his hands.

Sonny's fingers dug into Jay so deep, Jay flinched, but wouldn't let go.

"Easy," Jay said in a soft voice. "Just relax."

An intern hurried in and prepared an injection.

"The doctor is going to give you some medicine to help," Jay explained.

Sonny shook his head violently from side to side. He tried to fling his arms, but Jay grabbed on and held them.

"No," Sonny groaned. "Make it…just…make it stop."

"Easy, partner. The medicine will help, okay? But you have to relax. Work with me, okay? Come on. You can do it."

The doctor drove the needle into Sonny's arm. Sonny hissed. Jay flinched. Sonny dug his nails deeper into Jay's forearm. Jay clasped Sonny's other hand as tight as he could.

"Breathe, buddy," Jay said. "That's it. Just breathe."

One nurse busied herself with the IV. Two others tried to reposition Sonny.

"I got him," Jay said to them, still holding Sonny.

Sonny sucked air in through his gritted teeth. Eyes still tightly closed, he continued to groan.

Jay pried his hand from Sonny's grip. "Easy, buddy. I'm right here," Jay said to the man's pain filled face. He reached over to the side table for a wash cloth and some ice in a bucket. Wrapping the ice in the cloth, he placed it on Sonny's forehead.

Sonny hissed again, but when he put one hand on top of the washcloth to hold it in place, Jay knew it must have helped. He glanced down, and Sonny's other hand still clung to him.

"Just breathe," Jay said in a quiet lull. "Relax. That's good. Easy."

Sonny nodded without opening his eyes. Jay could feel the man's tension fade.

Jay began to move back but Sonny gripped him tighter.

"You're going to be okay," Jay said.

Sonny, eyes still shut, his hand holding the wash cloth to his forehead and his other hand fisting Jay's shirt sleeve, gave another nod. Little by little, his grip on Jay eased. Inch by inch, his hand lowered from his forehead. The pain dissolved on his face, and he fell asleep.

* * *

At two in the afternoon an orderly and nurse wheeled Sonny back into the room.

"How were the tests?" Jay said.

Sonny slid off the stretcher with the help of the orderly. Jay offered a hand. Sonny pulled away. "Don't. Touch me," he said.

Surprised, Jay took a step back.

"Oh, he's just a bit grumpy today," the nurse said in an overly cheery tone. "'Fraid we tired him out. Isn't that right, honey?"

"Screw you," Sonny said and closed his eyes. "Why is *he* still here?"

The nurse offered a weak smile when she looked at Jay. "Because he's your friend, honey. And he cares about you."

Without opening his eyes, Sonny said, "Tell him to leave me alone."

"Honey," the nurse said, "don't you remember when you had that awful headache the other day? Your friend was right here and helped you."

"I don't need his help," Sonny said, his eyes still shut. "And I'm not your honey."

Again the nurse kept the strained smile when she spoke to Jay. "Let's let him get some rest. Dr. Dixon would like to see you in his office."

Jay nodded. "Sure." He looked at Sonny who was asleep and then he adjusted the blanket, folding the covers back under Sonny's chin. After the nurse left the room, he bent to kiss Sonny's forehead, stopped himself, and with a disheartened sigh, left the room.

A knock on the office door, and Jay heard Dr. Dixon say come in.

Dixon, although the same height as Jay, was much thinner. He always had greased back hair every time Jay saw him. The thinness of his hair and whole body gave him a sunken face that was pitted in some spots. In his typical white shirt, but with a brown solid tie this time, his medical jacket was stiff and white. The brightness of the jacket only caused the man to appear more ghostly.

Dixon removed his glasses when Jay walked inside. He gestured for Jay to have a seat.

The doctor's office was quiet. The room simple. A desk, chairs and bookcase overstuffed with medical books and journals. The man's desk was buried in files, forms and scattered reports. Jay was certain Sonny's report was in there somewhere.

On the desk, Jay noticed the framed photo of Dixon's deceased wife. Next to that was a picture of a younger woman who held a baby and a young man who stood by her. Jay assumed one of them was either Dixon's daughter or his son with Dixon's grandchild.

Dixon rose and came around from behind his desk. He sat on the edge of the glossy lacquered desk. From where Jay sat, it felt like the man loomed over him.

Jay swallowed. "So how is Sonny doing?"

"Ken," the doctor began and slid a stapler out of the way, "we've been running tests on Michael and will continue that process for the next couple of days."

Uneasy in the chair, Jay said, "I know. I've asked how he's doing, and they keep telling me to wait."

"I'm sure you have many questions, and by the time we're done, you'll probably have a lot more. I have some information to give you." Dixon took some papers from the top of the pile. "I'd like you to read these. It should help with some of the questions. I'll also be sending copies and a full report to Michael's mother."

Jay took the sheets of paper and nodded. "I appreciate that."

"I hope it helps." Dixon readjusted his position, his feet firmly on the floor. "What I have to say is complicated, so please, stop me if you have a question, all right?"

Jay nodded. He leaned forward in his chair. But that placed him too close to the doctor so he sat back. "Go ahead. I'm listening."

"First of all, Michael has shown much better progress than I ever dared hope. I want you to know I never intended to write him off."

"I-I didn't mean that," Jay said. "This hasn't been easy."

"I understand. I want you to know that the fact that he came out of the coma at all is a miracle. By all rights, with the injuries he had, he should have, at the very least, remained in a coma permanently."

"I told you he would surprise you."

"Yes, you did," Dixon said. "And that brings us to the second part. The fact that Michael is able to speak and to comprehend is another miracle that I never thought would happen. The tests we completed over the last two days, while still very soon, show that he has many of his cognitive skills intact. He can read and write. He understands simple math. He's able to ask and answer many basic and general questions. He can follow simple directions and recall simple information. His short-term memory skills seem to be intact as well. Motor-wise, Michael is weak, which is understandable. He can grasp objects. He's able to use a pincher grasp… that is, pick up items between his index finger and thumb. Moreover, he's able to pull himself to a standing position. All of these facts are a miracle in themselves."

"That's great," Jay said.

Dixon acknowledged Jay's relief and then gently said, "That's all the wonderful things that Michael can do. Now we need to discuss where the damage is."

Jay's heart rate quickened. "Damage?"

Dixon moved a chair over to sit beside Jay. He turned it so they were face to face. "There is still so much we don't know about the human brain. It's a very complicated muscle. What we do know is that the brain houses different information and can perform different skills. If certain areas are damaged, then information and skills can be lost. What we know right now…and these words are going to sound frightening, is that Michael has irreversible brain damage."

Jay's stomach heaved slightly. He looked away from the doctor for a second and then back again. "I-I don't….That can't be right."

"Ken, I know you've witnessed some of this. That incident the other day, for example. His anger. His need to push you and anyone else away from him."

"I've seen that. But, come on. He's still recovering."

"Is that how Michael, the Michael you knew, might have reacted?"

Jay looked down at the floor. "I know he doesn't…remember. But, he will."

"From the beginning of this whole ordeal, I told you to expect brain damage. Now, it's here. No doubt about it. No chance of error. What we are dealing with…the type of brain damage Michael has…involves primarily the frontal temporal lobe. Michael has lost many of his memories for the past and yet retained some information as well. He can remember how to read and write and speak. He knows that he's learned certain things, but doesn't really know how. For example, he knows some of the various codes and procedures the police use for different crimes. But, he doesn't remember being a police officer or how he learned that information. He has no memories of events in his life. Where he went to school. His time in the army. Why he came to Florida. He also doesn't remember the people in his life…." Dixon's words trailed off as he placed his hand on Jay's arm. "Not anyone in his life."

"Right now. But…he will," Jay said. "He will, right?"

"No," Dixon said.

Jay cleared his throat. He needed to stand. He did. Then he needed to sit. He did. "This is….I don't understand how you could know something like that so soon."

"This is all very upsetting, I know. It's scary for you. And for Michael. Michael knows that he should know these things and can't really comprehend why he doesn't. That is upsetting to him to the point of making him angry. On top of this, Michael's social and emotional skills are impaired as well. That's due to the area of the brain that was injured. He's easily frustrated. Easy to anger. Easy to react. He's afraid and doesn't know how to deal with that. He feels weak physically and helpless. I've tried to reassure him that the physical weakness is temporary, but he's having trouble understanding that. I told you he could comprehend. But his comprehension is based solely on concrete matters. Basic. Real. He has limited understanding about emotions. It's a foreign concept to him. He's at the very basic level for emotions. Anger is the easiest to understand and to demonstrate. In addition, his social skills are extremely limited. He doesn't understand how to react in front of others. That means he doesn't know what's appropriate and what's not. How much cognitive information Michael has retained will have to be assessed over time. Right now, he's at the very basic concrete level in both his reasoning skills and his emotional skills."

"Okay. Okay. I get that. But he will. He will get better."

"Past events are gone, Ken. That area of the brain suffered significantly."

"I still don't....I'm not trying to be difficult, Doc. I just don't see how you could know that. Over time...."

"Over time, he may recall things he learned at different points in his life. But, as I explained, events in his life before the accident are gone. I want you to understand...to accept, that he has lost certain functions. Memories. His personality. He isn't the same and he won't ever be the same." Dixon stopped and took a breath. "Do you need some water?"

"No," Jay mumbled to the floor. "I just don't think I can accept that. I hear you. But...Sonny is here. He's alive."

"I know how much you want that. Ken, I'm not going to dash all your hopes. One thing is certain. Michael can learn. He can form new relationships. I just want you to understand that it won't be easy. It will be an honest to God struggle. You see how he is right now. He just wants to be left alone. He doesn't want to have to face what he doesn't know. What's also important, Ken, is that Michael's personality has been affected in different ways. It's difficult to say how much his unconscious personality has been affected. You may find that what made him laugh in the past doesn't any longer. However, you may also find that if he was a kind person, he still will be." Dixon paused. "Right now, he's on the edge. He's easily upset and may be aggressive at times."

"Aggressive?"

"Yes."

"Wait a minute. You mean that incident with the food tray? He's just frustrated. Who wouldn't be? Cooped up in here."

"It wasn't the first time."

"He's not violent," Jay said.

"He's angry. And how he handles that anger could be a concern."

With an edge to his voice, Jay said, "Sonny could never hurt anybody."

"Let's not go there right now," Dixon said and moved to lean on his desk again. "I know this is a lot to take in. I'm trying to be as clear as I can for something that is not clear at all. We all have to learn as we go along. You and Michael. Especially Michael, although I know this won't be easy for you either." Dixon drew a deep breath. "Ken, I know we've talked about your relationship with Michael."

"He's my partner," Jay said.

"He's more than your partner."

"I use that word to mean everything it could possibly imply," Jay said.

"I understand there's a lot at stake here," Dixon said. "Your careers. The understanding you and Michael had. The urgency that it be private."

"I'm not ashamed, doctor. I'm just cautious."

"The closeness that you and Michael share can be especially stressful and difficult at a time like this. Not just for…."

"Gays?"

"For any loved ones. It's difficult to see the person they love who talks and walks and looks the same, and yet is someone who just doesn't know who they are. The patient doesn't know what the relationship was. Doesn't remember the love and commitment. Families are devastated by this and heartbroken. I just think you should be prepared, Ken. Emotionally, this will be a struggle for you too."

"I can handle it," Jay said.

"I want to make it very clear. While Michael can learn, he will never be the same again. He will never be as he was. There was just too much damage. And it's not simply his memory. Emotionally, socially, his personality. All of it. Limited."

Jay sat speechless for a moment. He rose and walked the few steps to the opposite wall where all of the doctor's medical degrees were displayed. He ran a hand through his hair and turned back to look at Dixon. "No offense, Doc, but you were never very optimistic. I believe in Sonny. I believe he will make it back completely. He's just too stubborn not to."

Dixon sighed and went to sit behind his desk. "Well, as you've said all along, Michael and you could surprise me." He closed a file and put on a pair of glasses that hid his hazel eyes. "There's lots of information available on this subject beyond what I gave you. I suggest you read as much as you can. In the meantime, do you have any questions?"

"How much do I tell him about his life?" Jay said. "What do I say?"

"My recommendation? I suggest it not be a lot. It's best not to put a lot of expectations on him. Take it slow. You'll see changes in him for a while. Some days better. Some days worse. He may recall things that will give you tremendous hope, and then at times, not recall anything at all. Ken, Michael's brain was significantly damaged. I can't stress that enough. Areas were bruised and brain cells lost. He has to learn to reconnect. Other areas will have to develop over time and take the place of what was lost. The best advice I can give is to learn together. Don't expect him to react as he always did. Give it time and give him space. If you pressure him to be who he was, you could lose him completely."

"Wh-what about…us?" Jay asked. "I mean…our relationship? How do I tell him?"

Dixon was silent and then replied, "That was my earlier point. I don't think it's wise. I think it's too much for him to comprehend."

Jay frowned. "Too much to…but we have a relationship. We're together. We love each other. Don't you think that's worth telling him?"

"Not now," Dixon said flatly and then softened a bit. "Ken, emotionally Michael is at a…newborn level for lack of a better way to help you understand. In fact, he has no emotions. None."

Jay shook his head. "No. That can't be right."

"It is, I assure you, I know it's hard to hear, but that's what we have to contend with. He has no connections. No emotions he can either feel or understand."

"So he…doesn't love?" Jay said. "Me?"

"Not anyone. I'm not saying he can't learn to love or experience other emotions. Just not right now. Anger is rudimentary. In this case, the stepping stone."

Jay ran his hand through his hair with a heartbroken chuckle. "Well, he's got that down, doesn't he." He strained not to let the tears fall and said, "Still. I think I should tell him…unless he will remember on his own." Hope sprang for a moment and he asked, "Do you…think he might?"

Dixon shook his head. "No. I'm sorry."

"Maybe that will be another surprise, Doc."

"You say you need to keep this relationship private? Is that correct?"

"Yes," Jay said."I've explained that."

"What do you think Michael will do with the information? If he's confused by it, how will he make sense of it? Right now you have to establish just a basic relationship with him, don't you? He keeps pushing you away, and he doesn't even know exactly who you are. So you want to tell him you're more than friends and expect him to comprehend what no one else is permitted to know?"

Jay turned his back and let out a heavy sigh. "I guess you're right. It would make more sense just to get him to accept me…as a friend and trust me first." Another defeated sigh, and he looked at the doctor. "When can he leave the hospital?" he said. "What's next?"

"He'll need to stay for at least another week. That should give him time to regain his strength and start physical therapy, which he'll need no matter how he might fight it."

"Why should he fight it?"

"Because he doesn't understand how important it is. It's just one more thing he's told to do, and trust me on this, from what I've seen, he doesn't like to be told. I've tried to explain to him that he has some nerve damage. Some of that will improve and some of that is also permanent."

"Permanent? In what way?"

"Loss of feeling. Numbness. Perhaps some weakness on his left side. It all has to be assessed and monitored. We'll need his cooperation with this. Ken, I have another suggestion. A special care facility that I feel – "

"No," Jay said and shook his head.

"I know you don't agree. But I think we should consider at the very least short-term care for now. The nurses told me how good you were with him when he had the migraine the other day. And that's another factor. He will suffer with horrible migraines. That energy you displayed the other day is something you would have to have every single day."

Dixon sighed and continued, "I really believe a special care facility is best. One of the best is in Tampa. Michael could regain some lost skills. He'd be given the chance to learn again how to take care of his personal needs. He can start that process here as well. It's just that in cases like these, a rehab hospital can offer him more, and, of course, the continued physical therapy. There's life skill training. Occupational training. Whether he'll ever have enough skills to return as a police officer, I highly doubt. He may never have the temperament again."

"Whoa. Hold on. It looks like you're jumping the gun again."

"I've dealt with hundreds of cases like this, Ken. Denial from Michael is one thing. But denial from you won't help in the least, and I do believe you want nothing more than to help him."

"I do. Don't ever question that."

"Fair enough. Then listen to my advice. Of course, it's up to his family and you. He could go home or to a rehab hospital. I'll speak to his family."

"His mother left the decision to me."

"I know. She told me that. But in order for you to make the best decision you must have a clear picture of what we're dealing with. I won't stand in the way if you feel strongly about bringing Michael home with you. However, you must consider the type of care and supervision he'll require."

"I know his mom wants to come," Jay said. "And there are friends."

"I think it's critical for him to see the people that were important," Dixon said. "Just so long as they also come to terms with this. He's not the same person. He looks like Michael, sounds like Michael, but he doesn't react like Michael. You'll find in many situations, he doesn't act like the

Michael you knew either. There might be times when you'll see a glimmer, but when that happens, the worse you or anyone else can do is expect more. If you take anything out of this office, let it be that. He's brain damaged. It's crucial you come to terms with that. Don't expect more. It's important to treat him as he is now. If the people who love him can't, then it will only upset him and drive him further away. Michael's going to be confused. He doesn't understand what anyone wants from him or what he's supposed to do."

"That makes two of us," Jay said.

"The role you can play is to guide him. Help him. Reassure him. Michael thinks he's stupid now. Let him know it isn't his fault. He'll ask lots of questions. Answer them. Let him know it's all right to be confused. If you can do that, then he'll relax and let you in. If, of course, that's his nature."

"His nature? His nature was always to joke and take charge. He's never been the type to sit around. Moody, yes. Stubborn, sure. But with a lot of heart."

"Much of what you just described could still be intact. Exaggerated, in some respects. As for sitting around? The tests have shown a heightened adrenaline level. You will notice it's harder for him to sit still, and his attention span wanders easily.

"Ken." Dixon looked squarely at him. "Just remember. He's limited. His mind is like a child's at this point. How much improvement we'll see can't be determined right now. I just want to be perfectly clear. He's not going to wake up one day…not in a month or a year or five years from now and suddenly remember all that he's lost." Dixon sighed. "Are you sure you're ready for all this?"

"You've given me a lot to think about, Doc, that's for sure. But I'm not going anywhere. That part isn't even on the table. And the part about a rehab hospital? That's not going to happen either. He'll come home with me when he's ready. I know his mother will agree."

13

J ay kept vigil over Sonny like a protective father of a newborn. In order for anyone to get to Sonny, they had to go through Jay first. If Sonny were himself, and Jay kept hoping that he would be in time, Sonny would have teased Jay about how he kept guard. A tear gathered and Jay knew Sonny would also hate to see that. It's just that it was getting harder not to notice the differences he fought so hard not to admit.

Jay took what few private moments he had without nurses coming in to kiss his partner on the forehead and even once, on the mouth, careful not to wake him or be seen.

The area of Sonny's head that had received the brunt of the impact still had a bump. The black and blue had changed to a yellowish color.

Sonny's hair was slowly growing. He looked so young lying there, his face still pale with dark circles under the eyes, his darker than normal fuzzy hair against the stark white pillow. Jay missed the long brown curls.

At the window, Jay leaned against the sill. His partner might not remember them together, but Jay did. He remembered it all while it replayed in his mind.

They had been in bed together not long after they had confessed their love. In the dark, they held each other.

Sonny slept with his head against Jay's shoulder, their hands and legs interlaced.

"Son?" Jay said. "You asleep?"

"Mm-hmm," was the reply, and it made Jay grin.

"Can I ask you something?"

"Sure," Sonny said, eyes closed.

"You're happy, right?"

"You know I am," Sonny said without moving. "Now go to sleep."

"I just…I wonder if I hadn't told you how I felt, what would have happened?"

Sonny turned to his back and in the dark, he held Jay's hand. "Look, I know you get worried about all this sometimes. I get that your parents disowned you and you felt alone. But trust me, partner, I ain't gonna leave you."

"I'm sorry I get insecure sometimes. It's just me."

"It's okay. I get it. It's not easy keeping this secret. We have to keep acting like we're just two guys looking for love."

Jay chuckled. "That's how you describe it?"

"We go out. Girls hit on us. We flirt."

"They hit on *you*. And *you* flirt."

"No, Blondie, that isn't true. You get your share with no problem. But at the end of the day, it's about us. You and me. Nothing will ever change that." Sonny kissed Jay's shoulder. "Nothing. I love you."

"But this secret. How long before someone figures it out, or one of us slips?"

"Can't worry about that." Sonny flipped over and looked at Jay. "I wanna thank you, okay? Thank you for having the courage to say how you felt. I'd like to think I would've had the courage at some point, but…you did. That means a lot to me. You didn't know how it could have turned out. But it didn't stop you. You were honest. I'm thankful you were." He kissed Jay in a way that Jay returned with equal passion.

"So…are you really happy?" Jay said, anxious with the feel of Sonny's warm hand on his stomach.

Sonny kissed the tender spots along Jay's belly. "What do you think?"

"I mean giving up women?" Jay said, his excitement building.

"I think I got more than I can handle right here." Sonny smiled.

Jay purred with the moist licks of Sonny's tongue. "I just want you to be happy."

"Happy? I'll show you happy." Sonny kissed him long and full on the mouth. He nearly devoured Jay's lips. "How's that for happy?"

Jay was breathing heavily. "Not bad. Not bad at all," he had said.

Now, watching Sonny sleep, a warm tear dripped down Jay's cheek. A hospital cart squeaked in the hall. Not willingly wanting to leave the memory, he slowly opened his eyes. Sonny watched him. Before Jay could say anything, Sonny turned over in the hospital bed so his back was to him.

* * *

At home, Jay sat on a stool in the kitchen with the phone pressed to his ear.

"You want Mikey home with you?" Maria Santini said.

Jay nodded into the receiver. "Yes. I do."

"Then I agree," Maria said. "I just wish I could be there. Rachael's baby has pneumonia. Poor, sweet thing. Carla's only six months old, and with Paul out of town, Rachael needs help. Not that her husband usually is a help." Maria laughed, but to Jay's ears, it seemed tired. "He was an only child. Doesn't have a clue about babies."

"I'm an only child too," Jay said.

"Yes. But one day I know you'll make a wonderful father, and so will Mikey, and he'll marry…." The woman stopped short.

"He's going to be okay, Mom," Jay said.

"I know." Maria sniffed.

"You're feeling okay, aren't you?" Jay said.

"Oh, I'm fine. Just…worried. About the baby. Michael. You. You sound tired, Kenny."

Only Maria called him that. Jay grinned. "I'm fine. I promise."

"Kenny, I just want you to be honest with me. If caring for Mikey gets to be too much –"

"No, Mom," Jay interrupted, "it won't be. Home is going to be the best place for Sonny. You'll see."

"Oh, Kenny. I just wish I could be there. I should be."

"It's okay. You can do more for Rachael and the baby right now. Sonny…Sonny just needs some time."

"Well, as soon as Paul gets back, I'll be there. In the meantime, please, don't feel obligated to do this."

"I don't feel obligated," Jay said. "Sonny's my...you know. He's my best friend." Jay closed his eyes to stop the tears.

"I know. He's very lucky. We all are. You've been a blessing. When that social worker sent me all that information, I didn't know what to do. The thought of my son in some...some institution. I cried for days. Just knowing he'll be with you is a relief. Tell Mikey...tell him I love him. I'll see him and you soon."

"Mom, when you do come, it's best, for now, that it's just you," Jay said.

"I agree. The last thing Mikey or you need is the Santini-Rogatta family."

"How is Tony? With all of this?"

There was a pause. "Not good. He's convinced the doctors are idiots. Do...do you think they're wrong?"

Another tear threatened. Jay cleared his throat so his voice wouldn't crack. "I'm not sure, Mom. Sonny is...Sonny got hurt bad. But you know, I'll always have hope. It's worked for me in the past."

"I'm praying every day. My whole church is. I love you, Kenny."

"Love you, too." He hung up the phone and sniffed back the urge to cry. He glanced over at Dee and went into the bathroom.

Dee knocked at the door a minute later. "Jay? The hospital's on the phone."

Jay tore out of the bathroom and grabbed the receiver. He listened with Dee close at his side. "He does? Is he okay? You sure?" He hung up and smiled. "Sonny just got back from his tests. He wants to see me."

* * *

Jay practically skipped off the elevator and actually hummed on his way to Sonny's room. He knocked on the door and stepped into the room with a huge smile. "Hey there, partner."

Sonny looked blankly at him. "They tell me you keep asking questions about me."

"They?"

"Those...nurses. They said you never left when I was...was out of it."

Jay came closer to where Sonny sat on the bed. "Well, it's true. I stayed here for you."

"Don't," Sonny said, his voice flat.

Jay chuffed. "Don't?"

"Don't come round no more. Don't hang out here."

"Hang out here? I'm not hanging out here. I'm trying to make sure you're okay."

"Don't want it. Don't need you. Go away."

"Go away?" Jay said and eyed the expressionless face.

"Yeah. Go away."

Jay bit his bottom lip. With a slow nod, he said, "That's how you feel about it, huh?"

"They say I know how to talk. You don't listen. Go away." Sonny fisted the blanket.

"Okay," Jay said, forcing calmness. "Fine. Guess you don't want this cheeseburger I brought you or the fries." He opened a sandwich bag, took out a fry, and placed it in his mouth. "Still hot too. But I guess...."

Sonny perked up. He looked curious in a childlike way. "Cheeseburger?"

"Yep. An orange soda too. Lots of ketchup for the fries. Oh, well, guess I should go and take this with me." Jay turned for the door.

"Wait."

Jay stopped.

"I-I could eat," Sonny said.

Jay smiled before he turned. Hiding his grin, he looked at Sonny. "I guess you could."

"I could." Sonny's eager hand reached for the bag.

Jay pulled over the bed tray and adjusted it before he pulled out a wrapped cheeseburger and a large order of fries. He handed the soda to Sonny.

Sonny examined it, unsure of the opening at the top. Jay opened a straw and put it inside for him. A long, thirsty slurp, Sonny swallowed and then slightly smiled. "That's good. What is it?"

"Orange soda."

Sonny slurped more. "I like it." He watched as Jay unwrapped the burger. With big eyes he stared at the treat and seemed more animated than Jay had seen since he woke.

"Ketchup?" Jay said.

Sonny looked at him with his long lashes blinking.

"Try it without and then we can add it if you want." Jay handed the burger to Sonny.

Sonny nodded. He scooped up the burger and drove it into his mouth as if he were starving. "Good," he said with his mouth stuffed.

"You want to try a fry?"

Sonny nodded. He shoved one and then a handful into his mouth and worked overtime to chew.

Jay chuckled. "Easy there, partner." He opened the ketchup and plopped some on the plastic wrap. "Try dipping it. Like this." He demonstrated.

Sonny watched in amazement, then copied the action. He grinned more with the taste.

Jay smiled too. A connection. Food and Sonny. That hadn't changed. And Jay was more hungry for the link than Sonny was for the food.

Jay dangled a fry above his mouth and dropped it inside. Sonny chuckled and did the same. They both laughed. Jay dipped a fry in the ketchup. Sonny imitated. He even offered Jay a bite of his cheeseburger.

"No, buddy," Jay said. "That's all for you."

Sonny smiled wider.

"Hang on," Jay said. "You got…." He used his index finger to sweep up a drop of ketchup along the side of Sonny's mouth. "There." He put his same finger in his mouth and sucked it.

Sonny frowned. "Why…why are you looking at me like that?"

Jay stopped, His finger still in his mouth. His cheeks flamed with the desire he was unsuccessful at hiding, but before he could answer or change his expression, Sonny pushed everything off the table onto the floor.

"Stop it," Sonny shouted. "J-just stop."

"Son, I-I didn't mean to – "

"Get out. Get out," Sonny screamed.

Jay deflated. "Sure. Sorry. I'll go." He picked up the fallen soda cup and went for the door. "I'm sorry," he quietly said with his back to Sonny. Halfway out the door, he heard Sonny's tiny voice.

"No. Wait. I-I didn't mean it."

Jay turned, and what he faced reminded him of a naughty child ashamed of his actions. Jay's heart dropped.

"I…I get mixed up sometimes," Sonny said and hung his head. "I-I don't mean to."

"So you want me to stay?"

Slowly, without looking up, Sonny nodded.

"Okay, partner. I'll stay."

"I-I pushed it all on the floor."

"Yeah. The nurse is going to love that." Jay grinned. "Would you like me to get another burger?"

"Can…can I have more fries, too?"

"Sure. I'll be right back." Jay went out to the hall. He closed the door behind him and rested the back of his head against it.

"Ken?" a woman called to him.

Jay turned. "Mrs. Murphy. Diane. I thought you and Peter went home."

"We did," Diane Murphy said. "Peter had a slight relapse. Oh, nothing too serious. But the doctor wanted him here for a couple of days. I heard your friend, Michael, is awake."

Jay looked back at the door he still leaned on and nodded. "A few days ago."

"Funny, isn't it?" Diane said. "How we think that if they would just wake up, all the difficulties would be gone. We don't realize that what starts is a whole different set of problems."

Diane's clothes were wrinkled. Her once neat hair needed a trim. She wore little makeup and had bags under her eyes.

"How are you?" Jay said.

"Me?" Her voice broke, and she looked at the floor. "I'm okay. I decided to try and bring Peter home. My husband left me. Peter's younger brother decided to go with his dad. My daughter stayed with me, but," she brushed away a tear, "I think she wants to move in with her dad too. Peter is…agitated easily. He's begun to…scream. It's his way of getting out the anger."

Jay glanced at Sonny's door. "I'm sorry. That it's been so hard for you."

"Hard for me?" Diane looked at him with watery eyes. "It's been harder for Peter. I think we forget that. Imagine what they're going through.

Peter doesn't remember…how it was. At least, that's what the doctors tell me. But he can't speak. He can barely move. So how do they know? Sometimes, I think I see a familiar look in his eyes. A kind of…spark. But then it's gone. I wonder what it's like for him. Trapped in his body. In his mind. Wanting to do…to say things and, he can't. I know I'd scream, too, if it were me. I'd want to run as far as I could just to get away from everyone."

"You're very wise, Diane," Jay said. "Peter is lucky to have you."

Tears slipped down her cheeks. "I'm sending him to a special care facility. It wasn't easy to make that decision. But there are specially trained people there. People who might be able to give him more. Who might be able to…reach him. I think I'm holding him back. I think he sees me and…somehow he feels how sad I am. I don't want that for him. He shouldn't have to feel like that."

"Maybe he doesn't," Jay said.

"He does. I can see it. That's when he screams. That's his way of telling me to stop feeling so sad." Diane paused as she brushed away more tears and looked at Jay. "Oh, I don't mean Michael feels the same. Please don't think I meant that. Every case is different. You aren't Michael's mother. I think somehow Peter senses that I am and maybe that makes him feel… like a child. That might sound silly. The doctor thinks it is. He said that Peter *has* been reduced to a child. But he agrees that my expectations might be hurting him."

"I don't understand. Why shouldn't you expect anything?"

"I have to accept the way he is now. I just hope they can teach him a better way to communicate. And the fact is, I have two other children. They need me too. I'm not abandoning him."

"I know."

Diane grinned wearily. "I have to keep telling myself that because, in some ways, it feels like I am. I'm not. Not really. I'm just trying to give Peter a chance. With people who are trained to help. But, Ken, you and Michael. That's different. What facility will he go to? Maybe we'll see one another."

"Sonny, Michael isn't going to a facility. I'm taking him home."

"You are?" Diane's eyes frowned. "Oh. Home to…his family?"

"Yes. No. I mean. Home with me."

"That's a lot for you. Will he have a home health aide?"

"I…I don't think he'll need that."

Diane slowly nodded. "It's exhausting. I don't want to discourage you. But it is. I didn't accept it when they told me that."

"It's different with Sonny," Jay said. "He can talk. Boy, can he talk."

"Well, that's good. That's a start. Ken? When he talks? Listen to him. He may struggle to find the words. But just…listen. It's all so new. For them. And us. And don't worry if sometimes…sometimes you find your-self…angry or resentful. We're only human. But just remember, as hard as it is for us? It's got to be harder for them." Diane checked her watch. "I better go. Good luck, Ken. I mean that."

Jay waited while she walked away. He took a deep breath, let it out, and tried to shake off the doubt. Today was a step. At least he had that.

* * *

The small step Jay experienced led to two huge steps back. Beyond food, there was nothing much that held Sonny's interest. His eyes remained blank. The glint in them gone. They seemed to settle into a dark blue color. A color that reminded Jay of how Sonny had been before the accident when he was angry or upset. But now, that color never changed.

Sonny was quiet. It was hard, if not almost impossible, to draw him into a conversation. He stared or looked around like he was bored, and then he'd get distracted by noises, movement, the shadows on the ceiling. All those things seemed to capture his attention away from the person who was talking.

Captain Colby found Jay taking a break in the hall. "How is he?"

That question was getting harder and harder for Jay to answer. "Good news? He's walking better on his own. Still weak, though. Bad news? He just told me for the tenth time in ten minutes to get out and leave him alone."

Colby patted Jay on the shoulder. "Mind if I say a quick hello?"

"Be my guest. Just don't move too far from the door. He's a dead on shot with that plastic water bottle."

Colby eased in through the door with Jay right behind him. "Hi, Sonny."

Sonny looked at him, but did not acknowledge him.

"Everyone wanted me to say hi," Colby said.

"Everyone?" Sonny said, his frown making deep creases between his eyebrows.

"At the station," Colby said.

"The ones who sent all these flowers," Jay said, trying to sound chipper.

Sonny looked away.

Jay knew there was no meaning in the words he said. "Uh, Cap? Why don't we go get Sonny something to drink?"

"That orange stuff," Sonny said, his voice dull. He stared up at the ceiling.

"Orange soda. I'll be right back," Jay said.

Colby faced Jay in the hall. "I'm sorry, Ken."

"Ken? You never call me that unless it's bad. This isn't so bad," Jay said and offered a slight grin. "At least he didn't tell us to get out."

"What's going to happen when they discharge him?"

"He'll come home. With me."

"Are you sure that's such a good idea?"

"I still have time off to use. And like I said, if I need too, I'll take a leave."

"That isn't the point. What if Sonny doesn't want to go with you?"

Jay swallowed. That thought never occurred to him. "Let's go get his soda."

14

———

Sonny opened his eyes. Late afternoon sun filtered in through the hospital window. He turned his head and found Dee by a table reading the cards that people had sent – complete strangers as far as Sonny was concerned.

Dee grinned. "Hi, sugar."

"You're-you're that lady, Dee, right?" Sonny said, staring at her.

"That's right," Dee said.

Sonny stared harder, but not at her eyes. He was infatuated by her chest.

"Sonny?" She looked down at where his gaze was fixed and blushed. "Stop that."

"Stop what?" he said, not moving his gaze from her breasts.

"Stop staring at my chest."

"Well, if you don't want me to stare at them, how come you're wearing a tight shirt?" Sonny said.

"It's not tight." Dee glanced down at herself, adjusted her blouse, and looked back at Sonny's eyes still focused on her bosom. "You listen to me, Sonny, let me set you straight. I'm your friend. We've been friends for a long long time. So, if you want me to remain your friend, you better stop looking at me like that."

"Friend, huh? It ain't me you're friends with," Sonny said and directed his attention to the ceiling.

"Why do you say that? You *are* my friend."

"Not me. You don't even know me. How do you even know you'll like me?"

"Sonny, I know this is hard on you," Dee said.

"How can you know this is hard on me? How do you know anything about me?" Sonny said.

"If I was where you are? It would be hard on me. You should know this isn't easy on any of us."

Sonny sighed. "Us? How am I supposed to know that? I don't know you or who the hell *us* are."

"Okay. I think I get it. You're not the same person. You're different."

Sonny glared at her with cold eyes. "I ain't different. I ain't the same. I'm just… here."

"All right. Then let me tell you something if you're just here. You're acting like a brat. A spoiled brat."

Sonny smirked. "What's a spoiled brat?"

"Right now? You."

"Get out," Sonny said.

"I will. As soon as I make something clear. You're gonna need friends. You will. Listen to me or don't. It's up to you. But I'm telling you like it is. If you want to get out of here – I assume you do – and go out there" – Dee pointed at the window – "in the real world, then you're gonna need help. Like it or not. Now, Jay…Jay can help you."

"Jay? That tall blond guy? Yeah, he hangs out here a lot. How come?"

"How come? Because he cares about you, that's how come."

"Ain't me he cares about," Sonny said impassively. He laced his fingers together and put them behind his head.

"Oh no? Boy, you sure know a lot for not knowing anything."

Sonny glared at her.

"Oh." Dee returned his glare. "Is that look meant to scare me? Well, go ahead. Get mad. See if I care. Somebody's got to tell you, Mr. Smarty. Jay cares. And you should be grateful he does. He could be your friend if you let him. If you stop being so pig headed. Believe me, you're gonna need a friend. Someone you can trust. Someone who'll let you know what's going on. You think you can figure it out on your own? Go ahead and try. But if it was me in that bed? I'd pick Jay to help me. Are you listening to me?"

Sonny stared out the window a moment. Who was this woman? He looked back at her. "I ain't stupid," he said.

"No one said you were," Dee said, "so stop acting like it. If you wanna be smart, let somebody watch your back. Let someone be your friend. For what it's worth, I think Jay's the best choice." She picked up her purse. "Well. That's it. I'll go. Thanks for listening. Sorry if I bothered you."

She left the room. Sonny picked up the first thing his hand found – a box of candy Dee had brought – and he threw it at the door.

* * *

Marcy, a young brown-haired nurse who worked the eleven to seven afternoon shift, strolled into Sonny's room with his medication. "How are you today, Michael?"

"Okay," Sonny said, watching her every move.

"Good." She smiled.

He batted his eyelashes.

"Do you have something in your eyes?" Marcy said and put down the medicine.

Sonny looked down at his hands. "No."

Marcy giggled. "You aren't flirting with me, are you?"

Sonny looked up at her. "You smell nice," he said and winked.

"Oh. You *are* flirting," she said. "Guess you're on the mend. Here's your medicine." She offered a small cup with two capsules and another cup with water.

"Nope. Ain't gonna take 'em," Sonny said with a devilish grin.

Marcy rolled her eyes. "You always say that, and then you take them. Come on."

"You're pretty."

"Are we going to start that again? Come on. I have other patients to see."

"Nope. You gotta kiss me first. Then maybe I'll take 'em." He looked the young nurse up and down.

"Michael, you know it's against the rules."

"So? Door's closed. Who gives a shit about rules anyway?"

"Those of us who like our jobs," Marcy said. She glanced toward the door as if she considered either running or giving him the kiss. She turned back to him. He was an extremely good-looking man. His expression was seductive. His body, while still weak, was taut and firm. His voice was soft. His lips full and red. And that dimple that showed those raw times he smiled – hard to resist. Still, Marcy realized, the last thing she needed was to be reported that she came on to a patient…a brain damaged patient no less. "Just take the meds. Please."

"No. I wanna – "

"I know what you want."

"Then come on," he enticed.

Jay walked in. "Hey there, buddy."

Sonny rolled his eyes and leaned back on the pillow. "What the hell do you want?"

Jay scowled at the reaction and Marcy's red face.

Flustered, Marcy quickly handed the medication to Sonny. "Take these, Michael."

Sonny snatched the items from her and angrily handed back the empty cups.

Marcy slipped past Jay. "Mr. Jamison," she said nervously and scooted out of the room like a thief caught in the act.

Jay blushed. With his mouth open, he looked at Sonny.

Sonny laid with head still propped on the pillow. "What?" he said, his tone harsh.

"Were you? Were you trying to….?" Jay swallowed. "Were you trying to come on to her?"

"I was." Sonny huffed. "Then *you* came in." His eyes like steel stared up at the ceiling.

Jay shook his head and looked at the floor. "Sorry I spoiled it for you there, partner."

"Why do you do that? Call me partner?"

Jay considered the question and took a deep breath. "You and I…." He turned, glanced out the window, and then continued, "You were a cop."

"Yeah. You told me that."

"I was…your partner," Jay said hoping to see something in Sonny's blank eyes.

"What's in the box?" Sonny said, one brief conversation over, his attention on to something else.

Disappointed, Jay lifted the top of the box. "Pizza. I know you like…." He stopped. "I thought it was time for you to try something new."

"Smells good."

"Should be. It has the works. No anchovies though. You can try that another time."

Sonny was quiet while Jay fixed a plate, and then he said, "That lady. Dee? She said I should let you be my friend."

"She did, huh?" Jay licked pizza sauce off his thumb. "So what do you think about that?"

Sonny shrugged. He accepted the plate and put a huge corner of the pizza in his mouth. "She's got nice tits," he said with his mouth full.

"You really have to learn to take little bites," Jay said and laughed. "Lasts longer that way, and you actually limit the risk of choking." He glanced at Sonny and to his surprise, the man smiled just a little.

An orderly, timid, pushed open the door. He carried a food tray. Nervous, he set it down on the stand in front of the pizza.

"That stinks," Sonny said. "Take it outta here."

The orderly ignored him and left.

"I said, take it outta here," Sonny screamed to the closed door, and with one swipe of his hand, pushed the entire tray to the floor.

"Sonny, knock it off," Jay said.

"I told him I don't want this."

"Okay, partner, easy. That's not how to handle it. No wonder half the staff don't want to come in here."

"I don't give a fuck," Sonny said and slammed his head against the pillow.

"Well, I can't keep bringing you food," Jay said and looked at the mangled mess of mashed potatoes, brown gooey meat, and applesauce on the floor. "Serve you right if they left that there. You gotta learn to relax, partner."

"Partner," Sonny repeated.

"Yeah. You want me to stop calling you that, too? Gonna throw your pizza next?"

"No," Sonny said. "I like it. When you call me partner. It's kinda cool."

At first Jay wrinkled his brow, but he couldn't help smile at the sudden angelic look. "Cool, huh? Well, this mess isn't cool." He looked back at Sonny but the man had already forgotten it.

Sonny returned to eating pizza and looking out the window. He liked the blinds up as far as they could go so he could see the sky.

"Um, Sonny? Listen. The doctors said that in a couple of days, they might release you from the hospital." Jay waited for a reaction, saw none, and continued, "I-I was thinking. You could come home. With me. If you want. Or...."

"Or what?" Sonny said.

"Or...go to another place."

"Another hospital?"

"Well, no. Kind of. A place where you can keep having physical therapy. Or, I could take you home with me and bring you here for that."

"You think they'll be mad at me?" Sonny said and looked at the mess on the floor.

Jay frowned. "That? No. I'm sure they'll understand."

"That I'm a freak." An expression of sadness settled on Sonny's face.

"You're not a freak."

"They all think I am."

"No. You just...you have a temper. One hell of a temper. You need to learn control, that's all. So about...."

"I guess," Sonny said and stuffed more pizza in his mouth.

"Guess? What?"

"I'll go with you."

"Oh. Okay. Th-that's great. There's, just one thing. One rule."

"Rule?"

"Yeah. No throwing food at home, okay?"

Sonny looked at him and began to smile. "That's a joke, right?"

Jay grinned too. "Yes. And no. No matter how mad you get. Food stays put."

"I get it. Partner," Sonny said and went back to chewing. "What else you got?"

Jay placed the Sunday newspaper on the table. "Just something to read."

Sonny shook his head. "Nope. You're not gonna get me to read. They do that to me all the time."

"They?" Jay questioned.

"Them." Sonny gestured with his chin toward the door. "The doctors. Especially that one guy. Dixon. He makes me read stuff and then asks me dumb questions. Most of it I don't get." He sipped his soda. "I can't do half the things they're asking me to. And…." He stopped.

"What?" Jay said.

"Why you lookin' at me like that?"

The smile on Jay's face melted. "Like what?" He lowered his head and fumbled with the newspaper.

"I don't know. Weird. Like…." Sonny paused. When Jay dared to glance at him again, Sonny's mood and tone turned icy and defiant. "I don't give a shit."

"Sonny," Jay stumbled over the words. "Listen. Maybe I should tell you – "

"When they ask me stuff I don't know. I don't give a shit."

"Oh," Jay said and let out a breath.

"Tell me what?" Sonny looked up with an innocent expression.

"Huh? Oh. Nothing." Jay thumbed at the newspaper.

"You think I'm too dumb to understand?"

"No," Jay was quick to say. "I don't think that at all. I was going to say….You know something, partner? I know that feeling."

"What feeling?"

"When someone asks stuff and you don't know. I know what that's like. Especially when somebody reads me stuff. There's lots of times I don't get it either."

"Yeah?" Sonny seemed more at ease.

"Oh, yeah." Jay chuckled. "See this?" He held up the newspaper. "I read this all the time and most times…I don't get it."

Sonny sneered. "I hate it when that happens." He blinked his dark lashes at Jay. "It's annoyin', ain't it?"

Was that a hint of a smile on Sonny's face? "It is. Annoying."

"What's that page? The one with all the colors?" Sonny said.

"The comics. They're in the Sunday paper every week." Jay grinned at the first real conversation Sonny had initiated since the accident.

"Let me see," Sonny said, extending his hand.

Jay handed the section to Sonny who glanced at it with mild interest before he handed it back.

"Would you like to read it?" Jay said.

"Nope," Sonny said and stirred his soda with the straw. "You read it to me." He rested his head against the pillow and looked at Jay. "Will ya?"

"Really?" Jay's voice squeaked. "I mean" – he cleared his throat – "really? Well, sure. No problem." He sat in a chair, held the paper so both of them could see it and began to read. He did the character voices with his best impressions. Sonny laid back and listened. He looked at the pictures Jay showed him with little reaction.

Jay laughed at the jokes he read. Sonny didn't.

"I don't get it," Sonny said.

"Well, it means…you know what? That was pretty bad," Jay said.

"You can keep reading, though," Sonny said. "I like the way you say stuff."

Jay grinned. He continued to read until Sonny fell asleep.

"Have a good nap, partner," Jay said with the urge to place a kiss. He bit his lip, fighting the temptation. "I love you," he said under his breath.

15

___

J ay hummed "I'm A Believer," a tune by the Monkeys he'd heard on the radio. He pressed the elevator button for the seventh floor of the hospital and gripped the brown duffel bag. Full smile on his face, he continued to hum as he cruised down the hall.

"Big day," a nurse said and shared Jay's smile.

"Sure is," Jay said, about to knock at Sonny's hospital room door.

"I'll be in to give you his instructions in a minute," the nurse said.

"So. Partner," Jay said opening the door. "You ready? Time to come home."

Sonny turned from the window. "What took you so long?" he said with no expression.

Jay held up the canvas bag. "Can't very well go home in a hospital gown, now can you?"

Sonny snatched the bag and looked inside. "Cool." He pulled out a pair of jeans, a pullover brown shirt and sneakers. Starting to take off his gown, he eyed Jay. "You gonna watch me just like them? I know how to dress myself."

"Oh. Right. Sorry. I'll be out there. In the hall."

Dr. Dixon came out from behind the nurse's station and with his usual solemn face said, "Well, Ken, this is it."

"Yep." Jay glanced at Sonny's closed door. "This is it."

Dixon handed Jay two appointment cards. "This one is for Dr. Dean, Sonny's psychiatrist. I want him to continue with that. Dr. Dean is very experienced. He'll help Sonny work through his frustrations and identify his emotions. The other is for physical therapy. Three times a week."

"Got it," Jay said, with butterflies in his stomach.

"And I want Sonny to continue to use the cane. The weakness on his left side will improve. But the last thing he needs is another fall like he had this week."

"Right. Cane for left side," Jay said.

"And this is for his migraines." Dixon handed Jay a bottle of pills. "It's a painkiller and a muscle relaxant for the pain in his back and neck." He handed over another bottle with a few pills in the bottom. "Here is some medication for him to finish. It's an antibiotic to prevent further infection to his kidney. The instructions are on the prescriptions."

Jay's hands were overflowing. "Medicine for....Well, I'll look it over when we get home."

"I wish you both the best," Dixon said. "Good luck."

"Come on, Doc. Say what you really mean," Jay said with a smile. "Good luck. I'm going to need it."

"You know how I feel about all of this. It isn't going to be easy...."

Sonny ripped open the door. "Hey? We going or what?"

"For either of you," Dixon finished. "Take care, Michael. I'll see you next week."

Sonny didn't even listen. He dropped into the wheel chair and began to scoot it along before the nurse was ready. "Let's go. Let's go," he said.

Dixon patted Jay's shoulder. "It takes a brave soul to be a cop. A braver one to do this. Call me if you need anything."

Jay couldn't help but smile. He'd waited for this day for so long. He could tell Sonny was excited. Even though the clothes Sonny wore were a little baggy, he looked more and more like the old Sonny eager to leave this place.

"Let's go home, partner," Jay said.

* * *

A few minutes later the exit doors slid open, and they were outside. Sonny looked up at the blue sky, closed his eyes, and grinned at the sun on his face.

He took a deep breath and then another. Everything around him seemed huge and bright and wondrous.

He climbed into the front seat of Jay's rusted, 1970 blue Chevy. The thirteen-year-old car rattled and squeaked, coughing exhaust while Jay pulled out of the parking lot.

Sonny looked back at the hospital. The only place he knew grew smaller and smaller until it was gone. He rolled down the window, stuck his head out and felt the wind on his face.

Everything smelled different than the hospital. Smells he couldn't recognize. Some he didn't like. His nose itched. It was all so contrary from what he'd known all his life – a life only three weeks old.

The world, or at least what he could see from the car, was so much bigger than his small hospital room or the few other rooms he'd been in for tests. It was filled with strange sights and sounds. The air was different too. It was clear and fresh. Not the antiseptic smell he hated.

They drove past people on the street. No one stared at him or watched every move he made. They stopped for a traffic light. Everyone seemed occupied with things that were familiar to them.

There was a bus. He knew the name of that. People got on and off it. He didn't know where they came from or where they were going.

They passed a drug store, and he read the sign: Six pack of Coke Buy one Get one. He was puzzled by the meaning.

They went by a large, vacant dirt lot. Yellow caution tape was draped all around it. A large piece of machinery sat in the middle of the property with a huge shovel attached. He knew it was meant for digging but could not remember what it was called.

"Is that a...a....?" Sonny pointed ahead.

"A bridge," Jay said.

"Are we going on it? Can we?" Sonny said.

"Sure," Jay said and drove up the steep incline.

Sonny was practically out of his seat. His head out the window, he peered beyond the steel railing to the water below. "Boats," he said and pointed at the sailboats.

Jay held the back of Sonny's shirt. "Easy there, partner. Don't fall out."

Sonny sat back. He squinted up at the sun. It made him sneeze.

He heard Jay put on the car's blinker. The sound seemed familiar.

Jay turned left, drove, turned right, and headed down a tree-lined street.

There were brick houses, white houses, and a yellow house. Trees. Shrubs. Children on bikes. Kids on roller skates. A dog ran out from a backyard, barking at them, and chased them down the road.

There was a mailman. He spoke to two older people by a mailbox. A car passed them on the left. A school bus dropped off two little girls.

This was life. A life Sonny barely understood. A pang of nervousness buzzed in his stomach. Nothing seemed so wondrous all of a sudden. It all warped into something that made his head hurt.

Sonny rubbed hard at his temple.

"You okay?" Jay said.

Sonny grunted. He closed his eyes for a moment and fisted his hands.

"Sonny? You okay?"

"Don't," Sonny said. "Talk. Just. Quiet." He willed the buzz in his stomach to slow and the pounding in his head to stop.

Jay pulled into the driveway of 14 Tremont and shut off the engine. "Just take it slow, buddy. No rush."

Sonny put up his palm as if to warn Jay away. Gradually, he let out the breath he held and opened his eyes. "Th-this your house?"

"It's our...." Jay stopped. "We're roommates. We live here."

Sonny edged out of the car, took his cane, and hobbled, partly dragging his left foot. He waited for Jay to unlock the door and then peeked inside like a bear inspecting a new den. Finally, he took a small step over the threshold and then went in all the way.

Home, he thought. He didn't know what that meant. He could feel Jay's eyes on him, waiting for something, but Sonny had nothing to give.

"So?" Jay said. "What do you think?"

Sonny shrugged. "Looks okay, I guess." A deep open-mouthed yawn escaped, and he scratched his head.

"Tired?" Jay said.

"No," Sonny said, but it was a lie. His arms felt like the weights he used in physical therapy. His legs just as heavy. A sharp pain shot along his back. He tipped his head back and forth until his neck cracked. The sound was loud. He looked at Jay who had a weird expression. Sonny snapped his neck again. Jay looked away, fussed with the pillows on the couch and tried for a smile that didn't fool Sonny.

"So, this is it," Jay said and repositioned the pillow.

Sonny didn't move from where he stood. He glanced around at the living room and at the items decorating the shelves.

Jay picked up the duffel bag he'd carried inside and said, "How…how about lying down for a while. I'll make us some dinner. Wanna try spaghetti tonight?"

Sonny shrugged again. His insides tensed with the urge to scream. He clenched his fists and worked to stifle it. "Where's the bedroom?"

Jay's eyes opened wide. "Bedroom? Oh, right. Your bedroom." He chuckled nervously. "How about a class of juice or some water first, huh? It's time for your medicine." He showed Sonny the way to the kitchen, ran a cold glass of water from the sink and handed over two pills. "Be right back."

A few moments later, Jay returned to the kitchen.

"All set, partner," he said. "I'll show you to your room."

Sonny followed, and when he went into the room, looked at Jay. "I'm fine," he said.

"Oh. Sure." Jay again awkwardly chuckled and ran a hand through his hair. "I'll start dinner. You rest." He left, and Sonny closed the door.

* * *

From the moment that Jay headed for the hospital to pick up Sonny to the moment they both came into the house, Jay said his thanks to God and kept praying that this would be the thing Sonny needed to bring him all the way back. That thought evaporated quickly. The clothes Jay brought from home were Sonny's favorites. A faded pair of jeans with a torn back pocket, the brown pullover shirt with a hole under the right sleeve, and his worn down, broken-in sneakers. Jay could see none of it meant anything to Sonny.

The ride home meant nothing either. Sonny glanced around with curiosity but not the recognition Jay had hoped for. Deep inside, he wanted more than anything for Sonny to say, "Oh my God. I know where I am. Sorry I kept you waiting, partner. Guess I hit my head harder than I thought. But I'm okay now. I'm me. I'm back." But that acknowledgement didn't come.

Maybe when we turn down the street, Jay had thought. Maybe when he sees the house. Maybe when we go inside. Nothing. Jay worked to stay positive. He focused on the fact that Sonny was alive, here, and they were together.

It wasn't going to be easy. Being together without touching, without sharing what they had, it would be tough. Jay knew that he'd slipped a few times already. In the hospital when he looked with longing at Sonny, and Sonny caught those looks. In those moments, when Sonny had no way of knowing what the looks meant, it was clear to Jay that Sonny was angered even more. It crushed Jay.

Have to be careful, Jamison, Jay had warned himself. Just like when Sonny asked if this was where Jay lived. Jay almost slipped again. We're roommates, he heard himself say. How long could he make it all sound believable before he cracked?

And then the bedroom. Jay had completely forgotten. He would no longer share his bed with Sonny, but for how long? Jay couldn't let himself think about that. For now, he had to rush into his room, grab some of Sonny's clothes from the dresser and carry armfuls into what he would tell Sonny was his bedroom. Quickly, Jay filled drawers and the closet.

When he brought Sonny into the spare room, he noticed a sock he'd dropped in his hurry, snatched it up and hid it behind his back. Jay was going to have to do a lot of hiding, he knew it, but as fake as it felt, he tried to relax so Sonny didn't pick up on it. When he left Sonny in the room and the door closed, he told himself, *You've done this before, Jamison. For four years you hid the truth. You can do it again. You have too. So much more depends on it.*

* * *

Alone. For the first time Sonny was totally alone. At the hospital he was never really by himself. Nurses, orderlies, or someone was always barging in wanting to take him for tests, ask him questions, or sit in his room watching him. Even when he took a shower, the staff stood right outside the door. He'd go to the bathroom, and when he returned, someone was waiting for him. He closed his eyes to sleep and when he woke, he found more people hovered.

Sonny opened the bedroom door and peeked out to the hall. No one. He heard Jay banging dishes and running water, but there was nothing else. No beeping machines. No squeaky carts. He closed the door.

He glanced around. A bed. He sat on it. It was lumpy and squeaked. Two pillows. Both were too soft. There were a pair of black boots tossed in the corner. They were scuffed. He opened the dresser drawers. A few tee shirts of different colors. Cut-off jeans. Socks – one missing. Underwear. On top of the dresser was a hairbrush with some strands of brown hair. He touched his head. His hair was too short to use the brush.

The mirror above the dresser caught his attention. His reflection. It was weird. He didn't recognize the face that glared back at him. He shook his head. There was nothing in that mirror, in that room, or in the whole house, that meant one damn thing to him.

On the dresser there was a framed photograph of an older woman with gentle brown eyes and dark hair. In another frame, that same woman, younger, wore a wedding dress and stood next to a man with dark, wavy hair. There was another picture of a man who looked like Sonny smiling next to an older man in a police uniform. Next to that was a photo of a young woman with straight brown hair holding a baby and standing next to a man.

The images seemed to laugh at him. Strangers. All of them. A broken watch. Some discarded change. A crossword puzzle half done. The whole room seemed to taunt him.

Sonny's eyes drifted up to the mirror again. The face in it teased him the most. He touched his cheek. The image in the mirror imitated the act. His skin felt odd. His own hand even stranger.

Inside, rage boiled for no reason. Sonny had no place to go that felt even remotely normal. The anger rose until he felt as if he'd explode.

He gripped the hairbrush in his hand. Like a dagger, he stabbed the reflection and smashed the mirror. A sweep of his hand, and everything on the dresser flew across the room and crashed to the floor. He heard himself chuckle deep in his throat. He ripped open the drawers and grabbed whatever his hands grasped. Shirts. Socks. He tossed them into the air. He knocked over a chair. A lamp came next, and then he felt arms around him.

"Sonny. Stop. Stop it," Jay shouted and held him.

Sonny twisted. He strained and broke free and gave the other man a vicious smirk. "Get the fuck off of me! Don't fucking touch me." He went to the bed and tore off the sheets.

"Sonny. Stop. You have to stop," Jay shouted again.

"This is his room. His stuff. Not mine. Not me." Sonny turned with a harsh vengeance. He picked up the boots and threw them against the wall. "Not mine. He's dead. *Dead*," he screamed and pounded the wall.

From behind, Jay grabbed him again. "Okay. Okay. Easy."

"No," Sonny screeched. "Let. Me. Go." He strained with each word. He continued to struggle. He went on twisting, but he was tired. His body couldn't handle the fight.

"Easy," Jay said. "Just...go easy."

Sonny was breathing hard. Little by little, his body went limp. There was nothing he could do but surrender and let Jay hold him still.

"Okay," Jay said in a quiet voice, "you're okay."

Sonny nodded. He took a deep breath, and the rage dissolved.

Slowly Jay released his hold. "Just relax, okay?"

Sonny turned to him and the disaster. The room looked like a tornado had touched down and nothing was safe. "I-I didn't...I didn't mean to."

Jay ran a hand through his hair. He glanced around at the damage. "It's okay. I can clean it up."

"No. I-I will," Sonny said. He lowered his head like a naughty child.

"We both will," Jay said and patted Sonny's arm. "It's okay. Really."

"I shouldn't have....I didn't mean it," Sonny said.

"I know. It's a lot to take in. We just have to go slower, that's all." Before Jay could say more, Sonny left the room.

The front door opened. Jay was quick to follow. Sonny stood on the front steps and took in a deep breath.

"You okay?" Jay said.

"Where was it?" Sonny said, his voice small, the way it got when he was unsure.

"Where was what?"

"The accident."

"Oh. That. We…we don't need to go into that. Not right now."

"Tell me," Sonny said.

Jay hesitated. "Okay."

"Show me."

"Show you?" Jay swallowed and let out a heavy sigh. "Okay.

"It was a Sunday. Warm," Jay said. "You came out here to get the newspaper." He pointed down the driveway. "I came outside to water the plants."

Jay headed toward the street and pointed again. "You went over to Molly's house. Over there." He walked to that house with Sonny right by him. At the edge of Molly's driveway, Jay stopped. He paused and then said, "Danny. Her little boy. He was on a scooter." Jay pointed. "A car came from down there. It was swerving all over the road. Danny was in the street. You reached him and tossed him on the lawn, but…" Jay's voice quivered, "the car hit you."

Jay walked to the spot and looked at the ground. A shaky breath, he walked a little bit down the street and pointed once more. "You landed… here," he said and brushed away a tear. "You hit your head on a rock."

Sonny looked at the spot. He felt nothing.

"Mrs. Lowe must have taken it away," Jay said.

"Too bad," Sonny said. "Maybe I could have scraped off some of my brains."

"That's not funny," Jay said. "I can see it all so clear in my head. When that car crashed into you. The sound when you fell. The…blood. There was so much blood. It was the worse day of my life."

"Why? It's not like it happened to you."

"It matters to me, Sonny. Because you…you're important to me. Because I…." Jay swallowed hard at the word he couldn't say. "I care about you."

"Not me. *Him*," Sonny said, and his mood grew dark again.

"*You*," Jay said. "I know you don't remember. But I –"

"I don't remember," Sonny said. "And I don't…care."

"I care," Jay said. "I remember everything." He looked at the spot on the ground. "All of it."

"It doesn't mean anything to me," Sonny said. "It's not…" – he searched for the words – "there anymore. Just like the rock." He turned and slowly hobbled back toward the house.

16

Outside, just as the sun began to set, Jay watered his plants. He heard the front door slowly open and a moment later there was Sonny standing on the front steps. It seemed like old times.

Jay waved with a smile. Sonny went back in the house.

"Good luck," Jay whispered under his breath. "You're going to need it." *Give him space. Give him time.*

Jay set the hose to mist and heard Dixon's voice: *He'll be distant, remote...push people away....Don't get discouraged....*

The voice in Jay's head trailed off, and his own took over: "Go in low and, as Uncle Tony would say, duck."

Sonny came back outside. Jay directed the hose to a different set of bushes. He held his breath and waited, hoping.

Gradually, like a tiger getting the feel for the land, Sonny roamed over to Jay.

"Hey there," Jay said without looking up.

Sonny grunted.

The new Sonny. Grunts. Shrugs. One syllable answers.

"Get any sleep?" Jay said, picking off some dead leaves.

"I-I cleaned that room."

"Oh, yeah? That's good. Hated the idea of you sleeping where a hurricane touched down." He laughed. Sonny didn't. "Hungry?"

"Yeah."

"Good. Dinner will be ready...." Jay stopped when he heard Molly Connor call to him. She and her two daughters crossed the street.

"Dammit," he muttered under his breath. He turned with a cockeyed grin. "Molly. How are you?"

The young woman smiled from ear to ear. She carried a plate covered in plastic wrap. Her daughters rode their bikes, tassels hanging from the handlebars, and baskets filled to the brim with toys.

"Ken. Michael." She looked with adoration toward Sonny. "I'm so glad you're home. Out of the hospital. I made you some…."

Sonny walked away.

Molly's eyes watered. "He hates me."

"No," Jay said.

"He does," Molly said. "He won't even look at me."

"Molly," Jay said, "Sonny doesn't remember the accident."

"He doesn't….How is that possible?"

Jay swallowed the lump in his throat. He'd never said what he was about to say to anyone except Dee, and even then that made his eyes burn. "Molly, Sonny….he has brain damage."

Molly gasped and put her hand to her mouth. "No. That isn't possible. Is it?"

Jay swallowed again and nodded. "Traumatic head injury."

"Oh, my God. Ken, I'm so sorry. But…he'll get his memory back, won't he?"

The lump throbbed in Jay's throat and this time he shook his head. "The doctors don't think so."

"What do you think?"

Jay looked at the grass so she couldn't see the water form in his eyes. "I always have hope."

"Brain damage," Molly whispered. She watched Sonny differently this time. It wasn't with appreciation like before, but more like he was some alien from space. "My cousin was in a motorcycle accident years ago. He was brain damaged. He could walk and talk, but…." She gasped again. "Becky. Beth," she shouted for her twin girls. "Come over here."

Jay turned towards the source of Molly's apparent alarm. Sonny was talking to the kids while he fingered the brightly colored tassels. The girls showed him the items in their basket. Sonny silently took each one offered.

"Girls," Molly called again, more urgent.

"He won't hurt them," Jay said, annoyed with Molly's tone and the way she watched with accusing eyes.

"My cousin was…violent."

"Sonny isn't violent," Jay said, ready to tell her to go to hell and kick her off his lawn.

"Shouldn't he be in a special hospital for this kind of thing?"

"No," Jay said, his voice harsh.

"When my cousin was left alone with his little sister…." Molly's eyes grew big. "Girls? Come here right now."

Becky, balanced on her bike, rolled over to her mother. "Mom?" she said. "Michael wants to ride Beth's bike." The ten-year-old giggled. "We told him he's too big."

"Beth," Molly shouted to the other girl, "come here right this minute."

"Molly, you don't have to worry," Jay said.

"I'm sorry, Ken. I really am so sorry this happened." Molly took a small step back when Sonny joined them. "I'm sorry, Michael. Here." Her shaking hands offered the plate. "I made brownies for you. I'm glad you're out of the hospital. I'm so sorry, really but we have to go now."

"I don't care," Sonny said. He looked at Jay with an innocent shrug. "I don't care if I ride the damn bike."

Molly's mouth hung partly open. The girls giggled.

"He's funny," Becky said.

"Let's go," Molly said, and, as she gently pushed her daughters away, began to cry.

"Come on, partner," Jay said. His jaw flexed hard while he watched Molly hurry across the street. "Let's go in and check on dinner."

Sonny followed Jay inside. He sat at the kitchen table while Jay stirred the spaghetti sauce simmering on the stove.

"Stupid," Jay mumbled. "For her to even think…." He glanced back at Sonny who played with a small green figure at the table. "What's that?"

Sonny shrugged. "Some army guy."

Sonny flipped the green plastic figure between his fingers. He looked so serious and so engrossed in the toy that it made Jay wince. "Where'd you get it?"

"That kid gave it to me," Sonny said. He looked at Jay's concerned frown and threw the figure across the room.

"I don't want the damn thing," Sonny shouted. He pushed up from the chair so abruptly it fell. He stormed to his bedroom and slammed the door.

"Good luck," Jay muttered to himself. "You're gonna need it."

Later, the plastic toy incident forgotten, Sonny shoveled spaghetti into his mouth, slurped down the orange soda he insisted he have and gobbled the salad. Green peppers he spit out. He liked the cherry tomatoes.

"Had enough?" Jay watched in amazement. "Where do you put it all?" He patted Sonny on the back and brought the dishes to the sink. "So. How about a movie tonight?"

Sonny shrugged. "You…you mad at me?"

Jay frowned. "No. Why?"

"I threw that…that thing," Sonny said, his voice like a child again. "It wasn't food."

Jay's heart melted. "That's okay. I mean, it's not okay to throw things when you get mad."

Sonny twirled his fork. "What if I'm not mad?"

Jay laughed until he realized Sonny wasn't kidding. "You should never throw things."

"Or I have to clean it up, right?"

Jay nodded. He turned so Sonny wouldn't catch the pain on his face this time. "Plus you could break things you might want."

"What's that?" Sonny said, already distracted by something else on the kitchen table.

"That? It's your…it's a police badge."

Sonny picked up the shiny gold badge with the words Oakland City PD imprinted on the front. It shimmered under the light. "Cool."

"Yeah, cool," Jay said. Sadness welled up inside him.

"I do something wrong?"

"No. Why do you think that?"

Sonny shrugged. "You get this…weird look sometimes. Like I did something wrong."

"Sorry about that, partner. It's me. Not you." Jay took the badge. "This should be in its case. I must have taken it out and forgotten about it. Shouldn't be lying around. A bad guy might sneak in here and steal it." He made a sick laugh and turned with the badge fisted tightly. He hoped he hid the tears that begged to fall. "Hey," he said, trying to lighten the mood, "it's a nice night. How about a walk? Feel up to it?"

Once outside in the evening air, Sonny hobbled slowly alongside Jay. He glanced around with mild interest. The stars that began to poke out in the sky held most of his attention.

They walked slowly past Molly's house. Once more that spot and the street ahead flashed in Jay's mind. The car. The screech of tires. The horrific sound of bone slamming on pavement. It all played in Jay's head until he had to shut his eyes and steady himself.

"Why did she cry?" Sonny pointed back toward Molly's house.

"Molly? Well, she feels responsible for the accident."

Sonny scowled. "Why? Was she driving?"

"No. But it was her little boy you saved."

"She didn't want me to save her kid?"

There was so much innocence in the way Sonny asked everything that Jay's heart ached. It ached to the point he wished he could take it out of his chest and let it rest.

"It was good," Jay said. "What you did. Saving her little boy. But Molly…she blames herself. If you hadn't….If Danny hadn't ridden his scooter so close to the road, this wouldn't have happened."

"So she thinks I'm a freak, and it's her fault."

"She doesn't think…." Jay stopped himself. "The guy driving was drunk, Son. He's the one to blame. Not Molly and not her son."

"I don't blame anybody. Don't matter to me how it happened or why. She know I'm brain damaged? That I don't know shit about anything?"

"Okay, partner, let's drop it for now, huh?"

Sonny already had. His attention was back to the stars.

* * *

It was late. Sonny was restless. He tossed and turned in the bed, flopping from one side to the other. Finally, he got up and padded to the bathroom.

He flipped on the light, let his eyes adjust, and then stared at himself in the mirror.

He ran a cool hand over the stubble on his face. He combed his fingers through bristly hair and then stopped at the place he thought he felt a bump.

Brain damage, he thought. Missing pieces. Missing parts. He wondered if his brain actually had holes in it. Black, empty holes.

He didn't feel different, but then he didn't know how he was supposed to feel. There was nothing to compare anything to. One thing he did know: he was empty. Empty like when his stomach was hungry and it churned and made weird noises.

He wondered if what he felt was like food. When it was gone, there was just empty space left. Space that used to hold something good. He had no sense of anything. Nothing that meant anything. Even when he thought of the kids he'd met today, he realized he didn't have a clue what it meant to be a kid.

Then there was Jay. A small grin came to his mouth when he thought of the man. He liked him. Jay never pushed too much. He was the only one that Sonny felt…felt what? He wrinkled his brows in confusion. He didn't have a clue how he felt except he wanted Jay to like him, and he believed he could trust him.

Sonny shook his head. "It's either here or some damn institution," he said to the mirror. "No throwing food." He nodded to confirm the rule in his mind. "Got it."

* * *

Jay answered the doorbell's chime and found Captain Colby waiting on the step.

"Hey. Nice surprise," Jay said.

"Checking in," Colby said. He eased past Jay when he was invited inside. To Sonny, who sat in a chair with a magazine, he nodded. "Sonny. Good to see you."

"Huh?" Sonny glanced over. "Oh, yeah. You're that fat guy."

"I'm not fat," Colby barked. He looked at Jay. "I lost five pounds," he said and fitted his suit jacket around him.

Jay laughed. "Sorry, Cap. We're working on manners this week. Sonny? This is Captain Colby."

An indifferent wave, Sonny looked back at the magazine.

"Let's go in the kitchen," Jay said. "This is the first time all day I've gotten him to sit longer than five minutes."

Colby followed. "So, how is he?"

Jay shrugged. "Settling in, I think. Want some ice tea? I'm trying to get Sonny hooked on something besides orange soda."

"I can't stay. Just wanted to check in."

"You mentioned that. What's going on?"

"How are *you*?"

"Me? Fine. Why?" Jay looked at his captain and grinned. "I know you, Cap. Spill."

"I need you back, Jay. I've got cases coming out of the rafters. Two men on vacation, not counting you. One out with the flu. And the rest are idiots. I've got six homicides, one to be decided, three wanted suspects, and no one knows their ass from a donut hole. I need you."

Jay peeked around the corner. Sonny was playing with the TV remote and not too successfully. "Hey, there, buddy. Don't smack it. Try the power button." He looked back at his captain. "I can't. Not right now. He's still figuring his way around."

"Couldn't Dee help out?"

"She's got the bar to run, and Crocket went to New Orleans."

"For what?" Colby said.

"Don't ask. Listen, Cap, I would, but I got my hands full."

"Fine," Colby said with a disappointed sigh. "Think about next week. Two. Tops. But I need you back. With Sonny gone...." His words trailed off. "Anyway, I'm down to the bottom of the barrel." He pulled his pants up his middle-aged gut and headed for the door. "See ya, Sonny."

Sonny waved over his head while he switched channels faster than he could possibly see what was on the screen.

"Two weeks," Colby said as he went out the door. "Tops."

Jay ran a hand through his hair and turned back to Sonny. He took the remote and said, "Hey, how about we go someplace? The ocean. You haven't seen the ocean yet."

17

S onny gagged. "What the hell is this crap?" He spit a gob into the sink and with a God-awful face, looked at Jay.

"Sorry, buddy," Jay said. He set the blender filled with a thick brown mix on the kitchen counter. "I wasn't playing fair. You never did like my health drink concoctions, but I thought, what the hell, maybe with brain damage you would."

Sonny almost laughed, but not quite.

Jay glanced at Sonny. "One of these days, pal, I'm gonna make you laugh out loud."

"Why?" Sonny said with a blank look.

"Because it's good to laugh. Better to laugh than cry," Jay said.

"Why would I cry?" Sonny said.

"I got an idea," Jay said. "How about we go shopping?"

"Shopping?" Sonny scrunched his face. "What for?"

"Come on. It could be fun. You could get some new shirts."

Sonny looked down at himself. "I got a shirt. Looks new to me."

"That's at least five years old. And wrinkled. And you've worn it for three days. Something new. You pick it out."

Sonny grumbled, but got in the car. Before long, he was too busy staring up at the clouds to say anything.

Jay parked at the shopping center and tugged Sonny along beside him. In the store he gestured to all the racks of clothes. "See? So much to choose from." He looked back at Sonny who eyed a young woman who smiled at him. "Okay, Don Juan, let's go." He nudged the man forward and tried to distract him with stacks of shirts on a shelf.

Busy searching the display for the right size, Jay turned to check Sonny. He was gone. The bottom of Jay's stomach bounced. He darted his gaze around the store and rushed from one rack to another, down one aisle to another, calling for Sonny. The knot in his gut tightened. "Sonny? Sonny? Dammit."

A woman with the store's tag pinned to her blouse came over to him. "Is something wrong? Did you lose your child?"

Jay ran a hand through his hair. "No. My partner." He rushed down a few more aisles until he came to the toy section.

Sonny was there playing with a remote control car. He pressed the buttons, and the small race car zoomed across the floor.

"You scared the shit out of me, partner," Jay said, winded and relieved.

Sonny continued to focus on the toy. Jay hadn't seen him look so interested since he showed him how to use the blender.

Jay picked up another remote, and before long they were racing the cars, crashing into one another, and laughing. Sonny actually laughed. It was more of a snort, but Jay took what he could get.

"Excuse me, gentlemen," a stiff sales clerk said. "Either buy them or put them back."

Jay chuckled at Sonny who smiled with his dimple showing. "Guess we got caught, partner," Jay said.

Sonny crashed the toy car into the salesman's shoe. "Guess so. Partner."

They handed the remotes to the clerk and laughed all the way outside.

18

Jay banged on the bathroom door. "Hey," he shouted, "you drowning in there?" He snickered when he heard the shower shut off. "About time."

"What?" Sonny said. The door opened. Steam filtered out and swirled around his naked body.

Jay's stomach dropped and so did his mouth.

Sonny towel dried his hair as beads of water ran off his shoulders, his chest, and down his groin to that place that was hanging long and moist. The rest of his flesh was a warm pink color, tight and smooth.

Jay pulled his stare away, but his eyes had a mind of their own and looked once more. Physical therapy was doing its job. Sonny was more beefy, with muscles well defined.

Sonny cruised the towel along his chest and lower torso. Jay envied the towel. The urge to drop to his knees made his legs shake. The throb between his thighs grew nearly painful.

Once more Jay forced his eyes away. "Um, here. T-try this," he stammered and tossed Sonny a pair of jeans fresh from the laundry. He was jealous of those jeans as well.

Sonny caught the flying pants. "What's the matter?" he said. "You look weird."

"J-just put on some clothes," Jay said and went into his bedroom. "Your mother will be here soon. Don't walk around the house like that when she's here. In fact," he turned and looked again, "don't ever walk around the house like that." He closed his door, ripped off his clothes and jumped in the shower. The cold water created steam just by touching his skin.

"Hey? You gonna drown in there?" Sonny yelled.

Five minutes for Jay under a freezing cold shower barely did the trick.

"I wish," Jay mumbled with his head pressed to the tile, "that I could just tell him. Just say it. I love you. You love me. That's how it is." He closed his eyes, and saw the image of Sonny naked. "Get in that bed. I need...I have to...just let me touch you." He forced the faucet further toward cold. It was already as far as it could go.

"A bunch of people are at the door," Sonny shouted.

"What?" Jay turned off the water.

"People. At the door," Sonny repeated.

"Who?" Jay said from the other side of the bathroom door.

"That fat guy. A skinny guy and that lady with the nice tits," Sonny hollered back.

"Well, let them in," Jay shouted. "Sonny? Oh, for Christ's sake." He yanked on a pair of pants, tossed a shirt over his head and hurried for the door.

"Hey there," Dee said, standing on the stoop. "Glad to know I have nice tits."

"I'm not fat," Colby said.

"Well, dear, you could lose a little more," Ellen, Colby's wife said and laughed.

"I'll take skinny," Crocket said and snickered.

"You did say seven o'clock," Dee said.

"Is it that late already?" Jay held the door open for them.

"I brought beef stew," Dee said and headed for the kitchen.

"We have bread," Ellen said and followed.

"And cake," Colby said.

"I got the booze." Crocket patted the bag. "Lots of booze."

"Where's Sonny?" Dee said.

"In his room, playing with his trains," Jay mumbled.

"What?" Dee said.

"Nothing." Jay sighed. "He'll be out soon."

Sonny appeared in the hallway. He looked at them and didn't move.

"Well, there he is. Don't hide in the corner, sugar," Dee said and took him by the arm. "This is your party."

"Mine?" Sonny looked at Jay.

"They wanted to come over," Jay explained. "Kind of a welcome home thing. They brought dinner."

"Dinner?" Sonny said.

"And dessert," Dee added.

"That'll make him smile," Jay said and laughed.

"Here's a beer to wet your palate," Crocket said and handed Jay a cold bottle.

"I'll have one," Sonny said.

"Oh, no. Sorry, partner. You're on meds. Doc's orders," Jay said. "Pour him a tall orange soda."

They settled in with plenty to drink and eat, which made Crocket's stories tolerable. The bony man with large brown eyes and long narrow mouth was animated tonight. He told one tale after another, adding hand gestures that made them all laugh, except for Sonny. Crocket told stories about the tavern and the colorful characters that had been there. Before long, and a bit tipsy, he began to reminisce.

"So, in walks our esteemed host here," Crocket said and patted Jay's shoulder, "along with the guest of honor," he pointed to Sonny. "Detective Sergeants Ken Jamison and Michael Santini. aka, Jay and Sonny. Now, I personally taught them everything they know about the streets."

"Bull," Jay said with a laugh.

"I did," Crocket replied as if insulted. "Weren't for me, your white ass would have been handed back to you on a hanger. Who got you your first real bust? Me. Who got you the name of Benny the Burger?"

"Benny the Burger?" Ellen said.

"He was a burglar," Dee said.

"What did he steal?" Ellen said.

"Ladies underwear," Dee said and laughed.

Everyone around the table laughed except Sonny.

"No, seriously," Jay said through his own chuckle. "He stole jewelry, and he liked to try on ladies underwear. He broke into a department store and grabbed watches and rings. Then he went to the ladies section. Sonny was the one who caught him with his pants down." They all laughed louder.

"He was trying on thongs," Colby said with a chuckle that made his body shake. "These two bring him in still wearing them."

They roared. Sonny frowned.

"How did you all meet?" Ellen said.

"Oh, that's a hoot," Dee said. She patted Jay on the arm and smiled. "Isn't it?"

Jay grinned, the others smiled, and Sonny forced a grin on his otherwise blank face.

"It was all because of Smiley," Crocket said and shook his head. "Sad, sad tale."

"Oh, hush up. I'll tell it," Dee said. "You see, Mr. LaSalle here, Crocket, was in show business. No, really. One of his many interesting career endeavors. After traveling everywhere he could in the United States and getting tossed out on his skinny butt from most places, he ended up at Wally's Aquatic and Jungle World. A very fine dump about ten miles out of town."

"Dang, woman," Crocket said and smacked his lips. "Weren't that bad. It wasn't no dump."

"Right," Dee said. "Half dead fish in a cloudy aquarium. A robotic elephant that couldn't even spray water. And a bunch of masturbating monkeys hanging out in trees with birds that couldn't even fly."

"Don't listen to her," Crocket said. "I had an act there. Me and an alligator. I'd come out – "

"In swimming trunks," Dee interrupted. "With a red and yellow cape flapping in the wind. The Great Hector. Tamer of Wild Alligators. There was a poster and everything."

"Brought in business," Crocket said. "Anyway, I'd get in the water – "

"A swamp," Dee said.

"And wrestle an alligator," Crocket finished.

"Don't look so impressed," Dee said to Ellen while the others snickered. "The alligator was blind and had a bad right paw. Most of his teeth were gone, and he could barely move."

"I had him trained," Crocket defended. "We did all right. People paid to see this."

Dee laughed. "He'd roll around in the muck with this thing – fake blood oozing – and pretend that the alligator was getting the best of him. He'd go under water for a minute. Thrashing all around. Then he'd pop back up, and pretend he'd killed the gator."

"You think it's easy to train a gator to play dead?" Crocket said. "But then…" he lowered his head, "my gator disappeared."

"That's how we met Sonny and Jay. They were called in," Dee said.

"The Missing Gator Case," Colby said and jiggled. "They were still in uniform. Fresh to the department. It was their initiation."

"Did you ever find the poor thing?" Ellen said.

"No," Dee said with a sigh. "We think poor Smiley was made into boots and a belt."

"Don't laugh," Crocket said. "I loved that big guy. Named the tavern after him."

More laughter. Sonny looked back and forth at everyone like they all spoke another language.

Ellen leaned forward. "Why do they call you Crocket?" she said.

"Yeah, I always wondered that," Colby said.

"Well, that's a whole other story," Crocket began. "See, for a time I traveled Down Under. Me and a bunch I was acquainted with hunted for crocs. We'd get 'em and sell 'em. That's kind of how I got the idea for the gator show. Anyway, one of them crocs nearly bit off my foot. I kicked that beast square in the face. Then I shot him right between the eyes. I think he played dead, 'cause when I reached for him, he snapped at me again. One of my associates got in the lucky shot. People been calling me Crocket ever since."

Once more, everyone laughed. Sonny rose and left the room.

After a few moments Jay went to Sonny's room.

The door was shut. Jay knocked and opened the door. Sonny stared out the window.

"What's up?" Jay said.

Sonny shrugged.

"Hey," Jay said. "Come on. Talk to me."

Sonny was silent for a moment before he finally answered. "I don't get it."

"Get what?"

"Any of it." Sonny slowly turned toward Jay. "I don't understand anything that they're talking about."

"It's going to take some time, Son. Don't let it bother you, partner."

"Partner," Sonny sadly said. "I ain't that either."

Jay frowned. "Why do you say that?"

A shoulder shrug. "'Cause I'm not," Sonny said. "You always call me partner. But I'm not him."

"You are. Him." Jay sat on the edge of the bed looking at the back of Sonny's head and knew how much the man must hurt. If it was only half as much as Jay, it was still a lot.

"You don't get it," Sonny said, his voice deep. "I'm nobody's partner."

"You know why I call you that?"

"Because he was a cop and you worked together."

"That's part of it," Jay said. "But there's more." When Sonny turned to look at him, Jay once more fought the urge to tell him everything. "You and me...." He ran a hand through his hair, looked into Sonny's blank eyes, and tried not to say what he really wanted. "We need to talk." He huffed and said, "Why does that sound so familiar?" He saw nothing reflect back from Sonny and knew it all meant nothing. "You and me..." he swallowed, "are best friends." His heart sank. "The very best of friends."

"Not me. *Him.* I'm not a police officer. I don't remember being one, and I won't ever be one. And I don't know what it means to be...friends. So, I guess, we aren't – partners anymore," Sonny said.

So many things Jay wanted to say flooded his mind. How wrong Sonny was. How much they meant to each other. For a second he even considered shaking Sonny until he did remember – not only their friendship, but also the love they shared. Jay bowed his head.

"Whether you're a cop or not," he said, "or ever will be, or even remember it at all, doesn't matter. And you do know what it means to be a friend. You've been my friend."

"I have?"

"Sure. Absolutely. So we're partners because...because you're my best friend. Is that all right? Is it all right if you're my best friend?"

Sonny thought for a long moment. "I-I guess. Sure. That's okay with me."

"Good," Jay said and fought the tears.

"How long did you know him?" Sonny said.

"Almost five years."

"How'd you meet?" Sonny sat next to Jay on the edge of the bed.

"In the police academy. You just got out of Nam. Vietnam," Jay clarified. "You were in the army. Joined right out of high school. Lied about being eighteen. You weren't for another two months. You went through basic training in New Jersey, and the next thing you knew, you were halfway around the world. You never talked much about it. Said the things that happened just happened. But sometimes, when you'd see a disabled vet on the street, you'd get this really sad, faraway look on your face." He glanced sideways at Sonny. "It had to be tough. You were just a kid yourself. You got a purple heart. A special award," he said when Sonny frowned. "Your Uncle Tony told me the story."

Jay rose and went to Sonny's dresser. He picked up a cracked picture frame. "This is you with your Uncle Tony." He showed Sonny the photo of the older man in uniform. "He's a New York City cop. That's you standing next to him. He told me how you saved a bunch of guys in a Vietnamese village. Pulled them out of a fire when a building exploded. You stayed right there with them. Guarded them through the night until another troop could make it through.

"Anyway," Jay said while Sonny simply stared at him. "This picture?" He held up another photo, the glass of the frame also cracked. "This is your mom. Maria." He smiled down at the gentle older woman. "And this one is her on her wedding day. That's your father. He died when you were fourteen. And this picture is your sister, Rachel, her husband, Paul, and their daughter. Your niece. Carla." He placed the photos back on the dresser under the smashed mirror. "Guess we need to get some new frames and a new mirror. Seven years bad luck. Isn't exactly something we need, is it?"

"What about you?" Sonny said, his face blank. He scratched the top of his head.

"Me? I dropped out of law school. We were in the academy. Got to be friends. I liked you right away." Jay glanced at Sonny and wondered how much more he could say before he told him everything. "You told me once that you...you liked me right away too." He smiled at the memory and then had to turn his back. After he cleared his throat, he said. "We were assigned to the Oakland Police Department. Then three years later, we took the detective's exam and were promoted. Colby put us together and, like they say, it's been magic ever since." Jay turned and grinned at Sonny. "That's it."

"What kind of cop was he?"

"You were the best, buddy. Smart. Good instincts. Good at reading people. Very focused. And brave? None better. Hell, if it wasn't for you, I'd never have made it out of the academy. You taught me to fight and shoot. I helped you with the book stuff, but you got me through the physical stuff. We were good together. You saved my life more than once. Always backed me up. I knew I could count on you."

Jay sat next to the silent man and swallowed hard at the lump in his throat. "You were kind of cocky." He nudged Sonny's shoulder. "But that just meant you never took anything from anybody. We trusted each other. We always understood one another. Did from the first day, and that just kept growing over time."

Sonny lowered his head. "I-I guess you miss him, huh?"

"You know, when the accident happened, I was scared. I mean really scared. Never felt like that in my life. I mean, as cops, we faced some rough times. Bad guys with guns, knives, you name it. But we faced it together. We had one another. If it wasn't for that, I doubt either of us would still be here. But that accident was different. You were alone, and I had nothing. No gun. No way to fight. I prayed for you to be okay. To come back. And...you did."

"No," Sonny said. "You prayed for *him*. Not me. He didn't come back. Now...now you're just stuck with me."

"I'm not stuck with you. And I did pray. For *you*. You may not remember anything, and I know it's got to be tough. It's got to be damn hard to learn all over again. But you're alive. You were lying in the street after that car hit you. For a second, just a second, you opened your eyes and looked

162

at me. It was almost like…like you were saying goodbye. I won't lie to you, Son. I was scared. You looked at me and then…it was gone. I swear. I almost stopped breathing. All I wanted was for you to live. I wanted you to just live. And you did. You're here. Now. And for that, I'm grateful. I-I love you," Jay said and forced his voice not to betray him. "Always have. Always will."

"That's nice," Sonny said with no expression Jay could see. "What you said. But it…it doesn't…." He hummed what sounded to Jay like a painful cry and tried again. "I can't…." He tapped hard against his head in frustration.

"It's okay, partner," Jay said and placed a hand on Sonny's shoulder.

Sonny tensed and backed away. "I can't find the word."

"Just relax. It's okay."

"No. What you said. It doesn't mean anything to me. But it was nice. I just don't know what it means. I-I can't…feel."

Jay froze. Hearing that confession from the man he loved….He didn't even breathe. "Sonny, you do feel. You just – "

"No. I don't. I can't." Sonny said it like it was the most natural thing. But, when he saw Jay's face, he bowed his head. "I said it wrong, huh?"

Lump in throat, Jay tried to reassure him. "No. You said it fine. I want you to tell me those things. It's okay to tell me.

"I do wanna tell you…stuff," Sonny said. "It's just…hard."

"It'll get easier. But, Son, why did you pull away when I touched you?"

Sonny shrugged. "It hurts."

Jay creased his brows. "Hurts? Your shoulder hurts?"

"No. Being touched. I don't like it." Sonny looked at him with wide, innocent eyes. "Is that bad too?"

Jay began to reach for Sonny again and then quickly lowered his hand. "No. That's one of the things you should tell me. We're in this together. We have to learn as we go. I don't know everything. Hell, I don't know any of this, so you just tell me when I mess up, okay? Everything I said before I meant. That's how it is and why…you're my partner and still are my partner. You're not alone."

"I'm not alone," Sonny said. "I got you. Right? That's pretty cool, huh?"

"Yeah. Pretty cool." Jay patted Sonny's knee. He paused with the desire to wrap his arms around him. Jay licked his lips. They throbbed with the need to be on Sonny's mouth. He bit his lip and made himself go to the door before his strength failed him. "You coming?"

"No. I'll stay here."

"Okay. Good night."

"Good night," Sonny said. "Partner."

Jay's heart ached, but he managed to grin through it.

"Partner," he softly repeated and closed the door.

19

———⊤———

That night, as Jay lay in bed with the window open, he could hear the crickets chirping, calling for their mates. Bit by bit, his eyes drifted shut. The soft sounds of his breathing, the warm breeze through the window, seemed to sweep him up and lower him on a sandy beach. The sun reflected bright on the water in front of him. The tide rolled to the shore. The sand was moist. The waves gentle.

Jay stood with his hands in his pockets watching the water. The breeze felt damp and mild on his face. A seagull squawked and landed at his feet. It pecked at something on the ground.

As if he had always been there, Sonny stood next to Jay. He wore baggy, white cotton pants and a white shirt that blew in the wind. His hands hung at his sides, and he stared intently at the water that tumbled to the shore. With eyes set straight ahead, he finally spoke.

"How was it?" His voice was calm and light,

For some reason, Jay didn't look directly at him. "How was what?" he said and squinted in the sun.

"My death."

"You didn't die," Jay said and gazed at the water that lapped around his feet.

Sonny turned his head sideways toward Jay. "Yeah, partner, I did."

Jay chuckled. "No, partner, you didn't."

"How is he?"

"Who?"

"The new guy," Sonny said.

"What new guy?"

"The one you think is me. He isn't, Blondie. He's not me."

"You're nuts."

"He looks like me. That was kinda the plan."

Jay frowned. "Are you crazy?"

"I didn't want you to be alone. So, how is it working out?"

Jay was silent. The wind blew harder, and the water felt colder. Sonny's brown, curly hair waved with each movement of the air.

"Why did you have to go?" Jay said.

Sonny tilted his head. "It is what it is."

"It is what it is? That's an answer?"

Sonny bent and picked up some sand. He let the grains slowly seep through his fingers. "Answer me. How is he?"

Jay looked back at the water. "I love him."

Sonny smiled. "I know."

"I miss you," Jay said.

"I'll always be with ya. Always."

In the distance, someone called Sonny's name. Jay turned and creased his eyes in the bright light. There, near the dunes, was a short, balding man with a round face and round body.

"Hey? Isn't that Larry the Letch?" Jay said.

Sonny glanced over his shoulder. "Yeah. That's him."

"I thought he died two years ago."

"Three," Sonny corrected. "Now all he wants to do is play cards with me. Problem is, he cheats."

Jay grinned with a nod. "He always did cheat."

"Yeah," Sonny said. "Well, I gotta go. You take care, okay?"

"Sonny?" Jay said. "I love you. I'll always love you."

Sonny smiled. His form faded into the sunlight. Waves rolled up to the shore and back again. The seagull took flight.

Jay woke with eyes wet and burning. He reached over to what had been Sonny's side of the bed and gripped the pillow. Held tight to his face, he used it to muffle his sobs.

* * *

A knock on the door the next morning. Jay answered and found Maria Santini with a smile to match her son's and two worn out brown suitcases.

"Mom?" Jay was shocked. "I thought I was picking you up at noon."

"I got an earlier flight," Maria said. "I hope that's okay." A petite woman with dark, wavy hair, deep brown eyes, and rosy cheeks, her voice was gentle and still kept her Italian accent though she'd lived in New York City since she was fifteen.

"Of course it is." Jay bent to kiss the woman's soft cheek. "I-I just wanted to pick up the place. Come in. How was the flight?" He brought her luggage into the hall. When he noticed Sonny's rumpled shirt tossed on a chair and shoes Sonny left in the middle of the floor, he grabbed for them and gathered magazines and empty glasses – also left by Sonny.

"Don't fuss," Maria said. "I know how two bachelors live. The flight was fine." She looked around with a warm smile. "Oh, Kenny, I love the place. It's so…."

"Messy," Jay said, and when the older woman wasn't looking, kicked one of Sonny's dumbbell weights under the couch.

"Where's Mikey?"

"He's in the shower. Listen, Mom, remember what I told you on the phone. Sonny isn't…he-he doesn't remember…."

"I know. You explained that and so did the hospital. Rachel understands too. She would have come, but the baby…."

Jay noticed a pair of Sonny's discarded socks draped over a chair, and, while Maria wasn't looking, snatched them and held them behind his back and said, "That's good." When Maria turned in surprise, he clarified, "I mean, that's too bad about the baby."

"You mean it's best not to have too many of the family around," Maria said with a sparkle in her eyes. "That's why I convinced Tony not to come. Stubborn man. I thought I'd find him on the plane."

"He…he wouldn't…."

"Show up? I don't think so. And, Kenny, please don't fuss with me here." She stuck out her hand and took the socks. Jay felt a blush creep up his face and chuckled.

"I want to help," Maria went on. "I can cook. I'll do laundry and whatever else needs doing. You deserve some rest. I've read all the information the hospital sent me, and I've talked to Mikey on the phone. I know he doesn't know me. That's why I needed to come. He should know his mother."

"It's just that…he can get…."

"Upset. I know. I won't expect a hug or a kiss or for him to be excited that I'm here. But from you? I expect."

Jay let out his breath. He hugged her and kissed her again. "I'm excited to see you. Really."

"Good. And as for my son? I'll try not to upset him or let him see me cry. I just want to see him. I'm not expecting a miracle."

Sonny strolled into the living room tucking his white tee shirt into faded blue jeans. "Hey, Jay? How does that razor thing work?" He stopped and frowned with a question in his eyes. "Hello," he said to Maria and then glanced at Jay.

"Sonny," Jay said. "This is your mom."

Maria smiled.

Sonny continued to frown.

"Hello," Maria said.

"Hi." Sonny's tone was as flat as his expression.

"I thought it was time we met," Maria said. "I hope that's all right?"

Sonny tilted his head and shrugged one shoulder. "I guess."

"Is it okay to give you a hug? I'll understand if you're uncomfortable."

Sonny looked at Jay, who nodded encouragement. "Okay," he said.

Maria stepped to her only son and put her arms around him.

Jay admired the woman. He knew her and knew she fought not to break down and cry.

Sonny stood with his arms at his sides. He had made some improvements. He could tolerate more and didn't recoil as much when touched. He also relied more on Jay, and even now eyed Jay for some kind of reassurance, and then, cautiously, lifted his arms and put them carefully around his mother's waist.

Maria closed her eyes with the modest embrace and was quick to dry the tear that only Jay saw. Finally, she stepped back, sniffed and said, "So, where's my room?"

Jay caught his breath. "I-I, well…."

"Oh, just let me look at you both," Maria said. "You're both so thin. Are you eating enough? I plan to fix that. I am going to cook until you both burst. Mikey? How is your appetite?"

Sonny didn't say anything, but when they both looked at him, he realized she spoke to him. "Me? Mikey. That's what you called me when we talked on the phone. I forgot."

"You don't have to worry about his appetite," Jay said and squeezed Sonny's shoulder. "He's always hungry and never fills up."

"That's because he takes after his father's side of the family," Maria said. "They were all big eaters too. Okay. I'd like to freshen up and then, Kenny? Take me shopping. I have meals to plan."

"Yeah," Jay said. "Room. How about you take my room? I'll sleep on the couch."

Maria laughed. "That couch? I think it's a little too small for you, Kenny."

"Well," Jay began, "Sonny's bed – "

"It's got a big lump," Sonny interrupted. He glanced around. "Where's my weights?"

Maria walked down the hall and peeked into the first room – Sonny's – and across from that, Jay's room with a queen-sized bed. "Lumpy will make me feel right at home," she said. "Why don't you boys bunk together?" She went into the spare room. "I'll be fine in here."

"Bunk…together?" Jay's face flamed. "Right. Sure. Why not?"

"Okay by me," Sonny said with a shrug.

"Fine then. That's just…fine." Jay ran a hand through his hair.

* * *

"Maria, that was an amazing meal," Jay said. He sat back, patted his belly, and snickered at Sonny. "Where do you put it all? That's your second piece of cake."

"It's good," Sonny said and shoved more in his mouth.

"How does it all fit? Christ. It's amazing you don't blow up."

"Kenneth," Maria corrected. "The Lord's name. Anyone for more coffee?"

"I couldn't swallow one more thing," Jay said. "Unlike some people."

Maria chuckled. "Well, boys, put those few dishes in the sink. I'll finish in the morning. For now, *questa vecchia donna ha bisogno di dormire.*"

"You're not old," Sonny said and licked his fork.

Maria's mouth dropped. "*Scusi?*"

"I said you're not old," Sonny repeated.

Jay stared at Maria. "What did you say to him?"

"She said that she was old and needed to go to sleep," Sonny said. Maria nodded.

"*Ti Capisco?*" Maria said.

"*Si,*" Sonny said as if it was no big deal and put his dish in the sink.

Maria looked stunned. "He understands. Tell me, in Italian, that you liked dinner."

Sonny shrugged. "*Mi e piaciuta la cena.*"

"I liked dinner," Maria repeated and clapped her hands. "*Un miracolo.*"

"*Un miracolo?*" Sonny frowned.

"A miracle," Maria said with a teary smile. "My boy." She went to Sonny with her arms open wide.

Sonny stiffened and inched back.

Maria gasped, and her smile melted. "I'm sorry. I taught you as a child and to hear it...."

"It's all right, Maria," Jay said and guided her down the hall.

"I'm sorry. I got carried away."

"Don't worry. It's fine. He doesn't like to suddenly be touched. He just needs...."

"Time. I know. He knows Italian, Ken."

"I heard," Jay said and smiled back at her. "Thanks for dinner. You have everything you need? Okay. Good night." He placed a tender kiss on her cheek.

Jay went back to the kitchen. Sonny finished the last bite of his cake and was leaving the room.

"Hold on," Jay said. "New house rule, partner." He pointed to the floor, "No more leaving your crap lying around the house and dirty dishes go in the sink."

Sonny placed his glass in the sink and picked up his sneakers. "I'm going to bed. You coming?"

Jay's stomach dropped like a broken elevator with no stops. "Bed?"

"We're staying in your room, remember? Geez, you planned this."

"I did not plan this," Jay said. When Sonny frowned, he lowered his tone. "I mean, I remember. Yeah. Sure. I'll be right in."

"Whatever," Sonny said and went into the bedroom.

Jay picked up the remaining dishes and put them on the counter. He wiped the table, decided to sweep the floor, and then he paced outside his bedroom door. Brushing a hand through his hair, he took a deep breath and went inside.

Sonny was in bed. The lump of him on the side that before this nightmare began, had been his.

How did he know? For a brief moment, it felt like old times…except not.

Jay slipped into the bathroom. He paced in that room, too. "Okay," he said, stopping to look at himself in the mirror, "you can do this. Hell, for years you hid the truth from him. What's a few more? Few more what? Months? Years? Eternity?" Jay shook his head. "I can do this," he reaffirmed to his reflection. "He doesn't have to know that…that I want to toss him on that damn bed and feel every damn part of him." He huffed. "Get a grip. You did this before. You can fake it again." He glared at his image and put up his index finger. "But. I only lied to myself for those years and faked some of it, so if I did the math…." He shook his head again. "Oh, who am I kidding? This is nuts." He looked at the shower. "I cannot take another cold shower. I won't. I can do this."

He opened the door, flicked off the light, stood for a few seconds at the side of the bed and then grabbed his pillow.

He tossed the pillow on the sofa in the living room and tried to mold his long body to it. He curled up his legs. He twisted from one side to the next. Finally, he fell off the couch on his ass.

Frustrated, Jay snatched his pillow off the sofa and headed for the bedroom. The sleeping form he wanted so much and yet terrorized him, was still there, and not moving. Jay began to take off his sweatpants and then changed his mind. He left his socks and tee shirt on, too. Slowly, so he didn't wake the lump, he eased in under the covers. His body was as close to the edge as possible without falling.

He felt movement beside him. He sucked in his breath. The movement stopped. He let out a sigh. And then, Sonny's foot slipped between his feet. Jay gripped his pillow as if his life depended on it.

* * *

The window blind flapped gently with the breeze. The morning light teased. Jay found himself spooned in close behind Sonny. With his eyes shut, he sniffed the man. Vanilla. Cinnamon. Leather. For a moment, Jay grinned, ready to tell Sonny he'd had this weird dream where Sonny was hit by a car and….

Jay's eyes popped open.

He slid back from Sonny and worked to clear his head. He eased out from under the covers, went into the bathroom and headed straight for a cold shower.

Goose bumps to spare and shivering, Jay came out of the bathroom with a towel wrapped around his waist. At the dresser he took out a shirt. He happened to glance up, and when he did, realized Sonny watched him. Their eyes met. Jay's clear blue eyes melted into Sonny's deep velvet stare until Sonny quickly looked away.

"How'd you sleep?" Jay said, beginning to blush. He held the towel around his waist and prayed nothing bulged.

Sonny shrugged. "Okay."

Jay caught another quick glimpse from Sonny in the mirror. He held tight to his towel.

"Okay if I use your bathroom?" Sonny said. He slipped out from the sheets, seemed in a hurry to close the door, and the next thing Jay heard was the shower.

Dressed, Jay combed his damp hair and inhaled the aroma of breakfast. He found Maria humming in the kitchen.

"Good morning," she practically sang. "I made ham and eggs, home-made biscuits. Bacon. Orange juice."

"You're spoiling us," Jay said and sat at the table eyeing all the food.

"I love doing this for my boys," Maria said and squeezed Jay's shoulder. "I have so much to thank you for."

Jay placed his hand on hers. "No, you don't. I'm the one who should thank you. You trusted me with his care. If you hadn't, they would never have listened. If they had their way, they would have sent Sonny – "

"Sent me where?" Sonny said as he entered the kitchen.

Jay quickly sipped his coffee. Maria turned back to the sink.

"Holy shit," Sonny said, licking his lips at all the food. "This is cool." He tossed a piece of crispy bacon in his mouth before he even sat. He looked at Maria. "You don't have to leave soon, do you?"

Maria smiled. "The way to a Santini man's heart is through his stomach," she said. "Now, boys, I plan to make lasagna tonight. Here are a few other things I need. So you both go and do whatever you do, and I'll clean up and do some laundry."

"I can't let you do all that," Jay said.

"I want too," Maria insisted. "This is fun for me,"

"When you're done stuffing your face," Jay said to Sonny, "I'll meet you outside."

The day was warm. Not one cloud. Jay checked his flowers, and then he heard someone's throat clear. He turned with a start and saw Molly Connor in his driveway.

Timid, the young woman stood before him, eyes cast to the ground. When she gazed up at him, she said in a frail voice, "Ken? I-I wanted to apologize. For how I acted when you told me about Michael. That was… rude of me and stupid. Michael saved my little boy's life. He's Danny's hero and ours. What happened to him is unfair. To be left retarded – "

"He's *not* retarded," Jay said.

"I meant….Please, forgive me."

"I just don't want you or anyone to think that. He isn't," Jay said.

"I'm sorry. Michael is a wonderful man. I just wanted to say that."

Jay nodded. "Thanks. I'm glad you came by."

"If you or Michael ever need anything. I mean it. I'll do whatever I can."

Sonny strolled across the lawn. "Hey," he said.

Molly looked down at her feet and then back up again. "Hi. Michael."

"You're…."

"Molly. Molly Connor," Jay said.

"Right," Sonny said. "You made those brownies. They were good."

Molly smiled, more at ease. "I could make some more. How about a pie?"

"Sure," Sonny said with a shrug. "Say hi to…." He frowned and glanced at Jay.

"The kids," Jay said. "Pie sounds good. Thanks, Molly."

Sonny didn't say goodbye. He headed for the garage and lifted the overhead door. After he saw what was inside, he whistled.

The red Mach 1 Mustang with wide black pinstriping that started at the center of the hood and ran across the top where it ended at the bottom edge of the truck, shined in the light like something just wishing to be discovered.

"Sweet," Sonny said. "Whose car?"

Jay cleared his throat. "Yours, partner."

"Mine?" Sonny scoffed. "No shit?"

"No shit." Jay looked at the vehicle with a sorrow he tried to disguise. It wouldn't have mattered. Sonny paid no attention to him. He was too busy circling the car and touching the glossy hood.

"I want to drive it," Sonny announced. He tried to open the driver side door, but it was locked.

"Drive it? No. No way."

Sonny scowled. "Why? It's my car. You said it was."

"Yeah, I know, but, Son, come on."

"Why not?" Sonny demanded.

"Because…because it's a powerful…because you're not ready to drive yet."

"I can do this," Sonny said and grinned at the machine.

"We should check with your doctor first. Make sure you're ready."

"How would he know?"

Jay ran a hand over Sonny's short hair. "Because he's…he's your doctor. Come on, Son. Take it slow, remember?"

"I've been. Taking it slow. I can drive this. I can," Sonny said, his tone growing louder and more demanding.

"Don't lose your temper, buddy. How about…we could take it to the store, okay?"

"Cool." Sonny smiled.

"As in, I drive. You. You sit over there." Jay pointed to the passenger side. "If that's not good enough, then have a temper tantrum."

Sonny glared at him. "I'm not a baby."

"Then don't act like one. Passenger? Or no ride."

Sonny stared Jay down for a moment, clenching and unclenching his fists. For a second Jay was nervous. There were a lot of things Sonny could throw in the garage. But then, as quickly as the tension had built, it was gone. A slow grin spread across Sonny's tight face, and he nodded. "Okay."

"Okay." Jay exhaled. "Well, then. Okay." He unlocked the car, got in the driver's seat, and Sonny jumped into the passenger side like a kid getting on the Tea Cup ride at the amusement park.

Jay eased the car out of the garage. Sonny eyed all the knobs. He turned on the radio way too loud. Jay turned it off. Sonny reached for the shifter. Jay slapped his hand.

"Me drive," Jay said. "You sit."

"What's that?" Sonny pointed to the dash.

"That's a police radio."

Sonny lifted the microphone and punched some buttons. The radio was nothing but static at first and then squealed. Voices popped on, speaking codes and muffled sounds that grew clearer.

Jay turned it off. "It's not a toy."

Sonny looked around the inside of the car and then opened the glove compartment. He pulled out a gun.

Jay slammed on the brakes. The car behind them blasted its horn.

"Whoa," Jay said with his palms up. "Put that down. Put it down right now."

Sonny tossed the weapon in his left hand. "This mine too?"

"Put it down," Jay ordered. Traffic edged around him, blowing their horns or giving him the finger.

"Why?" Sonny said and pointed the gun at him.

"Sonny. You never, ever point a gun at someone."

"Then why have it?" Sonny examined the weapon. "Don't worry. It's not loaded. And the lock's on. See?" He opened the gun and checked the barrel and clip. He handled it like a pro.

"How...how do you know all that?"

Sonny shrugged. "Beats me."

Jay slipped the weapon out of Sonny's hand. "New rule. No touching guns until we have a chance to go to the firing range." He put the gun back in its place and locked the compartment.

20

S onny revved the Mustang's engine over and over again.

"Knock it off," Jay said from the passenger seat.

"I like how it sounds," Sonny said and revved it once more.

"Just pull it into the garage and help me pry my fingers off the dash."

Sonny snorted. "Your fingers ain't stuck to the dash."

"That's amazing. 'Cause that last turn you took at what? Sixty miles per hour, just about had me clawing my way out." Jay laughed. "I'm kidding. You're doing great. A real natural for only two weeks."

"I'm the best there is," Sonny said.

"Cocky, ain't ya?" Jay said.

"When can I drive someplace besides the damn hospital or Smiley's?"

"Baby steps, partner."

Sonny's expression turned hard. "I *ain't* a baby."

Jay patted his arm. "I know. Kidding. Got to work on your sense of humor. Here," he said and pulled out a map from the glove compartment." Let's look at this, and you can decide on a route."

Sonny looked away. "Can't."

"Why not?" Jay said.

"Can't read it. Looks like dots and squiggly lines. It doesn't make sense to me."

"Oh. Well, don't worry about it." Jay folded the map. "We'll come up with another idea."

Sonny was beyond all of it by the time Jay slipped the map back into the glove compartment. His attention now was on the dash and all the buttons.

Jay brushed Sonny's hand off the scanner control. "Will you stop playing with that? It's only for police business or emergencies. We aren't driving around as police, and, while that one turn could have been fatal, this isn't an emergency." He glanced over to Sonny, but the man stared off into the distance. "Sonny? Sonny?"

Sonny's eyes were glazed. He clenched and unclenched the steering wheel until a deep moan escaped his lips. He put his hand to his forehead and groaned louder.

"What's wrong? Sonny?"

Desperate to get out, Sonny fumbled with the handle. He moaned loudly and managed to open the car door. He slid off the seat, stood off-balance, and then gripped the side of the Mustang. Doubled over, he slipped to the garage floor.

Jay rushed to Sonny's side. "Talk to me. What's going on?"

"My...my head," Sonny said through clenched teeth. "Hurts." He groaned even harder and squeezed Jay's arm. Breathless, he moaned again. "Hurts. Bad."

"Okay, partner. Take it easy." Jay helped Sonny to his feet, got him to the passenger side of the Mustang, and this time, Jay was the one who left tire marks in the driveway.

* * *

"How is he, doc?" Jay said.

In the exam room, Dr. Dixon reviewed the tests and looked at the two men. "How's your head now? The medicine helping?"

"Yeah," Sonny said while he buttoned his shirt.

Dixon rolled his eyes at Jay. "I see conversation still isn't his thing."

"What did the tests show?" Jay said.

"There's a small, manageable blood clot on the brain."

"Blood clot?" Jay said.

"Manageable," Dixon repeated. "I'll put him on medication to shrink it. Should do the trick."

"If it doesn't?" Jay said.

"He might need surgery. But let's go this route first. It isn't all that uncommon."

"I ain't staying here," Sonny said.

Dixon took off his glasses. "Well, I guess that's been decided,"

"Does he need to?" Jay said. "Stay in the hospital?"

"I can allow him to take the medication at home," Dixon said. "Provided, of course, that he does." He spoke to Jay. "It could make him sleepy and maybe a little sick. But he has to take it three times a day. No matter what." The doctor eyed Sonny and said, "You can't miss even one. Understand?" He sighed at Sonny's flat stare. "Michael? Do you understand?"

"I'm. Not. Stupid," Sonny said.

Dixon sighed again. "Then answer when – "

"It won't be a problem, Doc," Jay interrupted. "Maybe we've just been pushing it a little too fast."

"No, we haven't," Sonny said. "This is about me." He glared at Dixon. "You should talk to me about me."

"I would if you would look at me," Dixon said. "If you would answer me. I'm not the one to be mad at, Michael. I know you're angry. It's part of the injury. Like it or not, you are brain damaged. But I am not the one to blame. You're pushing yourself too hard in physical therapy. You didn't finish your last medication. You refuse to continue treatments with Dr. Dean – "

"He's an asshole," Sonny said.

"If you won't listen to me or cooperate – "

"I'm done. Talk to him," Sonny said and threw open the door.

Dixon tossed up his hands. "He needs to learn to accept certain things. How is he doing? All he gives me are grunts, yeah, and fine. He won't tell me anything more."

"I know you're trying to help," Jay said. "He doesn't tell me much more. I know there's times when he's in pain. He just won't tell me."

"What have you noticed?"

"He stares off a lot," Jay said. "I call his name over and over. But it's like he doesn't hear me. He clinches his fist a lot. I don't think he's aware he's even doing it."

"Violent?"

"No. I mean, he gets mad. He throws things sometimes and then slams his bedroom door."

"But he's never tried to strike you?"

"No." Jay frowned. "Of course not."

"And what about you?"

"Me?" Jay said and ran a hand through his hair. "I'm…fine."

"Fine?" Dixon put down the file and sat on the stool. "Now who's the one not talking?"

"Really. I am. Fine. Yes, you were right. It can get exhausting. There were things I wasn't quite ready for. I try to slow him down. He wants to do everything all at once."

"You're doing a good job with him. Better than I thought."

"But?"

"No. No but. He trusts you. I can see that. He's come to depend on you."

"Listen, Doc, I was thinking…."

"I know how much you care about him, Ken. But this has to be hard on you. He isn't the same man."

"I love him," Jay said. "Always will."

"Even though he isn't the same man?"

"There's times. When he says or does something that's – "

"Like he used to say or do. I understand. But if *you* can't accept he isn't the same, what do you expect *him* to think?"

"I get all that. I do. I was thinking though, about telling him. You know. The truth about us."

"I wouldn't advise that. Not now," Dixon said. He rose and washed his hands at the sink.

"But, I think – "

"Ken, what do you think Michael will do with that information? Yes, he trusts you. But that only puts more expectations on him. And that kind of expectation only leads to more pressure to sort out things that are hard for him. Michael's level of thinking is very concrete. He has no abstract reasoning. No judgment to use in any situation. He acts in the moment. If you were to tell him, and he got upset, then what? How do you think he'd manage in the outside world without you to count on? You know as well as I do that his initial reaction to most things, especially new concepts, is anger. What if he runs from you? Gets into trouble. Maybe arrested. A judge would label him as incompetent and place him – "

"In an institution." Jay nodded. "Sonny would rather cut off his right arm and bleed to death than be in a place like that."

Dixon dried his hands. "On that, we agree. My best advice is *not* to discuss it with him. Not yet. Help him become more independent first. Help him learn some responsibilities and how to react without overreacting. Give it more – "

"Time," Jay said and bowed his head.

"He needs to learn a lot of things. Love is one of them. Especially that kind of physical love. If he runs from you, where would he go?"

"I don't know."

"I understand how hard this must be for you."

"Do you? You know what it's like to love someone only you can't tell them for reasons you can't control? I went five years without telling him. I never thought I'd be in that spot again."

"Like I said, help him to be independent. Having him so…dependent on you, copying what you do and say, isn't going to help him learn who he is. Right now, that's where Michael is. He imitates. Let him become a little stronger. In many ways, he's like a newborn."

"He isn't a baby. He hates that idea."

Dixon chuckled. "Of course he does. Anyone would. But in fact, that's where his development is right now. He hasn't matured emotionally and certainly not sexually."

"Really? He came on to a nurse while he was here. I've seen him look at women."

"And now you want to tell him he prefers men?"

Jay sighed. "Good point."

"You can't tell him that kind of thing and not expect some confusion especially if he's just beginning to be sexually aware. Don't undo all the good you've done. Give him…."

"Time," Jay said and nodded. "For the record. I like this Sonny very much. I actually get excited about the day. He loves to discover new things. And I love…."

"Teaching him."

Jay huffed. "I guess. I never thought of myself as a teacher or a damn tour guide."

"Or a parent. And in many ways you are."

"No. I'm not," Jay said. "That's one thing I can't be."

"Because you don't want him to think of you as a parent figure. Especially since you're still hoping one day you can tell him your feelings."

"Don't you think it's possible he could remember loving me?"

"Remember it? I highly doubt that. I know you're holding onto that idea. I just don't think it will happen."

"But if he loved me once?"

"Ken, Michael has to learn about his own feelings first. He doesn't really know what love is. You just have to give it – "

"Don't say time again," Jay said. "I understand. I won't push him. I've gotten damn good at cold showers."

"Just make sure he takes his medication. I don't want to have to operate if I don't have too."

Jay nodded. "Thanks, Doc."

Out in the corridor Jay found Sonny pacing.

"Good talk? 'Bout me?" Sonny said with an edge. "He tell you again how damaged I am? How dumb I am?"

"How's your head?" Jay said and punched the elevator button.

Sonny smacked the metal door with his hand. The elevator pinged, and the doors slid open. They both got in and Sonny smacked the wall.

Jay ignored it until they got to the car. "Why did you do that?"

"Do what?"

"Act that way. Not answer him. Walk out."

"He thinks I'm stupid. He treats me like an idiot."

"Well, if you act like one."

Sonny's deep violet eyes stared right through Jay. "Don't. Don't say...."

Jay knew the man struggled with the emotions, struggled to find the words. Dixon was right. There was too much pressure on him even for something this simple.

"Look," Jay said and calmed his own voice, "you're *not* stupid, okay? I don't think you are. So get that through your thick skull, will ya?" He smiled sweetly at the flame in Sonny's eyes.

Finally, Sonny snorted. "Thick skull." He laughed. "I got a thick skull."

"And you're pig headed."

Sonny frowned at that and then laughed after Jay did. But it was an empty laugh. Jay didn't need the doctor to tell him Sonny imitated, he recognized it more and more since Sonny had come out of the hospital.

How could Jay teach him to think for himself when nothing in the world was familiar? Baby steps, Jay thought. "Look, partner," he said, "you have to decide for yourself how you're going to act. But understand that if you act a certain way, like not answering when someone talks to you or getting angry right away, then people will treat you like you're stupid."

"They will anyway." Sonny traced his finger over the hood of the Mustang. "He knows I'm brain damaged. He's the one that decided I was. So that's what I'm supposed to be. If he wants to think I'm stupid, let him. He can go to hell."

Jay climbed into the car beside Sonny.

"Just...just try to listen to the doctors, okay?" Jay said.

Sonny stared out the window. "Why?"

"Because they're doctors, and they know. You have to trust them."

"Listen to them." Sonny turned towards Jay.

"Yes. They know what's best."

"They do?"

"Yeah, they do."

"Even if they think I'm stupid? Or-or how I feel is stupid?"

"How you feel?"

Sonny looked away. He tapped the door handle and for a second, Jay thought he might decide to run.

"Listen to me," Jay said. "You *aren't* stupid. But there are things you need to learn. So learn. Prove that you *can* do this."

"Jay? I-I gotta tell you something." Sonny didn't look at Jay at first, but slowly he drifted his eyes over to him, lingered for a second and then looked away before he looked back. Softly, he said, "This is all I remember.

I woke up in the hospital. I know they say I'm brain damaged, but…for me? It's like I was just born. Not a-a baby. I don't mean like that. And not damaged. Just…just new. And you help me. You help all the time. And not 'cause you think I'm dumb, right? But because you know that I'm… new." Sonny paused. "Does that make sense?"

"Yeah. It makes sense." Jay shifted in his seat so he faced Sonny. "Listen. If you don't understand something, that's okay. Lots of people don't understand different things. If you don't know something and you want to, then learn. You aren't stupid, or damaged, unless you think you are. Don't let anybody, including me, ever make you think you're something you know in your gut you're not. You have to be what *you* want to be. Whatever conclusions other people draw is their own problem. You don't have to prove anything to anybody unless you want to. You just be who you want to be. Got it?"

"I don't know who I want to be."

"You got time. Plenty of time."

"But I wanna know now."

"I get it. But some things just don't happen that fast," Jay said. "You just have to be patient. Can you do that?"

Sonny nodded. "Yeah. Patient. I-I get it."

* * *

At home, Maria waited anxiously at the door. "How is he?" she said.

"He's okay," Jay said. "A blood clot. It's okay." He consoled the woman. "It can be a common thing. The doctor gave him some medication."

"He'll be okay? You'll be okay?" Maria turned to Sonny.

"He'll be fine," Jay said. "Don't worry."

"All right then," Maria said. "Then I won't feel so awful for having to leave."

"Leave? Why?" Jay said.

"Who's gonna cook?" Sonny said.

Maria smiled. "I showed you how to make lasagna. You're a very good cook."

"See? A hidden talent," Jay said.

"I wouldn't even think of going," Marie said, "but Mrs. Antoine, my neighbor across the hall? I've mentioned her. She's a widow. She took a very bad fall. And she doesn't have anyone else, just a daughter who lives in Albany, and she can't come until the end of the month."

"It's okay," Jay said. "We'll miss you."

"And the food," Sonny said.

"But you and Michael come first," Maria said. "So if you need me...."

"No. It's okay. He'll be fine."

"I have a thick skull," Sonny said.

"And I'll be fine," Jay said.

"All right then." Maria went to her room and came back with her suitcases. "Only if you're sure."

"We are," Jay said. "Go take care of your friend. You're a good person. She's lucky, hell, we're all lucky to have you."

"I should stay. I should just stay here."

"Go," Jay said. "Really. It's okay."

Maria looked into the living room and watched Sonny toss a ball into the air, got bored with that, and began to lift his dumbbell. "Are you sure?"

"Yes," Jay reassured. "He's doing okay."

"Well, at least this way things can go back to normal and you can stop sleeping on the floor," Maria said. "Don't look so surprised. I make the beds, remember? Only one side of yours was slept on. I guess my son hogs the sheets, doesn't he? He was always a bed hog as a boy."

"I-I guess you caught me," Jay said. "I'll drive you to the airport. Sonny? Put down the weights and help your mom."

Outside, Maria dabbed her tear filled eyes. "I love you, Michael. Very much." She hugged him and smiled when he hugged her too. She got in the car, and as Jay pulled out of the driveway and Sonny waved, she glanced at Jay. "Will he be all right? Really?"

"Yes. He'll be fine."

"This has all been so much for you."

Jay smiled at her.

"You can tell me."

Jay frowned. "Tell you what?"

"How you really feel."

With red cheeks, Jay stammered, "H-how I-I feel? About…about what?"

"The accident. Lord, I hate that word. This thing that happened to Michael. I see it. And I know he's doing better every day. And I also know that's because of you. You're the center of his world. You know that, don't you? I don't know what he would do without you. Oh, he looks so much like his father. You know, women used to go crazy for my Mario." Maria giggled. "But he was always faithful to me. And the girls" – she giggled again – "how they were crazy for Mikey." She grew serious in a sad way and added, "Michael used to be so…full of life."

"He still is."

"But he's different. His eyes are so…empty. Even his voice sometimes." Maria wiped away her tears. "I don't mean to question. I just thank God he's alive."

"Me too, Mom. Me too."

"It must be hard on you. You've worked with him, been his best friend for years and now…this is new to both of you. But, Kenny, you need to have a life too. It can't all be about Michael. That isn't healthy for either of you."

"I'm fine," Jay said and squinted at the road ahead.

"You always say that. But you have to have other things besides Michael. I know if it wasn't for you, he'd be in some kind of hospital or worse, alone. I see how he doesn't let anyone else in, not really, except you. But you can't get lost in all that either. You deserve to be happy."

"I am. Happy."

"He depends on you."

"You don't think that's good?"

"I didn't say that. He watches everything you do so closely."

"But is that the right thing?" Jay replied and wondered.

"Maybe if it was anyone else he modeled, I'd worry. But you're good for him. I believe that. He'd be lost without you," Maria said.

"I don't want him to be lost," Jay said.

"He isn't. Not with you."

"I want Sonny to find out who he is," Jay said. "That's what he wants."

"And he will. You'll help him."

"Will I? You think I can help him find out who he really is?"

"I think so. Oh, at first he might be anything you tell him to be. But you'd never hurt him. That's why it's best he's with you. I'm sure of that."

"I'd never mean to. Hurt him, I mean," Jay said. "Dr. Dixon said Sonny depends on me. Is that what's best for him?"

"Why wouldn't it be?"

"Maybe…maybe it's stopping him," Jay said.

"Stopping him? I don't think so. Besides, it's better to be with someone who can guide you than to have to…."

"Figure it out on his own," Jay said.

"That's right. But you need a life too. I want you both to be happy. Anyway, I want you and Michael to come see me. When you think the time is right. He should know his family. Not that you aren't. Family. But…."

"I know what you mean."

"If you need me. If you need anything."

"I'll call. I promise."

They pulled up to the terminal, and Maria said, "Drop me here. No long good-byes."

"You'll be back, won't you?"

"I'd love that."

Jay handed the skycap Maria's luggage and grinned down at her. "I love you."

Tears slipped down Maria's rosy cheeks. "And I love you." She hugged him. "Thank you. For taking care of my son and…" she whispered in Jay's ear, "for loving him."

21

Jay stepped off the elevator on the fifth floor and inhaled the scent he knew so well. It was the smell of cold subs, sugary donuts, burnt coffee and floor wax. All of it blended in the hallway that led to the Detectives' Squad Room inside Oakland City Metro Police Department.

He had to admit it felt good to walk the hallway again. It was so familiar, like returning home after a long trip.

He opened the door to the squad room. Nothing had changed. Twenty-five detectives, some out on call, some busy at the typewriter, the phones ringing, the file cabinet drawer slamming shut, and Colby, as usual, barking orders in the distance.

Jay slammed the door to get their attention, and after the initial stares, was greeted by a dozen men.

"Well look here," one detective said, "a ghost from the past."

Detective Ryan patted Jay's back. "Is that really you?" he said. "Or my imagination?" A man in his early thirties, originally from Orlando, he'd been made detective a year ago and that's when, everyone kidded him, his hair began to fall out.

"Hey, how's Sonny?" Detective Weiss said and shook Jay's hand.

"Sonny's…okay," Jay said. "Getting better."

"Man, it sucks. What happened to him," Ryan said.

"Thanks, guys," Jay said, "for all the cards and the flowers. It meant a lot. Colby in his office?"

"Can't you hear him?" Weiss said and laughed. "He's reaming out a new guy. Don't think he'll be with us long."

"Griffin?" Ryan said. "That ass-wipe couldn't find a rhino in a fish tank. Sent to us from Daytona, and now we know why. We're short on men, and that's their way of helping."

"Cap'll be glad to see you," Weiss said. "That is, if you plan to return to our fair stage of comedy and drama."

Jay chuckled. "We'll see." He rapped on the captain's office door.

"Come in," Colby's gruff voice shouted. "And you. Get out."

Jay opened the door. A young man, dressed in a casual shirt and slacks brushed past him. Jay assumed that was Griffin

Colby, frowning, sat behind his desk. "Yeah? What?" He glanced over, and when he realized it was Jay, the frown turned up slightly. "Is this a dream? That really Detective Kenneth Benjamin Jamison?"

"Detective Sergeant," Jay said with his finger pointed upwards.

Colby rocked in his chair. "I'm rethinking the sergeant part. So. Here to put in for more time?"

"Actually," Jay began and ran a hand over the back of his neck, "I was thinking about returning to duty."

"Don't play with me," Colby said. "I'm on the edge."

"Not playing, Cap. If you really need – "

"Need? Look around, Jamison. What do you think all this crap on my desk is? Glamour magazines? Vacation brochures? I got so much sewage backed up in this tank we fondly refer to as our fair city, that even Roto-Rooter would run screaming."

"So I guess that's a yes."

"When can you start?"

"When do you need me?"

"Now," Colby said, and he almost grinned.

"How about Monday? I can tie up loose ends."

"Sonny? He doing okay?"

Jay offered a slow nod. "He's coming along. I think it's time. This will be good for both of us. He needs to…to be more independent. To learn to be okay on his own. I mean, for a few hours a day, anyway."

"And you need to get back to work. Get your mind on something else."

"That too, but honestly? I want him to figure out some things on his own and not count on me to tell him – even unconsciously – oh, hell. I want to do what's best for him and I think, hope, this will be."

"So, Monday it is," Colby said and walked Jay to the door. "I'm actually smiling."

"Really? Cap, it's hard to tell." Jay laughed and waved goodbye.

* * *

The next few days went by faster than Jay ever recalled days flying by. He hoped Sonny would be ready for this – for him to return to work. Sonny had no reaction when Jay told him, which was nothing unusual. He simply blinked his long lashes and then left the table when Jay was in midsentence.

Maybe something more visual, Jay thought. He showed Sonny the calendar and circled the day and his schedule. Sonny played with a rubber band the whole time.

Jay made a list of things Sonny could do while Jay was at work to keep him occupied. Sonny showed more interest in that.

Jay made arrangements for Dee to come over during the day and stay with Sonny, get him to his appointments, make sure he finished his newest medication and generally keep an eye on him. Jay balked when Dee referred to it like that.

"If I have to work late, can you stay?" Jay asked Dee.

"Depends," Dee said. "But don't worry. I'll get one of the girls to come over."

"One of the waitresses?"

"Yes, Jamison, one of the waitresses. What? Not good enough?"

"No. I mean, that's fine but…not Amy. She always flirted with Sonny too much. Jean would be okay. But I prefer Crocket and if – "

"You aren't being too fussy, are you?" Dee smirked. "Jay, relax, will you? He'll be fine. Give him some space."

"It's what he'll do in that space that worries me," Jay said.

* * *

Showered, dressed, Sonny checked that off his list. He vacuumed, checked that from his list, and after he finished the dishes, checked that off as well.

"You ready for therapy?" Dee said.

"Hang on," Sonny said. He went to his list on the kitchen counter and checked that item off too. "Ready."

The phone rang, and Dee picked it up. She didn't bother with hello, she knew who it was. "He's fine, Jay. Just like he was an hour ago."

"I just wanted to make sure – "

"I know," Dee interrupted and sighed. "You just want to make sure he's okay. He is. He was yesterday when you called fifty times."

"Don't exaggerate."

"Who's exaggerating? The day before, you called sixty times."

"So I'm calling less," Jay said. "Look, Dee, it's just that ever since I got back to work, it's been nonstop."

"Apparently not, Jamison, 'cause you stop all the time to call and check up. You've been back to work for less than two weeks. Lighten up, sugar. He's okay. He works off that damn list you make him every night like it's Gospel. And last night, didn't he make good lasagna? He did all that to surprise you."

"I know." Jay's voice softened. "And I didn't get home until midnight. He was already asleep. I'm seeing less and less of him."

"I show him your picture every night," Dee said.

"Very funny. Hey, he has – "

"Physical therapy. I know. We could have been there by now if you'd stop calling."

"He'll bug you to drive the car."

"Already has. Already told him no can do. I have to get my oil changed, and Jake, at the garage, told me he could squeeze me in.

"Thanks, Dee, for doing all this."

"Not a problem, sugar. But if you call me one more time, you're gonna find your telephone in the toilet."

Jay scoffed. "I may have to work late again. Can you explain to him?"

"Fine. In that case, you get one more call today. Now go to work, Detective, before I report your blond ass to whoever gets this kind of report."

"What kind of report?" Jay said with a hint of a chuckle. "Maybe I can direct your call."

"Stalking. Bye, Jay." Dee hung up.

"Was that Jay?" Sonny said. "I wanted to talk to him."

"He's got to get back to work, sugar. He'll call later. Trust me." Dee grabbed her car keys "Move it. We'll be late." She ushered Sonny out to her car.

"Why can't I drive *my* car?" Sonny said and climbed into Dee's Oldsmobile.

"I told you," Dee said. "Got to get my oil changed." Sunglasses on, she fixed the mirror and then pulled out to the street.

"So, get your damn oil changed some other time."

"And miss the free car wash they offer today? No way, sugar." She laughed and then noticed Sonny's pensive face. "You miss Jay, don't ya?"

"Yeah."

"He has to work late again tonight."

"Yeah."

"You know he'd rather be with you, don't you?" No response. "Don't you?"

"I guess."

"You're doing a great job, you know," Dee said.

"Yep."

Fifteen minutes later Dee pulled up to the front of the hospital. "I'll pick you up here. Two hours."

"You ain't coming in?" Sonny said.

"I think you can handle it."

Sonny shrugged. "'Kay," he said and climbed out of the car.

"Good talk, Sonny. Really good. " Dee shook her head as she drove away.

* * *

Colby flung his office door open.

"Jamison. Now," he shouted. His shirt sleeves were rolled up and his tie loosened.

Jay put down the file he worked on. Once inside the captain's office, he said, "Look. If this is the talk about me getting a new partner – "

"If this *was* the talk about you getting a new partner, I'd do the talking," Colby said. "What I was going to discuss with you is that I'm glad you're back."

Jay frowned. "Y-you wanted to tell me? That you're…glad? Okay, Cap. What gives?"

"Look. Sonny's on disability, and that's how we'll leave it for now. Sooner or later…"

"This *is* the talk. Well, I don't need….No, wait. I don't *want* a new partner. Sonny and I…."

"Were the best. I know that, Jamison," Colby barked out of one side of his mouth. "I'm the one who made you partners, remember? But what are the chances of his coming back? According to his doctors, if – and that's a big if – it could take a long time."

"So you want to stick me with someone else. Won't work."

"It damn well better work," Colby shouted.

Jay sighed and ran a hand through his hair. "I'm sorry, Cap. I am. I know you're right."

"You work for this department and…." Colby did a double take. "Wait a minute. You *know* I'm right?"

Jay walked to the file cabinet and stood leaning his head in his hand. "Yeah. I haven't wanted to face it. But…it'll be a long time, if ever, before Sonny comes back. I have to deal with it. I get that."

Colby scowled. "I had a whole speech ready about duty, and now I can't use it. You're a pain in my ass, you know that? You and Santini always were. Hey, hold on. Is this one of your games? The kind you both like to play to change my mind or something?"

"No. Cap. It's not." Jay looked over at him. "I have to face reality, as much as I'd like to fight it. I came back to work because you're right. I missed it. I need it. And because Sonny would have wanted me to. The idea of getting a new partner isn't something I'm jumping up and down about. I hate the idea. But I've got to do what I have too and Sonny…he's got to work on getting better, and so far, he is. So, that's how we play it."

Colby sat as if stunned. "That was part of my speech. So help me, Jamison, if you're playing me."

Jay chuckled. "I'm not."

"Okay. Well," Colby cleared his throat. "Then the next thing is, I need you to work this weekend."

"This weekend? Oh, no," Jay said and shook his head. "Cap, I've already put in twelve hour shifts for over a week."

"And now you can put in twelve hour shifts over the weekend. Something's coming down the septic system and I need you on board."

"Cap, please. I haven't seen Sonny – "

"Look, Jamison," Colby barked and rose quickly. "Either marry him and go on a damn honeymoon or concentrate on your job."

"You get little veins in your neck when you scream like that, you know."

Colby eased and smiled just the slightest. "You sound like –"

"Sonny," Jay said with a bittersweet grin. "And you sound like your old self. I missed that. You slapping your hand on the desk. Jumping to your feet. Yelling. Music to my ears."

"Get outta here," Colby said and waved Jay away.

"So? I can have the weekend off?"

Colby grunted. "No. Now get out and shut the damn door."

* * *

Myra Turner, a physical therapist assistant, was twenty-four, and stronger than her curvy, thin body suggested. She eyed Sonny from across the room like she had for the past few weeks. Like an alley cat on the prowl picking the right moment to pounce, she licked her lips, and swung her hips while she walked toward Sonny. He had just finished his reps. Sweat beaded on his face and down his bare back in all the right places.

"Looking good, Michael," Myra said in a voice she practiced to sound whispery.

"Thanks," Sonny said, putting the weights back on the ground.

"You've upped the pounds. Does Albert know?"

Sonny shrugged. "Who cares if he does?"

"You naughty boy," Myra said and giggled. "He's your therapist and my boss."

"So? Go tell him. I don't give a shit." Sonny huffed as he lifted the dumbbells.

"I won't tell. He's too serious, anyway. I bet you're like me. I bet you like to have fun."

Sonny worked his neck from side to side until it cracked. Feet placed shoulder length apart, he held the weights while he curled and uncurled his arms.

"So? Where's your keeper?" Myra said.

Sonny creased his brows. "My what?"

"The tall blond guy."

"Jay?"

"Yeah. Him. He's usually here. Watching every move you make. So, where is he?" Myra strolled behind Sonny admiring how his back muscles strained.

"He went back to work," Sonny said, focused on the reps.

"Oh, that's right. He's a...cop," Myra said. She stepped close to Sonny. "What about your girlfriend?"

"Huh?" Sonny scowled.

"The dark skinned lady with fuzzy hair," Myra said. "She hangs around you like you're a favorite toy. Are you?" She gazed at his chest and licked her lips. "A toy?"

"She ain't my girlfriend," Sonny said and continued to lift the dumbbells. "She went to get her car fixed."

"Oh." Myra batted her eyes. "So that means no guards."

Sonny ignored her.

"He's cute," Myra said. "Jay, I mean. Think maybe I should ask him out?" She circled Sonny. She got no reaction so she said it again. "Think I should?"

Sonny shrugged and snapped his neck once more.

"I mean. It gets lonely." Myra eyed Sonny in the mirror. "Don't you get lonely?"

Sonny stared into the long mirror and counted the lifts under his breath. Myra moved so he couldn't miss her. She bent to pick up the weights, showing her cleavage. She pretended to strain as she lifted the barbell. She grinned when Sonny noticed, but when he continued with what he was doing, she whined, "Oh. This is so heavy. I wish I was a big strong man like you."

Sonny sweated and continued counting under his breath.

Myra rolled her eyes and turned to bend so her buttocks curved in a way she knew men liked. "Could you help me?"

Sonny stopped and looked at her. "I'm not finished yet."

"Please." Myra batted her brown eyes. She pouted her pink painted lips and pulled down on her uniform top so more cleavage showed. "I have to clean up this side of the room. Albert's so mean. He always makes me do the heavy work."

"So tell him you don't wanna do it," Sonny said and went back to lifting the dumbbells.

"I'll buy you a soda," Myra enticed.

"Yeah?" Sonny said, grunting with each lift.

"Besides, you worked hard enough." Myra stepped close and ran a delicate finger over the curve of Sonny's bicep. "You don't want to strain yourself, do you?"

"Jay says I over-do sometimes," Sonny said.

"Jay? He's right. You could actually do more harm than good. And that," she said in a tempting tone, "wouldn't be good. For anyone."

Sonny put down the dumbbells and picked up the larger weights. "Where ya want 'em?"

"Over there," Myra pointed to a storage room. "Follow me."

Sonny followed her into an overcrowded room just beside the main office. He put the bar bells where Myra told him and turned. Myra snuggled in close to him. Her breasts brushed his arm.

"Small room," Myra said and smiled. She leaned into Sonny and grinned even more. "You smell good."

"I stink," Sonny said and slid past her.

"No. I like it. When a man, and I mean, a *real* man, sweats, he smells...." She purred close to his ear, "sexy."

"I'm gonna take a shower," Sonny said. He frowned at her. "Could you move back?"

Myra worked harder to turn on the charm. "You're very handsome. I bet you don't even know how handsome, do you? Those ripped muscles of yours." She ran the back of her hand like a feather over Sonny's arm. "Those tight abs...." She trailed down his chest. "Your back," she cooed and ran her hands around him. An inch shorter than Sonny, she licked her lips close to his mouth. "I bet you know how to make a woman feel good."

Sonny wrinkled his face. "You sick or something?"

"No," Myra said, impatient. "I'm just interested."

"In what?"

"In you, silly. Hasn't a girl ever come on to you?"

Sonny chuffed. "No."

"Well, I bet plenty of them wanted too. They were probably intimidated because you're so…" she groaned deep in her throat, "beautiful."

Sonny snorted. "I ain't beautiful. And I ain't a girl."

"Men can be beautiful. And believe me, Michael Santini, you are one beautiful man." Myra batted her eyes again and said, "You ever kiss a girl? Of course you have. I bet lots of girls. That's why you're playing so cool with me, isn't it? You have a girlfriend."

Sonny snorted again. "No."

"No? Playing the field?"

"What field?"

"The I-have-so many-to-choose-from field."

Sonny's forehead wrinkled. "Choose from what?"

Myra sighed. "You aren't making this easy, are you? Choose from girls, silly. I bet lots of girls too."

"I told ya, I don't have a girlfriend." Sonny moved her aside.

"How about that older woman I asked you about before?"

"Who? Dee?"

"Dee. That's her name? Well, the way she stands over you, you sure she isn't the other guard?"

"I don't have a guard."

"Then she must be your girlfriend, or," Myra giggled, "your mother."

"She ain't my girlfriend. And she ain't my mother."

Myra blocked Sonny from leaving. "Then come out and have a drink with me."

Sonny snickered. "I can't."

"Why not? You're a grown man, aren't you? Or won't Mommy and Daddy let little Mikey come out and play?"

Sonny's eyes narrowed, his face tensed. "I'm not a baby."

"Then be a man. I see how your friend, Jay? How he watches you. Every move you make when you're here. Like you're going to break or something. He met with Albert, you know. He told Albert that you get upset easily and to call him if you ever got out of hand."

Sonny's brows creased. "He said that?"

"Something like that. He said in lots of ways, you're immature. Well, I got news for him," Myra said and pressed in so close that some of Sonny's sweat dripped onto her breast. "You look damn mature to me. Especially in all the right places."

Sonny moved her away. "Leave me alone." He walked toward the showers. When Myra followed, he said, "You can't come in here."

"I work here. I can go anyplace I like. So? Come have a drink with me. I owe you a soda or something stronger if you want."

"Why you doing this?" Sonny said.

"You honestly don't know? Because I'm young. I'm free, and I like to have fun. What kind of fun do you have? You come here where everyone treats you with kid gloves so you don't bust a nerve. I read your report. Brain damage. You don't look damaged. Not in places that really matter. I heard them say you're slow. I don't think you are. And those friends who treat you like a kid? You're no kid either. I think you're bored with it all. The routine of coming here and then, where? Home? In bed by nine? You're here alone now with no guards. I bet they don't really let you out much by yourself, do they? I bet someone is usually babysitting you, aren't they?"

"Nobody is babysitting me," Sonny said, and his jaw muscles flexed.

"You sure? You got a car?"

"I drive."

"Then drive me someplace, and I can buy you that drink."

"I-I didn't drive today."

"They wouldn't let you, sweetie?" Myra pouted her lips. "Too bad. I got *my* car. We could go in that."

"I-I can't. Dee's gonna…Jay said…"

"Dee's gonna." Myra mocked. "Jay said. Well, sweetie, when you feel up to playing like a big boy, you let me know." She turned to leave and Sonny grabbed her arm. "Hey. Watch it."

"I wanna," Sonny said, his eyes intense enough to cause a spark. "I wanna play."

Myra grinned. "Okay then. You take your shower. I'll clock out and meet you in the parking lot."

* * *

"What do you mean Sonny didn't come home with you?" Jay said into the phone. Sitting at his desk in a room filled with detectives, he lowered his voice. "What do you mean?"

"Relax," Dee said. "He made a friend, and they wanted to go out for a soda. It's all harmless,"

Jay ran a hand through his hair and huffed. "Harmless? Wh-what friend?"

"He said her name's Myra. I've seen her at the hospital. She works – "

"In the physical therapy department. I know. I think she has a thing for Sonny."

"Really?" Dee said. "Well she's pretty. Perky boobs."

"Perky…are you kidding? She's a flirt."

"She seemed nice when I met her. She came over to the car. Very polite. Said Sonny did so well in his workout that she promised him a soda. Now, how bad can that be? Besides, he needs to start making friends."

Jay squeezed the bridge of his nose so hard it throbbed. "Myra never seemed the harmless type to me."

"You're just jealous. Sonny can't just have you or me. He has to start getting out in the real world. I think this girl will be a good start. She's a professional and she knows his case. She won't do anything to hurt him. She has experience."

Jay's expression soured. "Yeah. But what kind of experience?"

"What? Sorry, I dropped the phone."

"I said…never mind. Call me the minute Sonny gets home, okay?"

"Yes, Daddy," Dee said.

"I am *not* his father," Jay hissed.

"Then stop acting like it. Give him some space."

22

The days flew by, and Jay worked. His time with Sonny grew less, and Sonny's mood changed more. It was like the weather. Hot one day. Mild the next. Rain in between.

The tension in the house increased. Sonny argued. Doors slammed. He threw books across the room. He shouted he wasn't a baby, he didn't need a babysitter, and he sure as hell didn't need guards. Jay got the impression those words didn't come directly from Sonny.

Sonny just seemed to disconnect. What he did during the day, Jay didn't know since Sonny refused to have Dee come over or anyone else. He was asleep when Jay would leave for work in the morning and asleep when Jay came home late at night.

Nothing much was getting done in the house, either. Dishes piled in the sink. Laundry overflowed. Jay tried not to push too hard but even the simplest comments were either met with rage, or Sonny would walk away and ignore him. Things had to get better, Jay reassured himself, and was glad when he finally had a night off.

Jay knocked at Sonny's bedroom door. "Hey, partner, I'm home tonight. Wanna go for a walk or maybe get a pizza?"

Sonny lay on his bed, stared up at the ceiling, and didn't even look at Jay. "No," he grunted deep in his throat.

"You didn't even hear the other choice. How about we get Chinese? Or that Italian place you like?"

"No," Sonny said, still without eye contact.

"You've been really moody lately. I mean, you sit in here all night staring at the ceiling or out the window. You don't want to go anyplace or do anything. What's wrong? We used to talk."

"I go places. Myra and I went to the beach. We walked around the mall. We even went to a bar."

"A bar? Sonny...."

"What?" Sonny finally glanced at Jay. "Now I can't go to a damn bar? I'm old enough. I'm not a kid. And you're not my father."

"I know I'm not your damn father. I don't want to be."

"And you don't want to be...my friend either."

"Yes, I do," Jay said.

"You're never here."

"I'm here right now."

Sonny smirked. "Big. Fuckin'. Deal."

"Hey, watch the language."

"Screw you," Sonny said and slid off the bed.

"Sonny. Come on. Things were going good."

"For you. I'm bored."

"Okay. Let's do something."

"I am," Sonny said and snatched his car keys.

"Whoa. Where you going?"

Sonny headed for the door. "Out."

"Out? Now? Like hell." Jay blocked the way.

"Move."

"We need to talk."

"Get out of my way," Sonny warned with a look that was the harshest Jay had ever seen.

"I tell you what, buddy. You stay. I'll go." With long strides to the hall, Jay grabbed his keys and slammed the door behind him.

* * *

"Name your poison, Detective," Crocket LaSalle said with a snicker.

Jay slipped onto the bar stool. "Beer," he said. "And give me a shot with that." He put his head in his hands and let out a long sigh.

"You want a pillow, too? So you can lay your sad, pathetic looking face on it? Or how about a rope to hang yourself? Come on, man, I don't need someone depressed in here. You're bringing down my establishment."

Jay glanced around the tavern. There were two men already passed out and lying nose down at a table while three other men tossed back shots, barely talked, and played pool. "Yeah. Looks like everyone's having one hell of a good time."

"What's wrong? Trouble with Junior? Tough to raise younguns' nowadays."

"Don't start with me. If I tell one more person I'm not Sonny's father, I swear I'll draw my gun."

Crocket put up his palms. "Don't shoot, Sarge. Talk like that is bad biz. So, what gives?"

Jay gulped the shot of whiskey. "Sonny."

"Do tell," Crocket said and smacked his lips.

"He's…different."

"No foolin'?"

"Give me another one," Jay said and slid the shot glass to Crocket.

"You sure? You don't hold your liquor so good."

"Just do it," Jay said.

"So. Sonny's the problem, huh? Well, if it makes you feel better, I hear that slamming your head into a rock after getting plowed over by a speeding car can do that kind of shit."

"I don't mean that. Well, yeah. That. But…." Jay took a long sip of the foamy beer and shook his head. "It's more than that. A lot more."

Crocket poured another shot and wiped the top of the bar. "Psycho Doc is in and you're in luck. I got a discount this week. Talk."

Jay tossed back the shot. "I wish I could," he said. The whiskey burned his throat. He sucked down his beer to cool the heat.

"You were doing all right."

"That's just it," Jay said. He smacked his hand on the wood bar. "I was. We were. And now. This. Like nothing matters. Not before. Not lately. Not now. It's all…for shit. Everything."

"Right. Only, I ain't following," Crocket said.

"Me either." Jay gulped the last of the beer. "Me either. I'm not following this whole thing. I did all right, didn't I? Five years of all right. And for what? We were good together. Damn good. But no, I couldn't be satisfied with just that. No. I had to mess it all up. I had to go and tell him….But now I can't tell him. I want to tell him. I'm messing up this whole damn thing. And why? Because I can't tell him…." He glanced up at Crocket.

Crocket listened with his head propped in his hands. "Go on. You had to go and tell him, and now you can't."

Jay swallowed the rest of what he almost let slip.

"Can't tell him what?" Crocket said. "You was on a roll."

"Another beer," Jay said and turned to face the dismal crowd.

"For the record, my blond friend with a badge, you didn't mess up. You stuck by Sonny, and that counts for something. None too many I know would have done the same. Boy's lucky to have ya."

"I agree," Jay said. "Damn lucky. Ingrate." He smacked the bar again. "That's what he is. Slamming doors. Throwing my books. *Mine*. He doesn't read. Never did. Pissed because I have to work. You have any idea what the hospital bills look like? The national debt pales in comparison. Still haven't heard about the lawsuit. And I'm the one who handled that too. Wanted to make sure he was taken care of." Jay heard the bitterness in his own voice. "As if he even cares. No. Not the great Santini. Yelling at me. Ready to run out of the house. So I leave. And why? 'Cause he doesn't have a clue where to go or how to get there. That's why. Oh, he'd take off and not worry about anything. Not even how the hell to get home. And then what? Have everybody blame me? I should have transferred when I had the chance. Let him marry that bitch, Emma. Let her take him to goddamn Country Club dinners and pretend to be something he wasn't. But no. I wanted him to be happy." Jay sneered. "Happy. That's a joke. So you know what I did?"

"What?" Crocket said.

"I tell him…." Jay stopped.

"Tell him what?"

Jay froze for a long moment.

"What?" Crocket said.

"I-I tell him that she wants to change him, and he was a good cop and shouldn't let anyone change him. That's what I said."

Crocket went back to wiping the bar. "Guess he listened. He didn't marry her. Moved in with you instead."

"That's right. I said let's get a better place away from all the mud we crawl in all day long. And then you know what happens? I put up with his loud music. His leftover pizza stinking up the frig. His towels tossed all over the place. And for what? So a car with a drunk driver could smash it all to bits." Jay pushed aside the beer. "That's life. Full of damn surprises."

"Yep. Full of 'em." Crocket took the half empty beer bottle and tossed it in the trash. "Now what?"

"Now I go home. With all the other freaking surprises that I know are coming. I put on a smile and stand up straight."

"'Cause it's what you do, Detective. No sense trying to change now."

"That's right."

"Couldn't even if you tried. You and Sonny are like salt and pepper. Like butter and popcorn. Like nails and a hammer. A jaybird and a sunny day – "

"You talk too much," Jay said.

Crocket handed Jay a cup of coffee. "Better drink this before you go. It's hot, and it's strong. Then you can go home so you can tell him what you can't tell him or was it not tell him what you shouldn't have told him? Now I'm mixed up."

"Join the club," Jay said.

23

The next morning Jay was up and ready to leave for work while Sonny was still in bed. He wrote a quick note – *Sonny, Let's talk tonight. J.* He pinned it next to the household chore list that Sonny never bothered with anymore.

The twenty minute drive to work didn't seem long enough. With a heavy sigh, Jay locked his car doors and labored into the police station.

In the detectives' squad room a tall, well-dressed black man relaxed by the coffee maker, talking with Captain Colby.

Colby patted the man on the back and said, "There he is now. Detective Jamison? Meet Detective Bruce Harrison. Harrison's from Miami Metro. He's a new transfer."

"Hi," Jay said and shook the man's hand.

"Good to be here," Bruce said. He stood as tall as Jay, long in the torso, and looked to be about Jay's age. His hair was trimmed short, and everything about him appeared neat, from his clean shaven face down to his two-piece black suit and polished black Italian leather shoes. "I've heard a lot about you." Harrison smiled a toothy grin.

"Harrison transferred here about a month ago," Colby said. "He's been in Vice."

"I was really sorry to hear about your partner," Harrison said. "Detective Santini has an amazing reputation. You do, too. I never officially met him. Wish I had. But I've heard about the cases you both worked." He smiled again and offered his hand. "I'm looking forward to learning from the best."

Jay looked down at the offering and then at Colby who cleared his throat and said, "Harrison's your new partner."

"My what?" Jay said.

Colby cleared his throat again and from one corner of his mouth said, "Your partner. We discussed this." He patted Harrison on the shoulder. "Detective Weiss will show you around the office. Jamison? My office. Now."

"This is a joke, right?" Jay said while Colby shut the office door.

"We already talked about this," Colby said, his voice gruff. "Harrison showed a lot of promise in Miami, and while he was in Vice. We're lucky we got him. He's still wet behind the ears, but you can work with him."

"I can? No, I can't."

"Jamison," Colby barked. Jay swore the glass window behind the captain rattled. "It's time."

"I don't agree."

"This is an order. That's it. Harrison's nervous enough about filling in as your partner."

"Sorry. He'll have to manage his own confidence level. I've got a shitload of cases, and I've handled them just fine on my own."

"You know how many favors I had to call in?" Colby said.

"Ask for a refund. Send him back to Vice."

"What part about this being an order didn't you hear?" Colby said. "Maybe I'm not speaking loudly enough. Perhaps you'd like something in writing along with a suspension slip. Or better. A four week stint as crossing guard." When Jay lowered his head, Colby eased a bit. "Look, son, I know this part is tough. It always is. You said yourself you knew it had to be done."

"Yes, but… the timing is bad. It's too – "

"Soon? It's not. We could wait for another month or two, even three, and it would feel the same. Give him a chance. He's a quiet man with a good record, and he's eager to work with you. He's only seen you and Sonny from a distance when he first got here. Help him out. You know what it's like to be the new guy and to try and replace someone else."

"He won't replace Sonny," Jay said.

"You know what I mean. Take him around. Introduce him. Start with Crocket's place. That should give him one hell of an idea. But, don't, and I mean *don't*, scare him off. Now get out of here and be professional."

* * *

Sonny rolled out of bed and headed for the kitchen.

"Jay?" he called.

Garbage bag by the door, no coffee made. He went in Jay's bedroom.

In Jay's unmade bed and on the nightstand, he found medical journals and pamphlets all on the subject of traumatic brain injuries and brain damage. Some pages were folded down, and Jay had underlined some paragraphs. *Broad spectrum of symptoms contribute to the complexity. Irrational thought patterns. No sense of right or wrong. Reckless behavior. Disinhibition. Inability to understand or express emotions.*

Sonny ripped one of the articles in two. The rest he tossed on the floor.

He grabbed his car keys and headed out the door. He never saw the note pinned to the refrigerator. The words Jay had highlighted in the journal flashed in his mind.

* * *

"Jay, this is a surprise," Dee said and hugged him. She looked Bruce Harrison up and down with lukewarm interest. "Who's the suit?"

"Dee Santiago," Jay said, "meet Bruce Harrison. He's from Miami."

"Miami? I have an aunt who lives there. Lucy Santiago. You know her?" Dee said.

"Sorry. No," Bruce said.

"From Miami, huh? Everybody knows Aunt Lucy." Dee eyed Bruce.

"I went to the Academy there," Bruce said. "Worked for Metro about six months. Mostly homicide. If she wasn't dead or suspected of killing someone, I haven't heard of her. Which," he smiled with bright white teeth, "is a good thing when you think about it." His smile dissolved under Dee's stare. "Isn't it?"

"Where's Crocket?" Jay said.

"On another one of his dealings," Dee said. "Who knows? Guns. Booze. Bodies."

Nervously, Jay chuckled. "She's kidding," he said.

"Am I?" Dee said. "So, how's Sonny?" She eyed Bruce again and added, "Sonny is Jay's partner. His left hand actually. Sonny's left handed so… makes sense, don't you think? Sonny's the best damn cop there is. Right, Jay?"

Jay ran his fingers through his hair. "He knows who Sonny is."

"You've heard of him? Down there? In Miami?" Dee said. "But you never heard of Lucy? Interesting."

"Quit giving him the third degree," Jay said. "She doesn't even have an Aunt Lucy. Dee, Bruce is my new partner," Jay flinched from her icy gaze.

"Your new what?" Dee said. "Sorry, Jamison. We had a crowd last night, and my ears are still ringing."

"You heard me," Jay said.

"Excuse us, Officer Harry." Dee grabbed Jay by the arm. She yanked him to the kitchen and pushed him through the door. "What the hell are you doing? New partner? Really?"

"It's not my choice," Jay said.

"Then I'll call Colby and – "

"Put down the damn phone. Geez. You. Sonny. Colby. You're all driving me nuts. Look, I'm not crazy about this either, but let's face it. Sonny is on permanent disability at least for now. And that word – now – could be a long time. You've spent time with him. Is he anywhere near coming back to the force? Could you see him on the streets? I hate facing it just like you, but that's how it is. For now. So help me out, huh? Don't make it tougher. I already had an argument with Sonny last night. I don't need one with you."

"Yeah. Crocket mentioned you were in, and your chin was down to the floor."

"Sonny is…*was* doing better. I really felt like we were making progress. Like *he* was…."

"On the road to recovery?" Dee said. "Jay, you know that isn't going to happen."

"All I know is that now something is off, and I don't know why."

"You think it's all the hours you're working?"

Jay rubbed the back of his neck. "Probably hasn't helped."

"He misses you," Dee said.

He bit his bottom lip and thought, God, I miss him too. Avoiding Dee's eyes, he said, "This is why it's good to have Bruce. I can cut back a little. Two people chasing the nasties are better than one."

"Well...." Dee considered it. "If it helps you and gets you home to Sonny...then fine. But does he have to wear those fancy suits? Jay, he'll stick out like a pimp hanging around Mickey Mouse's Clubhouse."

"I'll talk to him about toning it down." Jay bent and kissed Dee on the cheek. "Thanks, sugar. I knew I could count on you."

"Jay, this thing about Sonny and recovery," Dee said, "tell me you don't think he'll ever really remember."

"Let's talk about it later," Jay said and turned for the door.

Dee took his arm. "You can't fool yourself."

"I'm not." Jay sighed. "Look, I've read all there is but I can't just accept it. You don't have to say it. But my head fights what my heart believes and then I go back and forth again. All I know for sure is this. I can't...I *won't* give up hope."

* * *

"So, what exactly do you have in mind?" Myra Turner said.

"Get off work. Let's hang out," Sonny said.

Myra placed some clean towels in a rack. "Well, it is slow today. Albert only has two more patients." She smiled and trailed her hand slowly back and forth across Sonny's chest. "But you better make it worth my while. You haven't exactly been Mr. Thrills."

Sonny creased his dark brows. "Who?"

Myra exhaled a heavy sigh. "I mean, we never do anything."

"I got drunk with you the other day."

"Drunk and high," Myra said. "You're smoking all my good stuff. But when I try to kiss you, you turn off. I've never had to work so hard. Am I losing my touch? Or maybe," she stepped in close, "you aren't into girls."

Sonny took her hands off his chest. "I like girls fine," he said with a hard glare.

"You're hurting me." Myra pouted. "I was just kidding. Don't give me the death stare. It creeps me out when you do that. You know, Albert said

I should stay away from you. He said you're...dangerous. Are you?" She stepped close again. "Dangerous?"

"Let's find out," Sonny said, his warm breath on her face.

"Mm-hmm. I'll meet you downstairs. But I'll have to follow you in my car. I have to be up early for work tomorrow."

* * *

"See you tomorrow, Bruce," Jay said outside of Smiley's. "Don't let Dee intimidate you. She's really a lot sweeter than she lets on, and if she likes you, she's the best one to have on your side."

"Listen," Bruce said, "I know I can't replace Sonny. And, man, I won't even pretend I can. I just want to learn from the best and fit in. Introduce me to the streets. I won't let you down."

Jay nodded. "Fair enough. Don't get lost getting out of here. Take a right at the next corner. Not a left. You'll be on the evening news if you do." He laughed and, as Bruce drove down the street, he waved.

Back inside the tavern, Jay rubbed his eyes against the cigarette smoke and plopped on a bar stool. He rested his head in both hands. Dee came behind the bar, and he tried for some kind of grin.

"Beer," she said, "or are you trying shots again tonight?"

Jay gave her a bitter smirk. "No shots. Just beer." He glanced around. "So Crocket's off again? Do you ever ask him where he goes?"

"So long as he don't bring it here, there isn't much I can do. His life insurance is up to date. I'm the beneficiary."

"Don't think I want to know that just in case."

"In case he's murdered and all fingers point to me? I got my own con-nections. You always said, if they can't find a body, they can't try you for murder."

Jay covered his ears. "Please. There's only so much I can claim I didn't hear." He laughed and looked at Dee. "That felt good. It's been awhile."

"So, how is Sonny? Really? We started to bond, you know. He was up to almost two syllable words with me."

"He's moodier. Quieter."

"Impossible. He'd have to be mute."

"Almost. I get that maybe he's upset with me working so much, but come on. Why can't he just talk to me?"

"That was the old Sonny."

"No. Sonny was starting to open up. Oh, shit." Jay looked at his watch. "I left Sonny a note that I wanted to talk tonight. I'll call him, pick up a pizza, and maybe I can get him to open up again."

* * *

Sonny chugged his fourth beer and inhaled a deep drag from the second joint Myra handed him. They sat in the parked Mustang. Windows cracked slightly didn't help – the car was filled with smoke.

In the passenger seat, Myra edged as close to Sonny as the T-stick between them would allow. It wasn't nearly as close as she wanted. "Can't we take this party inside?"

"I like it out here," Sonny said. His eyelids droopy, he heard himself giggle. "This shit is good." He took a longer hit and sucked back the smoke.

"You said that. Three times already," Myra said. "You're gonna have to start chipping in some money. This shit isn't cheap." She shook her head when Sonny offered the rolled cigarette. "I have to drive."

Sonny laughed, and a thick puff of smoke blew out of his mouth. "You have to drive." He laughed again as he said each word slowly, "Drive. Drive," and felt the V vibrate on his lower lip.

"You are so wasted," Myra said and purred close to his ear. She rubbed her hand down his chest and further between his legs. The lump in Sonny's groin made her grin harder and squeeze a bit more.

Sonny moved her hand. "You sure you don't want some? This shit is good."

"What gives, Sonny?" Myra whined. "I've seen you almost every day. You smoke my weed and drink my beer, but you never touch me. Aren't I pretty? Don't you like me?"

"I like you," Sonny said.

"Then what gives?" Myra eyed him. "You like to get high, huh?"

Sonny nodded. "Makes my head hum. Hummmm," he said and snorted.

"And sleepy. And hungry. And dull. Come on. If I don't start having fun soon, I'm leaving." She watched him suck down his beer and sighed. "Let's move to the backseat."

Sonny scrunched his face. "What for?"

"Oh for...." She tossed up her hands in defeat and then looked at him in a new way. "Hold on. Wait a minute. I forgot. You're brain damaged."

"Fuck you," Sonny said, and then he snickered. "Brain damaged. Who the fuck cares if I got a friggin' hole in my friggin' head?"

Myra sat up straight "The part of your brain. The part that got bashed. It means you have no memories of...of anything. Like high school. Your first date. Do you even remember the first girl you kissed?"

Sonny shrugged. "Nope." He laughed and popped his lips. "Nope, nope. Pa."

"So that means...." Myra got a devilish glint in her eyes. "You don't remember ever making love to a woman. Which makes you...a virgin." She laughed. "You're a virgin."

"Screw you," Sonny said.

"And that's why." She stared at him for a moment. "You came out of the coma but maybe...maybe something else didn't. Yet." She cupped Sonny's groin and once more squeezed gently. "Wakey, wakey. Time to play. Unless...." She looked up at him. "You're scared?"

* * *

Jay drove down the street with Dee beside him.

"Thanks for coming with me," he said. "Maybe with you here, Sonny won't run off."

"I wouldn't bet on that," Dee said.

"I just think both of us talking to him – "

"Bull, Jamison. You're just afraid of what you might let slip."

Jay snapped his head toward the woman. "Wh-what do you mean?"

"Calm down. You're as tense as Crocket's grip on a ten dollar bill. I just meant you can have a temper, too. And when he gets stubborn, you get mad. And when people get mad they say things they don't always mean. Not that you would. You just want to be sure I'm there to referee."

Jay relaxed. "I don't want him to feel like we're ganging up on him. I plan to do most of the talking. But, yeah. If you see either of us start to raise our voices, do that thing you do."

"What thing?" Dee said.

"That sweet oh-come-on-sugar-let's-just-relax thing you do. And food. Offer him food."

"He hates my cooking. I made him a grilled cheese last week and he spit it out."

"Offer him more pizza," Jay said. He glanced at his watch. "I don't know where the hell he is. He had therapy today, but he should have been home by now. He doesn't know that many places to go. I should've never let him have those damn car keys."

"Right. Lock him in his room. Please, Jay, whatever you do, don't say that to Sonny. He isn't a kid. He hates to be treated like one. We have to encourage him. Tell him it's okay to go out. But he needs to let us know. He needs to respect…oh my God. I sound like my mother."

"Maybe you better not say anything. Just keep pushing the food. I think I know what to say." Jay flipped the blinker on and turned onto Tremont Drive.

* * *

In the backseat of the Mustang, Myra put her mouth to Sonny's lips. Sonny stalled. The kiss she planted was different than the way she kissed him in the past. This time it was more firm and determined. He jerked back a bit but she was not giving up, and with his face held between both her palms, she prevailed.

He accepted the kiss and even lingered in it. His head buzzed, and his blood ran hot. There was an ache between his legs that throbbed. He took over and kissed her hard.

"Easy, baby," Myra coached. "Go a little slower,"

Sonny licked his lips before he placed them back on hers. He moved to the rhythm of her mouth. Turning his head from side to side, he was like an engine being revved. His lips, pressed firm to hers, were on fire. He groped her hair. The strands he tasted in his mouth slowed him for a moment until he pulled her hair back. She fisted his short hair in return and pulled it. It stung, but the pain excited him. He had never known anything like this. He could feel the blood race through his veins and his hands grab at her body.

"You taste so good," Myra said. She drove her tongue into his mouth and barely let him up for air. "This is fun? Isn't it?" she said while he lapped at her neck and kissed her chin. "You. Me. This is really nice, isn't it?" She grinned. He trailed his mouth over her lips. "That's it, baby. Let yourself go. Let Myra teach you, okay?"

His frenzy stopped with the rolling wave he suddenly felt. Gravity gave way, and his insides turned. He held her back.

"Wait. Wait," he said. His eyes were mere slits. "I feel…weird."

"That's because you want me," Myra enticed. "Here, baby, take a drink." She placed the bottle of beer to his mouth. Sonny chugged, almost choked, and hardly had time to swallow before Myra's mouth was on his again. Sonny groaned. She swirled her tongue around his, and he began to breathe harder. She stopped for a moment. It confused him. She smiled coyly and unbuttoned her blouse, lowered her bra straps and smiled bigger when Sonny licked his lips.

"Touch me," Myra whispered.

Sonny gazed at the breasts that rose and fell before him. Soft, round flesh with tiny goosebumps. Myra took his hand and placed it on her. Sonny squeezed the mound in his palm.

"Easy, baby. Not so hard. Relax." Myra guided his hand gently and nodded. "Like that."

Sonny massaged the flesh the way she showed him, surprised by the supple firmness and the desire it stirred deep within him. He played her right nipple, twirling it between his fingers and watched it rise and get hard. When she moved his head downward and placed her breast to his lips, he wasn't sure what she wanted, but, as the nipple teased his moist lips, he sucked it in with a sudden lust woken by greed.

His jaw open wide, her breast filled his mouth. He swirled his tongue around the raised nipple and fed on that. She groaned. He suckled.

Myra was breathless. She removed one breast wet and dripping out of his mouth and offered the other. Sonny savored the ripeness.

Myra's hair dangled across her face and stuck to Sonny's damp cheek. It tickled, and he scratched. Myra arched her back and offered as much of her bare chest as possible.

Sonny's hands ran up and down her back. He held her hips, and she rocked back and forth on his lap.

She made him drink more beer and, breathing hard, said, "Now let's see what you've got." She gripped his groin. "Nice," she hummed. "He's out of the coma now, doctor, and I bet he wants to come out and play too." She fumbled with the zipper of his pants.

Sonny fisted both breasts and squeezed them together while he glided his tongue across the flesh from one eager nipple to another. His lick impatient, and when, Myra pulled his hair and forced him to face her, his mouth was overpowered once more by hers.

She kissed him while she reached down into his pants and gripped him.

Sonny's eyes sprang open with the feel of her grasp. His head flung back. The sensation of being touched caused him to moan. He had never been touched there before except for his own hand. His mouth and eyes opened wide with the newness of it all, and he was fascinated by the urge he felt.

"You like that?" Myra said. "You feel so damn good. I bet you taste even better." She leaned into him and put her face to Sonny's neck where she began to suck the flesh like a starving man-eater. "You're so damn hot," she whispered.

Breathing hard, Sonny said, "I am? I don't think – "

"Shh," she said. "Don't think. Just let Myra teach you. I'll show you all the things you can do." Her hand caressed him, and with his head rested against the backseat, his lips curled into a roguish grin.

* * *

"Sonny?" Jay called out in the quiet house. He tossed his keys on the side table and yelled down the hall. "Sonny?"

"I'll put the pizza in the kitchen," Dee said.

"Hey? Partner?" Jay said. "I'm home and I got a surprise." He went into Sonny's dark room and then the bathroom. He came back scratching his head. Opening the front door, he glanced outside and noticed the lime green four door Subaru parked on the street.

"Is he home?" Dee said.

"I don't see him."

"Now, don't go call the Marines yet. Is his car here?"

"I don't know," Jay said. He headed for the garage.

* * *

Myra's blouse hung off her shoulders. Her bra undone. Sonny mouth was nuzzled between the deep crevice of her breasts.

"Now you know what that part of a woman feels like," she said. "There's a lot more I can show you." She clasped both sides of his face and lifted his head. "A hell of a lot more." She placed a long kiss on his mouth.

Sonny groaned deep in his throat. One hand ran up and down her bare thigh. The other palmed her delicate breast.

Myra reached down and began to unsnap his pants. "Let's get these off, baby. You're my sweet, innocent virgin, and it's time for another lesson."

Sonny nodded, and he forced his mouth to form the words. "Another lesson." Gravity fluctuated. Loops, whirls, buzzing in his head, he fought with the need to focus and the urge to pass out.

Myra worked the snap on his jeans. The prize she wanted bulged. "Come on, baby," she purred. "Stay with me."

"I'm with ya," Sonny mumbled.

* * *

Jay opened the side door of the garage. The room was filled with a light odor of smoke and a scent he recognized. The Mustang was parked, its windows foggy, and the car rocked.

"What the – " Jay pulled open the driver side door. "What in the hell?"

Myra, her skirt up to her crotch, straddled Sonny in the backseat. She had her hand down his pants and her mouth sealed to his.

Jay pulled the bucket seat forward and reached in to yank Myra off Sonny's lap.

"Hey," Myra screamed as she half fell, half stumbled out the door.

"What the hell are you doing?" Jay shouted. He looked back at Sonny. The man's zipper down, his face red and his lips swollen. "Get out of there. Now," he shouted again.

Sonny chuckled. "Whoa, man. Don't shout." He tripped getting out and fell into Jay's arms.

Jay caught him and forced him to his feet. "You're drunk. And high. Are you nuts? You're a cop."

"Cop. Cop. Cop," Sonny said and giggled. "You a cop. She a cop. Me a....No. Wait. No cop." He shook his head vehemently and laughed again.

"Get inside," Jay ordered. He nudged Sonny ahead of him. "And you," he turned and pointed at Myra, "get out of here."

"I don't have to listen to you," Myra said, holding her blouse together and lowering her skirt. "He isn't some damn kid. He's a grown man."

"That's right," Sonny slurred through half-closed eyelids. "I'm...a man." He laughed again and burped.

"Are *you* drunk too?" Jay asked Myra.

"Of course not," Myra said.

"Then go. That your car out front? Use it."

Dee came into the room. "Whoa. Ho," she said at the sight of Sonny's pants undone and Myra's breast exposed.

Sonny staggered to the door. "Hey there," he slobbered and made a half wave in the air. "We were having a party."

"I can see that," Dee said and looked at Jay's boiling face. "Um. Party's over. Time to come inside."

"No," Sonny said and nearly tipped. "Myra was teaching me...showing me...something. What was it?" He looked at her through slits. "Oh yeah. Her tits. Damn." He teetered. "The whole room is moving. Make it stop moving."

"Sonny, we have pizza," Dee said and shrugged when Jay eyed her.

"Pizza? Yeah? Man, I'm hungry. I ain't never been so hungry, have I, Jay? Nope. Don't think so."

"You," Jay said to Myra through gritted teeth, "leave." He took Sonny by the arm before the man ran into the wall and led him to the house.

Sonny muttered all the way. "We were having a party. Myra says I'm hot."

Myra began to follow. Dee stepped in her way.

"You heard him," Dee said. "Leave."

"I will if Sonny asks me too. He isn't a child. You and Jay treat him like one. Trust me, lady. He isn't."

"And trust me, girly," Dee said. "You better get your skinny ass outta here."

"Don't call me a girl," Myra said and buttoned her blouse.

"You're right. You aren't a girl. You're just like those women who hang around the corner near my bar. Friends of yours?"

"Get out of my way," Myra said, nose to nose with Dee.

Dee didn't budge. "You leave my boys alone. You got that? Unless you don't want one strand of hair left on that pretty head of yours. Now," Dee said and took Myra by the elbow, "get to your car. Drive to your house. Take a bath with ice cubes. It always works for me when I get hot and bothered. And then thank God Jay didn't arrest you for supplying drugs. That was your pot, right? I bet if he searched you, he'd find more, wouldn't he?"

Myra yanked her arm free. "I'm going," she said. "But Michael and I are in love. You can't stop us."

"Love? Girl – and I use that word very loosely – you should be ashamed of yourself. You took advantage of a young man who's still recuperating. I wonder what your boss would think of that?"

"Don't threaten me," Myra said, next to her car.

"Oh, you dumb bimbo," Dee said. "I already did. Now go."

* * *

"I can't believe this," Jay said. He had a strong hold on Sonny while he led him down the hall. But Sonny was tipsy and kept tripping and banging into the wall. A couple of times Jay almost lost his balance. Finally, he managed to get Sonny into the bedroom.

"You smell like a bar, for Christ's sake," Jay said. "How long have you been getting high? Is that why you've been so damn miserable? Why you're sleeping till noon? Why you lost interest in just about everything?"

"You spit when you're mad," Sonny said with a squeaky giggle. "I'm a virgin," he announced as Jay lowered him to his bed. "Myra says I'm hot." He laughed and squinted at Jay. "I wasn't hot. I don't get hot. Nerve damage, I think. Can't feel the cold either. I was sweating a little. But… whoa. This bed is moving. Why's it moving?" He groaned. "Jay? Make it stop moving, huh?"

"I should clean the damn floor with you, you know that? Getting drunk. High. Jesus, Sonny, we're cops."

"No," Sonny said and shook his head back and forth over and over again. "I'm not a damn cop. Never been a damn cop. Don't know what a damn cop is." He sat up and tried to steady himself. "Could you make this damn bed stop rocking?"

"You *are* a cop. Were a cop. And if you ever plan to be one again – "

"I don't. Don't you get it? I'm fuckin' damaged. A pile of shit is smarter than me. Fuck. I can't even get this room to stop spinning."

"Jay," Dee said from the doorway, "you need any help?"

Sonny pointed toward her and then at Jay. "You're not my mother. And you're not my father," he slurred. "I'm a grown man, and I don't need a babysitter. Or anybody else. I'm…." He flopped back on the bed, eyes closed and mouth slightly open.

"Stoned out of your mind," Jay said. He pulled off Sonny's shoes and slipped off his pants. "Is that a hickey?" He turned Sonny's head to look at the huge red welt on his neck and then harshly slid Sonny back on the bed. Lifting Sonny's legs onto the mattress, he covered him with a blanket. "Sleep it off. Tomorrow I'll kill you." Jay went to the door, turned once more to look at the passed-out lump, and shut off the light.

"I got Myra out of here. Bitch," Dee said. "I think we have a problem."

"You think?" Jay said and ran both hands through his hair.

"I think the cage has been opened, and the tiger's been let loose."

"No kidding. You still think Myra is harmless? A professional who's experienced?"

"Oh, she's a professional all right. And very experienced."

24

J ay heard a groan, shuffling of feet, and a thud followed by a hissed, "Shit," and then Sonny appeared. In the bright morning light, Sonny stumbled into the living room. He leaned against the wall, shook his head and all the while kept his eyes shut.

From the couch where Jay sat, he glared at the man who looked like he'd been run over by a Mac truck.

"Morning," Jay said, his tone as cutting as his glare.

Sonny put up a warning hand and labored into the kitchen.

Water turned on, Sonny spit, and when Jay went into the kitchen, Sonny's head was soaking wet.

Jay took a towel and was ready to place it on Sonny's damp hair, but Sonny backed away. Jay tossed him the towel. "You're dripping all over the place."

Sonny squinted at him. He ignored the towel on the floor and went to the refrigerator where he grabbed a carton of milk and drank from it.

Jay slammed a glass on the counter, and the bang made Sonny cringe.

"Use a damn glass," Jay said. "You're not a pig."

Sonny shuffled to the table, sat and laid his whole face in his arms. "My head. Hurts."

"Really?"

Muffled, Sonny said, "I need…my medicine."

"You don't have a migraine, genius. You have a hangover," Jay snarled. "And whatever you're feeling? You deserve." In a moment of sour pity, Jay placed a cup of coffee next to Sonny and slammed a bottle of aspirin beside it. "Here. Take two and don't choke. I'd hate to see you suffer more."

"What the hell is your problem?" Sonny said, lifting his ailing head.

Jay scoffed. "You're joking, right? I find you in the backseat of the Mustang, half dressed, for Christ's sake. With a nearly naked woman straddling you, and you ask me what's wrong?"

"Jealous?" Sonny said and swallowed some coffee.

Jay's face burned with contempt.

"You little shit," he hissed. "You were drunk and stoned. *Stoned.* You're a cop."

"I'm not a goddamn cop. You are. So fucking arrest me. I don't give a shit."

"You were stoned out of your mind."

"No shit?" Sonny shrilled. "Wow. You *are* a cop."

"Listen to me," Jay said, taking a deep breath and exhaling the urge to scream. "You never did drugs. You don't do drugs. You never *will* do drugs. Got it?"

Sonny inched bloodshot eyes upwards. Jay thought if Sonny could have spit fire, he would have.

"Got it?" Sonny said, his voice unnaturally calm for a second. "Well get this. I'm not him. He's dead. *Dead,*" he shrieked and stepped closer, "you son of a bitch. Got it? Dead."

"Stop saying that. You aren't dead. You're right here."

"No. You want *him* to be right here. He's not. I am."

"Sonny, come on. We were doing okay. What happened?"

"Okay?" Sonny squeaked. "You think so? You. You go off to work. You're too busy for me. You don't give a shit about anything, and you say *we* were doing okay?"

"I have to work," Jay said.

"Yeah. It's better to play with your buddies then hang out with a dumbass brain damaged shit like me."

"Stop it. You keep using that as an excuse. It's not. I never –"

"You always use it as an excuse to treat me like a kid. To tell me what to do and when to do it. You make me a goddamn list, and I'm supposed to be a good boy and follow what you say. I'm not your trained dog."

"I never said…I know you're not. But doing what you did last night? That was plain stupid."

"Oh well." Sonny flapped his arms. "Guess you finally figured it out." He turned to go out of the room, but Jay took hold of his arm. Sonny looked down at the touch like it was poison. "Don't," he growled, "touch me."

"Or what? You gonna punch me? Is that what comes next?"

Sonny unclenched his fist and yanked his arm away. "Leave me alone. You're good at that."

"If I leave you alone, then what, huh? So far you've done a great job."

"Fuck you," Sonny said and headed to his bedroom.

Jay held the door before Sonny could slam it. "Oh, no. Not this time, pal. No hiding. Let's get this fixed."

"Fixed?" Sonny huffed. "How? You got a new brain somewhere?"

"Stop saying that shit," Jay said. "You hide behind that like it makes up for everything."

"I hate you," Sonny said, his face cold as steel. "I really hate you."

"Do you? Really? 'Cause I love…I care about you."

"Screw you. Go to work. Leave me alone." Sonny pushed past Jay.

"New rule," Jay said. "No more drugs and no more Myra." He followed quickly behind Sonny's angry steps.

Sonny turned with a vengeance Jay had never seen. "New rule? I'm sick of your fucking rules. Every fucking one of them. Including" – he picked up a bowl with apples – "no throwing food." He sent the bowl flying. It smashed into the wall, and glass and apples scattered on the floor. "I'm outta here," he announced and headed for the door.

"Oh, no," Jay said and grabbed Sonny's arm. "Go ahead. Hit me. But you will clean up that mess, and you won't do drugs or see that slut again."

"Slut? Why? Because she wanted to kiss me? Because she likes me? You can't tell me what to do. You're not – "

Jay pointed a finger and warned, "So help me. If you say father, I'll blow. I am *not* your parent. Trust me, buddy, I've been a lot of things to you, and that isn't one of them."

"Get off me," Sonny said and pulled his arm away.

"As long as you live here…." Jay stopped himself.

"I won't live here. I'll leave."

"And go where?"

"Myra said I can stay with her."

"Oh, that would be perfect. Then you can sit around all day drinking beer and getting high. Then you can be like a hundred other losers making choices that morons do."

"Loser? Now I'm a loser and a moron?" Sonny rushed to Jay's bedroom and came back with an armful of medical articles and journals. "Why? Because that's what it says in here? 'Cause Dixon said so? Well, fuck you and all this crap." He flung the books into the air. "Go read about that." He went to the door again.

"Sonny?" Jay called, his voice tired and shaky.

Sonny stopped with his hand on the doorknob, but he didn't turn.

"How do you feel about me?" Jay said. "Really feel? About me? Us?"

If Sonny had turned, he might have seen the desperation and the longing in Jay's eyes. But he didn't. He paused for a moment looking at the knob and quietly said, "Go to hell, Jamison," before he jerked the door open.

"Sonny, you can't drive like this," Jay shouted to him.

"I'm going for a walk. Leave me alone," Sonny said. "Maybe a damn bus will run me over this time." He rushed down the steps toward the street.

Jay watched him go while tears he fought the whole time gathered. "Well, you can't say they didn't tell you this would be hard." He scoffed. "Hard? How about impossible."

He shut the door, and with a heavy, trembling breath, sat like a dead weight in the chair. Sweeping his hands down his face, he shook his head. "I hoped. I wanted him to…to come back to me. On his own. To remember…to at least realize…he loved me. And now?" He glanced at the broken bowl and the foreboding silence. "Now what?" He looked at the door. "Now what do I do?"

Don't put pressure on him, he heard Dr. Dixon say. *Don't tell him the truth. What if he runs from you?* Well, Doc? Guess who's running now? He doesn't even know and he's running.

Jay sighed, sitting in the middle of the empty house. "Five years of fantasizing. Hoping. Praying. Hiding. Six months living the dream, and now? Alone again." Tears washed down his cheeks, and he let out another long breath. He found himself in the same chair where he had sat the day he told Sonny the truth – that he was in love with him. The location was different but the room was decorated with the same bookcase he leaned on and the same coffee table where Sonny sat that afternoon. Sonny had run out the door that day too.

Jay faced the closed door, but this time it didn't burst open.

Funny, he thought, how things come full circle...almost.

* * *

Sonny walked for miles. His head hung low, his hands stuffed deep in his pockets, he kicked at stones along the way. He found himself well beyond any neighborhood houses and near a wooded area. The water tower appeared through the trees. He pushed through the brush while dried branches scratched his arms. Past all the tall weeds, there was a circle cut out among the oak and pine trees where the base of the tower sat. He squinted upwards in the sun and looked at it.

The gray steel beast with its thick black legs was huge. One hundred fifty feet to the top of the tank. Sonny grinned deviously and took to the ladder like an ape to the tree. He climbed straight up in the air. The wind blew harder. It whipped across his face. He still kept going beyond the sign printed on the side that read *Caution. Use safety straps.*

Further up he went, the cold steel ladder gripped in his hands. He looked down at trees that became smaller and houses in the distance like little dots.

Finally, at the very top of the tank that was rounded and slippery, he stood as if on the tallest mountain. The wind slapped his body, the force of it threatening to push him off if he continued to be so bold. Sonny planted his feet firmly like a king who ruled over all he saw. He stretched his arms out wide and tipped his head to the sky. He was as high as the birds, and the rush of adrenaline that coursed through his body made him feel more alive than he ever had before.

"Hey!" a voice from below shouted. "Get down from there. What the hell are you doing?"

Sonny looked down at two men in hard hats and nearly slipped. He regained his balance and smiled at them.

"I said get down from there," one man said. "Are you nuts? You can't climb up there."

Sonny flopped his arms. "I just did," he shouted back to them.

"Get your ass down here before I call the cops," the other man yelled.

"Go ahead. I know one you can call." Sonny laughed deep in his throat and faced the sky once more. "Call him," he mumbled with a nasty grin. "See if he gives a shit."

"Get down here right now," both men hollered.

"No," Sonny yelled back at them. He laughed at how small they looked and how unreachable he was.

"I swear," one man said, "if I have to come up there and get you...."

"Ah, shit," Sonny grumbled. "I'm coming. Just relax." He inched to the ladder and climbed down. When he was close enough, the two men grabbed him.

"Are you an idiot?" the shorter man said.

Sonny shrugged. "Depends who you ask."

"Get out of here. This is private property," the larger of the two men said. "I mean it. Get." He pushed Sonny making him stumble and fall to the ground.

Sonny got to his feet. The two men laughed.

"Serves you right," the short one said. "Now get."

"What an ass," the bigger one said and laughed again.

Sonny curled his fist and slammed it into the larger man's face. The man went down, his lip bleeding, Sonny paused for a second, surprised at the result.

"You stupid son of a bitch," the man snarled. "I'll teach you a lesson."

"I don't need no more lessons," Sonny said.

The man came at him.

Sonny ducked, sent his left fist into the man's gut and his right up to the man's chin. The man stumbled back. Sonny smiled at the power he had, bouncing with the excitement from one foot to the other. "Come on," he challenged. "Come on."

"Let's call the cops," the other man said and pulled his friend back to the truck. "That kid's nuts."

Sonny snickered at them both and took off running.

25

"Jamison," Colby barked, "you're late."

"Sorry, Cap," Jay said and began to loosen his gun holster.

"What the hell is wrong with you?" Colby said. "You look like shit."

"I-I didn't sleep very well last night," Jay said.

"Everything all right? Sonny okay?"

Jay couldn't look at the older man. He pretended to search his desk for nothing in particular. What he wanted to say was that no, Sonny was not okay. Jay found him with a seductive woman one step before it could have been worse. And if that wasn't bad enough, Sonny was drunk and high as a kite. He and Jay had argued. Sonny disappeared for hours and when he finally came home, he slammed his bedroom door and locked it. No matter how Jay tried to coax him out, Sonny didn't budge. But, he did throw something at the door and told Jay to fuck off.

"Is Sonny all right?" Colby said again.

Jay cleared his throat. "Sonny? Sure. Fine."

"Good. Don't get settled in. I need you to take Griffin out on the street."

"Griffin? The new kid?"

"Yes. The new kid," Colby mocked. "Damn rookies. He's one step closer to being sent back to uniform. I admit he isn't the sharpest tool, but if he could just get some balls, maybe he'd do okay. I need you to give him balls."

Jay wrinkled his face. "You need me to do what? What about Harrison? I thought –"

"He's your new partner. But he's got a mound of paperwork to finish for HR. So, today, Detective, you babysit the rookie. Drive the streets and find any lead you can to Rizzo. He's wanted for questioning in a missing waitress case. Which, as you know, fits his MO. So go. Explore. Take Griffin and get the hell out of my hair." Before Jay could say a word Colby turned and barked orders to another detective.

* * *

"Hey, sweetie," Myra said. She stood on the stoop in a low cut, tight shirt and dangerously high skirt. "Daddy put you to bed last night without any supper? Tell you that you can't play with me anymore?"

Sonny grabbed her and planted a rough kiss on her mouth.

"Oh. Feeling like a bad boy today?" Myra giggled and hoisted her breasts. "Nobody home?"

Sonny took Myra to his bedroom and closed the door. He pushed her to the bed. She giggled again. He took off his tee shirt and grinned wickedly at her.

"I'll show you how I feel," he said and edged closer.

* * *

Rick Griffin sat in the passenger seat of Jay's ragged Chevy. The young man grinned from ear to ear.

"This is so cool," he said. "Out on the streets with you. Me and Detective Jamison. Man, now that's cool. You and Detective Santini are like super cops. *Were* anyway." He stopped with a pale face. "I mean…are. You are anyway. I heard about Detective Santini. Man, that sucks. Brain damage. Geez. It's gotta suck, right? I mean, he had such a great career. And now. Gone. Friggin' drunk drivers. They should be shot. All of them. I mean – "

"Griffin?" Jay said, his gaze glued to the street. "Shut up. Do us both a favor and just…shut up."

"Can't I even ask a question?"

"If it's about police work? Yes. Anything else, and so help me, I'll use my gun." Jay slowed the car and glanced at a seedy looking man who dragged his feet along the street. "That's Manny. He's tight with Rizzo.

If anybody knows where that scum is, he will." Jay pulled over along the curb. "Stay in the car," he said and eased out to the sidewalk.

Manny walked with his head low and his hands in the pockets of his black hoodie. To Jay, he looked nervous even before Jay approached.

"Hey, Manny," Jay said with a smile. "How's it going?"

Manny took one look and ran.

Jay took off after him. He followed down a narrow alley, across the street where cars honked and slammed on their brakes, and down another alley.

"Stop running," Jay shouted.

Manny kept going stopping long enough to yank open the back door of a bar. He ran through, knocking into a waitress who dropped her tray full of drinks, and headed straight out the front.

Jay was a few feet behind him. He darted over broken beer bottles and shattered glasses. Manny ran down another alley and flipped a garbage can over. Jay leaped it like a marathon runner. His long legs cleared the can without a struggle.

"Stop," he hollered.

Manny reached the end of the alley. No place to go, he tried to climb the chain link fence. Jay grabbed him from the back and tossed him to the ground.

Manny scrambled to his feet, about to turn and run again. Jay was quicker. He fisted Manny by the shoulders and pushed him to the wall.

"I told you to stop running," Jay shouted and tossed Manny to the opposite wall. "I told you. Stop running," he said again and shook the dazed man.

Manny swung a wild fist. Jay ducked. Manny swung again. Jay landed a punch to the man's jaw. Manny went down. Jay jumped him and kept punching him.

"Why did you run, huh?" Jay screamed with spit spraying from his mouth. "Why, huh?" He slammed another punch. "Why did you run?" He lifted Manny's body by the shirt and prepared to bash him once more. "Why did you run from me?" He hit the dazed man again. "What do you want from me, huh? What do you want, Sonny? What?"

Someone pulled Jay off the half-conscious man. He turned ready to strike and realized in time it was Griffin, and that the face he had screamed at was Manny and not Sonny.

"Easy, Sarge," Griffin said, out of breath and hanging onto Jay. "You got him. He's down."

Winded, Jay stepped back. On the ground at his feet was Manny, bruised and bleeding from his mouth.

"Cuff him," Jay said. "And search him." He staggered over to the wall and held himself up, trying to catch his breath and calm his nerves. Sweat rained down his face. He looked at his right fist. The knuckles cut and bleeding. He shook off the sting.

"Crack cocaine," Griffin said, holding up the prize. "That's why he ran, Sarge."

"Read him his rights," Jay said, trying to steady himself. "Get him out of my face."

* * *

"You wanna get high first?" Myra tempted.

"No. Just shut up and don't talk," Sonny said. He kissed her again and again, running his hands through her long blond hair.

"Did Jay ground you? Tell you what a bad little boy you are?" Myra grinned as Sonny nibbled on her neck and palmed her breast. "Did you tell him we're in love?"

"I ain't. In love. With nobody," Sonny said and unbuttoned Myra's blouse.

"Maybe you just don't know what love is." She stopped him and looked into his eyes. "Maybe I need to show you."

"I don't need anybody to show me anything," Sonny said. He stood in front of her and whipped off his shirt. When Myra scooted back on the bed with a smile, he unzipped his pants.

* * *

Colby glared at Jay. "What the hell is wrong with you?"

At first the captain had shouted through the corner of his mouth, but then he began to shout with the whole thing open wide. He slammed his fists on the desk. A stack of files bounced and fell to the floor.

"In front of Griffin?" Colby yelled. "That moron. You beat up a guy? You beat the shit out of him."

"Manny ran."

"I don't give a shit. You know the drill. You had him. You cuff him. Did he land a punch? Don't answer that. I can see he didn't. He's cut up and black and blue. Any attorney worth his snot would have a field day with this. And in front of Griffin? Are you insane?" Colby slammed his fists on the desk again. The veins along his neck popped out. "Don't answer that. You lost it, Detective. Lost it. You're a pro. What in hell is wrong with you?"

Jay sank in the chair, his head hung low. "Cap. I – "

"Don't. Don't say one damn word. I get that doing this without Sonny is hard. I get that you're pushed to your limit. But you are still a cop. Still on this force. And you still have a job to do. This isn't kindergarten. You leave your problems at home and focus. On the job. No buts. No bull. For Christ's sake. You're one of my best."

"Was." Jay looked up at the burly man. "I was."

"You *are*, dammit." Colby pushed his chair back so hard it marred the wall.

"I can't do this. Not without Sonny."

"You can. Dammit, Jamison. I know it's hard to do without Sonny. But you're still good."

"Better with him," Jay said.

Colby eyed the man and then lowered his voice. "You were good together. Sure. But remember. You were one half of that team. Fifty percent. That doesn't mean alone you can't be one hundred percent. You have what it takes. You always did. Stop feeling sorry for yourself. Be glad Sonny is alive." He sat heavily in his office chair. "And be glad," he went back to barking out of half his mouth, "that I don't suspend your ass. Take the rest of the day. Get your head on straight. Report back tomorrow."

"For parking garage duty?" Jay said.

"Get out of here," Colby shouted.

* * *

Tired, Jay parked in the back lot of Smiley's and went in through the rear door. He lugged himself to a table in the corner and melted into the darkness. The scent of stale beer mixed with the stench of burnt French fries and vinegar was as pungent as he felt. The banging of pool balls whooshing across the billiard table and slamming into the pocket together with the scraping of bar stools on the floor didn't help either.

"Middle of the afternoon and you're here? Not a good sign," Dee said. "Beer? Ice tea? Rat poison?"

"Anything sounds fine. Surprise me," Jay said and lowered his head into his hands.

"You want my advice?"

"No. Please. No more advice."

"He's rebelling."

Jay frowned and looked up to her. "First. I assume we're talking about Sonny. Or, I should say, *you* are. I just came in for a break. Second, Sonny isn't a kid."

"Think about it," Dee began.

"I don't want to. My head hurts from thinking."

Dee chuckled and waved him away. "Don't give up, Jamison. That is so not you. Not in this case. Not with him."

"How do you know? Everything has its limits."

"You aren't even close to yours. Sonny is so much a part of you, you're lucky if you can piss without him."

"Are you drunk? Or maybe Myra gave you some of her pot, huh?"

"I'm just saying…."

"What? What are you saying?"

"You will never, could never, have never given up when it comes to Sonny. He's your…." she paused. "Family. And you're his."

"But he doesn't know that. He doesn't know anything."

"Then tell him."

"Tell him? I can't. What am I supposed to say? Hey, buddy, you and I are…."This time Jay stopped. The words caught in his throat. He couldn't tell her or anyone what he truly wanted to say. He swallowed. "That you and me are family." He ran a hand through his hair. "And then what? Let him call me his father again? I am not and have never been a parent to him."

"In some ways – "

"Don't," Jay warned.

"I'm just saying. In some ways you have become that. I don't mean in a true sense. But Sonny's young. He's going through all the stages from what I can see. He's at the stage now of – "

"Sexual awareness?" Jay dropped his head into his hands again. "Geez. That's just great."

"I was going to say rebellion. Didn't you ever rebel as a kid?"

"My idea of rebelling was joining the track team instead of the football team like my father wanted. Oh, and to be a cop."

"Wow, you did lead a sheltered life," Dee said and rolled her eyes. "I sure as hell rebelled. Never mind how. That's a story for when we're drunk, and you can't remember afterwards. But my point is, most kids, with obviously the exception of you, rebel."

"So what exactly do I do?" Jay said.

"You hang on tight."

"Hang on tight? To what? I've been holding on. To hope. To wishes. You name it."

"But not to Sonny. Talk to him. Make him face you. Tell him."

"Tell him what?" Jay frowned.

"I don't have to tell you. You already know." Dee paused and reached for Jay's hand. In a soft voice she said, "Tell him whatever you need to. Trust yourself. And trust that you can get through to him."

26

I t felt like a bowling ball was in Jay's stomach when he turned the corner. There was the ranch house on Tremont Drive. Sonny was either inside or he wasn't. Jay wasn't quite sure which was worse.

He parked the Chevy, and for the first time it didn't backfire. With keys in hand he was ready to unlock the front door, but it was ajar.

Instinct kicked in. He reached for his gun and held it firm. No sign of forced entry, he pushed the door open further and stepped inside.

With light steps he crossed the living room. Nothing was disturbed or missing that he saw. He peeked around the corner to the kitchen and then stepped into the hall.

Muffled sounds: a moan he didn't recognize and one he was sure he did.

At Sonny's bedroom he pushed the door open, and his eyes grew bigger than a full moon.

At the side of the bed, Sonny stood. His pants a tangled wad around his feet. His ass muscles strained and his hips bucked. Around his waist, legs were wrapped and painted pink toes curled.

Sonny turned his head toward Jay and looked at him with smoldering eyes. A look Jay missed along with a grimaced face he remembered.

Grunting while he strained to maintain the momentum, Sonny rasped, "Get. Out." He turned back to what held his desire and grunted again.

Myra moaned. She squeezed Sonny's white ass. Her nails dug into the flesh.

Sonny quickened the motion. The bed rocked. He twisted his head toward Jay again, and as he humped a bit slower, a slight grin curled across his lips. For Jay, it felt deliberate. As if Sonny wanted him to watch. As if he defied him to do anything about it.

Jay's legs went weak. His mouth hung open in shock. He shut the door and backed away until he touched the wall, and he slid to the floor.

At that moment, Jay wished it had been him struck by the car that Sunday morning in May. He wished it had been him that was run over, or, at the very least, that Manny had been smart enough to carry a gun and shoot him. All of those possibilities had to be less painful than this.

He rested his exhausted head in his cold, clammy hands.

That morning in May – a lifetime ago when Sonny had smiled and whistled as he went out the door. Jay heard his partner say he loved him and their life, that he was happy, that everything was perfect. And then the car slammed into Sonny. The *crack* of bone hitting pavement echoed over and over until Jay thought he'd go mad. His mind fired off one flash after another. Each image caused more heartache and a deep, inconsolable sense of loss he couldn't fight anymore.

He lifted himself from the floor and shuffled to the living room. Thoughts of running out the door and never looking back raced through his mind. But his body was too damn heavy, and it was hard enough just to breathe.

The bedroom door finally opened with the dread of Pandora's Box. Jay's body tensed, and his chest grew tight.

Myra giggled and said something that turned Jay's stomach even more.

"That was sweet, baby," the woman said. "You're right. You don't need anyone to teach you anything. You are damn hot."

Jay heard lips smacking. His throat burned.

Myra, in a breathy laugh, said, "You were worth the wait."

Jay found the strength to pull himself off the couch and the dignity to stand and face her. She ran her hands over Sonny's bare chest and kissed him full on the mouth.

"Can't wait for next time," Myra said. She strutted to the front door, her clothes disheveled. With a sassy turn she waved her fingers toward Jay. "Bye." A smug smile spread across her lips. "Don't be too hard on our boy.

We're in love." She went out the door, and Jay, with long strides, followed. He pushed hard against the already closed door and kicked it.

He turned with a look of disdain so acidic, the wallpaper should have melted. "Come out here," he spat at Sonny.

Sonny snickered from the threshold of his room. He shut the door, and Jay heard it lock.

"You think so?" Jay muttered. He stormed to the door and kicked it. The door splintered off its hinges.

Zipping his jeans, Sonny jerked his head. "What the – "

"What the hell are you doing?" Jay yelled. "You can't hide from me. And you sure as hell can't run."

"You wanna bet?" Sonny dared and headed for the door, shirtless.

Jay pushed him back. "Oh no. Not this time. You aren't going to run. Not again."

"Go to hell," Sonny said.

"No more running. I've had it. I've had enough."

"So kick me out. I don't give a shit." Sonny tossed a wrinkled shirt over his messed hair. He fumbled with his belt and shrugged. "I can stay with Myra."

"Myra. Right," Jay scoffed. "That piece of crap you're in love with?"

"I ain't in love," Sonny said and snorted. "I just like to…fuck."

Jay felt ill. "You think that's funny? Do you? What the hell is wrong with you?"

"What's wrong with me?" Sonny shouted. "What the hell is wrong with *you*? It's *my* life. I can do what I want with who I want. You don't own me."

"No shit. I think I got that. So what now? All of a sudden it doesn't matter to you what I think or – or how I feel?"

"How *you* feel? Give me a break. You go back to work and forget about me. You go off with your cop buddies, and screw me. Big deal. I don't give a shit. Now you're pissed 'cause I got a friend? You want me all to yourself and then don't bother with me. And then, when I say go ahead, I don't care, you go nuts." Sonny grew quiet and looked away. "I don't know what you want from me."

Jay stared at Sonny's back for so long, even Sonny twisted his head to see.

"What I want from you?" Jay swallowed the words. What he wanted was everything he wished so hard for and everything he'd lost. "I-I thought we were friends. Partners."

"Don't. Don't call me that. We aren't partners," Sonny said to the window.

"Since when?"

"I don't want to be your…your friend."

A million bees could not have stung Jay more. That one last sliver was gone now, too. "We're…we're not?"

"No. Even Myra wants to know why you keep me around. I'm just a pain in your ass. She's right. You want *him*. Not me. You could never want…not me." Sonny turned and faced Jay. It almost looked as if he had tears in his eyes. "So we aren't partners. I never was your partner."

"You're wrong," Jay said. "You were my partner. My friend. And…and a lot more. *We* were a lot more to each other. More than anyone knows. More than we let anyone know." He gazed at Sonny's back. "Look at me. Please."

Sonny didn't turn. Jay came closer. Slowly, Jay reached toward Sonny. He hesitated and then finally allowed himself to place his hand on the man's shoulder.

Sonny shook it off. "Don't touch me," he said. When he turned, his eyes were wet. But then they became icy and his voice matched. "Don't ever touch me."

Jay's heart sank as if an iceberg had ripped into him. "Don't touch you? Sonny, how can I not touch you? Don't you see? Can't you see?"

Sonny frowned. "See what? Just…just leave me alone."

"Leave you alone?" Jay nearly choked on the words. He lowered his eyes. "I loved you. I was always in love with you." When he gathered the nerve to glance at Sonny again, he saw only a blank look that threatened his last hope.

"I can't," Jay said. "I can't do this anymore. Sonny, we were a couple. You and me. I can't lose you. I can't. It took everything I had to get us to that place. And I can't let some damn accident rip us apart. Sonny, you and me. Our home. Our bills. We were a couple. We lived together in this house, and we slept in the same bed. You and me. Lovers." Tears filled his eyes. "Please try to remember."

Sonny said nothing. And then, his expression slowly changed. His mouth dropped a bit and he began to crease his eyes. "What? What did you say?"

"I love you. You and me. We...we were lovers."

Sonny's eyes opened wide. "You...you liar."

"I'm not lying," Jay said. "I didn't tell you because – "

"You're a liar," Sonny shouted and headed for the door.

"Sonny, listen."

"No. Stay away from me. Liar. Liar." With the back of his hand, Sonny slapped a lamp. It crashed to the floor, and the light bulb popped. "Just stay away from me."

"Sonny. Listen to me. Please," Jay begged.

Sonny sneered. "I trusted you. I trusted you."

At the door Sonny yanked it open but Jay slammed it shut. Sonny put both hands on Jay's chest and shoved him across the room. He stormed back to the door and ran down the steps. Jay hurried, but as he got outside, the Mustang's engine revved, and Sonny tore down the street.

"Shit," Jay said. He grabbed his keys and jumped in the Chevy. He peeled out, tires screeching.

Three streets and the main highway. Jay got to the intersection and lost sight of the red car.

He slammed his palms on the steering wheel. "Dammit, dammit," he screamed. "Dammit, Sonny." His voice grew quieter. "I never wanted to tell you like this."

Jay headed back to the house. Inside, he called dispatch.

"Listen, Larry, I need a favor. Put out an APB for a 1973 cherry red Mustang black stripes license Caesar Charlie Four....Yeah, I know that's Sonny's car. No, it isn't stolen. Just find it."

After he finished the call, he dialed Dee. "Sonny just tore out of here. I called in his plates. He doesn't know that many places to go but who knows what else Myra taught him. Could you – ?"

"I'll put out the word," Dee said. "You want my advice?"

"No," Jay was quick to say. "I love you, sugar, but please, no more advice right now."

He hung up, looked out the window and ran his hands through his hair. "Where would you run, partner?" A snap of his fingers. "Myra."

In the phone book, he found over twenty M. Turners. He picked up the phone.

"Mattie? I need the address for a Myra Turner. Yeah, not a common name. She works at Memorial Hospital. Physical Therapy. Find her and call me."

* * *

Hours went by, and Jay paced. The clock on the bookcase ticked. One minute. Another. Jay grabbed the clock ready to send it sailing across the room. He stopped and tossed it to the couch.

The shrill of the phone made him jump. He snatched up the receiver and pressed it to his ear. "Sonny?"

"Close. Crocket. They found your boy. Alibi Room. Yep. Pauley's place. Tore it up. I explained the situation to Pauley. As a favor he won't press charges if you promise to pay the damages."

"Is Sonny still there?"

"No. Your crew came and got him. Arrested. Drunk and disorderly conduct."

Jay hung up, and the phone rang again. "Hello? Sonny?"

"No, it's Morris. We got Sonny. Here. At the station."

"I know. I just talked to Crocket," Jay said. "I'll be right there."

* * *

Jay ran up the front stairs of Oakland City PD and to the area meant for arrested suspects and bookings. He recognized Officer Morris behind the glass panel and pressed the buzzer. Morris released the lock. and Jay entered.

"Picked him up at the Alibi," Morris said. "Knife fight. He's okay. Bandaged him up. Fought like a wild man, though. The owner and guys he fought said they wouldn't press charges so long as you paid for the mess."

"Guys?" Jay said. "How many?"

Morris huffed. "Practically the whole damn bar. Twelve? Fifteen? Got him here, and he was still fighting. Tossed him in lockup to keep him safe."

"Okay if I go back? Talk to him alone?"

"Sure. Good luck. What's got him so steamed anyway? That's not like Sonny to act this way." Morris unlocked another door. "We could have charged him for resisting arrest. Colby said to release him to you."

Jay headed down the hall and found Sonny behind bars. The man was pumped. He did pushups so fast it was like his motor was stuck in high gear.

"Sonny," Jay called, and the name echoed. "Sonny?"

Sonny huffed and puffed. Pushup after pushup, he didn't stop.

"Sonny," Jay shouted louder.

Sonny froze with arms extended. He posed like that for a moment and then leaped to his feet. His biceps were flexed, the veins along his arms strained. He had a gauze bandage wrapped around his right forearm. His white tee shirt was ripped and speckled with blood. He stared at Jay with eyes void of expression.

It was clear that Sonny was still drunk. Even six feet apart, Jay could smell alcohol, and it wasn't beer. Sonny had a bruised jaw, a swollen lip and a slowly blackening eye.

"Are you all right?" Jay said.

With a slow, vile smirk, Sonny stepped from the shadows toward Jay. "Slay away from me," he slurred. "I'll call an offsir if you don't."

Jay waved away the stench. "You stink, and you can barely talk."

"Oh, I can talk, budzy. And I will, too," Sonny said and staggered. The only thing keeping him from tumbling back was his hold on the bars.

"So talk," Jay said.

"You sure? 'Kay. Offsir sir?" Sonny yelled. " C'mere and meet a liar."

"Will you knock it off?" Jay said. "You're lucky that blood clot is gone or I'd think you were having a stroke. Can't you see what you're doing to yourself? Don't you care? About anything?"

"Like you?" Sonny poked a finger through the bars. "Liar."

"I didn't lie," Jay said and lowered his voice. "If you didn't feel like this right now, we could talk."

Sonny lifted his arms sideways. "I feel great." He laughed. "Don't I look it?" He wobbled backwards, tried to sit on the cot, but fell on his ass instead. "Who moved the bed?"

"I'll get you home," Jay said and was about to turn.

"Oh no. You stay away from me. I don't want your help. I don't want anything from you."

"Stop it, all right? Let's just get out of here."

"I'm not going anywhere with you." Sonny rushed to the bars and shook them. "Liar." When Jay didn't move, Sonny shook them harder. "I said I want to stay here. D'you hear me? I ain't going nowhere with you."

"Fine. Maybe it's better like this."

"Damn straight," Sonny said. He shook the bars again. One hand slipped, and then he gripped it again and shook the bars until they rattled. "Now get the fuck away from me."

"Okay," Jay said. "You want to act like a wild animal? Welcome to your cage. Where all the really bad boys end up." His footsteps echoed as he walked down the long hall to leave. With a wave over his head, he shouted back, "Night."

"Jay?" Morris said at the door. "What's happening? I was just coming back to unlock the cell."

"Don't. He needs to sleep it off. Let him stay put."

"Does this look like a hotel? I'm not so sure the captain will like this."

"If I take him out of here in his condition, he'll probably run off and do God knows what. Just let him sleep. I'll get him first thing in the morning."

* * *

At home in the dark house Jay flicked on a light and swore he could still hear the remnants of angry voices. In the harsh silence, he heard the crash of breaking glass, the crack of broken wood. It changed the whole feel of the house and made it something that turned his stomach.

He picked up the broken lamp. Shards of glass crunched under his feet. The door to Sonny's bedroom barely hung by a splinter of wood. Sonny's bed…Jay couldn't even look at it without the urge to vomit.

In the kitchen he reached for a bottle of Tequila Crocket had left in a cupboard. He popped off the top. The golden liquid shimmered in the dim light. He thought about it. Taking that golden liquid and drowning in it. Problem was, he and liquor never mixed. Two drinks at the most, and he was drunk and sick as a dog the next morning.

Tomorrow morning. Jay snorted at the thought. When he'd have to pick up Sonny from jail. He rubbed hard down his face. The ring of the phone startled him. He grabbed the kitchen extension.

"Hello?"

"Jay?" Dee said. "How's Sonny?"

"Sonny? Great, according to him."

"Crocket told me. Is he home? Is he okay?"

"No," Jay said with a heavy sigh. "He's spending the night at Grandma's."

"What the hell are you talking about?" Dee said.

"He wouldn't leave the jail. Can you believe it? That little shit puts me through freaking hell and he's pissed at me for…." Jay didn't say more. He just shook his head while his hand that held the phone also shook.

"I'll be right over."

"No. Thanks. Honestly, I'm exhausted. I'm going to take a shower and go to bed where I'll toss and turn like always and then get up and stare out the damn window. See? Nothing's new."

"You sound awful," Dee said. "You shouldn't be alone,"

Jay looked at the bottle of Tequila. "I'm not. I gotta go. I have to be up early to pick up our boy. I'll talk to you tomorrow." He hung up and poured a glass of the golden liquid. "To hell with it. Maybe me and you'll get to be new best friends." He toasted the glass. "To new partners and ex-lovers."

27

"**M**orning lover," Myra cooed from her side of the cramped bed.

Sonny frowned at first, the room strange to him. There were boxes scattered around the floor and on a chair. All of the boxes were crammed with clothes sticking out over the rims. The dresser was buried with more piles of clothes along with bottles of hairspray and empty containers of food. Sonny inhaled. There was a strong, odd odor of something spoiled. He coughed.

"What's the matter? Cat got your tongue?" Myra giggled.

Sonny glanced over at the woman, and she smiled. He pushed her hand off his chest and slid out of the bed. His bare feet touched a mixture of crumbs and dust on the floor.

"How'd I get here?" Sonny said in a dry, deep voice.

"You don't remember? You called me last night. Told me about the bar. Said I should pick up your car and come and get you. You were wasted, sweetie. Passed out the minute I got you inside."

Sonny squinted. "This…this your place?"

"Sure is."

"It smells."

"Kiss my ass," Myra said. "Besides. You and me can get a nice place once you move out of that prison. And I don't mean the jail. I mean the one you live in with Jay. He's a piece of work. But, hey. With your disability check and that big old sum of money you got from the accident settlement, we can afford something real nice. I can finally get out of that damn hospital with all those damn drooling paraplegics and those wrinkly mothball stinking geriatrics. I got me a real man now. I told people at the hospital about us. You should have seen some of those snotty nurses look at me."

"I'm going to take a shower," Sonny said and stumbled over some discarded shoes.

"You aren't exactly a morning person, are you?" Myra said.

Sonny squeezed through the bathroom door where more piles of clothes and towels were stacked on the counter and the floor. He pulled bras and panties from a clothesline strung across the shower and threw them on the floor with the rest of the junk.

His head throbbed. His mouth tasted like sandpaper. He caught a quick glance of himself in the medicine cabinet mirror. The left side of his lower jaw was bruised so bad it glowed purple. His right eye was puffy and yellowish brown.

He looked at his swollen knuckles. It hurt to make a fist. He ripped off the bandage to expose a two inch gash along his forearm and then looked at his forehead. There was a big bump. He touched the spot, and just that small amount of pressure caused him to wince.

The ache in his skull grew. Either a hangover or a migraine. He almost called out for Jay…but then he remembered.

The shower water sprayed lukewarm, and no matter how far Sonny turned the knob, it refused to get any hotter. He hung his tired head under the spray and let his muscles soak.

"Want some company?" Myra said and pulled back the curtain. She eyed his naked, soapy body. "You are just too damn beautiful."

Sonny yanked the curtain shut. "Leave me alone."

"Grumpy." Myra pouted. "Don't start being a bore, Michael. I hate boring."

"Get out," Sonny said against the pound in his head.

"You get out. This is *my* bathroom."

Sonny shut off the water. He climbed out of the shower, and, when Myra tried to touch him, he pushed her back.

"Oh, come on, Michael. I was just kidding," Myra said and followed him.

"Stop calling me Michael," Sonny said. "I ain't him. I don't know him. Don't want to." He pulled on his torn jeans, felt dizzy for a moment and had to sit.

"Okay. Fine. I'll never say Michael again." Myra sat next to him on the bed. "Even when you're being a really bad boy." With a lusty grin, she ran a smooth hand along his moist back. "You wanna get high?"

"No." Sonny groaned. "I got a headache."

"Oh, poor baby. Why don't you lay back and let Myra make you feel better?" She purred, "Mmm, I love your body. The curve of your back." She trailed a finger along his spine. "But mostly?" She squeezed his crotch and grinned. "I love – "

Sonny moved her hand. "Not now. Just…just stop it."

"You know, you're starting to get very dull. Maybe you should go home to that guy, Jay. He doesn't like you to have any fun anyway." Myra went to the dresser mirror and checked her makeup. "There's something weird about him. The way he acted when he caught us in your car and yesterday. Did you see the look on his face? Like he was gonna get sick or…cry." She laughed and turned to face Sonny. "Yeah. Like he was gonna cry. I remember when I caught my old boyfriend with this bitch in his apartment. I looked just like Jay did."

She turned back to the mirror and put on some lipstick.

"That's kind of freaky," she continued. "Like he wants you all to himself." She giggled and pressed her lips together. "You know what I think?" She swayed over to Sonny and put her knee on the bed next to him. With another giggle, she twirled her finger in one of Sonny's curls and said, "I think he wants to fuck you."

Sonny grabbed her by the wrist. "Shut up!" he said, his voice harsh.

"Ow. You're hurting me."

"Just shut up," Sonny said again, his eyes as dark as coal.

"What's the matter? Huh? Maybe you want to fuck Jay, too." She pulled free.

He rose, and she tried to prevent him from leaving. Sonny grabbed her by both arms and pushed her a little harder than he meant to. Myra flopped back on the bed.

"What the hell is the matter with you?" She looked at her arms. "You don't have to get so rough."

Sonny grabbed his ripped shirt off the floor and tossed it over his wet ringlet curls. "I'm outta here."

"Why?" Myra sighed and went behind him. She combed through his damp curls with her fingers, but when Sonny brushed her hand away and moved his head, she pawed his back instead. "You just need to relax. Come on, sweetie, let's just relax and" – she kissed his shoulder – "have some fun."

Sonny ignored her and zipped his pants.

"Come on. Let's smoke a joint and relax." Myra wrapped her arms around his waist and cupped his crotch. "I know what you need."

"No," Sonny said and tried to move. "You don't,"

Still from behind, Myra held him until Sonny unwrapped her arms and went out to the living room.

Annoyed, Myra said, "What's with you today?"

Sonny looked around the filthy floor until he found his shoes.

"Hey?" Myra said, standing with her hands on her hips. "I'm talking to you. Answer me."

Sonny pushed magazines and a bag filled with trash off the couch. He sat on some kind of wet spot and then moved to the coffee table covered with moldy take-out food containers and empty beer bottles. There he sat to put on his shoes.

"I said…" Myra went over and smacked his back, "answer me. Or are you too stupid to know that's what you should do?"

"I gotta go see Jay," Sonny said.

"What the hell for?"

"Where's my keys?" Sonny searched through more litter on the coffee table and couch.

"Why should I tell you?"

"Where are they?"

"Why? You gonna push me again? Find them yourself."

"Where are they?" Sonny demanded.

Myra snatched the keys off a table and dropped them in her blouse. "Come and get them."

"You're disgusting," Sonny sneered.

"Really? That's not what you said last night," Myra taunted.

"You don't wanna piss me off," Sonny said in a voice as dark as his eyes.

"Fine." Myra slapped the keys on the table. "Take the damn keys. Go back to Jay. Go back to being his good little boy. That's what you are, you know. A little boy in a man's body. See if he can make you feel good." She kept shouting even when Sonny was out on the street. "See if he knows what you're really like."

* * *

For Jay, the morning sun was relentless. It announced its arrival through partly closed blinds. Jay grunted and rolled away from it. With one eye barely opened, Jay found himself hanging half off the living room couch. Four empty beer cans were tipped over on the coffee table. The empty Tequila bottle lay on the floor.

With a mother of a headache, Jay exerted what little energy he had to stand. Big mistake. He fell back on the couch and waited for the wave of nausea to make a decision.

The urge to be sick passed. He gradually made his way to the kitchen and searched the cabinets for aspirin. When he finally found the bottle, he couldn't undo the child-proof cap. In frustration, he threw the plastic bottle across the room and sat heavily at the table. With head cradled in his hands, he rocked his throbbing head back and forth.

No matter how much he drank last night, nothing could wash away the reality.

Why did I tell him? How could I blurt it out like that? Jay shook his head, and even that little movement caused him to feel like he was on a roller coaster hanging upside down while all the blood rushed to his head.

He groaned, picked up the aspirin bottle, and worked to open it.

He pushed me to my limit, Jay thought as he forced the cap. That's why I said it. I'm not a freaking saint. Seeing him like that. With that... that bitch.

"Oh, for Christ's sake," he shouted at the plastic bottle, and the top popped off in his hands. He got a glass of water and swallowed two capsules, then decided to take two more.

Jay sighed. He never should have told Sonny like he had. What should he have done? Say, "Oh, by the way, buddy, there's a little something I forgot to tell you. You're supposed to love me. Yeah, that's right. Don't argue and don't ask questions. I'm telling you to love me." He shook his head. Pathetic. That's what he was. And now? Now Sonny would never trust him.

He rubbed hard along his forehead and noticed the light on his answering machine blinked. He pressed the button, and Mattie's voice came on. "Jay? I got that address. Took some time. That woman, Myra Turner? Moves around a lot. Here's the address if you still need it."

The machine clicked off. Jay, at the sink, drank another glass of water and looked at the clock. He had to pick up Sonny and somehow get him to listen. He was probably... what? Afraid? Ashamed? Confused?

He shuffled to the bathroom without a clue how to make any of this right.

* * *

Officer Harry Sims buzzed Jay into the booking area. "Who the hell dragged you through the gutter?" he said.

"I'm here to pick up Sonny," Jay said.

"Sonny? Detective Santini? You kidding?"

"Do I look like I'm in the mood to kid?" Jay said.

"What was he doing here?" Sims said.

"Didn't you check your morning roster?" Jay said. "The details should be there."

Sims shrugged one shoulder. "He isn't on it."

"What? That's not possible. He was brought in last night, and I had Morris keep him here."

"Why would you do that? What was he here for?"

"He got into a fight and...it doesn't matter. Check the roster again."

Sims turned a few pages and shook his head. "Let me get last night's guest book." He came back with a printout and scanned the names. "I usually go by my morning roster. But, oh, yeah. Here he is. Says here he was picked up just after two in the morning by someone you asked to come and get him."

"Me? I never....Who? Who picked him up?"

"Says here it was a Myra Turner." Sims looked up at Jay. "You never sent her?"

"No," Jay said and brushed a hand through his hair.

"You want her arrested for falsifying information?"

"No. I'll handle it."

"I got an address," Sims said.

"Don't need it." Jay sighed. "Thanks, Harry."

Back in his car, Jay shook his head. "Unbelievable. Fucking unbelievable."

"Cobra Three," Jay's radio squealed.

"Are you kidding me?" Jay said. "What now? My house blow up?"

"Cobra Three," the radio called again.

"Fine. Screw it." Jay clicked on the mic. "And good morning to you."

"Cobra Three? This is dispatch calling Cobra Three."

"Yeah, yeah. Cobra Three. Go ahead."

"Hold for Captain Colby," the dispatcher said.

"Jamison?" Colby's gruff voice shouted. "You think this is the Four Seasons or something? I said Sonny could be released to you last night, and you have Morris keep him here? You use police channels to put out an APB on Sonny's car that wasn't even stolen, and then use resources to search an address? This department isn't your private temp agency. You copying this?"

"Yes, Cap. Just had some problems. I wouldn't have asked if it wasn't important."

"You and I better have a nice long chat on what's important. Got it?"

Jay clicked on the mic. "Got it. Nice long chat. No problem."

Colby came back on the radio. "Well here's some real police work that does require our resources, which, by the way, the taxpayers are paying for. We got an anonymous tip. There's a robbery going down sometime this morning. Details are sketchy. Oakland City Bank on Visher. You copy that? V as in Victor."

"Visher. Copy," Jay said. "But, Cap? Couldn't you get Detective Weiss and McCann on this? I have a problem and – "

"And I'm interrupting. How inconsiderate of me." Colby's patronizing voice quickly turned harsh. "Get off your ass and get to work. I'm not running a daycare. I need you...as in *you*, Detective Jamison, on this. And I mean now."

"Yes, sir," Jay said.

"Now listen up. The tip we got says it's an inside job. Bank's supposed to be closed today for a payroll transfer. I want you to check it out. The bank's account manager is a man named Evans. Harry Evans, Late fifties. Five feet ten. Between one hundred ninety and one hundred ninety-five pounds. Usually wears a brown suit. He's going to accept the transfer. No one else is supposed to be there. I want you to keep an eye out if he lets anyone else in the bank. I'll have a uniformed car a block south of the place. If Evans lets anyone in, let them get settled and relaxed. We'll let them think it's going according to plan. Then I'll dispatch another team, and we'll take them down as they exit the bank. Hopefully, it'll go nice and clean. The streets will be busy with normal traffic, so the last thing we want is a shooting war. Copy?"

"Copy. Cobra Three out," Jay said. He hung up the radio and mumbled under his breath, "Focus, Jamison. Focus."

28

Harry Evans liked to gamble. He gambled on just about anything that moved, from the ponies to hockey and in between. And if it wasn't something that moved, then he loved to play cards. Married and twice divorced, Evans had two children with his first wife and three more with his second. The oldest two were in college. Between alimony, child support, college tuition and his new girlfriend, an ex-Hooters waitress, Evans was in debt up to his eyeballs.

A comb-over to hide the bald spots, middle-aged man, he should have been planning his retirement, instead, he owed a little over fifty thousand to a loan shark named Burton. It was fair to say Harry Evans was a desperate man. Hugo Burton knew it too.

Burton, with his squinty eyes and suntanned skin that offset his silver hair, enjoyed fine tailored suits and his thirty foot yacht. He was the owner of Burton Autos where huge deals were made. The auto shop wasn't the only place Burton made deals. He loaned money and collected his debts with high interest. It was something he'd done successfully for years. But when it came to Harry Evans, Burton was done waiting to be paid.

"I gave you a ninety day extension," Burton said. He sat behind his desk at the auto shop and watched Harry Evans squirm in the metal chair. Two brutish men, who made sure Evans didn't make a run for the door, stood on each side.

"I know," Evans said, his voice shaking to match the knocking of his knees. "And I appreciated that. I-I just need a little more time."

"More time?" Burton said and put the tip of his pencil in the electric pencil sharpener. The whir of the razor chewing the pencil to a small stub made Evans cringe even more. "You remember what the last extension cost you?"

Evans nodded. It had cost him a sprained wrist and a shattered windshield. "But I have a sure thing this time."

"You lose more than you win," Burton said and began to sharpen another pencil to a nub. "I told you the choices you'd have when the ninety days were up. Time to pick." Burton held up one stubby pencil. "Choice one. Should I remind you what it is?"

"No," Evans said and looked up at the two men who placed heavy hands on his trembling shoulders.

"Well then," Burton said, "why don't you tell me so I know you understand the terms." He rocked in his office chair.

Evans swallowed. The weight of the two men's hands on his shoulders made him sink further in his seat. "Gator bait," he said in a quiet voice.

"What was that?" Burton said.

"I-I said, gator bait."

"You do remember," Burton said. He laid the pencil down and held up the shortest one. "Or? Come on. Shout it out if you know the answer. Or do you need my friends here to remind you?"

"The other was…kill me."

"You and…? Come on. I'm getting really tired of this," Burton said.

"And my kids," Evans said and sank further in the chair.

"Very good." Burton rested the pencil next to the other. "Of course there is one more choice." He held up a fresh, unsharpened pencil and rolled it between his fingers with a slight grin. "You could pay me the money you owe plus interest. So, what'll it be? Should we gamble, boys?" He laughed along with the two men.

"If I could just have a little more time," Evans said. "I know this payout will be the big one."

Burton nodded at the two men. Both of them squeezed Evans' shoulder until the man winced in pain and nearly slipped off the chair.

Burton took the two sharp toothpick-sized pencils and held them up. "You ever gamble on what happens when a pencil this size and with this point is shoved up a man's nose? Or how about one this size?" Burton placed the end of the fresh pencil in the sharpener. The *whiz* of the razor chewed it to a pointy black tip. "How about one this sharp pushed into a man's ear? Think we should gamble on that too? You seem like a fairly bright man. Which one of my choices are less painful?"

"I don't have the money," Evans said. Sweat poured down his face even though there was a fan blowing on him.

"Well, that is a pity," Burton said. "But lucky for you, I figured as much." He chuckled. "Lucky. Something you definitely aren't. But maybe that'll change."

"How?" Evans said. He wiped his brow with the back of his hand and tried to sit up straight even with the hands still pressed on his shoulders.

"You're the Accounts Manager at Oakland City Bank, correct?"

Evans nodded. "Yes."

"How long you worked there?" Burton twirled the freshly sharpened pencil between his fingers.

"Twenty-four, twenty-five years. Ten in accounts."

"You handle some pretty large deposits and transfers, don't you?"

Again, Evans nodded.

"Well, this is how it'll go down," Burton said. "You'll be making a transfer. A transfer into one of my accounts."

"But…but you don't understand. There are paper trails."

"Like I said. You're a bright man, Evans." Burton took out a cigar and began to chew on the tip of it. "I'm sure you can figure a way around the paper trail, can't you?"

The heavy hands squeezed Evans' shoulder again.

"Speak up, man," Burton said. "I have another appointment in fifteen minutes."

The hands pushed down until Evans nodded. "I-I can come up with something."

"You see? This is why doing business together is so productive. But I wouldn't want you to strain yourself, so I'll tell you what I've come up with." Burton spit the tip of the damp cigar into his trash can. "You bragged once that you handle one of the largest payroll deposits in the city. Remember? You weren't just trying to impress me, were you?"

"No. I-I do," Evans said and squirmed.

"Good. I hate it when people put on airs. Now, when exactly do you get that deposit?"

"The last Saturday of the month."

"Top corporate account, right? How does it work? Exactly."

Evans cleared his throat. "It comes in around noon. Electronically. They wire the money, and I transfer it to an account."

"Good. But this time, you'll transfer it to an account I'm going to give you."

"But they'll know. They'll know it was me," Evans said in a panic.

"Oh, well, isn't that just so sad. Not my problem," Burton said and rocked easily in his office chair. "How long does the transfer take?"

"As soon as I enter the numbers…twelve hours. But – "

"Can it be undone?"

"No. Not if it's out of the country. You have to listen to me. I can't – "

"You can, and you will," Burton assured.

"I'll lose my job. I'll go to jail. They'll want to know who and where," Evans said, more sweat pouring down his face.

"You give them bogus information. How could they track that?" Burton calmly rocked. "You just said it can't be undone."

"It can't. But you don't understand."

"I understand. Do *you*? What's at stake here? How about I motivate you? Let's begin with this." Burton leaned forward. "First. You got two mighty fine looking daughters. One is really into soccer, isn't she? She's your youngest, right? You don't want anything to happen to her, do you? No. Of course not." He looked at his watch. "She should be coming in from school right about now. Here." He pushed his phone toward Evans. "Call home."

"Why?" Evans said.

"Do it," Burton said.

Evans started to dial. Panicked, he couldn't locate the right numbers.

"Allow me," Burton said and dialed the phone. "Let me put it on speaker."

When Evans heard his daughter, Maggie, answer, he glanced at Burton and said, "Hi, honey. How are you?"

"Daddy?" Maggie said. She sounded terrified. "A-a big man came up to me at soccer practice. He said he'd come back if I didn't give you a message."

"What message?" Evans looked at Burton who smiled.

"He…he said, tell your daddy I said hi, and I like going to the swamp. Daddy? What did he mean? He scared me. He looked at me funny. I don't want him to come back. Daddy? Why did he do that?"

Evans was pale. His knees bounced, and he tried to keep his voice from showing his fear. "It-it's all right, honey. Don't worry. He won't be back. I promise. Don't be scared, okay? I love you."

Burton hung up the phone. Satisfied, he placed the longest pencil into the electric sharpener again and let the razor chop it to a tiny stub.

Evans lowered his head. "I understand. Please don't hurt my daughter."

"So long as you understand," Burton said. "I want you to know I'm not completely heartless. This is business, Evans. You picked me, remember? I'm here to make money. That's all. I realize you have a pension and responsibilities to your kids. I'm not here to ruin you more than you've ruined yourself. So let's work together. You and me. And just so you know you're not in this alone, I have two men who will assist you. I want you to listen very carefully."

Burton sat forward in his chair, his eyes glued hard on Evans, he spoke slowly so nothing could be mistaken.

"You have free access to the bank on the day of the transfer, correct? Come on, Evans. Don't get close-lipped now. You were the one doing the bragging. Do you have free rein, as in no one else will be there? Good. After you get in the bank, you shut down the security system and then, unfortunately, you forget to turn it back on. I have two men that will be there to assure you make the transfer, and, just for shits and shots, they tie you up. They'll make it look like a forced entry, and poor old you were forced to comply. You tell anyone dumb enough to believe you that they put in the numbers and, with a gun to your head, two hooded men forced you to push the right keys. How's that sound?"

"I…I don't know. If they suspect anything, what will happen to me?"

"Well, either they fire your dumb ass or…I kill you." Burton looked toward the closed door. "Duke. Parks. Get in here," he shouted.

Two men, distinctly different and equally dangerous, entered the office

"I'd like you to meet Duke Reynolds," Burton said and introduced the first man. "Let me tell you a bit about him. He's a two time felon paroled eight months ago, and he's just been waiting for an opportunity like this. Haven't you, Duke?"

Duke was not an overly large man. What stood out about him was his cowboy exterior. Mid-forties, dirty brown hair and dark brown eyes, he had a long, thin face with thin lips and a pointed chin all shaded by the cowboy hat he wore. Originally from Arkansas, he'd spent time in prison for armed robbery. He moved to Texas, but after he was arrested and convicted for armed robbery, all he got to see of Dallas was behind a prison wall.

"Duke's no stranger to robberies," Burton said. "It's kind of his thing. During the last one he shot and wounded a night watchman. How long before they caught you, Duke?"

"Five months," the man said around a toothpick dangling from the left corner of his mouth. "I coulda lasted longer, but I ran outta supplies. Course, that was in Georgia. I ain't used to Georgia," he explained in his southern accent. "Sure do like their peaches though. Now, iffin' I could of gotten my hands on a horse and had some mountains nearby? Things might've been different. Yes, sir. Real different."

Burton chuckled. "Don't you love how he talks? So, tell us, Duke, why didn't you just head north? Toward the mountains?"

"Got myself a little mixed up," Duke said and adjusted his hat.

Burton laughed again and rolled his eyes at Evans. "He isn't the sharpest, but he's got no conscience, so, what the hell. I just need him to watch over you and try not to kill you." He began to chew once more on the tip of his cigar. "Now, that big bear of a man over there? That's Tyrone Parks. Say hello, Tyrone."

Tyrone, a black man, stood at a little more than six feet four and about 350 pounds. He had broad shoulders, a thick neck, and a square face with a misshapen nose broken more than once.

Waving an enormous calloused hand, Tyron said, "Hi. What's his name again, Boss?"

Burton puffed at his cigar and said, "His name is Evans. And," he laughed so his squinty eyes were reduced to narrow slits, "your name is Tyrone."

Tyrone waved Burton away with his huge hand. "Ah, you kiddin' me, right, Boss? I knows my own name."

"Tyrone was arrested for sexual assault and one suspicion of robbery. But he was never convicted on that charge," Burton said. "Were you?"

"Nah. I had me an excuse," Tyrone said.

"You mean alibi, don't you?" Burton said.

"No, Boss," Tyrone said. "Hers name is Ally Bea. I done told ya that. My ex-wife. Told the cops I was with her at a cook-out. She done left me after that. Don't know why she took off. Just did."

"Maybe it had something to do with you assaulting her sister," Burton said.

Harry Evans eyed both men. They made him nervous. The whole plan that Burton had devised made him nervous.

"Now listen up," Burton said. "I don't like to repeat myself. After the deposit comes in, Mr. Evans will transfer the money. Both of you make sure he does."

"How we gonna know, Boss?" Tyrone said and scratched his head.

"He'll push a button," Burton said.

"Which one?" Tyrone said.

"For shit and tits," Duke said. "The one that says push this one." He looked at Burton. "Right?"

"I'm sure Mr. Evans will explain it all to you," Burton said. "The only thing both of you need to do is to enter the back of the bank. Make sure the security cameras are off. Then Mr. Evans will put in the correct numbers and make the money magically appear in the account I have set. After that, his debt will be clear plus interest, and you boys will be paid. Any questions?"

"Do I kill him after?" Duke said.

Evans trembled in his metal chair so violently, it almost tipped.

"No," Burton said. "Only if he doesn't make this happen. If he doesn't, then take him to the swamp and go back after his daughter."

"I like the swamp," Tyrone said. "There's one big ol' gator there. I call her Susie. She smiles like my mama 'cept she's got teeth."

"All right then," Burton said. He smirked at Evans. "I know what you're thinking. Neither one of them are genius material, but don't underestimate their ability to get the job done. Here's the account information." He handed a slip of paper to Evans. "Make it happen. Or it won't be the last time you and my boys have a get-together."

That was two weeks ago. Ever since then, Harry Evans dreaded the thought of the last Saturday of the month. Sadly, as he parked his car in his usual spot in the back lot of the bank, the day had come.

Wearing his trademark brown suit, Evans unlocked the rear door of the bank and turned off the alarm. He glanced at his watch and waited.

There was a hard rap against the back door. Evans' already pounding heart nearly beat out of his chest. He peeked down the hallway. There stood Tyrone Parks. The large man was at the rear door, hands shoved in his pockets. With the black wool hat he wore on a day when it was eighty-five degrees, he stuck out like an elephant in a cluster of rabbits.

With quick hand movements, Tyrone motioned for Evans to come to the door. The over-sized linebacker glanced suspiciously around and bounced on his toes. Evans couldn't get to him fast enough.

"What are you doing here?" Evans said. "It's only eleven o'clock. You're supposed to bust in five minutes after noon. *Not* before."

"Duke said get here now, man," Tyrone said. "So that's what I do."

"Why? This isn't what we discussed. When the garbage truck comes to empty the dumpster, you're supposed to be hanging around out back. I need a witness that says they saw two men. Now get back outside."

"Can't," Tyrone said. "Duke said come in. Don't know why. Just 'cause he do."

"I don't like it. This is all wrong," Evans said, but Tyrone had already waddled toward the front of the bank.

"This is some bank," Tyrone said. "Hey? You got lollipops." He pointed to the dish on the counter. "Red." He smiled crooked teeth. "I like red."

"That's yellow, you idiot," Evans said and snatched the pop out of the man's hand.

"Hey," Tyrone whined, "give it. I want it."

Evans slapped the candy back in the man's outstretched paw. The pop was lost in his palm. "Here," he whispered, his voice harsh. "Just shut up and stay down, for shit sake."

"Why ya whispering?" Tyrone said. "Window ain't open. Got them blinds shut. Ain't no person gonna see. Just be cool, bro."

"I don't like this whole thing. I don't like it at all," Evans said.

"I got me a lollipop. I like red. I'm gonna say red." Tyrone ripped the wrapper with his silver filled front tooth and stuck the candy between his grinning lips.

* * *

Jay parked the Chevy just south of Oakland City Bank. From there he had a good view of the front of the bank and part of the rear alley parking lot.

The two story brick building sat on the corner of Visher and Second Street. A double glass entrance door with potted plants on each side faced Visher. The blinds on the front door and the large window were closed. A few people walked along the sidewalk. Just before the alley was a deserted store. Around the corner on Second, there was another opening for the bank's parking lot. Just past that was a dry cleaner.

Jay spoke into the police radio. "Cobra Three to Unit Twelve. Copy?"

"Copy, Cobra Three," the voice on the radio replied.

"You in position?" Jay said.

"East side," Officer Angie Rivera said. "Got a slight view of the front of the bank and the lot entrance on Second."

"Copy," Jay said. "Stay in position and leave this channel open." He settled back in his seat and pulled out his binoculars.

Nothing much was happening on the street in any direction. A few cars drove past. A city bus advertising a local TV station stopped briefly at the corner. One person got on and two got off. They crossed the street.

It was warm in the Chevy. Jay cracked the window and wished he had picked up some water. His mouth was as dry as pavement on a July day in Florida. He was grateful the aspirins he took earlier helped, but the dull hammer in his head told him he could use more.

Jay lowered the binoculars and squeezed the bridge of his nose. He ran a hand through his hair. Once more, he forced himself to watch the side alley and the street. His mind wandered.

"Focus, Jamison," he told himself. Now was not the time to be thinking about Sonny.

It was hard not too. His intention to go to Myra Turner and hopefully convince Sonny to come home with him had to wait.

In a way, this brief distraction was a good thing. He still had no idea what to say to Sonny, and the thought of facing him with Myra smirking in the background, was not something he relished. Just the thought of it put his stomach in knots and made the hammer in his head pound louder.

"I just wish," Jay said in a soft whisper, "that you could remember. Remember me. Us. Remember loving me." He sighed and stared out the window. "Okay. That's enough. Don't go there." Again, he fought to concentrate on the bank.

Ten minutes later a white Lincoln sedan pulled into the side alley entrance of the bank and parked in the lot. With his binoculars, Jay got a license plate number. A man in a brown suit got out of the car.

Jay called in the license. The search confirmed the vehicle belonged to Harry Evans.

That was his man. Jay clicked on the police radio. "I have Evans in sight."

"Copy, Cobra Three," Officer Rivera said. "I have visual,"

Jay kept a silent watch. Traffic was building along the street. A church on the east side had just ended services. Flocks of cars turned onto Visher.

"It's a funeral procession," Rivera's voice said over the radio.

"Dammit," Jay said to the street while the slow, long string of cars blocked his view. "Unit Twelve, can you see anything?"

Rivera clicked on and said, "Negative. I got a garbage truck entering the east side alley. Looks like it's stalled."

"Radio that in. Find out if this is its normal route," Jay said.

A man in a dark navy tee shirt wearing a cowboy hat strolled slowly, glancing about as he came down the street in Jay's direction. Near the front door of the bank and just before the alley, Jay's view was blocked by the line of traffic. He could only see the man's feet from under two vans that had stopped. He waited for the man to reappear, but lost track of him.

"Cobra Three," Rivera called. "The garbage truck is on its normal route but running fifteen minutes ahead of schedule. It's a new driver. He checks out. Looks like he's got engine trouble. His back end is in traffic. If he gets it started again, doesn't look like he'll make it at the angle he's at."

"Copy, Unit Twelve," Jay said into the radio. "I got a possible suspect, but my vantage point is compromised. I'm headed to the rear of the bank. Wait for my signal when I come back around."

"Copy," Rivera said.

Jay climbed out of the Chevy and weaved across the street through the stream of cars. Once he entered the side alley of the bank, he eased around the corner. From there, he had a perfect view of the rear door.

* * *

Angie Rivera, a uniformed cop in the department for three years, sat in the squad car with her partner, Dennis Johnson. Johnson, a seasoned cop with ten years of experience, kept tabs on the bank from the passenger seat.

"I got eyes on Jamison," Johnson said to Angie.

"I have him," Angie said.

They watched Jay cross the street. The moment he went down the side alley, they lost sight of him.

"Let's roll ahead a little. See if we can get a view," Angie said.

She drove the car ten feet forward.

"It's no good," Johnson said. "That damn truck is taking up the whole side."

Angie looked to her left. "When Jay comes around from the lot, we should be able to see."

"Yeah, if he can squeeze between that damn truck and the wall."

* * *

The man with the cowboy hat was nowhere in sight. Besides the white Lincoln, the small lot had no other cars parked there.

Times like these, Jay missed Sonny. The crunch of gravel in the alley, the smell of the street, the heat in the air – all of it was like any one of the hundred stakeouts he and Sonny had worked in the past. If he was here, right now with Sonny, this would seem like nothing more than another day on the job. As he darted his eyes around searching for any signs of the man he'd seen, he wished he hadn't thought of Sonny. He wished it wasn't Sonny's face that kept flashing in his mind. And, even more than that, he wished he didn't ache for his partner as much as he did.

Pushing the images out of his mind, Jay took a few more steps. Two windows in the rear of the bank had bars and the shades shut. He walked through the parking lot. Around the bend, there was the front of the garbage truck. He heard car horns honk behind it. Acting casual, he headed that way.

* * *

Rivera and Johnson kept their eyes peeled to the street. With binoculars Rivera scanned the building tops. Three buildings west she spotted a man on the roof.

"Call this in," Angie said. "We got a guy. Looks like a worker on the roof."

Johnson radioed the station. In less than two minutes, they confirmed the man was a worker from Ace Heating and Cooling sent to repair a ventilation system.

"The driver of the garbage truck got out," Angie said. "He's headed to the dry cleaners."

Johnson nodded. "Looks like he's looking for a pay phone."

"I think I have a visual on Jay," Angie said. "Hold on. I lost him again."

* * *

As Jay began to round the corner of the building next to the bank and head for the street, he realized the space between the garbage truck and the building walls on either side were too narrow. He turned around and, as he did, he saw one of the blinds on the bank window move.

Might be Evans, he thought. And if the man spotted him, he might get nervous. He passed the dumpster. Then he heard a sound. The crack of something under a foot.

Jay glanced to his right at the dumpster and looked toward the street. There wasn't much room between the stalled truck and the wall. He heard the crackle of something hard again. He slowed just beyond the dumpster. There was about ten inches between that and the wall. He stopped. Just as he turned to look over his shoulder, he felt the gun in his back.

"Don't even blink, pardner," a deep southern voice ordered. "You in it now."

* * *

"I don't see Jay," Rivera said. "He hasn't come back out."

"Give him a few more minutes," Johnson said. "He probably had to go back around."

* * *

"Move. Real slow," the man said close to Jay's right ear. "Keep your hands up so I can see 'em." He reached under the front of Jay's nylon jacket and removed the gun from Jay's holster. "Now just head on over there, and we'll both be as happy as a foal tucked in next to his mama."

Jay stepped gingerly with the gun pressed hard to the center of his back. When they got to the rear door, Duke kicked the bottom of it twice, waited, and kicked again.

Tyrone opened the door. His mouth dropped.

"Get in there," Duke said and pushed Jay inside.

"What ya got, Duke?" Tyrone closed the door, locked it, and followed.

"A pony on a lead line. Whatta ya think, you imbecile? A cop." Duke used the gun to press Jay further inside and told him to stop. "Search him. I got one gun. I don't trust these here cops to carry only one weapon."

"Oh my God," Evans cried. "What are you doing? This is not – "

"Shut up," Duke said. "I hear your whiny voice one more time, and I'll shoot ya just for cause."

"He's clean," Tyrone said. "How'd ya catch him?"

"He was sniffing around out back," Duke said and took off his cowboy hat. "Sit down," he told Jay. "Tie him up," he ordered Tyrone.

In the main area at the front of the bank, Jay was pushed into a chair set between two desks. When he looked up at his capturers, he knew he recognized one of them. When Duke removed his hat again to wipe away some sweat, Jay was sure of it. Duke Reynolds was a man he and Sonny had arrested two years ago for holding up a liquor store.

"Nice day for a robbery," Jay said.

"It was. Till you showed up," Duke said. He squinted at Jay. "Well, set my boots on fire. I know you. Jane...no. Jamison, right? Or you the other one?"

"Gee, I didn't think I looked anything like my partner," Jay said.

Duke snickered. "Don't matter none to me which you are." He back-handed Jay across the mouth. "I owe you both. Now just sit there and shut up."

"Thought you were sent to jail," Jay said. He licked blood off his lip. "Banks your new thing now?"

"I told you. Shut up," Duke said and slapped Jay again. "Hurry up, Tyrone. Christ. I could tie down a bull faster than you move."

"I never agreed to this," Evans said, his hands shaking. "A cop? Police? There's more. There has to be."

"Where's your partner?" Duke said. "Answer me."

"You told me to shut up," Jay said and smirked.

"Boy, you really wanna beatin'? I ain't gonna ask again. Where's your partner?"

"I'm flying solo on this one," Jay said.

"You 'spect me to believe that?" Duke said. "I remember you two. Tighter'n a new pair of boots."

Jay stared down at the floor. "Believe what you want. I'm alone."

Duke grabbed Jay by the front of his shirt and growled. "Where's the others?"

From behind Jay, Tyrone tightened the ropes around his wrists. "How this be, Duke?"

"Shut up," Duke said. "Where's the others? Talk."

Jay frowned. "Who? You want me to shut up and him to talk or me talk and him shut up?"

Duke grabbed a handful of Jay's hair and pulled. "I ain't gonna ask again."

"What others?" Jay said.

"Don't play me, boy. Why you hanging around the back of the bank?"

"This is my bank. I wanted to cash a check," Jay said.

"Bank's closed," Duke said.

"It is? Oops," Jay said with a wry grin.

"You're real funny for a cop. Kind of like a damn rodeo clown. Well, ya know what?" Duke reached into Jay's inner jacket pocket and took out the badge. "You know what, Detective Jamison? I'm the bronco in this here rodeo, and I'm gonna stomp you to tiny bits. Your own mama won't know ya."

"Detective? He's a…a detective?" Evans face froze in panic. "This isn't right." He glanced up at the wall clock. "It's almost noon. You two were supposed to be here *after* the garbage truck came for the dumpster."

"I don't know how to tell you this," Jay said. "But you got a little problem with your plan. That garbage truck? It's already here. Broke down. Side alley."

"Dammit," Evans said, pacing in a circle. "This isn't how we planned it. Who's going to witness you breaking in now?"

"I hate to bust your bubble again," Jay said. "But, I don't think you're gonna need to worry about that either. In case you haven't noticed. Hi. I'm a cop."

"Yeah. A real clown," Duke said and smacked Jay across the mouth again.

"Will you stop that?" Evans shrieked. "Why did you two show up early?"

"Mr. Burton don't trust you. And I don't either," Duke said. "Tyrone? Keep an eye on the front." He pointed a gun at Jay's temple. "In case you ain't noticed, this here's a gun. Where's your back-up? Huh? You really want to die over this?"

"Put that down," Evans said, his voice trembling. "No one gets hurt. That was the plan."

"Plans change," Duke said, his gun still aimed at Jay's head. "Now I ain't gonna ask again. Why you here?"

"We got a tip," Jay said. "Your little stick-up is shot to hell. No way you're walking."

"Oh, I'm walking all right," Duke said.

Jay shrugged. "Robbery is one thing. You really want to add killing a cop to it? That's a whole other problem I don't think you or your partners want."

"He's right," Evans said. "I don't want any part of shooting a cop."

"Any sign of anything?" Duke shouted to Tyrone.

"Nothin' I can see," Tyrone said.

"Move them desks to block the front door," Duke said. "And push whatever you got to block the back door, too." He kept the gun aimed at Jay's chest. "You said tip. Who gave you a tip?"

"Anonymous," Jay said.

"Bull. Who? You got to ten. And I ain't patient."

"They teach you to count in prison?" Jay said.

Duke pressed the gun harder to Jay's chest.

"Please," Evans begged. "Tell him."

Jay grinned. "I told you. Anonymous. That's all. What difference does it make? We know. It's over. Give up…shit. What the hell was your name?"

"Duke," Evans said. "His name is Duke."

"Shut the hell up," Duke said.

"That's right," Jay said. "Duke. Yeah. I remember now. The cowboy wanna be. Isn't your real name Eugene?"

Tyrone laughed. "Eugene? You ain't never told me that."

Duke snarled. "Shut up," he said to Tyrone. "And block the door. You" – he pointed the gun at Jay's head – "I'm about ready to blow that stupid grin off your face."

"Oh God," Evans whined. "Please. Just put down the gun. This isn't going to work."

"He's right, Duke," Jay said. "You should put down the gun and trade in your horse while you can. You'll get five to ten if you stop now, and with a lenient judge, maybe out in two."

"I-I was forced to do this," Evans explained. "They made me."

"Shut up, you piece of cow shit," Duke said. "You ain't getting outta this nohow." He looked at Jay. "Anonymous, huh?" Duke's narrow eyes trailed to Evans. "You worthless pig snout. You did this to get the attention off you. You set this up." He punched Evans in the face.

Evans fell back into the desk. Like a scared rabbit, he scurried behind the desk as if it would protect him.

"I-I didn't," he said. "I swear. Why would I do that? I didn't want to get caught either." He wiped the blood from his lip and with wide eyes looked at Duke. "I swear. I'd lose my job. My house. Everything."

"Then you let your mouth flap to someone," Duke said.

"Are you insane?" Evans said. "Why would I tell anyone? I wanted this to be over and done." Still behind the desk, Evans begged Jay, "Tell him. Tell him it wasn't me."

"Then who?" Duke glanced at Jay who shrugged, and then he looked over at Tyrone.

"What?" Tyrone said. "I didn't say nothin' to nobody. Not nobody. 'Cept…."

"Except?" Duke said. He fisted the gun until his knuckles turned white.

"My girl," Tyrone said and lowered his head.

"Your girl?" Duke said. "That bony, skinny mouse? That junkie whose so high on meth, she don't know what a fat, dumb, rat ass ugly mother-fucker you are? I should shoot you now just to save air. You homegrown piece of horseshit."

"Ah, Duke. Don't be talkin' like that. She won't have said nothin'."

"No? For a snort of meth, she'd sell her right tit. I bet you your dumb black ass she made a deal with somebody."

"Well this is perfect. Just perfect," Evans said and nervously twisted his hands. "Now what? Huh? Now what do we do?"

* * *

"We've lost contact with Detective Jamison," Johnson radioed dispatch. "He circled back to the rear of the bank. It's been eight minutes. No audio. No visual."

"Even if he couldn't make it past that truck," Rivera said, "he should have been back to his car by now."

"He said he was following a suspect." Johnson peered through his binoculars. "If they got suspicious…." He clicked the radio again and said, "Report to Captain Colby. Detective Jamison is MIA. How should we proceed?"

* * *

"Where are the other cops?" Duke said to Jay.

"All over the place," Jay said.

"You're a real smart ass, you know that? Get him to his feet," Duke ordered Tyrone.

With one burly hand, Tyrone lifted Jay out of the chair.

Duke slammed a fist into Jay's face and another into his gut.

Jay folded. His wrists tied tight behind his back, he wheezed to catch his breath. Duke pulled Jay's head up by the hair. A punch to the jaw, Jay flew back to the carpet. He turned to his right side, coughing. Duke kicked him in the ribs. Three, four times, the pointy tip of Duke's boot landed exact each time.

"Stop it," Evans cried. "You're making it worse."

Another direct kick, and Duke shouted, "I'm madder than a coyote stuck in an electric fence. You want me to take it out on you? Than shut your face and watch the goddamn back door." He pulled Jay's hair forcing him to his knees.

Duke turned to Tyrone. "Get this piece of crap off the floor and tie him tight in that chair. I gotta think."

Tyrone hoisted Jay to his feet. Jay spit blood on the floor. Winded, he managed to say, "Give it up, Duke. This is too hot even for you. You give up now, it won't be so bad, but every minute on that clock gets you deeper."

Duke paced. "We can still pull this off." He turned toward Evans. "Turn on your damn computer. You're gonna make that transfer."

"But then what?" Evans said. "How are we going to get out of here?"

"We got ourselves a cop for a hostage," Duke said.

"What about me?" Evans said. "They'll know I helped you."

"They won't know shit. Tell 'em you were forced," Duke said.

"Forced? They were tipped off," Evans screeched. "They know. Oh God." he gripped the edge of the desk. "They know."

"So? Make a deal. Give 'em Burton's name," Duke said. He laughed for the first time. "See how far that gets ya."

"I'm a dead man," Evan said. He looked at Jay and shook.

* * *

The police radio clicked on. "Unit Twelve. This is Captain Colby. Any sign of Jamison?"

"No, sir," Johnson said. "It's quiet. That damn truck is still broke down. Cars all backed up."

Rivera focused on the front of the bank. "I got some movement at the window. Can't tell what it is. But the blinds moved."

"Copy that," Colby said. "Sit tight." He hung up the radio microphone. "Get the bank on the line," he told Bruce Harrison. "And the snitch. It's time to talk."

Bruce dialed the bank. Ten rings. "Nobody's picking up."

Detective Weiss came out of a side room dragging a young, haggard looking woman with him. "This is Tess Fry."

Tess tried to yank her arm free. Her arm so skinny the bones showed. "I told ya all I know."

Colby approached Tess. His weight alone dominated the pencil-thin woman. Her complexion was nearly blue. Her face sunken so her eyes bulged and her cheek bones appeared sharp. Bleached blond hair, frizzy and brittle, was uncombed and ratty. Sticks for legs, she wobbled on her two-inch wedge heels. The added height did nothing for her. A breath could knock her over.

Colby eyed her. "You told your dealer a nice story. He gave you crystal and in exchange, made a deal for himself with us. Now it's time I hear it straight from you."

"I told ya. All I knows is something going down at the bank," Tess said. "That's all."

"You better hope you know more," Colby said. "And you better start talking. How long you think you'd last in a cell?"

* * *

Evans nearly jumped out of his skin when the phone rang. He stared at it, barely breathing. The phone kept ringing. No one moved.

"You should answer it," Jay said. He was tied in the chair between two desks. "I have a feeling it's for you."

"What should I do?" Evans said.

The ringing stopped.

"You should talk to them," Jay said.

The phone began to ring again.

Evans' voice quivered. "Who…Who could it be?"

"I can pretty much guarantee it isn't Publisher's Clearing House," Jay said.

The shrill of the phone filled the room.

"Duke?" Tyrone said. "Ya wants me to answer it?"

"Shut up." Duke sneered. "Get the fuck outta my way." He pushed Evans back and snatched the phone. With the receiver pressed to his ear, he finally growled, "Yeah."

"Duke Reynolds," Colby said. "This is the Captain of Detectives Oakland Metro Police. I understand that you and Tyrone Parks decided to pay the bank a little visit. Guests of one of the bank managers? A Mr. Harry Evans?"

"Guess you know a lot," Duke said.

Evans tugged on Duke's arm. "What? What does he know?"

Duke pushed Evans backwards. "Whatta ya want?"

"I'm a little sketchy on the details," Colby calmly said. "Something about a payroll deposit. Tess didn't seem to know much more."

"Tess," Duke snarled over at Tyrone.

"Tess?" Tyrone came to stand next to Duke. "Is my Tess on the phone? I wanna talk to her." He reached for the receiver. Duke jerked away and kicked him. Tyrone yelped and stepped back.

"Guess ya wanna know who else is at the party," Duke said.

"You aren't smart enough to pull this off," Colby said. "Or to plan it. I understand it was someone who owns a car dealership. Tess wasn't quite sure of the name. She said sometimes she doesn't listen to Tyrone."

"To bad she listened at all," Duke said and swatted Tyrone's hand away when he tried to take the phone again.

"Don't you think that person should come to the party?" Colby said. "Let him take some of the heat?"

Duke grinned. "What I think is, we got ourselves a cop right here. That's all we need. Now here's what we's gonna do."

"Hold on a minute," Colby said. He put the receiver to his chest and looked at Bruce. "Radio Unit Twelve. Tell them we're sending back-up. This is going to be treated like a hostage situation and an officer down."

29

S onny slammed the door to Myra's apartment. He could still hear her screaming at him to come back. He trotted down the stairs and climbed in behind the wheel of the Mustang. The whole car reeked of cheap perfume, stale smoke and spilled beer. He turned the key in the ignition. The Mustang roared with a charge of power he enjoyed.

His head still pounded from the night before and the scratchy shrieks of Myra's voice in his ears. The police radio under his dash squawked with static. He reached to turn it off but then he heard a rapid succession of excited voices calling out codes.

The codes that were familiar caught Sonny's attention. There was a major crime underway and a possible officer injured.

Sonny turned up the volume, and then he heard a voice he recognized.

"All units," Colby announced. "All units. Possible 10-35. 10-78. Officer needs assistance. Detective Jamison badge number 306 possible down or hostage."

"Hostage?" Sonny said. He adjusted the signal and strained to understand.

Colby fired off more codes. Some Sonny knew. Others he didn't.

"Come on," Sonny said to the radio. "Where, dammit? Where?"

The radio squawked again. "Suspects armed and dangerous. We believe Detective Jamison was taken inside. All units proceed to 34 Visher Street corner of Second. Wait for my orders."

"They got Jay? Who?" Sonny said. "Thirty-four Visher." He searched under the bucket seats for the map. He opened it and studied it. It was no use. All he could make out was a bunch of wiggly lines, numbers and colors. He could not get his brain to process the information into anything concrete or meaningful. Frustrated, he ripped the map to shreds.

Sonny rushed toward Myra's apartment. He burst through the door and found Myra smoking a joint.

"Change your mind, lover?" She giggled and took another hit.

"Where's 34 Visher Street?"

Myra giggled again and leaned her head against the couch. "Want some?" She offered the joint.

"Where is it?" Sonny said, standing in front of her.

"Why?" She took another long pull and held her breath.

"Just tell me, dammit. Where is it?"

Myra puffed a cloud of gray from her mouth. "Where's what?"

"Thirty-four Visher, dammit," Sonny shouted. "Corner of Second. Tell me where it is."

"Um…let's see," Myra said and giggled again. "Fisher?"

Sonny took her by both arms and shook her. "Visher, dammit. Tell me now. Tell me."

"Back to the rough stuff, huh?" Myra cackled. "I like it."

Sonny shook her harder. "I mean it. Tell me now."

"Hey. Knock it off or I'll call a cop." She laughed. "I might even call Jay. Let him arrest you. Maybe *he'll* wanna party afterwards."

Sonny clenched his teeth. "Tell me now or so help me…."

"All right. All right. God. It's four blocks down. Turn right at the Omni Gas Station, then up one block."

"What is that place? What?" Sonny grabbed the joint from her hand and crushed it in the ashtray.

"Hey. That's not nice," Myra said. "It's a bank, genius. Geez."

Sonny tossed Myra back on the couch.

"You're welcome." Myra giggled.

Sonny slammed the door on his way out.

Back in the Mustang, he followed the directions Myra gave him. He began to turn at the gas station. The street ahead was blocked by police who redirected traffic.

Sonny made a quick U-turn and parked. He ran down the back streets using the alleys. When he got to a building that blocked him from going further, he wasn't sure which way to head.

With no other direction to go, the only option was up. Stuck between two brick buildings, he shimmied up a drainpipe, got to a ledge, and pulled himself up to the roof of the building.

He ran along the connecting roofs until they separated. A five foot distance between one roof to the other, he jumped. When he landed, he tore the knee of his pants and skinned his hands. No time to stop. He could hear police sirens.

Sonny looked over the side of the building. Below him, he saw the tops of police vehicles that lined the entire block. The cars were parked haphazardly. More sirens blared, and more police cars screeched to a stop. Barriers were quickly placed to prevent anyone from getting down the surrounding streets. Five more buildings from where he stood, a swarm of police had planted themselves across the street. By the way they kept watch of the building in front of them, Sonny knew that had to be the bank. Ahead of him roofs looked like a long train with very little space between them. He could use that route to stay above the police and get where he needed to go.

He ran across three more rooftops and again checked the street below. He could make out a tow truck that had a garbage truck hooked to it. As the tow truck pulled away, a dozen more police cars circled like a wagon train.

Sonny paused. He was so close with no idea how to get inside the bank. No gun. No way of knowing what the bank looked like inside. All he knew was that he couldn't just stand around trying to figure out his next move.

He turned from the edge of the building and spotted a man who stood a few yards away and nervously watched him. The man had an open tool box by his feet and a wretch held anxiously in his hand.

"Stay right there," the man warned as Sonny came his way. The same height as Sonny, he weighed about twenty pounds more.

Sonny put up his hands and stepped closer. The man wore a light gray shirt with the words Ace Heating & Cooling printed above the right pocket.

"Who are you?" Sonny said. "What're you doing up here?"

The name Ed was printed on the opposite side of his shirt. "What are *you* doing up here?" Ed said and fisted his wrench. "Don't come any closer. I mean it."

"See that building over there?" Sonny pointed.

"Yeah. The bank. What about it?"

"I gotta get over there and inside," Sonny said.

"Why? Is that why all the cops are here?"

"Yeah. I gotta get over there."

Ed backed away. "Don't hurt me, okay? I got kids."

"I don't plan to hurt you," Sonny said. "I need your help. I gotta get inside the bank. Someone's trying to rob it."

"No shit. You serious?" Ed glanced toward the building.

"How would someone get in it?"

"I know that building," the man said. "Worked on the air conditioning. There's a vent system on the roof. Someone could go in through there. Is that what they did?"

"Beats me. So if I went in through the vent, that could get me inside?"

"Along the duct work. Tight squeeze, but yeah. Takes you along the ceiling and from there, you could drop down. Hey? Who the hell are you? Why don't the cops know this?" Ed backed up again and tightened his hold on the wrench. "You got blood all over your shirt. Just who the hell are you?"

"Take off your shirt and give it to me," Sonny said.

"What? Why should I?"

"'Cause I'm a…a cop. Yeah. A cop. And I'm telling you to."

"A cop? Yeah, right. Where's your badge?" Ed said.

Sonny lunged at Ed. He slapped the wrench out of Ed's hands so fast Ed didn't know what happened. He looked at Sonny with huge round eyes. Sonny grabbed him by the front of his shirt, and Ed froze with fear.

Sonny gestured with his head toward his raised clinched fist. "That's my badge. Got it? Can you see it real good? Good. Now give me your damn shirt."

"Sure. Sure," Ed said. "I don't want no trouble. I got a wife. Kids."

His fingers shook so much, he could barely undo the buttons. He took off the shirt and gave it to Sonny.

"That belt thing too," Sonny said.

"My workbelt?" Ed said. He unsnapped it and handed it over while Sonny put on the gray shirt and buttoned it.

With the tool belt fastened to his waist, Sonny said, "How do I shut down the air conditioning?"

"From inside," Ed said.

"Can I shut it off from the roof?"

"Ah, yeah. Yeah. There's a main power switch next to the fan box."

"Okay. Come on," Sonny said.

"Me? You want me?"

"Just stay low and follow me," Sonny said.

"But I got – "

"Kids. Yeah. Just stay low."

"You really a cop?" Ed said.

"That's what they tell me," Sonny said and nudged Ed to follow.

Hunched over, Sonny led the way across two more buildings. When he got to the end, there was a ten and a half foot span from one edge to the other.

"Guess we'll have to jump it."

"What?" Ed shrieked. "I-I can't jump that. It's impossible."

Sonny pointed to a silver box on the opposite roof. "Is that thing sticking up the vent?"

"Yeah. You pop off the top and slide down it."

"And the switch?"

"That red button next to it." Ed said. Sonny backed up several feet. "Man, you're nuts. You can't – "

From the farthest end of the roof, Sonny took off running.

"Jump that," Ed finished.

With sheer determination, Sonny leaped from one building to the other. When he landed, barely an inch from the edge, he rolled. His palms, already skinned, were cut even deeper with bits of gravel embedded. He ignored the sting.

"Go back," Sonny shouted to Ed. "And keep your mouth shut."

Ed nodded with his hands up. "Never saw a thing."

* * *

"Do you see the police out there?" Evans said and put his head in his hands. "I'm ruined. Ruined. This has gone far enough." He marched over to Jay.

"Hang on," Duke said. "What the hell you think you're doing?"

"You have to get me out of this," Evans begged Jay. "Tell them I was forced into this. I was. By their boss. I never wanted any of this." Over his shoulder, he pleaded with Duke, "We can let him go. We can end this."

"You touch those ropes, and you'll be on the floor," Duke said. "You got two choices."

"Please. No more choices," Evans cried.

"Shut that squeaky, whiny voice," Duke said with a corrosive tone. "Or I'll shut it for you."

"There's just no point in going through with this," Evans said. "The police know. They know everything."

"Yeah, well, we got one way outta here," Duke said and eyed Jay.

"None of this would have happened if he'd kept his mouth shut," Evans said and pointed at Tyrone.

"Tess should of said nothin'," Tyrone said. "'I's kind of mad at her 'bout that."

"You think?" Duke said. "You're lucky I got my hands full right now or I'd shoot you and that dumb bitch." He pointed the barrel of his gun at Evans. "And you too. I should put two slugs in you just 'cause you make me sick. But Burton wants his money, and dead means no paying back a loan."

"Paying back a loan?" Evans shrilled. "Are you kidding? We'll all be in jail. Who cares about a damn loan?"

"You better," Duke said and grabbed Evans by the back of the neck. "You better give a shit." He dragged Evans over to a desk and tossed him in a chair. "Get that transfer going. Now."

"But you heard that cop," Evans said. "If we let him go, it'll mean two years jail for you," He looked at Jay. "You could fix things, right? You could get them to go easy on me too, right?"

"Burton won't," Duke said. "He'll come for ya sure as a frog gobbles up a moth. Jail or no jail. No way I'll sit in a cell and wait for someone to slice me. No, sir. I think a cop is more leverage. So while you're crying over there, you're making me rethink this whole plan. Whatta you think, Tyrone?"

"Don't care none no way, Duke," Tyrone said. "Just so long we get outta here. How we plan to do that?"

"Well, the way I figure it. We got ourselves one cop and one sissy. One owes money. One owes me 'cause he put my ass in jail."

"The one that put your ass in jail was the cop, right?" Tyrone said.

"Yes, you giant rat turd," Duke said and sighed. "And outside, we got cops lined up all along the street."

"That's not so good, is it?" Tyrone said.

"Shut up. Just…shut the fuck up, or so help me, I'll empty this gun into your dumb empty head," Duke said. "Now where was I? Yeah. The way I figure it is to hell with Burton. In jail, we're sitting like frogs just waitin' to get their legs torn off. But out there, we got ourselves a chance. We got a cop. A ticket out. So all we need is money. Screw transfers and all that shit. Ain't gonna do us a damn bit of good. But money in this here hand of mine, and we got it made."

"Think you got it all figured out, huh?" Jay said. "There is no way in hell, they're going to let you step one foot out of here unless you throw down the gun and give up."

"You better hope that ain't so," Duke warned. "Or your ass is the first thing they'll be wiping off the floor."

The phone rang. Even Duke jumped.

He tore the receiver out of its cradle. "Yeah?" he barked, listened and then said, "So, you want to speak to Detective Jamison, Captain Colby?

Well, I want a few things too." Duke smirked. "I want a car, and I want all those cops out there gone."

Tyrone tugged on Duke's sleeve. "Tell 'em we wants a pizza, too. A big one with pepperoni and bacon."

Duke pushed Tyrone away. "Did you hear me?" Duke said into the phone. "You do that, and the cop lives." He slammed down the phone and glared at Evans. "This here's a bank, right? It's got money. Get me some. Now."

"I-I don't have the combination to the vault," Evans said.

Duke fisted both sides of Evans' suit jacket and lifted the man out of the chair. "Find me some. Now."

Evans trembled. "I-I can't. I'm telling you…it's not possible."

"You gonna wet your pants, boy?" Duke said. "You got keys to open this here place. They better open somethin' else too," He tossed Evans back into the chair.

"The small safe," Evans said. "I-I could open that. There's about forty thousand in it."

"Forty's better than nothin'. Do it," Duke said.

"Don't," Jay warned. "Once you do, they won't need you anymore. Duke is itching to kill you. I've seen that look before."

Duke placed the tip of his gun at Jay's forehead. "You are really biting me in the worse way, ya know that?" he said. "Now I say you keep that mouth of yours shut or the next thing you'll be hearin' is a loud bang and your brains sliding down that there wall."

* * *

Bent low, Sonny inched along the roof so no one on the street below could spot him. He made it to the tall, square vent and hid behind it. The button Ed had told him about was within reach. Sonny pressed the switch. The fan stopped, and the hum that had been constant was suddenly quiet.

Slowly, carefully, he pried open the top of the metal vent. It was dark inside. He shined a flashlight. It was a long way down and curved. He lifted his head and peered over the edge. The police were in position, but they made no move to get in the bank.

He could see Captain Colby. The large man had his suit jacket off and his sleeves rolled up to the elbow. He held a megaphone to his mouth.

"Duke Reynolds," Colby yelled. "Tyrone Parks. This is the Oakland Police. Release Detective Jamison now and come out with your hands up. Harry Evans. We need to see you. Open the front door and surrender. Surrender before someone gets hurt." Colby lowered the megaphone and waited. A moment later, he raised it and shouted again, "There is no car coming for you. There's no way out. Surrender."

* * *

Duke opened the front door a crack. "Ain't gonna surrender," he shouted. "You want a dead cop on your hands?" He pulled the door shut and locked it.

"Oh my God," Evans said. "My kids. Missy. What will they think? Oh, please, Saint Michael, help me."

"Shut the fuck up," Duke said. "Only help you're gonna get is if you open that safe and hand over whatever you got. You wanna stick around after that and surrender, go ahead. But me and that cop are gonna be headed elsewhere."

"What about me?" Tyrone said and sulked.

"If you can move that fat ass fast enough," Duke said.

"There sure is a lot of cops out there," Tyrone said.

"Really?" Duke said and snickered. "Can you count the cars?" He looked at Jay and added, "Boy can't count past nine."

"More than nine," Tyrone called over his shoulder.

"See?" Duke said. "Looks like you're pretty important, Jamison. All them cops out there just to save little ol' you." He scratched the bottom of his chin with the barrel of the gun and said, "Even if I don't make it out. Knowing that I killed you, just might make it worth the trouble. Thought of you a lot when I was in the joint. You and that partner of yours thought you were pretty slick catching ol' Duke like that. I never even saw you boys coming that night. Like two alley cats sneaking up on a mouse. Well, you know what?" He pointed the gun at Jay. "I ain't no mouse no more." He went back to the door and shouted, "Get me that damn car and move outta here, or so help me, you'll get this cop back, all right. One body part at a time."

* * *

Sonny heard everything Duke threatened. He also heard Colby's answer.

"All right, Reynolds. Don't do anything you'll regret. I'll have a car here in one hour."

"Make it twenty minutes," Duke called back. "I think I'll start with his fingers."

"Give me forty," Colby said. "I'll call you, and we can figure this out."

Sonny had to make his move now. Cautiously, he climbed on the vent box and slipped in feet first. Ed was right. It was a tight fit.

Inside the metal shaft, the opening he found himself in was barely wide enough. He managed to twist onto his belly. His foot kicked the casing, and he paused when the tin echoed.

On his elbows, Sonny crawled for nearly a hundred feet around a slight bend and fifty feet more where he could see an office below through the vent screen. The room was quiet. He slid further and the vent began a slow decline. Straining to slip along the shiny surface and careful not to knock into the sides, Sonny got to a place where once more he could see through the grates of a vent.

He spotted Jay tied in a chair, his wrists and ankles bound. There was also a taller man with a gun pointed at Jay's chest.

From the distance, Sonny heard a husky voice say, "It's hot in here. You know that, Duke? How come it got so hot in here?" The voice came closer until Sonny could see a bear-sized man take off his wool hat and swipe an enormous arm across his forehead.

Sonny sweated as well. Beads of perspiration ran down his neck and back. He pressed forward a bit to see if there were more men.

A shorter man in a brown suit came into view. He took off his jacket and huffed in the heat as well. "Something must have happened to the AC. I thought I heard a noise before."

"Me too," Tyrone said. "A kinda bang or somethin', huh?"

"A bang or somethin', huh?" Duke mocked. "Check the back, asshole. Make sure that bang wasn't a cop sneaking inside." He peered through the front window blinds. "I swear, if those cops think they can roast me outta here, they got a big surprise comin'."

Tyrone headed for the rear of the bank and then stopped. "Hey, Duke? What if it is cop? What if he's got a gun and shoots me?"

"Then I'll shoot him back," Duke said.

"Oh. Right," Tyrone said and continued to the rear door.

The phone on the desk rang. Sonny watched Duke answer it, never taking the gun off Jay.

"Well," Duke finally said, "ain't that just too damn bad, Colby, you don't get time to clear traffic. I wanna see those cop cars gone now."

There was a short pause, and then Duke said, "Yeah. Jamison's alive. Not for long if you don't do what I want." He held out the phone to Jay and said, "No tricks. Tell 'em I'll start with your fingers and work my way down. Tell 'em to turn the air conditioner back on, too."

Duke held the phone a few inches from Jay's ear. "Cap?" Jay said,

"Jay? You all right?" Colby said.

"They want the AC back on," Jay said.

"We didn't shut it off," Colby said. "How many men are in there?"

Duke took the phone away. "That's enough chatty." Into the phone he said, "How many of us? You figure it out. Maybe that bitch Tess didn't know everything, huh? Turn the air conditioner back on."

"I'm telling you, we didn't shut it off," Colby said. "There was a man working on the roof a few doors down. Maybe there's a malfunction."

"Get me that car, and get the cops away," Duke said. He paused and then said, "I'm not sending Evans anywhere. I need him. The only thing I'm gonna do is *not* kill this cop. For now. But if you try to screw me? Two fingers. Right hand. For starters." He slammed the phone back in the cradle.

Duke snickered. "Says he'll come after me," he said to Jay. "Says he'll take it personal. Guess you're more important than I thought."

"He's not kidding," Jay said.

"Well, you better hope he gets me what I want," Duke said. "'Cause if he don't? You're going down. I ain't letting them take me back to prison. No way."

"Please, oh, please," Evans begged. "Just let him go and let's give up. It's over. There's nowhere to go. Murder won't help any of us."

"Maybe not," Duke said with a smug grin. "But it sure as hell could make *me* happy. The way I see it, we got insurance. Those cops back off. We use this cop as a shield and take that fine looking Lincoln out back."

"And go where?" Jay said.

"Don't talk yourself outta a few more hours to live," Duke said. "Once we're clear, we dump your body and high tail it outta the country."

"Hawaii?" Tyrone chimed in. "I always wanted to see Hawaii."

"Dump his body?" Evans said. "You can't be serious."

"What else I'm gonna do with him?" Duke said. "Take him on a honeymoon?"

Tyrone scratched his head. "He is a cop, Duke.

"That just occur to you, Tyrone?"

"Well, how come you want them to bring ya a car?" Tyrone said.

"To keep 'em busy." Duke peered out the window. "See? They moved a couple of cars all ready."

"But…but what about me?" Evans said.

"You? Open the damn safe," Duke demanded. "And if you don't shut up, you'll be the first one I put a bullet in just to show I mean business."

* * *

Sonny unscrewed the ceiling grate and let it drop to the floor.

The clatter of the grate between both desks made Evans cower with hands over his head while Duke aimed his gun to the ceiling

"What the hell?" Duke said.

"Don't," Evans shouted, still covering his head. "There's gas pipes up there. You'll blow us all up."

"Who's up there?" Duke said. "Who? Answer me."

"Might be rats," Tyrone said and backed into a corner.

"Ain't no rat," Duke said and kept his gun pointed at the ceiling. "So help me. If you're a cop – "

"Cop?" Sonny's voice shouted from above. "I'm from Ace Heating and Cooling. We got a main power break."

"Bullshit," Duke said. He cocked his gun.

"Don't shoot," Evans said. "Please. We use Ace. We have problems with the system all the time."

"It sure is hot in here," Tyrone said.

"Are you shitting me?" Duke asked Evans

"Listen to me," Evans said. "There are gas pipes up there, and we do use that company. I swear." He glanced toward Jay and back up at the ceiling.

"This is just great," Duke said. "This here party just keeps getting better. What's next?"

"Maybe some beer and a pizza," Tyrone said. "I'd really like a pizza right now."

"Will you shut the fuck up?" Duke groaned. "You. Ace whatever guy. Get down here. You better hope to hell you ain't no cop."

Through the ceiling, Sonny shouted down, "What? Can't hear ya." He banged on the metal vent. "You got any AC?"

"I said get down here," Duke demanded.

"Hold on, will ya?" Sonny stalled. "I got a problem here. Shit. This unit's in bad shape."

"I swear to God I'm surrounded by jackasses," Duke said and then shouted at the ceiling, "Get out here now or so help me, I'll come in after you."

"Hang on," Sonny said and lowered his head through the grate opening. "Whatta ya want, huh? You want this unit fixed or what?"

***

The moment Jay heard Sonny's voice, his heart skipped a beat. But, when he saw the man's curly head hang down from the vent, he nearly stopped breathing.

Jay twisted the knots that held his hands behind him. Sonny was out of his league here, and Jay, more desperate than before, was panicked to do something. There wasn't much he could do at the moment. He watched the anger build in Duke who already was on edge and tried once more to loosen the rope.

***

"Well," Sonny called down. "Do you want it fixed or not?"

"Duke, I want it fixed," Tyrone said.

"What the hell are you doing up there?" Duke said. "How the hell did you know the AC was out?" He stood just beneath Sonny and eyed Evans. "Something ain't right with this."

"You got that right," Sonny said. "This unit's a mess. Whole block is out, but we got power. Don't make sense."

Duke frowned up to the ceiling. "Do you see that I have a gun pointed to your head?"

"Yeah," Sonny said. "I see that. How come?"

"Are you stupid or something?" Duke said.

Sonny grinned. "Might be something. Don't know."

"Duke, man," Tyrone said. "It's-it's really hot. I can't do nothin' good in the heat. Let him fix the damn thing, will ya?"

"Are you crazy?" Duke said. "We got a shit load of cops out there and you want this here buck poking around? Maybe he's a cop. That ever occur to you?"

"No," Tyrone said. "Why's a cop be in the ceiling? You a cop?"

"I wish," Sonny said. "Think it's fun to be squeezed in here like this? It ain't. Now, you want it fixed or not? Don't matter to me."

"I'm gonna shoot you outta there," Duke said.

Jay worked the knots that held him as fast as he could. His wrists burned with every try. He spotted a letter opener on the desk. If he could just move the chair a little to the left he might have a chance.

Evans stood next to Jay and whispered, "You and I know there's no gas pipes up there. He's not from Ace either. You help me get out of this, and I'll help you."

Jay struggled with the knot. He looked up at the ceiling and then at Duke anxiously waving the gun.

"Clear it with the DA," Evans whispered. "I'll make sure Duke doesn't shoot him."

Jay nodded. "Get that letter opener."

"Hey," Duke bellowed, when he saw Evans next to Jay. "Move your ass over here. Now. And you," he looked up at Sonny, "you got two seconds to get your ass down here."

Evans quickly placed the letter opener in Jay's waiting hand. He walked over to Duke and said, "You want this whole place to blow sky high? Including the money? I swear the air conditioner is always going out." He pointed up at Sonny. "That's Fred. He's from Ace."

"Ed," Sonny said and pointed to the name sewed across the shirt.

"Ed. From Ace," Evans said. "The whole place will blow."

"Don't want that, Duke," Tyrone said. "'Sides, if you gonna shoot him one way or the other, let him get the AC on before you do."

"You cannot be this stupid," Duke said.

"He can't be a cop," Evans said. "No cop could be that crazy."

"Maybe," Duke said and eyed Sonny. "Maybe not."

"We use Ace all the time," Evans said.

"Ain't got time for this shit," Duke said. He looked up again. "Fix it. And" – he waved the gun at Sonny – "don't get cute. Gas or no gas, I'll shoot holes up there so fast you won't know what hit you."

"All right," Sonny said. "Geez. They don't pay me enough for this shit." He pulled his head back into the ceiling and slid away from the opening.

Jay strained with the letter opener to cut the ropes. They were thick, and he couldn't get the right angle.

The phone rang. Duke grabbed the receiver. "You better say what I want to hear. I got myself another hostage. Either he's one of yours or he really is here to fix the AC. But either way, I'll use him to show you I ain't clowning." Duke paused and glared up at the open vent.

He fisted the gun. "Oh yeah? If he's that worker, you should have cleared him outta here."

He listened a moment.

"You got twenty minutes," Duke said. "I want the streets to the north clear. You got that? All the way outta the city. That worker'll be the first if you try to screw me." He slammed down the phone.

Sonny banged with a hammer in one spot along the vent and then another. The sound echoed. One more bang, and the wrench fell through the opening to the floor.

"Shit," Sonny said. He looked down through the space. "Hey? Can somebody hand me that wrench, huh?"

"Leave it," Duke said. "We're outta here in twenty minutes."

Tyrone's face dripped with sweat. His shirt was soaked. "Duke. I gotta have air. I ain't gonna make it. Let him fix the damn thing. I feel sick."

"Oh, fuck," Duke said. "Fine. But hurry up."

"Gotta have my wrench," Sonny said, his head hanging down.

Jay sawed at the ropes. Sweat rained down his face just as fast as his fingers worked the letter opener.

Duke gestured to Tyrone. "Get the damn wrench."

Tyrone bent down on one knee to pick up the wrench and then huffed as he struggled to stand back up. He held it up to the ceiling.

Sonny's hand reached down just short of taking the wrench. "Can't get it. To tight in here."

Tyrone, on his toes, tried once more and still the wrench was just out of Sonny's grasp.

"Get a chair, will ya?" Sonny said.

Tyrone moved a chair just under the opening where Sonny leaned out. With effort, he stepped up and handed Sonny the wrench.

Sonny gripped the tool and said, "Hey, man, don't go anywhere. I need somebody to hold this wire."

Evans eyed Jay. Jay sawed faster against the nylon rope. Duke came closer to him. He stopped.

"You," Duke said to Evans. "Get that safe open."

Evans nodded, looked nervously at Jay and then fumbled with the set of keys he held. He dropped them once and then once more.

"Stop stalling," Duke said.

With Tyrone still teetering on the chair, Sonny lowered his head through the grate opening once more and said, "Hey? Big guy? You think you can reach in and hold this?"

Jay fought the ropes that held him. He worked the letter opener and felt the rope give slightly.

Standing on the wobbly chair that began to bend with his weight, Tyrone stretched as much as he could to look in the vent. "What's you want me to hold?"

"This damn wire," Sonny said. "Come on, man, reach a little more. Stay still. Hey? Somebody hold the big guy's chair before he falls."

"Duke," Tyrone said breathing hard, "Don't let me fall."

With Evans at the safe, Duke huffed. "Fuck this. It's taking too long."

"Almost got it if you hold the damn chair," Sonny said. "Feel that? You got it?"

Tyrone stretched and almost fell off the chair. "Duke? Ya gots to hold it."

"I got the damn chair," Duke said.

"Don't lets me fall, Duke. Promise," Tyrone said.

"Ya damn crybaby, shut the fuck up," Duke said. "Just get this over with."

Tyrone reached up into the vent. "Yeah. I-I think I feel something."

With Duke holding the slowly bending chair and Tyrone's arm stretched as far as it could go, his pudgy head close to the ceiling, Sonny took the hammer and bashed the man in the skull.

Tyrone fell like a mountain that caved in.

Jay flew out of the chair and pushed Duke.

Duke stumbled. Tyrone crashed on top of him so fast, there was no time to move.

Duke's gun slipped out of his hand.

Sonny swung out of the vent on top of Tyrone's round body. With the hammer still in his grasp, and Duke crushed under Tyrone's weight, Sonny bashed Duke in the head and knocked him out cold.

Evans turned from the safe in shock. Sonny grabbed the gun off the floor and pointed it at Evans. "Get over here," he said.

Evans nodded with his hands up. "Don't shoot. I helped you. I did."

Jay had fallen to the floor. His ankles still tied, he hurried to untie the ropes. Once he was completely free, he got to his feet and grabbed Evans by the scruff of his neck. He twirled the hysterical man around and tossed him into a chair.

"Don't move," Jay said.

Sonny stood with one foot on Tyrone's back like a hunter with his kill. He aimed the gun at Duke who groaned, but remained pinned under Tyrone's huge body.

Jay took the gun from Sonny and stared at him for a moment. When he could finally speak, all he could think to say was, "Ace Heating and Cooling?"

Sonny shrugged.

Jay yanked Evans to his feet and led the man to the front door and opened it. "All clear," he shouted. "Send in some uniforms."

"I helped you. I helped," Evans said. "We had a deal. I kept Duke from shooting that officer. They would have killed him if I didn't stop them."

"Yeah. I'll be sure to let the DA know everything you did," Jay said in disgust.

Colby, along with ten uniformed officers and Bruce Harrison, rushed inside. Fifty more men remained outside with weapons trained on the bank.

The captain took one look around, and, when he caught sight of Sonny, his mouth dropped.

"Whoa," Harrison said, his eyes as wide as the captain's jaw.

On the floor at Sonny's feet was a man the size of a whale. Sticking out from under that was the skinny upper torso of another man.

"What the hell is going on?" Colby barked.

"I was just about to ask that myself," Jay said.

"What is *he* doing here?" Colby demanded.

"Pretty cool, huh?" Sonny said.

"I'll say." Harrison laughed and then coughed when Colby eyed him.

Jay started, "Cap, I – "

Colby put up his sweaty palm. "Don't say anything. This man is supposed to be on disability. What in hell am I gonna tell Internal? A disabled cop, off duty on medical leave shows up like this. He gets in past a hundred cops? My ass'll be ground meat." The veins on his neck bulged. "Get him out of here," he shouted. "I got press all over the place."

"Yes, sir," Jay said and tugged Sonny's shirt.

"Not out the front. Use the back and keep it quiet," Colby said. "And Jamison, my office in the morning."

"Yes, sir," Jay said again and ushered Sonny through the rear door.

Two steps onto the parking lot, Jay spied the cameras and reporters that peeked around the corner. "Oh shit," he said.

One reporter shouted. A frenzy of others joined him, and rushed toward Sonny and Jay like a stampeding herd of cattle.

Jay pulled Sonny along by the shirt tail.

Sonny waved at the cameras.

Jay slapped his hand down and nudged him to move faster.

They scooted toward the other side of the building, and all the while, Sonny smiled at the cameras and waved again.

"Knock it off and move your ass," Jay said and hurried him.

They took a few side alleys and lost the reporters.

When they got to Jay's car, he wasn't smiling.

"Pretty cool, huh?" he said. "Is that what you said to the captain? What the hell were you thinking? You could have been killed in there."

"But I wasn't," Sonny said.

Jay ran a hand through his hair. "That isn't the point. You had no business being there. Ace Heating and Cooling for Christ's sake. Fixing the AC. In a vent? Lucky for you those guys were morons. That was the dumbest – "

"Nobody got hurt," Sonny said, his tone flat. "You're welcome."

Jay ran both hands through his hair this time and let out a long breath. "How the hell did you even know?"

"I heard it on the police radio in my car."

"I told you. That isn't a toy."

"It was on," Sonny said. "Myra must have turned it on last night."

"Right. Myra."

"I figured you needed help," Sonny said and shrugged.

"So let me get this straight. You came down here and almost got yourself killed? That's just great. What did you think you were doing?" To Sonny's blank stare, Jay added, "You could have been shot. Can you understand that?"

"When I was your partner, I could have been shot, too. Did you act like this then?"

"That was different," Jay said.

"Why? I got the bad guys. I helped you. I didn't get shot. Nobody did. Can't you just say I did okay? Huh?"

Myra Turner ran down the sidewalk and straight into Sonny's arms. "I saw it on the news," she said. "When you asked where the bank was, and I heard all the sirens….Were you in there? What happened?"

"I saved Jay's life," Sonny said.

"What in the hell are *you* doing here?" Jay said.

"I told you," Myra said. "I heard it on the news. I guess I saved your life too because without me, Sonny didn't know how to get here. Right, sweetie?" She trailed a finger along Sonny's arm. "Come on, baby. Let's go celebrate." She wrapped her arms around Sonny's neck.

Sonny pulled her arms away and shook his head. "No."

"No? Are you kidding?"

"Go home. Leave me alone," Sonny said.

Myra scoffed. "You're telling me, you'd rather go with him than come home with me? Listen, lover, that's not how it works."

"I'm not your lover," Sonny said.

"The last time I looked up, you were." Myra raised her voice.

"Go home," Sonny said. "I ain't going with you."

"Lover…" Myra purred and reached to touch Sonny again.

Sonny pushed her hand away. "I said. Go. Home."

Myra backed away. With fire in her eyes, she said, "That's just sweet. Why don't you two go fuck yourselves?" She walked off in a huff.

Jay's lips curled into a relieved grin. He rubbed the back of his neck and glanced at Sonny. "You okay?"

"We need to talk."

"We do? I mean…yeah, we should," Jay said.

"Back at the house?"

"Sure. Th-that's great," Jay said. "Fine. Okay, then. So, talk. Good. How'd you get here?"

"My car's back there. I-I just don't know how to get back to the house."

"No problem. You can follow me," Jay said. "And, Sonny? Make sure that damn radio is off."

30

J ay pulled into the driveway, and Sonny parked the Mustang behind Jay's Chevy. Silently, they walked to the front door. It was locked. Jay turned the key, and they stepped inside.

The broken lamp was still on the floor and fragments of shattered glass greeted them.

Head hung down, Sonny said, "I-I'm sorry. About the mess."

"It's been a busy morning," Jay said and tossed his keys on the table. "I haven't had time to clean."

"I'll clean it," Sonny said.

"That's okay. It can wait."

They faced one another. Sonny was the first to lower his eyes and look away.

"Listen, Son," Jay began.

"Why'd you lie to me?" Sonny said, not looking up.

Jay's stomach flopped. "I-I didn't lie. You and me...before the accident...."

"Why didn't you tell me?"

Jay huffed. "Lots of reasons. There were lots of...reasons."

"You lied." Sonny lifted his head.

His sapphire eyes were the darkest blue Jay ever remembered seeing. It almost hurt Jay to look at him. He took a step closer but when Sonny backed away, he stopped.

"No," Jay said, "I-I haven't lied. I know it's not easy to hear. About... about you and me. How it was. Is. But it wasn't something I could just say to you." Jay looked at the floor this time and said, "I just couldn't tell you."

"So you did lie. Not telling is like lying."

"No, it's not," Jay insisted. "Sometimes a person doesn't tell something because they don't want someone to get hurt or worry or…scared."

"Scared?"

Jay went into the living room. Silent for a second, he turned so he could look straight at Sonny. "I wanted to tell you. I did. But the doctors said…Dixon thought – "

"Dixon's an asshole."

"He knows about these things. It's his job."

"So Dixon knows about us? Who else?" Sonny said.

"No one. No one has ever known."

"No one?" Sonny said and frowned. "Why?"

Jay shrugged. "That's how we wanted it. You and me. How we feel about each other is just for us. No one else. We're cops, and there was no point."

Next to the living room window, Sonny moved the curtain so he could look outside. He was quiet to the point that Jay grew more nervous.

"Sonny, you have to understand. People don't accept this kind of thing."

"Why?" Sonny said without turning.

"Because…because they don't. It's not….normal to them."

"So it's…wrong?"

"No. Not…wrong." Jay squeezed the bridge of his nose as he struggled to find the words. "You and I never cared what anyone thought. It wasn't wrong for us. But…."

"But? You said we were friends. When I asked who you were. You said my partner and my friend."

"We are. Friends. And partners," Jay said.

"Cop partners," Sonny said.

"More than that."

"But you didn't tell me. When I asked you why you called me partner, you went on about cop stuff."

"I-I shouldn't have. But there were reasons," Jay said.

Sonny continued to look out the window and said, "If I was a girl. If I was your wife or your girlfriend, you would have told me. So you lied."

"I didn't lie. I just wanted to…to protect you."

"Protect me? From what?"

"From…." Jay lifted his shoulders. "From…I don't know." He shook his head. "I honestly don't know."

Sonny flipped the curtain back into place and turned. "So it's okay to lie. To not tell something if you wanna protect someone?"

"Yeah. Something like that." Jay frowned. "Wait a minute. You keep saying I lied because…you're mad because I *didn't* tell you?"

"I'm not mad. I was at first. But now? I don't get it."

"Wait a second. Let me understand this. Are you…I mean, *were* you mad because you thought I lied about us? About us being…you know, gay? Or were you mad because I didn't say anything about us, and you're okay with us being gay?"

"You're giving me a headache."

"That makes two of us," Jay said and sat in the chair.

"You should have told me. You didn't."

"So I've got to know. You're okay…I mean you're not confused or anything else about us?"

"You didn't tell me. So you must be ashamed."

"I'm not ashamed. I've never been ashamed of us," Jay declared.

"Then you thought it was wrong. Just like Dr. Dean said."

"Not wrong. I just wanted…whoa. Hold on. Dr. Dean? The psychologist you saw a few times and refused to see again?" Jay rose out of the chair.

Sonny bobbed his head. "He said it was wrong. What I was feeling."

"What do you mean, what you were feeling?"

"I told him I liked you. He said I was confused."

"You like me. What's wrong about that?"

"No. I mean I *like* you."

"You like me," Jay said and frowned.

Sonny walked over to Jay and looked him deep in the eyes. "I like you" he said. "Like this." He planted a long, firm kiss on Jay's mouth and then backed away.

Jay's jaw dropped. "Whoa. Hang on. You…you *like* me?"

"Who's the slow one here?"

"Why didn't you tell me?"

"I'm brain damaged, remember? I didn't know what it was, and then I started to think…you said to listen to the doctors. That I should trust them. I thought if I told you, you'd kick me out, and I had no place to go."

"You thought I'd kick you out?"

"I heard what you said to that lady, Maria, about sending me away."

"Sending…No, Sonny, I would never send you away. I didn't want anyone else to send you away."

"And Myra said you just kept me around 'cause you felt sorry for me."

"That's not true," Jay said. "And what about this thing with Myra? If you like me…like that, then why her?"

Sonny shrugged. "I thought that's what I was supposed to do."

"So all this time…? Everything we went through…." Jay huffed. "You're right. Dixon's an ass."

"I still don't get why you didn't tell me."

"Oh, Son. You don't know how many times I wanted to. But I couldn't. I didn't want to pressure you or…or scare you."

"I still don't get why it should scare me?"

"For the same reason you thought I'd kick you out if you told me. It's not…normal."

"Normal? You said it's not normal to pour orange soda on my cereal," Sonny said.

"Well, come on. That *is* gross."

"Not to me," Sonny said. "I think it's a normal thing to do."

Jay scratched his head. "You have a point."

"So how come Dixon knows?"

"He wanted to send you to a special hospital," Jay said. "When you were still in a coma. I fought him on it and he got suspicious, I guess. He asked me and I was too damn tired to…."

"Lie?" Sonny said. "Does that lady know? Your captain know?"

"Dee? Colby? No. I told you. No one knows. We worked together, as partners. But after work, when we were here, alone, it was just about us. We never needed anyone's approval. We loved each other, and that was all.

"But like I said, we're cops. It isn't something you announce. I mean, most of the guys we worked with would hate us. Our lives would be in danger all the time. The streets aren't the right place for this kind of thing. So to protect ourselves, we kept it private. Just us."

Jay considered Sonny's silence for a moment and then stepped closer to him.

"I'm sorry. All of this…mess, could have been avoided. I-I guess we were still trying to protect each other. You didn't say anything because you thought it was wrong. I didn't say anything because I thought it might scare you. We both listened to the wrong people and the wrong advice. But, Sonny? That's all over now. What you need to know…what I want to tell you is…I-I love you."

"Me?"

"Oh, yeah." Jay nodded with a sweet smile.

Sonny was silent, and, when he turned his back, Jay creased his brows. "Sonny? Say something. You're making me nervous here, buddy."

Sonny turned. "I-I don't know what that means. You love me."

"It means I *really* like you. Like this…." He leaned in and kissed Sonny longingly with a hunger that was finally fed even though he craved more. When the kiss ended, he hugged Sonny close to his chest. "If I'm dreaming, don't wake me." He gazed into Sonny's eyes. What he thought reflected back made his heart beat like never before. "I've missed you. I've missed you so much. I love you, Sonny. Always have. Always will. Always."

"Me?" Sonny took a step back. "Or…him?"

Please take a moment and review this book. We independent authors live by word of mouth from readers like you.

Truth Can Kill (Santini & Jamison Vol.2) coming soon.

Excerpt from Truth Can Kill:

Thunder clapped outside. A lightning bolt illuminated the still house for only a second. It was long enough for Sonny to aim the gun. Jay froze.

The barrel of the gun pointed at his face, he watched in horror while Sonny shook, and a blank, dazed look filled his eyes.

Look for more information on this book and others at
www.LindaThomasCook.com
or friend me at Facebook: Linda Thomas-Cook.

www.ingramcontent.com/pod-product-compliance
Lightning Source LLC
Chambersburg PA
CBHW071254170626
46809CB00001B/212